INTO THE FIRE

The President waited until he and Brognola were alone. His stage presence was gone, and he seemed tired and weary.

"I said I was putting all my cards on the table this morning. That wasn't absolutely true. This one has to be played close to the vest. The CIA is convinced that all of our anti-drug operations have been penetrated... probably even our military personnel in South America. I have to work on the assumption that it's true. I have to have some people down there that I know I can trust—people who can find things out and who will not be afraid to take decisive action if I authorize it. You and your people are what I need. I want you to support operation Blast Furnace with everything you've got. Any questions?"

Brognola shook his head. It was plain enough. Stony Man was going to war.

Other titles in this series:

DON PENDLETON'S
MACK BOLAN®

STONY MAN™

NIGHT
OF THE
JAGUAR

A GOLD EAGLE BOOK FROM
W⊕RLDWIDE®

TORONTO • NEW YORK • LONDON
AMSTERDAM • PARIS • SYDNEY • HAMBURG
STOCKHOLM • ATHENS • TOKYO • MILAN
MADRID • WARSAW • BUDAPEST • AUCKLAND

First edition November 1997

ISBN 0-373-61915-4

Special thanks and acknowledgment to
Patrick F. Rogers for his contribution to this work.

NIGHT OF THE JAGUAR

Printed in U.S.A.

NIGHT OF THE JAGUAR

CHAPTER ONE

The White House, Washington, D.C.

Hal Brognola sat quietly in the Oval Office as the director of the Central Intelligence Agency finished his briefing. The director was pleased with himself, and he glowed with triumph. The CIA had not looked good during the past two years, but this time he knew he had a winner.

"You requested the CIA make an all-out effort to help solve the current crisis, Mr. President, and we have done so. I don't want to disclose Intelligence sources, but our Office of Current Intelligence is almost certain that a major shipment of cocaine will be flown to an airfield in northern Mexico in the next forty-eight hours. There, it will be transferred to a group of light planes and flown across the border into the United States for distribution. It gives us a perfect target, an incredible opportunity to strike the drug cartels a crippling blow. All we have to do is act quickly."

The chairman of the Joint Chiefs of Staff looked skeptical. He had been burned by the CIA before.

"You say a major shipment. Just what does that mean?"

The director of the CIA smiled. He was ready for that one, ready and waiting.

"I can't tell you the exact amount, General, but the aircraft carrying the shipment will be Boeing 727 jetliners. There will be at least two of them, perhaps three. And we believe some or all of the shipment will be the new type of cocaine that has been causing so much trouble. We consider that to be a major shipment."

General Grant Ross whistled softly. Three jetliners loaded with cocaine impressed even him. He began to suspect why he was there, but he said nothing. The ball was in the President's court. If the United States was going to take action, the decision was up to him.

"That's damned fine work, Paul," the President said. "You and your people have done an outstanding job. I have only one question before I stick my neck out—are you sure?"

The director hesitated for a second. That question haunted every Intelligence agency in the world. He had been at the game long enough to know that you could never be absolutely sure of anything.

"Yes, sir," he said quietly. "Satellite reconnaissance confirms that the 727s are at an airfield in western Brazil near the Bolivian border, ready to fly in and load. Our La Paz station reports unusual activity in the Bolivian cocaine growing areas. Unless there's a major change in the weather or the cartel learns that we know about the operation, we're sure the shipment will occur sometime in the next twenty-four to forty-eight hours."

"That's good enough for me. Those bastards are getting as bold as brass. Imagine—727s full of cocaine! Well, they're not going to get away with it. That leaves only one question. Where and how do we hit them? General, you're our expert."

The general gave it a moment's thought.

"We should hit them on the ground. Intercepting them

in flight is too risky. If we go after them in Brazil or Bolivia, we'll have to use strategic bombers. I recommend we attack after they land in Mexico. How we do it depends on our objectives. If we want to destroy them, an air strike will be best. A squadron of F-15-E Eagles will do the job nicely. If, on the other hand, you want to capture them, we'll have to send in a ground team, Rangers or Navy SEALs.''

The secretary of state, sitting quietly, did not like what he was hearing. Air strikes or commando raids into a friendly country? The damage to U.S. foreign policy could be immense, but the President seemed as enthused as the CIA and the military. He needed someone to help him persuade the Man not to do this. He decided to stall for time.

''The attorney general should be consulted, sir. After all, the FBI and the DEA report to him.''

''You're quite right, John, but the attorney general is testifying before Congress today.'' the President said. ''I don't believe you've met Mr. Brognola. He represents the attorney general in this matter. We haven't heard from him yet. What are your recommendations, Hal?''

Three pairs of eyes turned speculatively to Hal Brognola, and they belonged to three of the most powerful men in Washington. All they knew about Brognola was that he had to be important in some way, and the President had called him ''Hal.'' Anyone who was on a first-name basis with the President had to have some influence. None of them spoke. It was better to wait until he committed himself and they found out which side he was on.

Brognola smiled. He did not like Washington politics, but he knew perfectly well how the game was played.

''I agree with General Ross,'' he said. ''The airfield in Mexico is the logical place to hit them. I think we should try to capture the planes on the ground and fly them to the United States. That way, we'll have clear indisputable evidence that we were acting against the drug cartel. No one will be able to claim that it was a U.S. military action against Mexico.''

''That's easy to say, Mr. Brognola,'' the secretary of state said, ''but if anything goes wrong and we have dead U.S. military personnel in Mexico, all hell will break loose.''

''For that reason,'' Brognola replied. ''I recommend that we don't use military personnel or CIA paramilitary people. That way we maintain plausible deniability if anything goes wrong.''

The CIA director smiled. He loved plausible deniability, and he liked the way Brognola thought.

''This is really more of a law enforcement or counterterrorist action than a military mission. I recommend we use—''

The smile vanished from the CIA director's face. ''Excuse me for interrupting you, Mr. Brognola. The use of FBI or DEA teams is out of the question. We have reliable information that both agencies have been penetrated by the drug cartels. The security risk is much too great. All the drug cartel needs is one leak, and they cancel the operation. We simply can't risk it.''

''I agree. I was about to say we have to use a strike team composed of men who can't be traced to any U.S. government agency. They'll capture the planes if possible or destroy them if it's not.''

''These miracle workers had better be absolutely trustworthy,'' the CIA director stated. ''Once they have control of airplanes loaded with hundreds of millions of dollars' worth of cocaine, what's to prevent them from simply flying off with them? Do you know anyone you can trust that much?"

"So," General Ross stated, "all we need is a highly trained, top secret, completely trustworthy strike team that cannot be traced to the United States military or Intelligence services. That's a perfect solution. There's just one little problem. Where the hell do we find people like that?"

The President smiled.

"You can leave that to me."

Northern Mexico

DEA SPECIAL AGENT IN CHARGE Teresa Antonio plodded on through the sand and the dark and wondered what she had done to deserve this. She was a small, dark-haired woman with large dark eyes and an almost elfin face that belied her age. She might have been a middle-aged camper, lost in the high deserts of northern Mexico, except for the silenced Colt R-0636 9 mm submachine gun slung over her shoulder. She almost bumped into the dim form of Jack Grimaldi as he stopped in front of her. Grimaldi produced a small black box from his pack and stared at it intently as red numbers flickered across its face.

Antonio looked around. It was nearly midnight. The faint crescent moon was setting. She could see arid soil broken by outcrops, and occasional clumps of sagebrush. She was surprised that it was so cold—she had always thought that deserts were hot—and glad to be wearing her black nylon raid jacket. She was not impressed by what she saw: a godforsaken wilderness. Antonio was a big-city girl, born and raised in East L.A. Her normal duty station was the DEA Miami Division Office.

If this was the great outdoors, somebody else could have her share.

She wondered if she had time to shake the sand out of her shoes. No such luck. Grimaldi slipped the black box back inside his pack.

"Let's go," he whispered.

"I don't suppose you'd like to tell me where we are and where we're going," she retorted.

"No problem. We are approximately four hundred yards from our objective, and we are going straight toward it."

Antonio frowned. She believed in secrecy and security, but this was too much.

"You wouldn't mind telling me what our objective is, now that we're almost there?"

"Of course not," Grimaldi said. "Our objective is to get you to Mike Belasko before midnight. If we get moving now, we'll make it."

Antonio suppressed the desire to swear and followed Grimaldi through the dark. After all, she was there only because of the cryptic message she had received from Belasko. She did not know who Belasko really was or who he worked for, but she had seen him in action against international drug dealers, and he had saved her life in a desperate firefight against heavy odds. If he said she was needed immediately to participate in a critical mission, she was ready to go.

A voice suddenly hissed in the dark. "Saber!"

Adrenaline shot through Antonio's body as she started to reach for her submachine gun.

"Freeze!" Grimaldi told Antonio.

Then he called out "Crossbow!" in a louder voice.

"All right, Jack, come on in," said the voice from the dark.

"Sorry I yelled at you, Teresa, but my friend's an ex-Ranger. You don't want to startle him. He's a little quick on the trigger sometimes," Grimaldi said.

They approached carefully as a tall man rose from behind a clump of sagebrush. He was wearing a nonreflective dull black raid suit and night-vision goggles, and he held an M-16 rifle. Antonio found herself looking down at its muzzle and into the gaping maw of the 40 mm M-203 grenade launcher clipped under its barrel. Grimaldi was right; she did not want to startle him. It looked as if Mike Belasko associated with some very serious people.

"This is the lady Striker's waiting for, T.J. Where is he?"

"Down in the control tent. You might remind him I was supposed to be relieved ten minutes ago."

"I'll try to remember," Grimaldi said and motioned to Antonio to follow him. She blinked as T. J. Hawkins seemed to vanish back into the dark. She knew he had to still be within twenty feet, but she could not see the slightest trace of him.

"Who the hell was that?"

"We call him T.J., or sometimes Hawk. He likes sneaking around in the dark. He's dependable, though. You can get a good night's sleep when he's guarding the perimeter."

That was reassuring, but Antonio sensed that whatever was about to happen, she was not going to sleep tonight. She followed Grimaldi up the slope of a low ridge. She almost stumbled over a small, low-lying camouflaged tent half buried in the ground. A plastic sheet was draped to block the light when the tent flap was opened. Grimaldi lifted the flap and motioned for Antonio to enter.

The tent was dimly lit, but it seemed bright compared to outside. The interior was crowded. Antonio recognized the big man working at a laptop computer. Mike Belasko looked different from the last time she had seen him. He was wearing a dull black raid suit and was festooned with pistols, spare magazines and assorted grenades. She glanced around the tent. The five other men were similarly dressed and equipped.

Antonio smiled. "Mr. Belasko, I presume. Or should I call you Striker?"

Bolan looked up and smiled. "My friends call me Striker. Welcome to the party. You're just in time. We just got a report from the Air Force AWACS that its radar has picked up our friends. They should be here in fifteen minutes."

"All right, Striker. Now that I'm here, do you mind telling me what the hell is going on?"

"No problem," Bolan said. "We are about to make an extremely large drug bust. I can't do that without my favorite DEA agent, but let's talk while we're moving. We have to be in position when our friends get here."

FIFTEEN MINUTES LATER, they were in position on a sandy ridge overlooking a concrete airstrip and some old, rusty metal buildings. Teresa Antonio was still having trouble believing her ears. She had been fighting the war on drugs for many years. The idea of seizing or destroying two jetliners full of cocaine seemed too good to be true. If they could pull it off, it would be the drug bust of the century.

Mack Bolan listened intently. At first, all he could hear was the soft sighing of the wind and the mournful howl of a distant coyote. Then he heard the faint rumble of jet engines from the south. He glanced at his watch. Right on time. Whoever was flying the 727 knew his business. The rumble of the engines became a shrieking roar as the big plane made a low pass over the airfield. He could see the Boeing 727 clearly through his AN/PVS-7B night-vision goggles. He watched as the jetliner turned and lined up with the runway.

The Executioner felt the adrenaline start to flow. His team was in position. The men of Phoenix Force and Able Team were stone-cold professionals, and they knew what to do. Now all they had to do was do it.

The sky seemed to blaze as the 727's pilot turned on his landing lights. A truck near the far end of the runway responded by turning on its lights. The pilot seemed satisfied. He throttled back his engines, put down his flaps and started his final approach. Bolan watched as the aircraft touched down. He heard the roar of the thrust reversers and the screech of tires as the big plane slowed and rolled down the runway. He could see it clearly in the light from the truck's headlights. It was painted white and gold in the color scheme of Mexicana Airlines, but Bolan was willing to bet that it had never seen the inside of a Mexicana hangar.

The pilot taxied to the end of the runway, turned the plane around and put on the brakes. The low whine of the three Pratt & Whitney JT8D turbofan engines faded away as the pilot cut the power. Bolan frowned. The pilot was a cautious man. He had positioned the 727 for a fast take-off in an emergency. The Executioner hoped the entire crew would leave the plane before he made his move. If not, it might be tricky. If the 727 started a takeoff run, he could try to shoot out its tires, but that wouldn't be easy in the dark. If that didn't work, he would have no alternative but to destroy it.

The forward door in the jetliner's fuselage opened, and the self-contained boarding stairs deployed. The men from the truck moved quickly to the foot of the stairs. Bolan could hear a buzz of conversation in English and Spanish. The drug smugglers seemed relaxed, happy that the plane had landed safely. They were off guard, not expecting trouble. It would have been easy to open fire without warning and kill them all, but Brognola had stressed the importance of taking prisoners if possible. The big Fed would not have asked them to do it if it were not important. The door on the side of the aircraft just behind the cockpit opened and boarding stairs swung down. A man in a white shirt started down the steps. All the men on the airstrip were looking at him and the plane. Now was the time to take them before the situation changed.

"Moving out now," he said into the microphone of his tactical radio. "Let's go."

The group moved quietly forward, Antonio in the center, Bolan to her right, Carl Lyons to her left while McCarter and Rafael Encizo moved toward the parked truck whose headlights were still illuminating the runway. Bolan made one last check of his equipment. His M-4 Ranger carbine was an improved and lighter weight version of the M-16 rifle. It had a 30-round magazine in place and a multiple projectile antipersonnel round was loaded into the M-203 40 mm grenade launcher mounted under its barrel.

They were almost into the lighted area, thirty feet or less from the six or seven men grouped around the 727's forward boarding stairs. They could not hope to get much closer without being discovered. Bolan stopped and signaled to Carl Lyons. The Ironman's cold blue eyes stared through the sights of his Atchisson assault shotgun, his finger ready on the trigger. He took a deep breath and roared, "Freeze! Move and I'll blow you in two!"

Stunned as Lyons's voice suddenly blasted out of the

dark, the group of men was frozen by utter surprise and the cold, deadly certainty in the voice.

Teresa Antonio broke the sudden silence.

"This is the DEA. You are all under arrest for attempting to smuggle narcotics into the United States. Lay down your weapons slowly and carefully. Resist and you will be killed."

A tall man in the center of the group glared back at the dim figures at the edge of the light.

"Your DEA has got no authority here, *hija de la puta.* This is Mexico!"

Antonio did not appreciate being called the daughter of a whore. She kept the sights of her 9 mm Colt submachine gun centered on the man's chest.

"Last chance. Drop your weapons now!" she snapped.

"You are the ones who are under arrest! You are in Mexico illegally. I am a Mexican police officer. I will show you my badge."

His hand reached suddenly under his jacket, and Carl Lyons did not wait to see what he was pulling out. Antonio heard three rapid booming roars as he pulled the trigger of his Atchisson assault shotgun and sent three blasts of 12-gauge buckshot into the man's chest. He went down instantly. The rest of the group exploded into action, swinging up their weapons and trying to fire.

Bolan had his sights centered on the chest of a big man with a folding stock AK-47. The penetrating power of its steel-jacketed bullets made it dangerous even to men wearing body armor. The Executioner had the selector lever of his M-4 carbine set for full automatic. He squeezed the trigger and put a burst through the big man's chest. The human target staggered as the high-velocity, full-metal-jacketed bullets struck, but he was still on his feet, still holding the AKS-47. Bolan took no chances, knowing the big man might be wearing body armor and that a long burst from his weapon could be deadly at short range. The soldier sent his next burst through the man's head.

He heard firing to the left and right as the Stony Man team exchanged shots with the drug traffickers. It was a short, one-sided fight. Caught by surprise, facing superior firepower and skill, the drug cartel's men went down. Bolan saw a flash of white to one side. The man who had gotten out of the 727 was racing toward the boarding stairs. Bolan swung his M-4 carbine and centered the sights on the man's back, but hesitated. He did not like firing toward the plane. Grimaldi might not be able to fly the 727 if it was damaged.

He heard Carl Lyons shout.

"Freeze! Drop your weapon. Move and I'll kill you!"

The man in the white shirt stopped at the foot of the boarding stairs, but he did not drop his weapon. He whirled toward Lyons, and Bolan saw the muzzle-flash as he opened fire with a 9 mm automatic pistol. Lyons was running forward with the Atchisson held against his right side in the assault fire position. He pulled the trigger and his semiautomatic shotgun boomed repeatedly. It was not precisely aimed shooting, but every time the Able Team leader pulled the trigger, he sent a charge of double-aught buckshot shrieking toward his target. The man in the white shirt dropped his weapon and fell heavily, down and dead.

Bolan stiffened as a low whine came suddenly from the Boeing 727. The pilot was trying to restart the engines. Lyons also knew what that noise meant. His shotgun was empty, so he dropped it and drew his big Colt revolver.

The two men sprinted to the foot of the boarding stairs. If the steps were pulled up and locked in place, they would never get inside the 727. Bolan took a flash-stun grenade from his harness, pulled the pin and threw the bomb up through the open door. Designed for hostage rescue, the grenade was not supposed to damage an airplane.

The grenade detonated with an eye-searing flash and an incredibly loud blast. The 727 shook and vibrated, but it was still intact. Lyons went up the stairs three steps at a time, his .357 Magnum Colt Python in his hand. He went through the door crouching low. Bolan drew his Beretta 93-R and charged after him. He heard the angry buzzing snarl of an automatic weapon and the answering blasts of the Able Team commando's .357 Magnum pistol.

The Executioner shot through the door, swinging the muzzle of his Beretta to cover the interior of the plane. The body of a man lay near the door, a 9 mm Glock pistol near his hand. Lyons had moved forward into the cockpit.

"All secure, Striker. Tell Grimaldi we're ready for him."

Bolan spoke rapidly into his tactical radio, heard Grimaldi's answer, then moved forward into the cockpit. The pilot was slumped over the controls. A stray round had hit him in the back of the head. Bolan pulled him out of the pilot's seat as Grimaldi walked through the cockpit door. He slipped into the pilot's chair and ran his eyes quickly over the instrument panel and the controls.

"Can you fly her, Jack?" Bolan asked quickly.

"Probably," Grimaldi said with a frown. "Everything seems to be working. There are bullet holes in the fuselage, so the cabin won't hold pressure. We'll have to stay below eight thousand feet, but we've got plenty of fuel. One thing, Sarge. The takeoff's going to be a bit hairy. She's very heavily loaded. They were planning on unloading the drugs here before they took off again. I'm going to need full power and every last foot of the runway.''

Bolan understood. Grimaldi was the best pilot he knew, and he had complete faith in his judgment when it came to flying.

''You call it.''

''I like a challenge,'' Grimaldi said with a wicked smile. ''Go! Coming with me?''

Bolan nodded. ''Antonio and I will come with you. She can handle the law at El Paso. The choppers will pick up the rest of the team.''

''All right, tell everyone else to stand clear. I'm restarting engines in sixty seconds.''

The Executioner had just reached the door when he heard Gadgets Schwarz's voice in his headset.

''Heads up, Striker. There's a second large aircraft approaching from the south.''

Up on the ridge line, T. J. Hawkins heard the rumbling whine of jet engines growing louder. He swung his Stinger launcher over his shoulder and pointed it at the runway. The second Boeing 727 roared down the runway, but it had not braked to a stop. Hawkins heard Mack Bolan's voice crackling in the headset of his tactical radio.

''T.J., this is Striker. The second plane is trying to take off. Take him out.''

Hawkins did not hesitate. He had no sympathy for the men who made and imported cocaine. He aimed, centered the image of the 727 in the range ring and pressed the Identification Friend or Foe interrogate button at the rear of the Stinger launcher's grip stock. That was force of habit. Hawkins knew there were no friendly jets in the area. The IFF unit emitted a series of rapid, strident beeps. It had received no reply to its challenge. Hostile target! The image of the 727 was swelling larger and larger in

Hawkins's sight as it rolled down the runway and swept past him, moving faster and faster. They were not going to stop. He pressed the tracker activation switch and kept the aircraft centered in the sight's range ring, hearing a steady tone as the tracker activated.

The steady tone suddenly changed pitch. Lock-on! The tracker had the target. Hawkins pressed the uncage switch. The Stinger was locked on the 727 and ready to fire. The whine of its jet engines rose to a roar as the 727's pilot went to full power and started to climb out. Hawkins raised the launcher on his shoulder so that he could see the three sight notches just below the range ring. No need to lead the target. The aircraft was flying almost straight away from him. He centered the 727 in the center notch, pulled the trigger and held it back. The booster charge fired, and the Stinger shot from its launcher. Its solid propellant rocket motor ignited, and the missile flashed toward its target.

The Stinger's guidance unit was locked on the heat radiating from the plane's engines and would follow it and home in. The missile struck the tail of the 727 and detonated in a flash of yellow fire. The stricken jet shuddered and began to belch flame and smoke as it fell toward the desert sand below. Hawkins saw a bright flash of fire as the aircraft smashed and vanished in a huge ball of orange flame. Pieces of blackened, twisted aluminum shot up into the sky, then rained to the ground.

Hawkins spoke softly into his tactical radio.

"Mission accomplished, Striker. He's not going anywhere."

Bolan had no doubt of that. He turned to Grimaldi.

"Wind her up, Jack, and let's get out of here."

CHAPTER TWO

The White House, Washington, D.C.

Sitting quietly, Hal Brognola looked around the conference room. Everyone was there: the chairman of the Joint Chiefs of Staff, flanked by half a dozen admirals and generals, the secretary of defense, the secretary of state, the attorney general, with the heads of the FBI and the DEA, the Director of the CIA, and the chairmen and ranking members of the key congressional committees. There was enough power concentrated in the big conference room to change the official policies of the United States. No one paid any attention to Brognola. He was lost in the group of makers and shakers. That did not bother him at all. He was not in the business of attracting attention.

The buzz of conversation stopped as the President swept into the room and moved to the speaker's rostrum. He touched a button, and the lights in the room dimmed. Images began to flicker across the giant projection TV screen. The camera zoomed in on the big Boeing 727 sitting on the runway surrounded by a swarm of heavily armed federal officers. Some men and women were unloading large plastic bags of white powder and loading them on waiting trucks.

The camera closed in on two women standing by the

big plane's nose wheel. The tall redhead spoke rapidly into her microphone.

"This is Anne Baync, World Wide News, in El Paso, Texas, with a breaking news story. In a stunning move that goes a long way to answer the criticisms of those who call our war on drugs a failure, an elite U.S. government strike team has just seized a jetliner that was attempting to smuggle a huge cargo of cocaine into the United States. This is by far the largest shipment of hard drugs ever confiscated by U.S. authorities, and its seizure is a crippling blow to the international drug cartel."

She thrust her microphone toward the woman standing next to her.

"This is DEA Special Agent in Charge Teresa Antonio, who led the Operation Snow Fall strike team."

Antonio stared at the camera. She did not look like the leader of a strike team that had just made the greatest drug seizure in U.S. history. She looked small and ordinary beside the tall, glamorous TV journalist.

"Agent Antonio, you were in command of the raid into Mexico?"

Antonio smiled modestly.

"Let's say I was the highest ranking law-enforcement officer directly involved in the operation. But I would like to make one thing clear. This wasn't just a DEA operation. Personnel from other federal agencies and the U.S. military were involved. Without their hard work and dedicated cooperation, Operation Snow Fall wouldn't have been successful."

"Can you tell us the names of your team members, Agent Antonio?"

"I'm sure you'll understand when I say that I can't do that," Antonio replied. "I would certainly like to give them the credit they deserve, but you know the war on drugs must often be carried out undercover. To reveal their names would destroy their future effectiveness.''

Bayne smiled her best professional smile, showing the camera her remarkably even white teeth. Antonio's answer had not made her happy, but the woman was smart enough to know that she was not going to get Antonio to say anything on camera that she did not want to say. She switched gears smoothly.

"I understand, Agent Antonio. I have heard rumors here at the airport that your team seized twenty tons of cocaine. That sounds incredible. Can you confirm this?"

Antonio looked straight into the camera.

"No, Miss Bayne, that isn't correct. Our preliminary inventory indicates forty tons of cocaine and—"

"Did you say forty tons?"

"Forty tons of cocaine and four tons of heroin. The cartel is branching out."

"Can you tell us how much that's worth?"

"Approximately. The wholesale price of pure cocaine in Miami is twelve to fourteen thousand dollars per kilogram. Heroin is worth more—fourteen to sixteen thousand per kilo. If the cargo had been delivered to dealers in the major U.S. cites, it would have been worth about five hundred million dollars."

For once, Anne Bayne was speechless. She caught a signal from her assistant.

"Thank you, Agent Antonio. We will now switch to the nation's capital, where the Attorney General is about to hold a news conference."

The videotape came to a stop and the lights came up.

The President was beaming. He had seen the El Paso tape four times before, but he still loved it. Hal Brognola smiled, too. The operation had been completely successful. None of his people had been killed or wounded, and

Stony Man's secrecy had been maintained. It was popular with the audience. Brognola could hear a buzz of approval. But the members of the audience were puzzled, wondering why the President had called them there.

The President looked around the conference room.

"What you have just seen was a remarkable achievement. Most of you don't know that there was a second 727 loaded with cocaine. Its crew refused to surrender and attempted to take off and escape. Agent Antonio's team destroyed the plane. In doing so, they were carrying out my orders."

"And this happened in Mexico, Mr. President? Did we have the approval of the Mexican government?" someone asked.

"Let's just say that they made no objection. Now, you're probably wondering why I asked you here. Let me tell you that this isn't a celebration. It's a major policy meeting. The United States is under attack. You might even call it chemical warfare. Most of you know that a new, much more powerful form of cocaine has been coming into our country. It has already caused the deaths of hundreds of people. If this shipment had gotten through, thousands of people would have been killed by the cocaine on those planes. We've just won a battle, but the war is still going on. There's a lot more cocaine where that came from. We have to decide what to do next. That's why I've asked you here."

He smiled as he looked around the room. He had taken a lot of flak from the media and the opposition on the failure of the war on drugs. At last, he had won one.

"Before we start, I'd like you to meet someone. I think we get too isolated here in Washington. I think we need to get the facts on the war on drugs from someone who's out there fighting in the trenches. I'd like you to meet

Special Agent Teresa Antonio and hear what she told me today.''

Everybody clapped enthusiastically as Teresa Antonio stepped up to the podium. She was nervous. She was a federal government employee, and she was about to tell the Washington establishment things they did not want to hear.

"The President asked me one question," she said quietly. "Are we winning or losing the war on drugs? He asked me not to pretty it up but just tell him the truth. I did, and it's not hard to understand. We are losing."

A murmur ran around the room. Brognola noted that some people were nodding in agreement, but others were looking skeptical.

"Would you tell us just what you base your conclusions on, Agent Antonio?" a distinguished looking senator asked.

"I could give you tons of statistics, Senator, but there is one fact that I think tells it all. I joined the DEA in 1983. My first assignment was to the Miami office. When I started there, a kilogram of pure cocaine sold for $55,000. Last week, you could buy a kilo in Miami for $12,000. And it's not just Miami. It's the same in any big city in the country. The wholesale price of cocaine has gone down nearly eighty percent. That means just one thing. Despite everything we've done, there is far more cocaine available now than when we started the war on drugs. That's the only thing that's really important. When you or I can buy cocaine on half the street corners in Miami today for less than one-quarter of what it cost in 1983, that tells it all. We're losing."

Brognola looked around and saw the unhappy faces in the room. He was not surprised. The truth was often a bitter pill to swallow.

"Thank you, Agent Antonio," the President said. "Now before I ask for comments and recommendations, I'd like you to meet one other person."

A gray-haired woman walked to the rostrum.

"I'm Dr. Margaret Klein of the DEA Special Testing and Research Laboratory, McLean, Virginia. Our drug ballistics section has completed a preliminary analysis of the cocaine shipment seized by the DEA in northern Mexico. We've succeeded in identifying the source. The cocaine was produced from the leaves of coca plants grown in the Chapare region of Bolivia. It's identical to small samples seized by the DEA offices in New York, Miami and Los Angeles. DNA analysis indicated that the genetic material of the basic coca plant has been altered to produced a new variety of cocaine. This is the cocaine that has been responsible for the significant increase in deaths among cocaine users. If this shipment had reached the United States, thousands, perhaps tens of thousands of people would have died."

A senator held up his hand.

"Just a minute, Dr. Klein. Are you saying someone has deliberately created this new variety of cocaine?"

"Yes, that's what I mean. The odds against it being a natural mutation are extremely high."

The senator shook his head. "I don't get it, Doctor. Why would the cocaine cartels produce something that could kill their customers?"

"Do you know what cocaine does to people who use it, Senator?"

The senator smiled. He was used to ducking hard questions.

"It makes them high and happy, I guess."

Dr. Klein smiled coldly. She did not think any aspect of cocaine was amusing.

"It's not as simple as that, Senator. Cocaine in any form places great stress on the body. Cocaine acts on the brain's pleasure-reward system. It stimulates a strong release of dopamine, a chemical manufactured by the body that's associated with sensations of intense pleasure. That's why, as you said, it makes the user 'high and happy.' But there is a potentially deadly, unwanted side effect. It activates the central nervous system's fight-or-flee response. Normally, this is the body's response to situations of great danger. The body floods with adrenaline, the heart rate and respiration accelerate and blood pressure rises dramatically. The chances of heart attack and cerebral hemorrhages are significantly increased. Death may result even if the user is in superb physical condition. That's what's killing people, and nothing short of making cocaine completely unavailable is going to stop it."

The senator stopped smiling. "I'm sorry I asked."

"It gets worse," she continued. "As a person continues to use cocaine, the nervous system builds up an increasing tolerance to its pleasure-inducing effects. The user has to take more and more cocaine to duplicate the original feelings of pleasure. After a while, what the user thinks is just a 'recreational' dose may become lethal. For some reason we don't understand yet, this new variety of cocaine intensifies and shortens the whole process. It makes the fight-or-flee response longer and much more intense. That's how it kills people."

She looked around the room. Her expression was somber.

"That's all I have to tell you, gentlemen, but I would like to emphasize one thing. If this variety of cocaine gets into the United States in quantity, large numbers of people are going to die. I'm an analyst. I don't make policy, but for God's sake if there's anything you can do to stop it, do it now!''

The President stepped back to the rostrum.

"Gentlemen, you've heard the facts from the people who are fighting the war. The situation is bad, and it's going to get much worse unless we do something. Now, what do we do?''

Everyone looked at the attorney general who did not look happy. Of all the members of the President's cabinet, he had the most direct responsibility for the war on drugs, and he had just heard the President call it a failure. He was on the hot seat, but he was a skilled politician. Perhaps he could turn this situation to his advantage.

"I agree with the President, gentlemen,'' he said. "The situation is very serious. I think the main problem is a shortage of resources. There are only six thousand sworn agents in the DEA, men and women who carry badges and guns and can make arrests. That's less than one agent per mile of our northern and southern borders. That's clearly inadequate. I recommend that we double the number of agents as rapidly as possible.''

A tall, black congressman stood up immediately.

"I agree with the attorney general,'' he said. "But let's not forget that we need more police officers on the streets in our inner cities. I have legislation to provide funding for twenty-five thousand federally funded officers for our large cities pending in the House. I propose we double that figure and move the bill through Congress as rapidly as possible.''

The President frowned. He was looking for new and innovative ideas, but he was getting business as usual. People were using the crisis to enhance their own positions.

"Those suggestions are certainly worth considering.

But does anyone have anything new and different to suggest?''

A tall Army officer wearing the two silver stars of a major general stood up. He was an imposing figure in his dark green uniform with the dagger patch of the Special Operations Command on his shoulder and the four rows of ribbons on his chest. Brognola did not know them all, but he recognized the Distinguished Service Cross, the Silver Star, the Purple Heart and the Combat Infantry Badge. Conrad Stuart was not just a paper pusher. He had earned his rank the hard way. Brognola had worked with Stuart before. It would be interesting to hear what he had to say.

Stuart glanced around and steeled himself. Since he had been a Ranger for many years, it would take more than a room full of politicians to frighten him.

"You have asked for recommendations, Mr. President," he said formally. "I have one. I've been involved in special operations for twenty-five years. Many of those operations were part of the war on drugs. I agree with Agent Antonio. We're losing that war, and unless we change our strategy, we'll continue to lose it."

He took a breath.

"I'm a soldier. I think in military terms. We're losing the war on drugs because we're fighting the battle in the wrong way and in the wrong place. Most of our effort is concentrated here in the United States or close to our borders. We're trying to seize cocaine after it's already in our cities or interdict the flow as it reaches our borders. You can double the size of the DEA and the Coast Guard. You can put fifty-five thousand more cops on the street. Those are good ideas. They would help, but they won't solve the problem. There's really only one way to do it. Reinstitute Operation Blast Furnace."

Many people looked puzzled, Hal Brognola included. It seemed to him that he had heard of Operation Blast Furnace years earlier, but he could not remember the details.

The President also looked puzzled, but he had worked with Stuart on a number of highly classified covert operations. He respected his abilities.

"Fill us in, General," he said. "Just what was Operation Blast Furnace?"

"It's easier to remember if you were there, sir, and I was. Cocaine is made from the leaves of coca plants. They grow only in the four Andean countries—Bolivia, Colombia, Ecuador and Peru. Most of the production is in Bolivia and Peru. The coca leaves are converted into cocaine in drug factories in those countries, then shipped to the United States. Blast Furnace was the only time we ever went after the cocaine producers on their own home ground. It was a joint U.S. Army-DEA-Bolivian government operation. For six months, it worked. We persuaded the Bolivian government to cooperate. We destroyed several major drug factories. The price of coca leaves in Bolivia dropped more than ninety percent. Most of the big drug traffickers left the country and hid out in Brazil. If we had only kept it up, we might have broken the back of the cocaine trade."

Stuart looked around the room, wearing a bitter expression. It was obvious that his memories of Operation Blast Furnace were not happy.

The President was interested.

"Why, General? What happened? Why did we quit?"

Stuart hesitated. He was not a political soldier, but he knew how things in Washington worked. If he told the truth, he would be stepping on the toes of some important people and several powerful government agencies. He had never been the kind of man who told lies or distorted the truth to protect his own position. He was not going to start now.

"Politics," Stuart said. "People in the administration got worried that we were going to suffer heavy casualties. The DEA was concerned that too many of their agents would get killed. Some Bolivian politicians started to scream that the American Army and the DEA had occupied Bolivia. There were some well organized anti-American demonstrations in the streets. The State Department started to say Blast Furnace was creating strong anti-American feeling in Bolivia and other South American countries. We didn't have the guts to stick it out. We pulled out. Three months later, the drug traffickers had come out of hiding, and it was business as usual. People in Washington started to say Blast Furnace was a failure. Well, I was there, and it wasn't. If we had stuck it out and kept on carrying the war to the drug traffickers, we wouldn't be having this meeting today."

"So, you're recommending that we reinstitute Operation Blast Furnace, General?" the President asked.

"Yes, sir. That's what I recommend, and this time, damn it, let's go in to win!"

The President asked for any additional comments. Brognola could see that several people had not liked Stuart's blunt words, but they offered no alternatives.

The President made sure he had everyone's attention. "I want to thank you all for attending the meeting on such short notice. I appreciate your advice and support. I'm going to implement several suggestions made here today. I've thought it over, and I can come to only one conclusion. General Stuart is right. We aren't going to win this war arresting small-time pushers and trying to seal our borders. We must take the war to the enemy and destroy their base of supply. As of this minute, I am reinstituting Operation Blast Furnace. Ladies and gentlemen, this time we are going in to win!''

A murmur ran around the room and it seemed to Hal Brognola that not everyone approved of the President's decision. But the majority of the key players seemed to be on his side. Brognola saw the Man smile. He read things the same way.

The President's smile faded.

''I have one more thing to say. This isn't going to be business as usual. This isn't a partisan political effort. All U.S. government agencies will give it one hundred percent support. If there is any interagency fighting or back stabbing, the heads of those agencies will be immediately replaced. Believe it! Now, I want reports from all major agencies within twenty-four hours. I want to know all our options, military, legal, diplomatic, everything. That's all, thank you.''

Brognola felt satisfied. He had worked with several United States presidents. This one was a consummate politician, but he was not afraid to make decisions and accept responsibilities. The big Fed liked to work with a man like that. He stood up and started to follow the group out the door. The President caught his eye as he passed.

''I need to see you before you leave, Hal.''

Brognola was not surprised. He did not think he had been invited to the meeting because of his sparkling personality. The President waited until he and Brognola were alone. His stage presence was gone, and he seemed tired and weary. He looked at Brognola with a question in his eyes.

''You've been around here a long time, Hal. What do you think? Did I make the right decision?''

Brognola considered his answer. He did not make policy, he carried it out. But it was an honest question and it deserved an honest answer.

"Yes, sir. I think you were right."

The President felt gratified. He knew Brognola was not a flatterer. He said what he meant. That was what made his opinions worthwhile.

"I hope so. If I can't get this drug problem under control, the nation is in deep trouble. Now, on Blast Furnace, any recommendations?"

"Yes. Put General Stuart in charge in South America. I've worked with him before. He'll get the job done, if anyone can."

"That sounds like good advice. Now, there is one more thing before you go."

He drew a thin folder out of his briefcase. Brognola could see the red-and-white covers and the letters that stated Top Secret-No Foreign in bold letters.

"I said I was putting all my cards on the table at the meeting. That wasn't absolutely true. This one has to be played close to the vest. It's a report from the director of the CIA. I asked him to use all the resources of his agency for the past week to evaluate the situation. The CIA is convinced that all of our antidrug operations have been penetrated by the cartel, the DEA, the FBI, the attorney general's office, probably even our military personnel in South America. Their evidence looks very convincing. I have to work on the assumption that it's true. I have to have some people down there that I know I can trust, people who can find things out and who won't be afraid to take decisive action if I authorize it. You and your people are what I need. I want you to support Operation Blast Furnace with everything you've got. Any questions?"

Brognola shook his head. It was plain enough. Stony Man was going to war.

"No, sir, I understand. If I can use a secure phone, I'll get on it immediately."

CHAPTER THREE

El Dorado International Airport, Bogotá, Colombia

Mack Bolan checked his watch and looked around the airport terminal. Big and modern, it featured snack bars, restaurants, shops that sold Indian handicrafts, a tourist information office and a branch of the national bank. The airport was situated eight miles northwest of Bogotá, and the Executioner just had time to make his meeting at Colombian National Police headquarters, provided the U.S. embassy staff did their share. It would be very difficult to explain the contents of his team's luggage to the Colombian customs officers.

An earnest young man in a gray three-piece suit had introduced himself as an assistant attaché from the American embassy. He knew the airport security procedures, and the Colombian National Police officers knew him. Diplomatic immunity and the news that the director general of the National Police wished to see these Americans immediately worked wonders. Their luggage was whisked through customs, and they were ushered to the rental car company in remarkably short order.

The embassy had reserved a Volkswagen van. Bolan would have preferred something faster, but he did not have time to request a change. David McCarter took the keys from a young woman at the rental desk. He was automatically elected to be the driver. All the members of Phoenix Force and Able Team were excellent drivers, but McCarter was superb.

The Briton put the van in gear and pulled past the rental agent's booth. The woman who had given him the keys, whose blazer had a big tag that read "Maria", showed her gleaming white teeth as she smiled at the handsome, well-dressed Englishman..

"Enjoy your stay in Bogotá, sir. Will you be here long?"

"Unfortunately, no, to my great regret," McCarter said.

Bolan looked at McCarter with a raised eyebrow.

"Charming young lady," McCarter said as he pulled onto the highway. "She obviously knows a gentleman when she sees one."

Bolan shook his head. He was used to Jack Grimaldi seeming to have a girlfriend in every airport in the world, but McCarter?

"You think so?"

"Certainly. Charming, absolutely charming. She has a lovely face and did you see her—"

McCarter studied the traffic around them.

"I hate to change the subject, old chap, but I think someone's following us. A blue Mercedes-Benz and two or three vans."

Bolan checked the side rearview mirror. There were several cars behind them, but this was the main road from the airport to central Bogotá. There was bound to be traffic. It might be nothing at all, but this was Colombia and he trusted McCarter's judgment. Better safe than sorry.

"Speed up. Let's see what they do."

The soldier studied the rearview mirror as McCarter stepped on the gas and the van accelerated smoothly. He could see the blue Mercedes and at least two minivans following closely.

Bolan frowned.

"All right, everybody, get your weapons out and lock and load. Keep them down out of sight."

McCarter's face tightened. "You think they'll try something as soon as this, Mack?"

Bolan nodded. "Even if they knew we were coming, they weren't going to try anything in the airport. There were too many National Police and soldiers around. But if they want to get us out of the picture, they'll try to hit us on the road, now, before we get into Bogotá."

McCarter reached under his jacket and pulled out his 9 mm Browning Hi-Power pistol. He would have to keep one hand on the wheel to drive, but McCarter was a formidable shot. Mack Bolan unzipped a black nylon case between his feet and pulled out his M-4 Ranger carbine. The weapon was loaded with a 30-round magazine, and it had a 40 mm M-203 grenade launcher clipped beneath the rifle barrel. The Executioner pumped the action of the grenade launcher to chamber a high-explosive round and placed the M-4 across his knees.

Bolan looked at McCarter. "What do you think?"

The Briton frowned. "Soon. There's a clear stretch of road ahead. I'd say there." He checked the rearview mirror.

"Heads up, men. The Mercedes is coming up."

Bolan glanced at the rearview. The big blue car was almost overtaking their Volkswagen van, and the Mercedes had far more power. McCarter was a superb driver, but if there was going to be a race, they would lose.

"Don't speed up," Bolan ordered. "Act as if you haven't noticed."

McCarter nodded. "They're probably not going to start

the party. I'd say they want to get ahead and block us. I could be wrong, though. We'd better be ready, just in case."

McCarter was right. Bolan gave his orders quickly.

"Gary, you and Cowboy take the left side windows. Rafe, you and T.J. take the right. Gadgets, you take the rear window. Remember, we don't shoot until they initiate hostile action. Got it?"

Gary Manning nodded. He had a .30-caliber Heckler & Koch sniper's rifle across his knees with a 20-round magazine inserted. The weapon was one of the most accurate rifles in the world. It was also extremely powerful, with far more penetrating power that the high-velocity .22 bullets from the M-4 carbines. If worse came to worst, Manning could riddle the Mercedes in three or four seconds of aimed semiautomatic fire.

"Where will you be, Mack?" he asked.

"I'll take the sunroof. I need to work on my tan."

Manning grinned. The sunroof was the most exposed position, but Bolan would be able to fire in any direction.

The Executioner unlatched the sliding sun roof but kept it closed. He pulled on a set of plastic goggles. It was going to be breezy up there.

"Here they come," Schwarz shouted.

"They're pulling out, passing on the left, Mack. Their windows are still up. No sign of hostile action," McCarter reported.

They waited tensely, half a dozen weapons poised for action. The temptation to open fire and gain the advantage of surprise was strong, but Bolan resisted it. They were in a foreign country, and so far, the people in the Mercedes had done nothing but follow them down the road. He watched out the left side window as the blue vehicle shot by in a smooth display of power. It changed lanes again, and now it was in front of them, its driver perfectly matching McCarter's speed.

"There's a white minivan coming up to pass us," Schwarz announced.

"I see him," McCarter answered, "and there's someone coming up behind him. A yellow minivan with tinted windows."

"Keep your eyes open, Gadgets. There'll probably be one more."

"Roger, Mack," Schwarz acknowledged. Bolan took a quick look over his shoulder. Gadgets had a 9 mm Calico submachine gun in his hands with a 100-round magazine snapped in place. He could make life very exciting for anyone who came up on their rear bumper. Bolan glanced around the interior of the van. Everyone was in position and had their weapons ready. It was not going to be easy. The body of the van looked solid, but it would not stop bullets, and the odds were at least two to one. Only fast, accurate shooting could save them now.

"Do you want me to take evasive action, Mack?" McCarter asked quietly.

Bolan shook his head. "The minute you do that, they'll know we see them. Act like you don't know they're there. We might be able to surprise them."

McCarter smiled in appreciation. He liked that kind of surprise.

"Got it. What do you think they are going to do?"

Bolan glanced into the rearview mirror.

"They've got at least two vehicles, maybe three. They should also have one other vehicle acting as the observer and to follow us in case we get away. That's probably the blue Mercedes. If they're smart, at least two vehicles will try to cut us off and hold us in place while the third one comes in for the kill. They'll have something like a heavy, a grenade or rocket launcher.''

"That's simply wonderful,'' McCarter said. "That's why I like working with you. There's so seldom a dull moment. Let's see if we can lure them in.''

The Briton accelerated. Behind them, the white minivan sped up as well, changing lanes to come up alongside them.

Bolan watched as the yellow minivan came slowly up behind them, recognizing the setup as a textbook case of a moving ambush. Both vans had large sliding doors in each side and wide windows in the back. There could be a lot of men and weapons in those vehicles. In another minute, they would be sandwiched between them, trapped in a deadly cross fire.

McCarter checked his rearview mirrors for the third vehicle, then spoke quietly without taking his eyes off the road. "There's your third van, Mack, another minivan. It's black with tinted windows. Just pulled onto the road behind us from that on ramp and is coming up fast.''

Bolan checked his mirror again. The third van was accelerating rapidly, coming up behind them. The trap was closing fast. He did not believe in coincidence. The people in those vans were going to kill them. There was no point in waiting any longer.

"Go!'' he shouted.

McCarter accelerated slightly, holding the steering wheel in his left hand and his big 9 mm Browning pistol in his right, keeping its muzzle just below the upper edge of the door. Bolan heard the whine of electric motors as the Briton pushed the master control switch and lowered the windows. Air began to howl through the interior of the van at sixty miles per hour.

Bolan slid open the sun roof and stood up, his head and

shoulders above the van's roof, the M-4 carbine in his hands. He flipped the weapon's selector switch to full-auto.

The white van in the fast lane began to accelerate steadily up alongside them, its windows starting to open. Bolan's right hand moved to the M-203 grenade launcher's trigger assembly in front of the M-4 carbine's magazine.

The yellow van was coming up fast on the other side, followed by the third van. A bullet struck the Volkswagen's roof. The people in the white van were getting hostile. McCarter snapped up his Browning Hi-Power and fired shots into the van's front seat as fast as he could pull the trigger. It was hard to aim well and drive at the same time, but McCarter was a superb driver and an excellent shot. Most of the full-metal-jacketed bullets tore into the front of the van. Broken glass sprayed from the white van's windshield and the vehicle lurched and swayed as the driver fought for control.

Two men with AK-47s were trying to fire through the side windows. The sudden lurch threw off their aim, but the Volkswagen van was a big target. Not all their bullets missed. McCarter heard the sound of bullets tearing through metal and someone swearing. He had no time to look. He concentrated on holding the van steady so that his passengers could shoot. He heard a snarling roar as Gary Manning fired his Heckler & Koch PSG-1. The white van lurched again, but it stayed beside them.

Bolan aimed his M-4 carbine at the white van's front window, looking steadily through the carbine's grenade sight despite the wind tearing at his hands and face. He aimed at the front window and pulled the M-203's trigger, feeling the push of the recoil as the M-203 sent the 40 mm high-explosive grenade on its way. He had not allowed enough for the wind, so the slow moving heavy

grenade was blown to the rear. Bolan saw glass shatter
and splinters fly as the heavy projectile struck the rear
window and detonated inside the van. He saw a flash of
orange flamc, then the gasoline tank exploded, and the
van was enveloped in a ball of orange fire. He felt the
heat and shock of the blast against his face, then the white
van was gone, a shattered burning wreck spun away behind them as McCarter accelerated away.

Something plucked at Bolan's sleeve. The yellow van
was to their right now, weapons blazing from its windows.
The M-203 grenade launcher was a single-shot wcapon,
and the soldier had no time to load another grenade. He
snapped the M-4 carbine to his shoulder and looked
through its sights. Three men were firing from the van's
open windows, two with AK-47s, the third with a 12-
gauge riot shotgun. Bolan pressed the carbine's trigger
and sprayed the van's interior with four quick bursts. He
saw a red dot fly as he fired the last burst. He had used
the old soldier's trick of loading a tracer as the last round
in the magazine. His carbine was empty.

There was no time to reload. He dropped the carbine
and let it swing on the black nylon sling across his shoulder, drawing his .44 Magnum Desert Eagle. Hawkins had
already aimed his M-4 carbine and was shooting short
bursts into the van alongside them. Glass flew as the van's
rear window shattered under the multiple bullet impacts.
Bolan saw flickering muzzle-flashes as the men in the
attack vehicle fired back, and he felt a series of hard fast
jabs as a charge of 12-gauge buckshot smashed into his
body armor.

Hawkins fired again as McCarter pulled the Volkswagen into the vacant fast lane to the left and tried to take
them out of the hail of gunfire. For a second, the yellow

van fell behind, then the driver floored the gas pedal, and the vehicle began to creep forward.

This couldn't go on. At any moment, a bullet might hit the Volkswagen's gas tank or blow out a rear tire. Bolan ignored the shrieking wind and the screeching tires. As he pushed off the big Desert Eagle's safety, he saw a swarm of yellow-white flashes as Gadgets Schwarz fired a burst of 9 mm hollowpoints into the pursuing van's hood. The burst was ineffective and Bolan knew why. Gadgets's submachine gun was silenced, his magazines loaded with subsonic hollowpoint rounds. His bullets were striking the slanted hood and glancing off, failing to penetrate the engine compartment. Faster than their Volkswagen, the yellow van was slowly pulling alongside.

"The tires! The tires!" Bolan shouted, but Gadgets did not hear him over the roar of gunfire and the shrieking rubber. The Executioner would have to take his own advice. The man with the shotgun had stopped firing. He was probably reloading. It was now or never.

Bolan leaned farther out of the sunroof, rested both elbows on the van's roof, gripped his big .44 in a firm two-handed grip and sighted on the yellow van's left front wheel. He pressed the trigger rapidly, firing as fast as he could, pausing only a fraction of a second to check his sights. He fired six or seven times, but nothing seemed to happen. Suddenly the enemy vehicle's front tire blew. The van swerved wildly as the driver fought desperately for control. Bursts of AK-47 rifle fire streamed high over Bolan's head as the men firing through the van's windows were thrown around as the vehicle spun and skidded.

The driver lost his fight. The yellow van suddenly skidded out of control and struck the outer lane's guardrail. Tearing through the barrier, it flipped over and over until it smashed into an outcrop and burst into flames.

There was no time to watch the wreck. The black van was still behind them. Bolan holstered his Desert Eagle and snapped a fresh 40 mm grenade into the M-203.

McCarter checked his rearview mirror.

"Behind us, Mack!" he shouted.

The black van was closing in. A big man was awkwardly shoving his head and shoulders out of its sunroof while he clutched something in both hands. For a moment Bolan could not tell what it was. He could see a round black circle like the muzzle of a weapon, but it was far too big to be a 12-gauge shotgun or even a 40 mm grenade launcher. Then he realized it was a Russian rocket-propelled grenade launcher.

"Rocket launcher," he yelled as he snapped up his M-4 carbine and fired a fast burst.

McCarter understood the danger perfectly and did not waste time in conversation. He twisted the wheel and yanked the Volkswagen to the left. The tires screamed and the boxy van shuddered on the edge of turning over, but McCarter managed to straighten out and roar down the road.

Bolan held on grimly and glanced at the black van behind them. He saw a sudden puff of gray-white smoke, and something long, slender and deadly shot toward him. The RPG-7 rocket passed close enough for him to feel the hot exhaust gas from the rocket motor on his face. It shot past the Volkswagen, streaked down the road ahead and struck the ground ahead, its five-pound high-explosive warhead detonating into a ball of fire.

The man in the black van's sunroof suddenly ducked inside the vehicle. The RPG-7 had to be reloaded through the muzzle, a task that was impossible to complete on the roof of a swaying van.

Bolan aimed the grenade launcher and pulled the trigger, sending a 40 mm high-explosive grenade toward the black van's front window. He saw glass shatter as it struck the window, penetrated into the van and detonated in an orange flash. The vehicle's other windows were shattered by the blast. It fishtailed, rolled over and slammed into the freeway's center divider.

The Executioner was full of adrenaline. He scanned the area, looking for targets, but there was nothing left to shoot. The Phoenix Force van was roaring down the road alone. The blue Mercedes, and who knew what else, was somewhere ahead of them. They might be rushing into another ambush. Bolan ducked back down through the sunroof and yelled, "Stop!"

McCarter hit the brakes, and the Volkswagen screamed to a smoking stop by the road's center divider. Behind them, the three vans were strewed along a thousand-yard stretch of road, burning and exploding, sending up huge plumes of thick black smoke. Bolan searched the road ahead. The blue Mercedes was gone, but he knew that it was somewhere ahead, its occupants reporting what had happened to their superiors.

Behind them, traffic had come to a halt, as dozens of astonished motorists slowed to inspect the carnage. A huge traffic jam was already starting. The traffic ahead was gone and the empty freeway stretched out in front of them. Bolan surveyed the vans.

Nothing moved.

He got out of the Volkswagen and pushed a fresh magazine into his M-4 carbine. He worked the M-203's breech and slid in a defensive multiple projectile. They ought to report what had happened, but he was not sure just how. He considered checking the vans for survivors, but it was probably going to be a waste of time.

He heard the familiar sound of helicopter rotors and

looked up. A Bell UH-1 military helicopter was approaching rapidly from the direction of the airport. Bolan saw the red, yellow and blue insignia of the Colombian military painted on its side as it turned and started to come in for a landing. McCarter climbed out of the Volkswagen, snapping a fresh magazine into his Browning before holstering it.

"What do you think?" Bolan asked. "Were they just waiting at the airport for some Americans to kill, or were they looking for us?"

"They weren't just hanging around the airport, Mack. Think it over—twenty or thirty men, four vehicles, that's a major effort. They wouldn't be waiting at the airport for days just on the chance someone would turn up. They were there waiting for us, and they were there to kill us. You see what that means, don't you?"

Bolan frowned. He did not like it, but McCarter was right.

"Yeah," he said quietly, "they were waiting for us. They knew which flight we were on. Our security has been penetrated. They have someone inside Blast Furnace."

CHAPTER FOUR

National Police Headquarters, Bogotá, Colombia

Bolan and McCarter were quickly ushered to the top floor of the National Police headquarters building. The heavily armed, uniformed guards were careful to check their ID, but the news that the director general wished to see them immediately prevented any bureaucratic delays. Their escort delivered them to the director general's secretary, a pleasant, gray-haired woman in a tan uniform. She poured each man a cup of coffee and assured them that the director general would see them as soon as he finished a phone call to the minister of national defense. Bolan and McCarter looked at each other. It was the same the whole world over. Hurry up and wait.

At least, the coffee was superb. The man who once said Colombia produced the finest coffee and the finest cocaine was probably right. Bolan was working on his second cup when the secretary motioned for them to follow her into the director general's office.

General Julio Arias was a tall, thin man with closely cropped gray hair. He wore a tan cotton summer uniform, and the two multipointed stars of a Colombian major general on his blue shoulder boards. He carried a 9 mm Browning Hi-Power pistol in a belt holster, and it was not for show. Bolan could see that the hammer was cocked and the safety set, ready to draw and fire in an instant. Arias sat at a large desk looking at some photographs and papers in front of him.

He stood up and smiled as his secretary led Bolan and McCarter, who was using his David Green alias, into his office.

"Mr. Belasko, Captain Green, I am General Julio Arias, the director general of the National Police. Your attorney general has requested that I brief you on the drug situation here in Colombia and to discuss possible Colombian cooperation with the United States in the new action in your war on drugs, Operation Blast Furnace. I am happy to do so."

He paused and stared at them for a moment, and his smile faded.

"Before I do, let us, as Americans like to say, get one thing straight. There is a bad joke here that says that in Colombia, everyone works either for the drug cartels or the Americans. Well, I do not work for either. My allegiance is to the legally elected government of Colombia and to the constitution of 1886. And, gentlemen, be sure that I will do my duty."

Mack Bolan could think of nothing to say to that. Arias motioned for them to be seated. The Executioner snatched a quick look at the photos on the general's desk. That might not be polite, but he was not sure how he stood with the general. After all, he and Phoenix Force had killed a number of Colombian citizens on Colombian soil a few hours earlier. It had been self-defense, but the director general of the National Police might still take a dim view of it. It was as he suspected. The large glossy black-and-white prints showed burned-out minivans and burned and riddled bodies.

Arias saw Bolan's quick look.

"Yes, Mr. Belasko, part of your welcoming committee. We have identified some of the bodies. All are known gunmen for the Cali cartel. You have saved the national prosecutor's office a great many pesos."

He looked at another paper on his desk.

"I see that you are a British subject, Captain Green. Is the British government participating in Operation Blast Furnace?"

McCarter smiled disarmingly.

"No, sir, at least, not yet, although cocaine is becoming a major problem in Great Britain. I am here merely as an observer."

The general looked at the small silver pin in the lapel of McCarter's sports jacket, a double-edged winged dagger. He was not close enough to read the tiny letters on the badge, but he knew that they said—Who dares wins! It was the badge of McCarter's former regiment, the Special Air Service, England's counterterrorism team.

"I understand, Captain," Arias said. "The SAS is famous for its powers of observation. I am sure your report on Operation Blast Furnace will make fascinating reading. May I offer you more coffee? No? Then let me brief you on our war with the drug cartels.

"I am responsible to the president of the republic for our war on drugs. I command the National Police Force. I have fifty-eight thousand officers and men in my force. I can call on our army, the navy and the air force for support, as well as the ministry of justice and other civilian agencies. We have formed an integrated task force. We are going after the drug cartel's drug factories, drug crops, chemicals, bank accounts and political connections. We have a special military and police task force in the city of Cali. Its mission is to crack down on the drug cartel and disrupt its drug operations and communications. We have placed military garrisons on all of the Colombian-owned Caribbean islands to intercept drug shipments and confiscate the cartel's ships and airplanes. If we can keep it up, in another year or two, we will see the beginning of the end of the Cali cartel in Colombia.''

Arias stopped and looked from face to face.

''That is a wonderful speech. It impresses even me. I am sure it makes the narcobarons tremble in their boots. But you gentlemen are men of the world. You know I would say exactly the same things if I was in the pay of the drug cartel. Such words are easy. Perhaps I can show you something more convincing.''

He stood up and walked to the wall beside his desk, stopping beside a large map of Colombia flanked on either side by two boards covered with black cloths.

''As you Americans say, you cannot tell who is winning the game unless you know the score. These are my scoreboards.''

He pulled the black cloth off the left-hand board.

''This is what we have accomplished so far this year. We have destroyed twenty-five thousand acres of coca plants and fifty-four hundred acres of heroin crops. We have confiscated more than four hundred forty thousand gallons of liquid chemicals and eight million pounds of solid chemicals used by the drug cartel to process coca into cocaine. We have destroyed two hundred forty-three drug factories, and twelve hundred drug cartel criminals have been arrested and have been convicted or they are in prison or awaiting trial.''

''Very impressive, General,'' McCarter said.

''I believe so, myself, but it is only part of the score. He pulled the black cloth off the second board.

''This is the other half of the score. This is what it has

cost us. In the past ten years, the cartel has killed more than three thousand National Policemen and soldiers, twenty-three federal judges, four presidential candidates, sixty-three journalists and hundreds of innocent Colombian civilians. We are fighting the war on drugs, but we are bleeding, gentlemen.''

Bolan looked at the somber figures on the chart. He knew Colombia was a small country with one-tenth the population of the United States. Losses like those shown on the chart would really hurt. He saw something the general had not mentioned. In the lower right-hand corner of the chart was a red, hand-printed number three. Someone had crossed it out and printed four next to it.

''What's the red number, General?''

Arias smiled. ''It is of no importance. My staff likes to keep track of such things. That is the number of attempts to assassinate me so far this year. They have tried car bombs, snipers and putting a bomb in my staff car. The cartel is very ingenious. Perhaps next they will put poison in my coffee.''

Bolan nodded. He knew Arias was not joking. If a man in his position was not willing to sell out to the drug cartels, he had one of the most dangerous jobs in Colombia.

''Now, to business. Your General Stuart stopped here yesterday on his way to Bolivia. He explained Operation Blast Furnace to me and my staff. I think it is an excellent idea. I hope you are very successful. General Stuart also talked to the minister of national defense and the commanding general of the armed forces. The United States is very anxious that Operation Blast Furnace be seen as a multinational operation. They would like the Colombian armed forces and the National Police to participate by sending units to Bolivia. Frankly, I do not think that will happen. We have more than enough problems to handle here. Perhaps the army will send a Ranger battalion to make your government happy, but that is all.''

Arias looked at a file on his desk.

"I am sure you gentlemen are here for some specific purpose. You seem to be a highly efficient group. You rid Colombia of twenty-three cartel gunmen this morning. I am grateful for that. Keeping in mind that I have no people I can deploy to Bolivia, what can I do for you?''

"I'll leave questions of national policy to people who are paid to worry about them," Bolan said. "What I need is information from your Department F-2.''

"The Intelligence department, Mr. Belasko? I am surprised you know so much about my organization. Perhaps that can be arranged. What do you wish to know?''

"Our information is the same as yours. Cocaine production has shifted south to Bolivia during the past few years. We understand that many Colombians have gone to Bolivia and are involved in drug production there. I would like all the information your Intelligence department has on these people—names, descriptions, capabilities, current locations.''

Arias nodded. That would not cost him much, and it would make the Americans happy.

"We are always glad to assist our allies. I will notify the head of Department F-2 immediately. You will have the information you request in twenty-four hours.''

Someone knocked on the office door. The general's secretary entered and handed him a sheet of paper.

"This is a message from the American embassy in La Paz. You are in demand, Mr. Belasko. General Stuart wishes to see you in Bolivia as soon as possible. A place is reserved for you on an American Air Force plane that will stop here tomorrow morning. It will fly you directly to La Paz. I will give the Intelligence data you requested to Captain Green. I wish you a safe journey. Good luck in Bolivia.''

The meeting was over; the general's secretary ushered them out.

"It looks like I'm on my way to La Paz," Bolan said. "It seems like we're going to get what we wanted here. I'll see you in Bolivia."

McCarter was frowning. Something was bothering him, and Bolan had learned long ago that when the Phoenix Force commando was unhappy, there was usually a good reason for it.

"There's something wrong?" he asked.

"Too right. Do you know General Stuart?"

"I know who he is, but I've never met him. Why?"

"I keep on top of the Stony Man security files. There's a *very* short list of people who are cleared to know who we are and what we do. General Stuart's name isn't on the list. If he doesn't know who you are, why does he want to see you immediately? If he does know, who told him? I don't like it."

Neither did Bolan.

"I don't know the answer," he said. "I guess I'll have to go to Bolivia and find out."

CHAPTER FIVE

La Paz, Bolivia

Mack Bolan got to his feet as the big Air Force C-17 braked to a stop. He was glad the flight from Bogotá to La Paz was over. The C-17 Globe Master was a miracle of modern technology, but its seats were as uncomfortable as those in any U.S. military transport plane in which he had ever flown. He picked up his two black nylon bags and walked down the ramp, blinking in the bright midday sun. A Captain Swenson from the U.S. embassy was supposed to meet him. He hoped the captain had not forgotten. It would be extremely awkward trying to explain the contents of his bags to the Bolivian authorities.

He slipped on his sunglasses. A sign proclaimed that he was at Kennedy International Airport, altitude 4,018 meters, the highest commercial airport in the world. He could believe that. A cold breeze was blowing across the runways. He had a heavier jacket in one of his bags, but he was not about to open it in public. The small terminal did not seem to have much to offer. Groups of soldiers and civilians were exiting the huge C-17. A harried U.S. Army master sergeant was herding them toward a row of waiting buses. Bolan did not see an Army captain who seemed to be looking for him.

A tall Army sergeant first class, standing by a jeep, was wearing camouflaged combat fatigues and had a 9 mm Beretta pistol holstered at his side. He held a card with Belasko printed on it in large black letters. It did not look as if Bolan rated deluxe transportation, but at least he would not have to walk. He walked over to the jeep.

"I'm Mike Belasko, Sergeant."

"Right, I'm Sergeant Johnson. Welcome to La Paz. Got all your gear?"

Bolan nodded.

"Let's go, then. The general wants to see you in a hurry."

Bolan put his bags in the jeep and swung into the passenger seat.

Johnson drove smoothly down an access road next to the runway. They came to an open gate guarded by a small man in a khaki uniform with a rifle slung over his shoulder. Bolan saw two more men in similar uniforms with their rifles ready in their hands. The first man took one look at the jeep's diplomatic plates and waved them through.

"Army?" Bolan asked.

"*Carabineros,*" Johnson said. "Part of the National Police Force. They've been tightening up security since Blast Furnace started. By the way, are you armed?"

Bolan nodded. His Beretta 93-R was under his left arm, and his .44 Magnum Desert Eagle was holstered on his hip. "Are you expecting trouble?" he asked casually.

"Not exactly, but the general says all military personnel had better be ready for trouble. He says the drug cartels aren't going to take Blast Furnace lying down."

Bolan sensed that the general was a man who knew his way around. He checked to be sure that the selector switch on his Beretta was set for burst fire.

"Heads up and hang on," Johnson warned. "Here we go."

Bolan glanced up. They seemed to be running out of road and driving over a cliff. He saw a sign that said PARA ABAJO! in bold letters. He had just enough time to translate that into "downhill" before Johnson pulled a hard left turn and started down a road that twisted along the side of the plateau toward the city below. They passed through shabby groups of houses and shops. Then suddenly there it was, twelve hundred feet below, La Paz filling the bowl of a huge canyon three miles wide from rim to rim.

It was a remarkable view, a city of a million people with a cluster of modern high-rise buildings at its center, but Mack Bolan concentrated on hanging on as Johnson snaked the jeep down the winding road.

"This is the back road," he said cheerfully. "It's a bit rough, but it's quicker this time of day." Bolan could believe that. It was a white-knuckle ride all the way. He hung on grimly until suddenly they were down, driving along tree-lined streets decorated here and there with bronze statues of generals from forgotten wars. Johnson turned left into the center of the city, drove three blocks and pulled up in front of a building. It did not look much like an embassy, just another commercial building, but with the American flag flying and Marine security guards at the door.

"This is it," Johnson announced. "Not much to look at. It used to be the U.S. Consulate until it got upgraded last year. Things are a real mess right now. People are pouring in for Blast Furnace, and we've got to try and coordinate the whole damned show. Come on, Belasko, we don't want to keep the general waiting."

They waited while the Marines checked their ID. There

was no way that Bolan could see a man on the second floor of the commercial building across the street who took several pictures of him with a 35 mm camera with a superb telephoto lens.

Johnson ushered Mack Bolan into the building and down the hall. He stopped at a desk outside an office manned by a tall, thin, blond woman wearing a U.S. Army camouflage battle dress uniform and a captain's bars. The sergeant saluted.

"Mr. Belasko, sir," he said and was gone.

The captain stared at Bolan without enthusiasm. Her desk was stacked with papers, and waiting lights were glowing on her phone. It was obvious that she had never heard of Mike Belasko and did not need any new problems.

"I'm Captain Swenson. Just what can I do for you?"

Bolan smiled and extended his passport.

"Mike Belasko, Captain. I'm attached to the Blast Furnace Task Force. I was told General Stuart wanted to see me here immediately."

Swenson glanced at a list on her desk and nodded.

"The general does want to see you as soon as possible, Mr. Belasko. He's meeting with General of Brigade Gomez, our liaison with the Bolivian army. Have a seat and have some coffee while you wait."

Bolan nodded and sat in a battered wooden chair. He would have liked to ask the captain what was going on, but she had no time for casual conversation. She was on the phone answering one call after another, switching rapidly from English to Spanish and back again. Bolan stood and poured a cup of coffee, then settled down to wait. Even if Swenson had not been busy, he doubted that she knew the answer to the one thing he really needed to know.

Why did General Stuart want to see Mike Belasko? Bolan was sure that he had never met Stuart as Mike Belasko or under any other name. If Hal Brognola had set up a meeting with the man, he would have told him. He did not like it. Stuart should not know who Mike Belasko was or what he did. If security had been breached and his cover had been blown at the start of the operation, things were bad.

The door to the general's office opened. A tall man wearing a khaki uniform with a six-pointed gold star on each shoulder came out and walked down the hall. He had to be General Gomez. He looked as if he had things on his mind. His meeting with General Stuart had obviously not been a happy one. The captain did not seem to care. She ushered Mack Bolan into the general's small office and closed and locked the door.

General Stuart, a big man over six feet tall with iron gray hair, was sitting behind a desk. He was wearing a leaf stripe camouflage battle dress uniform and well-worn combat boots. A nylon web belt around his waist supported a holstered .45 automatic and a Randall fighting knife. Bolan appreciated the Ranger tab on his left sleeve and the silver parachutist's wings on his chest. There were generals, and there were generals. Stuart did not look like the armchair type.

"Glad to see you, Belasko," he said. "You and I need to talk as soon as Swenson fills you in on the situation. She's the assistant military attaché at the embassy here. I've drafted her as my aide while I try to get things organized."

Swenson set up a chart under a map of Bolivia on the wall, then pointed at the chart.

"This shows the organization of the Bolivian armed forces and the national security forces. Antinarcotics activities are the mission of the security forces. Bolivia doesn't have local police forces. All police units report to the director general here in La Paz. We are interested in the Fuerza Especial de Lucha Contra el Narcotrafico, the Special Force Against Narcotics, FELCN, for short. It has about six thousand officers and men and is responsible for antinarcotics efforts throughout the country. It can call on the army, navy, air force and other branches of the police for support as necessary. Obviously, the FELCN is going to be involved in Blast Furnace.''

She turned to the map.

"Bolivia is about the size of California and Texas put together. It has approximately seven million people. About half of them are Aymara and Quechua Indians. Thirty percent are mixed blood, and the rest are of Spanish descent. They're the elite that really run the country. In most cases, if you're dealing with government officials, you will be dealing with them.''

Bolan nodded. He did not expect that he would be spending much time hobnobbing with high-ranking government officials.

She pointed to two areas outlined in red in the center of the map.

"These are the two main cocaine production areas in Bolivia, the Yungas and the Chapare regions. More than sixty-five percent of the cocaine entering the United States comes from there. Cocaine is made from the leaves of the coca plant. The coca bushes will not grow above two thousand meters or below one thousand. That limits the area of cultivation and production. The objective of Operation Blast Furnace is to destroy cocaine production in those areas.''

Bolan nodded. "I understand. Our objective is to destroy the coca plant fields?''

Swenson glared at him.

"Certainly not, Mr. Belasko! We can't do that. That would be a major violation of Bolivian law. It's not illegal to grow coca plants here. About one-half million people, mostly small farmers, grow coca plants. Coca pumps about two billion dollars a year into the Bolivian economy. The coca growers don't think they are criminals, and they have a lot of political influence. It's illegal to convert coca leaves to cocaine. That's what we have to go after, the drug factories that convert coca to cocaine."

"All right," Bolan said. "We go after the factories. Where do I come in?"

Stuart smiled. Whoever Belasko really was, he did not beat around the bush.

"As far as I know, I can't order you to do anything, but I'm going to request that you and your people take on an extremely important task. The CIA and the National Reconnaissance Office are making an all-out effort to locate the cocaine factories. They think they've already found several. The President wants action, and he wants it now. It will be days, maybe weeks, before we get things straightened out with the Bolivian government. We have to settle questions of command and control and rules for the use of U.S. military personnel before I can move officially. We can't wait. We need to take action in the Chapare region. There's really only one organization that can do anything immediately. I want you to go to the Chapare and support their operations as soon as possible. Tell Mr. Belasko about UMOPAR, Swenson."

Captain Swenson pointed to her chart.

"UMOPAR is the Rural Area Police Patrol Unit. They are based in the Chapare."

"I'm sorry, General," Bolan said. "I don't think I'm the man for the job. I don't have any law-enforcement experience. Neither do most of the people on my team. It sounds like a job for the DEA or the FBI, not for us.''

''UMOPAR is not your average rural police force,'' Stuart said. ''They are a special paramilitary force organized to go after the narcotics traffickers on their own home ground. They were organized in 1983 at the request of our government, and we pay part of their costs. Nobody calls them UMOPAR down here. People call them Los Leopardos, the Leopards, from their jungle-camoflage combat fatigues. The drug cartel's people are well armed and willing to fight. It's the Leopards' job to take them out. I have a great deal of confidence in you, Belasko. I'm certain you can handle the job.''

Bolan frowned. What Stuart said was flattering, but how did he know about him at all? Had someone in Washington been talking?

''Before I say yes or no, General, there's something I have to ask in private.''

Stuart nodded. ''I'm sure Captain Swenson will excuse us.''

Swenson swept out of the office with the air of someone who had wasted enough time on the mysterious Mr. Belasko.

''General,'' Bolan said ''there's something I've got to know.'' His face was grim. He did not want to anger Stuart, but something was wrong. The Stony Man team's effectiveness was based on its security, and it looked as if that security had been breached.

''You say you have a great deal of confidence in me. I need to know why. The existence of the organization I work with and its roles and missions are highly classified. Information about it can be distributed on a need-to-know basis only. There are only a few authorized people with a need to know. It's a short list, and I know every name on it. Yours isn't one of them. If you had been briefed since I left the United States, my mission controller would have informed me. There appears to have been a breach of security. I need to know what you know and how you know it.''

"Take it easy," Stuart replied. "I'm not trying to find out who you really are or what your organization does. If you told me, you'd probably have to kill me. Let's just say that a few months ago the President directed me to support a special operation in New Guinea. The operation was controlled by Hal Brognola in the Department of Justice. You may remember a submarine and some cruise missiles. I organized that part of the mission. I know Brognola's team accomplished a very difficult mission under extremely hazardous conditions. You are on my personnel list as an observer from the Sensitive Operations Group of the Department of Justice, which my sources say is headed by Hal Brognola. Not all generals are stupid. I can put two and two together and get four. I think you are the head of Brognola's special team. That's why I say I've got a lot of confidence in you, and I'm sure you can handle the job. I can't order you to do it. You can walk out the door if you want, but this is an important job. Somebody has to do it.''

Bolan thought it over. What Stuart said made sense. Perhaps he owed the general one. He had been awfully glad to see that submarine that day, as his helicopter had been running out of fuel over the ocean. Besides, he had not come to Bolivia to sit behind a desk and shuffle papers. If the action was in the Chapare, he was ready to go there.

"All right, when do I leave?" he asked.

"You fly out to Santa Cruz first thing in the morning. From there, you take a helicopter to the Leopards' base at Trinidad. Captain Swenson will go with you to carry the latest Intelligence information. She will introduce you to Colonel Suarez, thc Leopards' commanding officer and the head of the DEA team at Trinidad. Be careful what you say to the local DEA agents. The CIA believes they have been penetrated by the drug cartel. I'll have your team flown into Santa Cruz as soon as possible. We'll put you up at a local hotel tonight. Sergeant Johnson will drive you over. I'll have Captain Swenson bring some background briefing folders to your hotel when she gets off duty. Read them tonight. They'll help put you in the picture. Any questions?"

Bolan shook his head. It all seemed clear enough. He would find out the details when he got there. But come to think of it, there was one thing he did need to know.

"Suppose I locate a drug factory, and for some reason, the Leopards aren't willing to hit it. Am I authorized to destroy it?"

"No, I can't tell you to do that. Just keep an eye on it," Stuart said. "It just might take care of itself. You know drug factories use large amounts of very dangerous chemicals. Who knows? It might just catch fire and explode."

Bolan nodded. He and Stuart were going to get along just fine.

He shook hands with the general and started toward the door.

"One more thing, Belasko," Stuart added. "Watch your back."

EL VIEJO WAS studying a thick file of papers at his desk when he heard a soft knock on the door. He glanced at his watch. His assistant, who was in charge of the surveillance teams at the airport and the American embassy, was due to report, but he took no chances. He flicked off the office lights and aimed a cocked 9 mm mini-Uzi at the door. His nickname meant "the old one." He was only fifty-six, but he had been through the cocaine wars from the beginning. He had not survived long enough to be nicknamed "the old one" by being careless.

His assistant came through the door very carefully. He held the large manila envelope in front of him and made no sudden moves. He knew his superior shot first and asked questions later when in doubt.

"Good afternoon, Roberto," El Viejo said politely. He set his Uzi on safe and put it back on his desk. "You have today's reports?"

Roberto nodded. "Yes, everything through five o'clock today."

"What do they tell us?"

"The Americans continue to pour in. They appear to be serious about this Operation Blast Furnace. Two of their big military transport planes came in today. We have photographs of the passengers. There were many military men. U.S. Army, Marines, and Air Force, and many civilians, probably DEA and FBI. We are undertaking normal measures to find out who these people are and what assignments they will have."

"What else have you learned?"

"We have a report from Washington concerning this General Stuart. He is the second in command of their Special Operations Command. He has been a Ranger for twenty-five years and has planned and led many American special operations. He speaks excellent Spanish, and he was here in Bolivia in the 1980s. We must be careful. He is a very dangerous man."

El Viejo nodded. "I am sure he is, but he obviously

leads a very dangerous life. Perhaps he will have an accident. A fatal one."

Roberto smiled. One of the reasons he liked working for El Viejo was that he had no trouble making up his mind. He did not pass the buck. If you showed him a problem, he solved it.

"Is there anything else?" El Viejo asked.

Roberto hesitated. He wanted to seem intelligent and full of initiative, not frightened by shadows. Still, as vague as his information was, it might be very important indeed.

"There is one other thing. It may not be important, but I feel that you should know."

He reached into the envelope and took out six glossy 8 by 10 prints.

"See the man in these pictures? He arrived this afternoon. The American in uniform is Sergeant Johnson. He works for Captain Swenson, that blonde who coordinates things for the new American general. Johnson picked up this man at the airport and drove him directly to the American embassy. He was taken at once to a private meeting with General Stuart and Captain Swenson. We have not been able to penetrate Stuart's organization, so I do not know what they talked about. We do have contacts inside the embassy, of course, so I was able to learn that this man's passport says his name is Michael Belasko. He did not contact the local DEA or FBI after he met with Stuart, but I think he might be the same man who killed several comrades of mine when I worked with the Medillín cartel. The resemblance is striking."

El Viejo stared at the photographs.

"Where is he now?"

"At the Hotel Emperador on the Stadium Plaza. But I must stress that I cannot be sure it is the same man."

"It does not matter," El Viejo said coldly. "Kill him."

CHAPTER SIX

The Emperador Hotel, La Paz, Bolivia

Mack Bolan sat in his room on the second floor of the Emperador and finished checking his weapons. They appeared to be in perfect condition, but he would like to have test-fired them to be sure that nothing during the trip had affected their zero and shifted the point of aim. That seemed a little impractical in the middle of downtown La Paz.

He was feeling hungry but had no idea where to eat. Bolan looked at his watch. Captain Swenson should be coming by with the briefing folders. She looked like a woman who knew her way around. He would ask her to recommend a restaurant. Perhaps she would dine with him.

He heard a soft knock. He could not answer the door with a .44 Magnum pistol in his hand, so he curled his left hand around the 9 mm Smith & Wesson in his pocket. It might not be the most powerful handgun in the world, but it was remarkably better than no gun at all. He made sure he was not standing directly in front of the door. Hotel-room doors will not stop bullets.

"Who's there?" he called.

"Captain Swenson, Belasko. The coast is clear. Let me in."

Bolan opened the door. Mary Swenson stepped into the room quickly. He might not have known her if he had passed her on the street. There was nothing military about her appearance. She had changed to a dark blue dress and high heels, and a large black leather handbag had been slung over her left shoulder.

She glanced at Bolan and smiled. She had not missed the ready stance and the left hand slipped casually into his pocket. General Stuart was right. Mike Belasko was a very dangerous man.

"I'm sorry to have kept you waiting," she said. "I thought I'd better be careful. I went home, changed my clothes and drove around for a while before I came here. I don't think anybody followed me, and I came in the back door."

"Expecting trouble?"

"Not exactly. Maybe I'm getting neurotic, but I've been seeing the same car too often lately. I think somebody may be following me. I didn't want to take any unnecessary chances."

Bolan agreed. He had learned long ago that your subconscious mind often could pick up small details and warn you when there appeared to be no rational reason to be alarmed. He would have been dead a long time ago if he ignored that kind of warning. Bolan thought quickly. If someone was following Swenson, the U.S. embassy was probably under surveillance. He could easily have been followed to the hotel.

"Are you armed?" he asked.

Swenson patted her big leather handbag.

"I've got my pistol and three spare magazines."

"Good. Maybe we had better get out of here. Do you

know anyplace where we can spend the night? Not your place or the embassy. Someplace where no one is likely to look for us.''

"I know a couple of low-cost hotels near the embassy," Swenson replied. "If we look like we are planning a one-night stand and wave a few dollars at the desk clerk, they won't ask any questions.''

Bolan nodded. Better safe than sorry.

"All right, I'll get my gear and—"

Someone knocked on the door.

Bolan was no longer concerned about raising a few eyebrows. He drew his .44 Magnum Desert Eagle with one fluid motion.

"Who's there?" he called and aimed the big pistol at the center of the door.

"Sergeant Richards from the embassy, Mr. Belasko. General Stuart sent me with some papers for you. You have to sign for them.''

Bolan looked at Swenson, who shook her head. She did not know a Sergeant Richards. Her right hand shot to her purse, and she drew a large, flat black pistol. Bolan recognized a .45-caliber SIG-Sauer P-220.

"Just a minute," Bolan called. "I just got out of the shower. I have to throw on some clothes.'' He motioned to Swenson to move to the left, out of line with the door. She nodded and complied, holding her pistol in a two-handed grip and aiming at the center of the door. Bolan walked forward, reached out with his left hand and turned the doorknob.

The door seemed to explode. Bolan heard the snarl of an automatic weapon, and a swarm of hard-nosed full-metal-jacketed 9 mm bullets tore through the panel, showering splinters of wood into the room. Anyone standing in line with the door would have been cut to pieces. The lights suddenly went out, and the firing stopped abruptly. Someone kicked the door hard, and it flew open. Two weapons fired from the hall, sending long bursts criss-crossing into the corners of the room.

Bolan heard the dull boom of Swenson's P-220 as she snapped four quick shots through the door. Bolan waited tensely, holding the big Desert Eagle in a firm two-handed grip. He was an old hand at combat in hotel rooms. He was sure he knew what was coming next, and he was right. A man dived through the door and rolled into a prone position on the floor. In the dim light, Bolan saw that he had a flat black automatic with a remarkably long magazine protruding from its butt. The man was waiting for Swenson to fire again. He would fire at her muzzle-flash and cut her to pieces.

Bolan put the Desert Eagle's dimly glowing night sights against the man's left side and pulled the trigger twice. The big stainless-steel .44 Magnum pistol bucked and roared, its muzzle-flash startlingly bright in the dim room. The man jerked convulsively as the two huge hollowpoint bullets tore through his body and ripped into the floor. The big black automatic dropped from his nerveless fingers and he lay still.

The muzzle-flash from Bolan's big .44 had revealed his position. Instantly, he rolled to his left, toward the center of the room, hearing the ripping snarl of more automatic weapons. The floor behind him exploded in a gout of splinters and shredded carpet as a burst of bullets ripped into the spot where he had been. He saw a blur of motion as someone jumped into the doorway and emptied his magazine in one long continuous burst that raked the room.

The Executioner swung the sights of his Desert Eagle onto the man's chest and fired a double tap. Simultaneously, he heard the repeated boom of Swenson's P-220 as she snapped four quick shots at the man. She was not shooting as well as Bolan, but then, few people did. She fired rapidly and got two fast hits. Struck by two .45 bullets and two .44s in half a second, the man was thrown back into the hall and lay sprawled on the floor.

The sight was not encouraging to the people outside, who had expected to attack one man alone and kill him before he could fire a shot. Now they were facing two people or even more, and they had utterly failed to achieve surprise. Now they seemed to be thinking it over. For the moment, it was a standoff. The door was a death trap for anyone trying to charge into the room. That was the good news. But if Bolan and Swenson tried to escape, they would be caught in a murderous cross fire the moment they stepped through the door.

Swenson was crouched behind one corner of the couch, covering the doorway with her P-220. Bolan caught her eye and pointed to the telephone. She picked up the receiver and listened for a moment, then shook her head. The phone line was dead. No help there. She caught his eye and pointed at her automatic. She held up her left hand with four fingers spread. Bolan understood. She had four rounds left. That wasn't good. He had spare ammunition in his two nylon cases, but he did not use .45 cartridges. Nothing he had would fit her pistol.

He could give her one of his two pistols but that was not a good idea. Both the Desert Eagle and the Beretta 93-R were difficult to use. They required long practice to be effective, and he probably did not have time to check her out on even the simplest things such as the location of the safeties and magazine releases. Bolan suddenly had an idea. Mary Swenson was a regular Army officer. The answer was as close as his two black nylon cases.

He moved quietly to the cases and pulled open their closures. He pulled his M-4 Ranger carbine out of one case and pushed it into Swenson's hands. Even in the dim light, he could see her face light up with savage glee. The M-4 was a shorter, lighter version of the standard U.S. Army M-16 rifle. She knew how to use it perfectly. Bolan handed her a nylon web pouch that held four loaded 30-round magazines. She put her pistol back in her handbag, then inserted a magazine and chambered a round in the M-4. It was impossible to prevent the clack sound of the carbine's bolt, but Bolan did not care. If the men in the hall knew what that sound meant, it would discourage them mightily.

That was not the only surprise he had for them. He pulled four grenades from the elastic loops on one side of the case. They were not conventional fragmentation grenades. They were shaped like small soft drink cans with grenade fuses and safety handles protruding from one end. Swenson was impressed. There seemed to be no limit to what her companion could pull out of the case.

He put his lips next to the captain's ear and spoke softly.

"We're getting out of here. I'm going to shake them up, and when they're confused, I'm going to throw two flash-stun grenades. Close your eyes when you see me throw, and keep them closed. You're going to see bright-as-hell flashes through your eyelids and hear two very loud bangs. As soon as that happens, I go through the door. We won't try for the elevator. The stairs are to the left. You follow me through the door as fast as you can. I'll fire to the left. You fire a couple of bursts to the right, and we run for the stairs. Got it?"

He looked at her as he spoke. She seemed to be all

right, perhaps a little shaken up. This was probably her first firefight, and that could be remarkably exciting.

"Got it. Keep my eyes closed until the grenades go off, follow you through the door and fire to the right." She kicked off her high heels. "Any time. I'm ready."

Bolan nodded. They were as ready as they could ever be. He needed to know where the enemy was. He picked up a large leather cushion and threw it through the open door. He heard it hit the floor, and someone yelled in Spanish. Two automatic weapons snarled into life, one from each side of the door. The cushion was caught in a cross fire and torn to pieces. Bolan was satisfied. The other side had murderous intentions, but the attackers were not very professional.

He pulled the safety pin on the first grenade and hurled it through the door, then immediately pulled the pin on the second grenade and sent the bomb after the first. He closed his eyes tightly. Someone in the hall shrieked a warning, but he was too late. The first grenade detonated. Even through his eyelids, Bolan saw an intense yellow flash. The explosion in the hall sounded like the crack of doom. The second grenade repeated the performance. The scene outside the room was a close approximation of hell. Bolan could hear men screaming and cursing in Spanish. It was now or never, while they were dazed and confused.

"Go!" he shouted and dived through the door, crouching, his Beretta 93-R in his hands, its selector switch set on burst mode. He had no time to look behind him; he could only depend on Swenson to do her part. The Executioner was through the door, then he pivoted left. Three dim shapes loomed five feet in front of him. The man in the center was swinging up a weapon, trying to fire. Bolan pulled the trigger. The Beretta 93-R spit three 9 mm hollowpoints in two-tenths of a second tearing into the man's chest. Bolan swung on another man and fired. The man was hit and spun away. The Executioner swung toward a third man and found himself looking down the barrel of a big, flat black automatic pistol. He pressed the trigger of the Beretta, but too late. He and the man fired together.

Something struck Bolan in the chest like a hard jab from a skilled boxer. He staggered but held on with grim determination and squeezed off two quick 3-round bursts. The man in front of him fell heavily. He would not need shooting again.

Bolan heard the ripping snarl of the M-4 carbine behind him as Swenson sent a long fast burst down the hall. Someone yelled in Spanish, and the captain fired again. The Executioner pivoted and threw another grenade down the hall over the woman's shoulder. It landed and exploded with a soft pop, thick red smoke spewing forth.

"Come on," Bolan yelled and ran toward the stairs. He could hear Swenson charging after him. They were almost to the exit when the door suddenly swung open. Two men stood there, both holding AK-47s.

The Executioner pulled the Beretta's trigger, but the pistol fired one shot and stopped. Something was wrong. He had no time to waste struggling with jams. He dropped the Beretta, threw himself to the left and tried to draw his .44 Desert Eagle.

Bolan heard a flat, dull boom behind him as Swenson pulled the trigger of the carbine's M-203 grenade launcher. Bolan had loaded it with a 40 mm multiprojectile antipersonnel round. The M-203 discharged its buckshot load in one huge blast like a giant sawed off shotgun. The buckshot spread fast as it cleared the M-203's gaping bore. The swarm of heavy shot cut the two men to pieces. They went down instantly, bleeding from a dozen wounds.

Bolan had his weapon up and ready to fire, but there was no need to shoot. Both men were dead.

"Come on!" he yelled and shot through the stair doors. He swept the area with the muzzle of the Desert Eagle, but there was no one there. Swenson burst through the doors behind him. She had the M-4 carbine in one hand and his Beretta 93-R in the other. As she handed him the Beretta in the lighted stairwell, she looked pale and was trembling slightly. He did not blame her. She had just killed two men at point-blank range and stepped over their bleeding bodies.

Long ago, Bolan had been a Green Beret sergeant and a good one.

"Just don't stand there, Swenson. Reload!" he snapped in his best command voice.

Swenson was a soldier, and she responded instantly to the iron ring of authority in Bolan's voice. She pulled out a fresh 30-round magazine, snapped it into the M-4 and chambered a round. The familiar routine seemed to steady her nerves.

"Where's your car?" he asked.

"In the parking lot back of the hotel. Down the stairs and turn right."

Bolan checked his Beretta 93-R. It was obvious why it had quit firing. The special 20-round magazine protruded two inches below the bottom of the butt. A bullet had torn the bottom of the magazine away. The cartridges the magazine had held and the feed spring were simply gone. Nothing else seemed to be wrong. He discarded the damaged magazine and snapped in a fresh one.

He looked up. Swenson was staring at him.

"You're hit. There's a bullet hole in your shirt. Better let me take a look at it."

Bolan looked down. She was right. He opened his shirt

and saw a gleaming copper jacket. A 9 mm bullet had stopped halfway through his soft body armor.

Swenson continued to stare. She was used to the heavy-duty body armor that soldiers wore over their uniforms. She had never seen the soft, flexible body armor that a man could wear undetected under his shirt.

"That's bullet proof?" she asked skeptically. "It doesn't look like it."

"It's a top brand body armor soft vest. It'll stop most pistol bullets except for the Magnums and most shotgun rounds. It won't stop rifle bullets, but it's a lot better than nothing at all."

Swenson could believe that. The 9 mm bullet was neatly placed in the center of Mack Bolan's chest. If he had not been wearing the vest, he would be dead or badly wounded.

"I've got to get one of those. Where did—"

She stopped abruptly. The wailing, undulating sounds of police sirens were echoing up the stairwell. Bolan glanced at his watch. The fight had started just four minutes ago. Actually, the response time of the Bolivian police had been admirably short, but he did not want to stay to talk to them. Swenson undoubtedly had diplomatic immunity. He did not. He did not want to discuss the bodies littering the second floor of the hotel or the unusual weapons he was carrying with the local law.

"Let's get out of here, now!" he snapped and started down the stairs. It was taking a chance, but the police did not know what was going on. It was not likely that they had surrounded the hotel and closed all the entrances, but it would not stay that way for long.

He reached the ground floor and opened the door a crack. He saw nothing but a deserted hallway. He motioned to Swenson to follow him and moved toward the back of the hotel. The security guard was not around. Perhaps he was off somewhere responding to alarms. Bolan looked cautiously out the door. There were about two dozen cars and vans parked in two rows. No one was in sight. It looked too good to be true.

Bolan had not stayed alive as long as he had by taking things for granted. It was better to assume that the opposition had staked out the parking lot than to walk blithely out and get his head blown off.

"Which car is yours?" he asked.

"The white Honda Civic in the second row."

"All right. Walk out casually as if you don't have a care in the world. Look in the back seat. Someone could be lying on the floor, waiting for you to come back. If you see someone, just keep on walking. I'll take care of him. If it's all clear, get in, start the engine, and pull up by the door and pick me up. Here, you'll look a little funny carrying my carbine. Give it to me. You won't need it. I'll cover you. Got it?"

Swenson nodded and handed him the M-4. She would have felt safer with it in her hands, but not much. She had seen Bolan shoot and the thought that he would be covering her was very comforting. She stepped through the door and walked toward her Honda. She remembered what Bolan had said and checked the back seat. All clear. No one was there. She was about to unlock her Honda's door when a tall, thin man seemed to appear from nowhere. He had to have come from the orange Toyota parked next to her car. His hands were empty, but the captain did not like his looks. He had a cruel smile on his face, as if he were enjoying an unpleasant joke at her expense.

"Stay just where you are, *gringa.* You do not really

want to go anywhere. You will not like what will happen to you if you try."

Swenson acted frightened, which was not hard. The thin man radiated a cold, deadly menace.

"Leave me alone," she gasped. "I'll scream if you touch me."

The man laughed and his hands moved with blurring speed. She heard a sharp click and found herself staring at the gleaming blade of a switchblade knife an inch in front of her nose. His left hand gripped the neck of her dress.

"If you scream, I will cut your face to the bone. You are not a very pretty woman now. When I am through with you, no man will look at you, and children will scream when they see your face."

Swenson waited for the crack of the M-4. She was looking forward to seeing Mike Belasko shoot this bastard dead, but no shot came. Why didn't he shoot? Then she realized what had happened. Her back was toward the hotel. Her body was screening the man with the knife. Belasko could not fire without hitting her. She had to do something, create some kind of diversion to give him a shot.

The thin man touched her left cheek with the point of his knife, and Swenson winced. She could feel a drop of blood running down her face.

"Tell me you will be a good little girl and do just what I say. Tell me that you will not scream."

"Please. I won't scream. Please don't cut me. I'll do whatever you say."

The thin man smiled broadly.

"Of course, you will. Now you will come with us. We will walk over to that yellow van, arm in arm like two lovers. I will introduce you to my two friends. We will take you away to a quiet place and have a nice, long talk. Who knows, you may look prettier with your clothes off."

"Oh, God, no," Swenson whimpered. "I have money, lots of money, here in my handbag. I'll give it all to you. Just let me go. Don't hurt me."

Her right hand moved to her handbag. "Here, take it all."

The thin man laughed. It was not a pleasant laugh.

"It is not your money I want, *gringa.*" He pointed with his knife at the yellow van. Someone inside opened the back door. "Move. Now!"

Swenson's right hand was inside her handbag now. Her strong slender fingers closed on the black plastic grips of her P-220. She whipped it out as fast as her hand could move. Out of the corner of her eye, she could see that the knife was flashing back toward her. As soon as her SIG-Sauer's muzzle was pointed at the man's chest, she pulled the trigger as fast as she could move her finger. She was firing at a range of six inches. She could not miss. Four heavy .45-caliber bullets struck the thin man with terrible numbing force. He staggered back a step or two and tried to swing his knife.

The captain heard a familiar crackling snarl as Bolan put six high-velocity bullets through the man's body. Two men leaped out of the yellow van with AK-47s in their hands. Swenson heard the M-4 snarl again as Bolan cut the two men down with two fast, well-aimed bursts.

"Are you all right?" Bolan shouted.

The captain thought so. There was blood on her blue dress, but it did not seem to be hers. "Yes," she yelled back.

"Get in the car. Start the engine. Let's go," he shouted.

Swenson forced her numb body to obey. She started the engine, and the Honda's tires screeched as she put it in gear and shot out of the parking slot. Bolan stepped out of the hotel's back door. The M-4 snarled again as he shot out the yellow van's rear tires. He snapped a fresh magazine into the carbine as she slammed to a stop.

The woman tried to shout a warning as she saw the muzzle-flashes of an automatic weapon firing from inside the yellow van. A swarm of green tracers flashed past the roof of her car. Bolan saw it, too. He pulled the trigger of the M-203 grenade launcher and sent a 40 mm high-explosive grenade into the van. The bomb detonated, and the van shook and began to burn. Then it exploded as its gas tank blew. Whoever had been inside the van would not cause any more trouble.

"Go!" Bolan shouted as he leaped into the front seat. Swenson pulled the Honda out onto the street. Behind them, flames and thick black smoke were billowing upward from the van. Sirens could be heard, wailing in the distance, coming closer.

"Where to?" she gasped.

"The American embassy. We may need diplomatic immunity as fast as we can get it."

CHAPTER SEVEN

The Airport, Santa Cruz, Bolivia

Mack Bolan was awakened by the sound of the C-130H's engines changing as the Air Force pilot reduced power and started its final approach. He had not had much rest the night before. It had taken some determined intervention by General Stuart and the American ambassador to recover his equipment from the hotel and persuade the Bolivian National Police that they did not need to hold Mike Belasko as a material witness. It had helped that several of the dead men had been identified as well-known drug cartel gunmen. The police seemed happy they were dead. The official story was that Mary Swenson had heroically defended herself against a kidnap attempt by a group of terrorists.

He looked out the window. The appearance of the land below had changed dramatically. They had been descending steadily ever since the plane had left La Paz. Now, they were nearly ten thousand feet lower, and the rugged Bolivian highlands had given way to lush green plains and clumps of green forest, cut here and there by muddy wandering rivers. He was surprised to see how large Santa Cruz looked as the C-130H flew lower and lower. Swenson had told him it was the second largest city in Bolivia.

Thirty years earlier, it had been a sleepy country town with dirt streets, living on cattle raising and farming. Now it was swollen with money, the cocaine capital of South America.

He glanced at Mary Swenson. She was sitting next to him, wearing her Army combat fatigues and staring at some papers from her briefcase. She seemed to have recovered from the stresses and strains of the previous night. He had to admit she had handled herself quite well during the fight at the hotel. Bolan frowned. Perhaps she had done just a little too well. She seemed to know a bit too much and be a little too good. She had handled her weapons skillfully, firing double taps with her .45, reloading rapidly, and firing an M-203 grenade launcher without any instruction. She had to have had some specialized training that the average young Army officer, particularly a woman, would not have received. She might not be just the simple assistant military attaché she said she was. She could be a Defense Intelligence Agency operative or work for the Army Counter Intelligence Corps. He would call Stony Man as soon as he got the chance and ask Barbara Price to check Swenson's records. Until he could find out more about her, he would just have to be careful. He remembered what General Stuart had told him: "Watch your back."

He looked around the C-130's passenger-cargo compartment. Most of the people he saw were Army and Air Force personnel going to Santa Cruz to set up communications equipment and aircraft cargo handling facilities. In the back of the plane were two dozen men in civilian clothes. They had kept to themselves during the flight, staring curiously at Bolan and Swenson now and then, but making no effort to talk or be friendly. He thought they looked like law-enforcement types, DEA or FBI. It looked as if Operation Blast Furnace was going to make Santa Cruz a lively place. That was all right with him. He was ready to do his share.

The C-130H touched down and rolled along the runway. Bolan collected his gear and followed Swenson down the transport's tail ramp. He felt the tropical heat the moment he stepped off the ramp. It was still an hour before noon, but the temperature was already above ninety degrees and climbing, and the humidity was nearly one hundred percent. He began to sweat instantly. He was wearing his soft body armor under his shirt, and a light nylon jacket to conceal his pistols. It had been a comfortable combination in La Paz, but it was not going to be pleasant in the humid heat of the lowlands.

He looked around quickly. The Santa Cruz airport was remarkably large and modern, accommodating several small airliners and an incredible number of light planes. The military team began to unload its equipment from the big C-130H. The law-enforcement people were boarding two small buses. No one seemed to be waiting for them.

Swenson looked at her watch.

"Somebody is supposed to meet us with some transportation. I think we had better wait. It's about five miles into town, and I don't want to ride any public transportation while I'm carrying this."

Whatever she had in her briefcase, she seemed to think it was very important. He was not about to argue with her. After all, it was her responsibility.

"Fine. I'm in no hurry, but let's get out of the sun."

He started to follow Swenson.

"There you are. I've been waiting for you," a woman called out from behind him. He knew the voice, but he could not place her. He pivoted smoothly, keeping his hands at his sides but ready to draw and fire if he had to.

He found himself staring at a tall, red-haired woman who was thrusting a microphone in his direction. Of course, he knew that voice. He had heard it dozens of times from Bosnia, Somalia, Haiti, anywhere in the world there was trouble. It was Anne Bayne, the WWN news anchor. Her cameraman was right behind her. It was not surprising to find her in Bolivia, but how did she know him? He had been careful to stay out of sight at the El Paso airport.

Bolan thought fast. The last thing in the world he needed was worldwide TV coverage, but if he rushed away or tried to duck back into the plane, it would attract attention and be recorded on camera. Maybe he could say that—

"Sir," Anne Bayne said coldly, "please move at least ten feet to the left or right. Do it now."

Bolan stared at her. He saw no sign of recognition on Anne Bayne's face. Maybe he was getting paranoid, but if she did not have any idea who he was, what did she want?

"Please move, sir. I'm about to do an interview, and you're in the middle of the scene. Please move now!"

Her tone of voice was not pleasant, but she was telling Bolan to do just what he wanted to do—get away from the camera's lens. He moved quickly to one side. Mary Swenson started to follow him.

The tall redhead stopped her with a quick gesture, motioned to her cameraman and spoke rapidly into her microphone.

"This is Anne Bayne, World Wide News, in Santa Cruz, central Bolivia, with a breaking news story. U.S. military personnel are pouring into Santa Cruz as the controversial Operation Blast Furnace gets under way."

She thrust her microphone toward Swenson.

"This is Captain Mary Swenson, United States Army,

attached to the U.S. embassy in Bolivia. Last night, Captain Swenson was the target of a vicious kidnapping attempt in La Paz. She shot her way out. I think that says something to those people who say that American women have no place in combat. Can you tell our viewers anything more about what happened in La Paz?''

Swenson blinked. She looked nervous and stared at the microphone as if she were hypnotized. Apparently, her training at West Point had not included how to deal with world famous news anchors.

''No, Miss Bayne. I was off duty, visiting a friend at a local hotel. A group of men attacked me. I'm not sure why. I was armed, complying with General Stuart's orders. I managed to fend them off until the police arrived. The matter is still under investigation. I'm not supposed to say anything more at this time.''

Anne Bayne smiled beautifully, radiating sympathy and understanding.

''I understand. Can you tell our viewers what you are doing in Santa Cruz, Captain? Has it anything to do with Operation Blast Furnace?''

''I'm just acting as a courier, Miss Bayne. We are establishing a logistics base here in Santa Cruz to support Operation Blast Furnace. I brought some of the necessary paperwork from La Paz. If you will excuse me, I'm on duty now, but I'll be glad to talk to you later.''

Bayne motioned to her cameraman to stop recording. She smiled her high-voltage professional smile.

''Of course, Captain Swenson. I understand that you're busy. I would like to talk to you later about a number of things, how you feel about U.S. policy in Bolivia, women in the American military, that sort of thing. See you later.''

She turned and walked rapidly toward the law-enforcement types who were loading their gear onto their buses. Swenson stared after her in open-mouthed amazement. The idea of discussing Pentagon policy with Anne Bayne on network TV frightened her far more than drug-cartel gunmen. At least, she could shoot them.

"Watch out for that lady, Mary," Bolan warned. "She can get you in a lot of trouble."

"She is a pushy bitch, isn't she?" a man said from behind him. There was something familiar about that voice, but Bolan could not place it.

He turned smoothly, not drawing his pistol but poised for action just in case. He found himself looking at a stocky, strongly built man in his late fifties. He had short, closely cropped gray hair and was wearing dark, European-style wraparound sunglasses. He did not appear to be armed, but Bolan thought he detected a faint bulge on the man's right hip. He did not seem to be hostile. He was looking at Bolan with a friendly smile.

"Well," he said cheerfully, "things are going to start heating up now that you're here, Belasko."

Bolan knew he had seen the man before, but when and where? He had a minute to think. The stocky man was looking at Mary Swenson, reading the name tag on her fatigue jacket.

"I can see why you're a soldier, Captain. You certainly look fit, hard as a rock."

Bolan was surprised. It seemed a stupid thing to say to a young woman, even if she was in the armed forces. But Mary Swenson did not look offended. She smiled as if she were enjoying the conversation.

"Hard as the Rocky Mountains," she said.

"Right, Captain Swenson. I'm sorry about that stupid challenge and response. I always wonder who the idiot is who thinks them up."

Swenson smiled again. "That's all right. I like it. It's just like a movie. It makes me feel like a real spy."

The stocky man chuckled. "That's a dirty word, Captain. Other countries have spies. We have agents."

Bolan had heard those words a thousand times before. CIA. Of course. It was Fred Byrnes. He had been a CIA agent with their Moscow station the last time he had seen him. It was obvious he had a new assignment.

He held out his hand. "How are you, Fred. It's been a while."

Byrnes shook Bolan's hand and beamed.

"Damned right it has. What are you doing down here, if I'm cleared to ask?"

"Operation Blast Furnace."

Byrnes smiled. "Aren't we all?"

He looked at Swenson.

"We need to talk, Captain. Can you vouch for Belasko? I know him, of course. He and I were on one hell of a mission a year ago, but can you certify his need to know on the mission we're working on now?"

Swenson nodded. "I'll vouch for him. General Stuart says he is cleared for all in-country Blast Furnace information."

"That's good enough for me. I'm pretending to be a crusading freelance journalist. I've got to go over there and look like I'm interviewing those cowboys from the DEA. I'm staying at the Hotel Viru-Viru on Junin Street, room 309. Meet me there in two hours, and I'll buy you a drink. Be careful here, Captain. There are some dangerous people in Santa Cruz. Of course, you've got Belasko with you. He's better than a company of Marines. See you later."

Swenson looked at Mack Bolan and lifted one eyebrow.

"A company?"

Bolan grinned.

"Fred likes to exaggerate. Certainly not a company. A squad, maybe."

Two hours later, Mack Bolan and Mary Swenson walked into the lobby of the Viru-Viru. It was not the most luxurious hotel in Santa Cruz, but it was neat and clean, and Bolan knew that Fred Byrnes was too old a hand to attract attention by staying at the most fashionable places. The desk clerk offered them a double room with private bath and telephone for twenty dollars. He apologized for the steep price, saying that there were so many new people in town, but he offered to throw in a free breakfast the next morning.

Bolan agreed that it was more than reasonable and promised to think it over. He glanced around the lobby. It seemed to be deserted, but he took no chances. He motioned to Swenson to follow him up the stairs. The woman did not seem to enjoy the walk, but she understood. If anyone was watching them, they would not be able to tell which floor they went to by watching the elevator floor indicators.

As they walked down the third-floor hall to room 309, Bolan kept his hand close to the butt of his Desert Eagle. He knocked carefully on the door. He remembered that Fred Byrnes was fond of 12-gauge shotguns and .357 Magnum revolvers and believed in shooting first whenever possible. Bolan was careful not to stand in front of the door when he knocked just in case the agent was feeling nervous.

Byrnes looked through the peephole, unlocked the door and let them in. Bolan smelled the familiar scent of gun cleaning fluid. A 12-gauge Remington pump shotgun was lying on a small table, its gaping muzzle pointing toward the door. Byrnes held a Colt Python .357 Magnum revolver in his right hand.

Bolan raised an eyebrow.

"Expecting trouble, Fred?"

Byrnes grinned. "I always expect trouble when I'm in the field. I figure I'll live a lot longer that way. Besides, you have to clean and oil your guns once a day in this climate, or you'll end up with a pile of rust. Sit down, and I'll pour you a cool one. You can have anything you like, as long as it's beer or whisky."

Bolan normally drank very little if at all when on a mission, since anything that reduced his awareness or slowed his reflexes could be fatal. Still, he remembered that being hospitable was important to Fred Byrnes.

"I'll have a beer," he said.

Byrnes pulled two bottles from the small hotel-room refrigerator.

"I'll join you. How about you, Captain?"

Swenson shook her head.

"No, thanks. Maybe in a little bit. What I'd like to do is use your shower and change. This uniform is fine in La Paz, but it's murder down here."

"Be my guest," Byrnes said. Swenson was a clever young woman. She knew Bolan and Byrnes might have things to say to each other they would hesitate to say in front of her. Byrnes waited until he heard the water running.

"How have you been, Mike? Still living a life of travel and adventure?"

Bolan took out a small flat black box that Gadgets Schwarz had given him. He turned it on and scanned the room. No red lights came on. If any bugs were in the room, they were not the electronic variety.

"I'm doing all right, Fred. What about you? The last

time I saw you, you were going to retire and go fishing. I'm surprised to see you here in Bolivia."

Byrnes sipped his beer and shrugged.

"You know how it is. When you've done this kind of work as long as I have, civilian life can get awfully boring mighty fast. You can only go fishing so many times. What the hell would you do if you retired?"

Bolan frowned. He did know how it was. When you have risked your life a thousand times, peace and quiet may be unendurable. He could not imagine what he would do if he gave up his War Everlasting.

"I was starting to climb the walls when I was contacted by the assistant director of operations. He said he had real problems. The CIA had to step up their support of the war on drugs. It's got too many satellite jockeys and computer geniuses and not enough old hands like me. He said he badly needed someone who could speak Spanish, had a lot of experience operating in the field and establishing networks of local agents rapidly. Everybody back at headquarters thought old Fred was the only man for the job."

Byrnes smiled cynically.

"I knew they were shining me on, but what the hell. I wanted to get back in the field, so here I am. How about you? Still working for the same people?"

Bolan smiled again. He had no reason to distrust Fred Byrnes, but he was not cleared to know about Stony Man and probably never would be.

"Yeah," he replied.

Byrnes sighed. He had the natural curiosity of a good Intelligence agent, but he knew that sustained probing by the CIA's Moscow station had not been able to find out who Belasko was or who he worked for. He would find out only if the big man decided to tell him, and that was not likely. He took another sip of beer and changed the subject.

"How well do you know Swenson? Do you trust her?"

That was interesting. Maybe Byrnes knew something Bolan didn't.

"I met her yesterday in La Paz. I don't know her well, but I don't have any reason not to trust her. Do you?"

Byrnes scowled.

"Nothing concrete, but she's been in-country for two years. If she can be bought by the cartel, she has been. We'd better keep an eye on her."

Bolan was puzzled. That sounded like CIA paranoia, but maybe Byrnes had survived twenty-five years in the field because he suspected everybody. Still, that left one obvious question.

"If you don't trust her, Fred, why is she your contact?"

Byrnes snorted. "Because she's all I could get. Bolivia was a backwater as far as the Agency was concerned until last month. The La Paz station is a joke, and the cartel knows everyone we have stationed there. Besides, she's bringing some interagency stuff. General Stuart wouldn't let any of our people carry it. He's been a Ranger for twenty-five years, and you know how those army special operations people are. They never trust the CIA."

Bolan knew that was true and he knew why, but it was not the time to discuss it if he and Byrnes were going to work together. Maybe he was getting paranoid, but could he trust Fred Byrnes? Probably. The Russian Mafia had not been able to buy him. Unless Fred had changed in the past year, he would not sell out to the drug cartel.

Swenson came out of the bathroom. She had changed to a white dress that showed off her long legs quite well. She would never win a beauty contest, but she was an attractive young woman in civilian clothes.

"I'll take that beer you offered," she said with a smile. "I feel halfway civilized now that I've had a shower and gotten out of that damned uniform."

She took a bottle from Byrnes and grinned at the two men.

"If you two have had enough time to drink beer and tell war stories, maybe we should get down to business."

"All right," Byrnes agreed. "What do you know about my operation?"

"Not much. General Stuart told me you are in charge of CIA operations in Santa Cruz. He gave me your description and the contact phrases. That's all I really know. Why don't you fill us in?"

"All right. About two months ago, the President put pressure on the CIA to do a lot more in the war on drugs. The director of operations knew that we had very little field capability in Bolivia. He sent a group of people down here to get things going. I'm handling the Santa Cruz area. I'm developing a network of agents to provide human Intelligence capability. My objectives are to locate cocaine factories, gather information on the leaders of the drug cartel and find out who's sold out to the cartels."

Swenson looked puzzled.

"What do you mean when you say you're developing a network of agents? Doesn't the CIA have plenty of agents they can send in?"

Byrnes chuckled.

"You've been seeing too many movies, Captain. Things don't work that way. CIA agents don't do the actual spying. Look at me or Belasko. Could we pass for Bolivians? Even if we could, there's a special Bolivian accent that takes years to learn before you could pass for a native. No, what we do is recruit people who live in the country we're going to operate in. CIA agents like me control these people and direct their operations.''

Swenson shook her head.

"I don't understand. How can you just come in here and recruit Bolivians to spy for the CIA?''

"You can always find people if you know how to look. Cocaine production is big business. A lot of people are involved. Where there are a lot of people, some of them are unhappy. Some of them want something very badly, to get rich, to change the government, to get revenge because they think they were treated badly. My best agent is a woman who buys food for the people who work in the drug factories and helps smuggle it to them. She has two young daughters in the women's prison in La Paz. They're serving long sentences for narcotics violations. Bolivian prisons are pretty brutal. She will do anything to get her daughters out.''

Swenson looked both fascinated and repelled. She had found out how things really worked, and she did not like it. Bolan understood how she felt. It sounded cold-blooded and ruthless. Byrnes seemed to think of the people he recruited as pawns on a chessboard, not real human beings. If some of them were killed, he would shrug his shoulders and recruit replacements. Bolan knew that most Intelligence services work that way. It was why he never really trusted any of them, American or foreign. Fred Byrnes did not see anything wrong with it. After twenty-five years in the CIA, it seemed as natural as breathing.

Byrnes had not noticed Swenson's look. He would not have understood what was bothering her if he had. It would never have occurred to him that anyone would be upset by standard CIA operating methods.

"Getting any results?'' Bolan asked.

Byrnes thought for a second.

"Yes. Not as much as I'd like, but I'm starting to get there. The real problem is time and the pressure I'm getting from Washington. If I'd had six months to set up my network, things would be running smoothly. But I've had five weeks, and I can't start slowly. I've got to go for broke and get results right now. I don't really know the people I've recruited. Some of them may have been sent by the cartel to find out what I'm up to. That means I've got to be careful not to blow my cover. Anyway, let me show you what I've got."

He moved to a small desk, took a map from a pile of papers and unfolded it. Bolan took a quick look. There was nothing remarkable about it. It was a large-scale topographical survey map of central Bolivia. He could see Santa Cruz in the lower right-hand corner. Byrnes spread the map out on the table. He took a small flashlight out of his camera bag and pointed it at the map.

"Watch this, Mike. It's really neat."

He pushed the switch and shone the flashlight on the map. Instantly, a group of a dozen or more glowing yellow points appeared on the map. Byrnes clicked the flashlight off. The glowing points vanished. He turned the flashlight back on, and they reappeared.

"Those are the prime targets," Byrnes said happily. "I've had my agents investigate over sixty possible drug factory sites. These sixteen look good. I've got at least two or three independent confirmations on all of them. I'd bet my next month's pay that there are people at each one of those sites making cocaine."

Bolan did not want to spoil the Fred Byrnes show, but there was one critical question.

"Just how current is your information, Fred?"

"You're a hard man to get ahead of, Mike, but you're right. That's the problem. I'm depending on the human eyeball, not some super scientific nonsense. I don't dare give my agents radios. They'd be killed instantly if they were caught with them, so I have to wait until they have been out to the site and then get back and report in person. My latest information on these sites is twenty-four to forty-eight hours old.''

Bolan frowned. He knew from personal experience that a raid based on forty-eight-hour-old Intelligence could be a disastrous failure.

"I know, Mike, it's not perfect, but it's the best I can do with what I've got. But you don't have to just depend on me. I think Captain Swenson has some information for us.''

Swenson opened her briefcase and put some papers on the table. Her fingers moved carefully as she manipulated the lining and pulled out a sheet of clear, transparent plastic. She laid it carefully across Fred Byrnes's map. Bolan saw that the plastic sheet was marked with a series of small red circles and ovals.

"Here's the superscientific nonsense," she said with a grin.

"You don't hear me complaining, Captain. Look at that, Mike.''

Bolan looked. Nine of the red marks circled Byrnes's yellow points.

"What's the source of your data, Mary?" he asked.

"It's the latest data from Washington. It came in from D.C. via satellite about two hours before we left for the airport. It represents the best satellite reconnaissance data available, optical, infrared and radar. We have been promised we will get an update every twenty-four hours and a flash report if anything changes.''

Byrnes looked at the map and nodded.

"Well, there are our targets, Mike. Now, what the hell are we going to do about them?"

CHAPTER EIGHT

Santa Cruz, Bolivia

Mary Swenson looked at Fred Byrnes. Mack Bolan grinned. Fred had been right when he said the Army did not trust the CIA. Still, Blast Furnace was supposed to be a joint operation in which all U.S. government agencies supported one another. Swenson shrugged her shoulders. She knew the agent had a high-level security clearance, and a senior CIA agent should know how to keep his mouth shut.

"We don't have any U.S. strike capability in-country at the moment. The USS *Hornet* will be off the coast in forty-eight hours. It will stand by to support Blast Furnace operations."

Byrnes looked impressed. "The *Hornet*'s an aircraft carrier?" he asked.

"There aren't any carriers available. The *Hornet* is what the Navy calls an amphibious assault ship. The Navy gave us a briefing on it. It's an impressive ship. It looks like a carrier. It's got a flight deck, but it can't operate regular Navy jet aircraft. It can carry twenty-two hundred troops and forty transport helicopters and helicopter gunships. It has a squadron of Marine Corps Hawker Harrier vertical take off and land attack jets, and there are U.S.

Army Rangers, a Navy SEAL team, and Marine Force Recon troops on board.''

It sounded great, but Bolan thought he saw a problem.

"I looked at a map before I flew down here. Bolivia is landlocked. Isn't that going to give us problems using the *Hornet?*"

"You're right. They lost their coastline in a war with Chile a hundred years ago. If we use helicopters or planes from the *Hornet,* we will have to overfly Chile or Peru. The State Department is working on it.''

Swenson paused briefly.

"That's the good news, but there's a problem with the Bolivian government. So far, they've only agreed to the use of U.S. troops in a supporting role. We're still working on getting their agreement to use U.S. combat units inside Bolivia. We believe we can get it, but General Stuart thinks that it will take a few days.''

Byrnes sneered.

"Damned politicians! Don't we have any in-country capability at all?''

"Well, there's Mike,'' Swenson said. "He's here, and his team will be flying into Santa Cruz tomorrow.''

Byrnes smiled. He did not know who Belasko was, who his team was, or where they came from, but he had seen them in action and he was favorably impressed.

"What's your mission, Mike? What are you authorized to do?'' Byrnes finished his beer and grinned wickedly. "Assuming I'm cleared to know.''

Bolan thought it over. There was no point in not telling Byrnes where he was going. If the CIA agent's network was any good, they would report Bolan's location, anyway.

"General Stuart's asked me to support the Bolivian National Police's special antinarcotics unit, UMOPAR. I expect to go to their main base tomorrow. I think I'll move my team out there as soon as they get here.''

Byrnes nodded. ''The Leopards? Well, that makes sense. If anybody's going to really do anything in the next few days, it will be Colonel Chavez and his merry men. Maybe I'll go with you, if you don't have any objections.''

''It's all right with me, Fred, but won't it blow your cover?''

''Hell, no! I've got a perfect cover. Officially, I'm Fred Byrnes, crusading freelance journalist. I'm here in Bolivia to write a book about the cocaine trade that tells it like it really is. I'm interviewing everybody, promising them anonymity. I can go anywhere and talk to anybody. Hell, I'll really publish a book. How would you like to be famous, Mike? I could give you a whole chapter.''

Bolan laughed. ''Thanks, there are a lot of things I need, but publicity isn't one of them.

Chimore, Bolivia

JACK GRIMALDI REDUCED power, brought the MH-60K special operations Black Hawk helicopter to a perfect hover and set it down smoothly, precisely in the center of the landing area. Bolan looked around as Grimaldi cut power and the whine of the twin turbine engines died away. They had flown out along the Santa Cruz-Chimore road, flying over the lush greenery of a tropical rain forest, broken only by wide muddy rivers and an occasional small village.

As usual, Grimaldi had flown superbly. They were exactly where they were supposed to be and precisely on time. Bolan was not surprised. He would have been astounded if it were any other way. Fixed wing or helicopters, Jack Grimaldi was the finest pilot he had ever seen.

Bolan unfastened his safety belt and slipped out of the copilot's seat.

"Let's get her unloaded, refueled and checked out, Jack," he said. "David and I are going to pay a call on the commanding officer."

He went back into the passenger compartment and out the side door. David McCarter and Mary Swenson were waiting there, looking around. The captain was wearing camouflage fatigues, and an issue 9 mm Beretta M-9 automatic was holstered on a hip. Two stocky men wearing green-and-black-spotted camouflage uniforms were staring at her in amazement. They were accustomed to captains, but a tall, blond female captain was something new.

McCarter had decided to project a military image and was wearing the distinctive British army disruptive-pattern-material camouflage fatigues. His desert sand beret was set at a rocky angle.

The Leopards' base camp was in a wide jungle clearing dotted with many white-washed prefabricated metal huts and surrounded by razor wire. The Bolivian flag with its three horizontal red, yellow and green stripes hung limply from the flag pole. Bolan and company had landed on the camp's airstrip. Across the clearing, Bolan saw a cluster of larger prefabricated buildings surrounded by their own wire fence.

"Is that the jail?" he asked.

Swenson exploded with laughter, her face turning a bright red.

"Oh, that's great, Mike, just great! Wait till I tell Frank Latimer that!" she gasped.

Bolan looked at Mary inquiringly. She laughed again.

"Those buildings are the quarters of the local DEA

team. About twenty-five of them are stationed here. Latimer is the DEA special agent in charge. Wait till he hears this!''

Bolan was not amused. He would have to get along with the local DEA contingent. It would not help if it looked like he had started out by insulting them.

"Let's not tell him. Let's just keep it among ourselves," he said.

"All right, if you say so, but you owe me a beer. Heads up. Here comes the welcoming committee."

An old style U.S. Army jeep with National Police Force markings drove up to the landing pad. A smiling young man in the Leopards' uniform got out and saluted. He seemed impressed by McCarter and pleased to see Swenson. He appeared to give Bolan a casual glance, but the Executioner had been looked over by experts before. He was sure that the smiling young captain could give an accurate description of him from that one short look.

"Good afternoon. I am Captain Vargas. Colonel Suarez regrets that he was not able to greet you personally, but the commander is a very busy man. He is eager to see you and asks that I bring you to his office immediately."

Bolan looked around as they drove across the base. It seemed to be a beehive of activity. Small groups of men were checking their weapons and equipment and getting ready to climb on a strange collection of cars and trucks. Another group seemed to be practicing some form of unarmed combat. Others were guarding small groups of men and women in ragged clothing who were working at various jobs around the base.

"Your people seem very busy today, Captain," he commented.

Vargas smiled. "Today and every day. The colonel believes in the American saying, 'The devil finds work for idle hands.' He is determined that no Leopard shall be idle.''

Bolan had known a few colonels like that in his day.

The jeep stopped in front of one of the white-painted prefabricated metal buildings. It did not look any different than any of the other buildings except that a hand-painted sign proclaimed in Spanish that it was the headquarters of UMOPAR.

A sentry armed with an M-16 rifle stood guard at the door. He and Captain Vargas exchanged salutes, and Vargas ushered them inside. The building was set up as one large room. At the far end, a tall, dark man wearing the Leopards' spotted camouflage uniform sat at a large desk staring with obvious distaste at several folders stuffed with papers. His shoulder boards showed three silver stars on a black field, the insignia of a Bolivian colonel. Bolan did not need to be told that this was the commanding officer. Even sitting at his desk, the tall man radiated command authority.

Captain Vargas stopped in front of the colonel's desk and saluted smartly.

"My Colonel," he said formally, "allow me to present our visitors from La Paz, Captain Green, Captain Swenson and Mr. Belasko."

Colonel Suarez looked up, returned Vargas's salute and smiled faintly. It was not a happy smile. He stared at Bolan coldly.

"I am pleased to meet you. Particularly you, Mr. Belasko. I have had several messages concerning you and your group. It is very kind of you to come to such an out-of-the-way place to teach me how to conduct my business."

Bolan knew he was about to tiptoe through a mine field,

but if he and Suarez could not work together, he might as well get on a plane and fly back to La Paz.

"I'm pleased to meet you, Colonel," he said, "but there has been some mistake. There's no way I can teach you your business. You know the situation, your men and their capabilities, and what the drug cartel does here in this area. I know none of these things. I'm here to learn them and to help you if I can. My team includes specialists in several key areas, and General Stuart has promised to help with equipment and logistics support wherever he can. We are at your service, Colonel. Perhaps if you would brief us on the situation, we'll see where we may be able to help you."

Suarez looked at his visitors and smiled.

"I am glad that you are here to help me. God knows that I can use all the help I can get. Very well, I will explain the situation here as best I can."

He pointed to a map on his office wall.

"I have 720 officers and men in my unit. About 460 of them are here. We patrol the area around Chimore, which we call the red zone, because most of the action happens there. The others are in our northern base camp at Trinidad about 180 miles from here. My force is split. We maintain two camps because the coca is grown here, and the drug factories that turn it into cocaine are in the jungle around Trinidad. My battalion is not particularly well equipped. We have 450 of your M-16 rifles. The rest of my men carry old U.S. Army surplus .30-caliber M-1 carbines. We have no night-vision equipment, so we cannot operate effectively at night. Our trucks and jeeps are old and difficult to maintain. We have six Bell Huey helicopters available. They are ten years old and are getting tired. We have few radios, and those we have do not work very well. My men are all volunteers and their morale is good, but this is not a pleasant place to be stationed. If you can help me solve these problems, I will bless your name."

"We'll do the best we can, Colonel. I would suggest that the members of my team inspect your weapons and equipment and make recommendations. If we uncover problem areas, I'll contact General Stuart and try to get them fixed. Of course, I'll review any recommendation with you and get your approval before I make it."

"Very well, Mr. Belasko, I can ask for nothing better. Now, I have told you my situation. Do you have any questions?"

"How is your security, Colonel?" McCarter asked. Bolan nodded. It was a good question. Success in this kind of operation often depended on keeping your plans secret until they were carried out.

"My security is terrible," he said bitterly. "I am sure that the *narcotrafficantes* have many people in their pay inside my camp."

McCarter was astounded. If Suarez suspected some of his men had sold out, why didn't he get rid of them?

The colonel noticed his expression.

"Does that surprise you, Captain Green? It is simple enough when you know the situation. My men are members of the National Police. The basic pay of a policeman is the equivalent of sixty dollars U.S. a month. Men who volunteer for the Leopards are paid an extra forty dollars a month by the American government. A hundred dollars a month is not very much, even in Bolivia. Now suppose this young man is in charge of a checkpoint on a back road. A man comes up and says 'I am a farmer. I must get my crop to the market before it spoils. If you could see that my trucks are not delayed at your checkpoint, I would be extremely grateful.' With that, he hands him a thousand dollars. That is almost a year's pay for looking the other way for five minutes. Do not be surprised that, more often than not, my young man will take it."

He looked at Captain Vargas.

"Of course, the opportunities for officers and sergeants are much greater. Vargas is our operations officer. What have you been offered lately?"

"Twenty thousand dollars and the friendship of a beautiful young lady for next week's patrol plan, Colonel."

Suarez smiled. "It is good that Vargas comes from a rich and respectable family in Santa Cruz so that money does not tempt him, but if the *narcotrafficantes* keep importing beautiful young ladies, I may have no one left that I can trust."

"What about the local people? Can you count on their support?" Bolan asked.

Colonel Suarez smiled bitterly.

"Do not make the mistake of thinking that the people love you, or me and my men, for that matter. If they have to choose between us and the drug lords, they will choose the drug lords every time."

McCarter looked puzzled.

"I don't doubt what you say, Colonel, but I don't understand. From what I have been told, you and your men have a good reputation. Why would the local people support the drug traffickers?"

"Because we are the police. We give the people nothing but raids. I have no money, no food, no medicine for them. I can do nothing for them. The drug lords are different. People can go to them and say, 'My daughter is ill, sir, and I am very poor. Can you give me a little money to buy her some medicine?' The drug lord will give him money, enough to pay for a doctor or a plane trip to Santa Cruz. If they go to a village, they behave well. They pay very well for hotel rooms and meals in the local restaurant. They never molest the local women. They give money to build schools and churches. And they pay very good prices for coca leaves. Most people do not think of them as criminals but as rich and respectable businessmen.''

Bolan shook his head. He was sure Colonel Suarez knew what he was talking about, but it was bad news. If the drug cartel was really that popular with the locals, wiping out the drug factories was going to be a damned hard job.

''Very well. If there is nothing more, Captain Vargas will show you to your quarters. They are not very good. I am afraid we seldom have visitors here in Chimore. Most people have better sense,'' Suarez said.

''I have a request, Colonel,'' Bolan said. ''An American journalist, Fred Byrnes, will be flying into Chimore later today or tomorrow. General Stuart would appreciate it if you would grant him a personal interview. If possible, I would like to be present.''

Colonel Suarez looked skeptical.

''A journalist?''

''Mr. Byrnes is a man of many talents, Colonel,'' Swenson said. ''I'm sure you would be interested in some things he could tell you.''

''Ah, that kind of journalist. I would be happy to meet with your Mr. Byrnes as soon as he arrives. Is there anything else?''

''Yes, Colonel,'' Bolan replied. ''Captain Green and I would like to get a feel for what's going on in your red zone. We would like to go out with one of your patrols. Strictly as observers, of course.''

''Nothing could be easier. Captain Vargas is leading a

patrol tomorrow morning. If he has no objections, you may accompany him. What do you say, Captain?''

Vargas smiled, flashing his white teeth.

"No objection, Colonel. I will try to show our visitors an interesting time."

CAPTAIN VARGAS SHOWED THEM to their quarters. Gadgets Schwarz had already set up and checked out their lightweight LST-5C satellite communications radio.

Its antenna was pointed at a spot in the sky. He pushed a button and waited until a green light came on. The radio was locked on a United States military communications relay satellite standing motionless 22,300 miles above the equator and ready to transmit.

Bolan pushed the button.

"Granite Home, this is Striker. Acknowledge, Granite Home."

His voice flashed upward into space and was retransmitted to a second relay satellite over the continental United States and down to the satellite communications antennas at Stony Man Farm. He knew someone would be there. The operations center's SATCOM radio was monitored twenty-four hours a day when a team was in the field. Bolan waited for a few seconds and heard a familiar voice.

"Striker, this is Granite Home. Over."

Bolan was always impressed by satellite communications. Barbara Price's voice was as clear as if she were standing next to him. He reminded himself to keep it short as he pushed the transmit button. The narrow beam of the LST-5C SATCOM was focused on the relay satellite. In theory, it could be intercepted only by another satellite in a similar orbit, but Bolan did not like to trust theories when his life might be at stake. He had learned years earlier that if you want to survive, you had better keep your radio traffic to a minimum.

"Team insertion accomplished. At planned location. Contact made with Leopards' commander. Situation favorable. Starting operations tomorrow morning. Is Hal available? I have an urgent request for mission support that's going to require some high-level action. Striker out."

"Negative, Striker. There are political complications. He's in a meeting with our friend in Washington. I'll relay your message as soon as possible."

"Roger, Granite Home, I understand. I need four hundred M-16 rifles, forty M-203 grenade launchers, twenty M-249 SAW, ammunition, spare parts and two hundred sets of night-vision equipment. I need them delivered here to the Leopards' base at Chimore as fast as possible. Also find out whatever you can about a Captain Mary Swenson."

"Message understood. Will comply. Are you planning on starting a war, Striker?"

"Maybe, but just a little one."

"Stand by, Striker," Price said.

He could hear Price speaking to someone else at the operations center, but he could not make out the words.

"Striker, Granite Home. We'll take action to obtain requested equipment immediately. I have just received a message from Hal via secure phone. He says that diplomatic and political problems are developing with Blast Furnace. Some immediate public successes are needed. Do the best you can."

"Message understood, Granite Home. Will comply. Striker out."

Santa Cruz, Bolivia

EL VIEJO LANDED at the Santa Cruz airport two hours later. He did not attract any attention as he stepped off the small Bolivian airliner. He wore old, comfortable clothes and carried a battered leather suitcase. He looked like a poor but hard-working man who had come to visit his relatives. He walked past several National Police troopers with carbines slung over their shoulders. They did not give him a second glance. El Viejo smiled. It was amusing to think how they would react if they knew who he really was and what his mission was in Santa Cruz.

No one was there to meet him. He boarded an old bus and rode into town. He got off at the Plaza de 24 Septiembre in downtown Santa Cruz. He did not think he had been noticed or followed, but he was a careful man who took no unnecessary chances. He strolled around the plaza as if he did not have a care in the world. The plaza seemed to be dozing in the tropical heat of midafternoon. On benches around the central fountain, men in immaculately ironed linen shirts and dark sunglasses sat and idly watched the passersby and each other. Their shirts were cut loosely enough to conceal pistols. They were either plainclothes policemen or *trafficantes*.

An old man with a cart was trying to sell ice-cream bars. A nun was herding a wistful group of schoolgirls in white uniforms past the ice-cream vendor. El Viejo loved ice cream, and he was fond of children.

"With your permission, Sister, it is a very hot day. I would like to buy you and your charges some ice-cream bars."

The schoolgirls looked expectantly at the nun, who smiled and nodded. She could see nothing wrong with it, and it would make her girls so happy. El Viejo handed the vendor some money and smiled as the man handed the girls their ice creams. The girls smiled happily. It showed the sister was right when she talked about the power of prayer.

"Many thanks, sir. You are a kind and generous man. How may I thank you?"

El Viejo tipped his battered Panama hat.

"Remember me in your prayers, Sister," he said as he walked away. "I have much to be forgiven for."

He walked casually across the patio toward the cab stands. The nun smiled after him. In a world with so much wickedness, it was nice to meet such a kind and generous man. El Viejo selected an old, cheap cab without air-conditioning. He gave the driver the address and sat back and looked at the streets as they drove along. He had not been in Santa Cruz for a year. It did not seem to have changed much.

It seemed like a sleepy, tranquil city where nothing ever happened. But appearances could be deceiving. Behind closed doors and security fences, men wearing dark glasses and gold chains were running Bolivia's most profitable industry, cocaine production. The cab stopped and El Viejo got out. He walked idly around until he was sure the cab had not been followed, then he walked a few blocks until he reached an exclusive residential neighborhood. The street was lined with huge tile-roofed mansions surrounded by high brick walls topped by razor wire and sharp spikes. The mansions were outstanding examples of what cynical Bolivians call "narcoarchitecture."

He stopped at the gate of a particularly opulent mansion and rang the bell. A hard-faced young man wearing dark sunglasses and a large automatic pistol came to the gate, but he did not open it. He stared contemptuously at the shabby, gray-haired man.

"Whatever you are selling, we do not want any. Be off!" he said harshly.

"A thousand pardons for disturbing you, sir, but if you would tell the owner of this house that El Viejo is here and wishes to speak to him, I would be very grateful."

The guard's face froze. He had never seen El Viejo before, but he had heard of him and knew that only a man with a death wish would insult him. He opened the gate with remarkable speed and ushered El Viejo inside.

"Come with me, sir. I know Don Roberto will want to see you immediately."

El Viejo followed him to a large patio. Seven men were sitting around a table, eating and drinking, served by two lovely girls in skimpy bikinis and high heels. The men looked like rich businessmen, and in a way they were. Between them, they ran Bolivian cocaine production.

Don Roberto saw his guest and stood up immediately.

"My house is your house," he said in the formal Spanish welcome. "Please be seated. What is the news from La Paz?"

"It is bad, I fear. That is why I am here. What we have heard is true. The Americans are coming again and this time, in force. They have a general in command, and many airplanes and soldiers. Our contacts inside their embassy say that their objective is to destroy every cocaine factory in the country. If our government will let them, the Americans will use their soldiers and Marines directly against us."

"Damned Americans," Don Roberto said indignantly. "Surely, our government will not agree to this?"

"I am afraid they will. The President of the United States himself is demanding it."

The men around the table frowned. They did not like Americans, but they did not underestimate them. The idea of elite American troops sweeping the jungle and destroying their drug factories was appalling.

"Can their general be bribed?" Don Roberto asked.

"I do not think so. He is a hard man. I doubt that he will compromise."

"What are we to do, then? We cannot just wait for the Americans to destroy us."

"I have thought this might happen for a long time. I have prepared a plan to defeat the Americans. I call it Operation Thunderbolt. With your permission, I will explain it to you."

Don Roberto smiled. He liked the sound of Operation Thunderbolt.

"Proceed, please," he said.

El Viejo talked for nearly twenty minutes, explaining his plan in detail, answering skeptical questions skillfully.

"It is an excellent plan, but it will cost huge amounts of money," Don Roberto said.

"That is true," El Viejo conceded. "But what is our business worth to us? And if we succeed, we will own Bolivia, and the Americans will be thrown out for good."

There was a brief discussion, but no one disagreed. El Viejo was right. There was no alternative.

"Very well," Don Roberto said, "you have our blessing. Implement Operation Thunderbolt, and to hell with the Americans!"

CHAPTER NINE

The Red Zone, Central Bolivia

Mack Bolan was enjoying deep, dreamless sleep when someone tapped him lightly on the foot and a fiendishly cheerful voice begin to sound off in his ear.

"Rise and shine, Mack! Time to be up and at them. It's a beautiful day, and Captain Vargas will be here in a few minutes. Roll out and get ready. I've made some tea. A cup or two will get you going."

Bolan grimaced. Having to drink McCarter's tea was almost a fate worse than death. He pushed the mosquito netting aside and got out of bed. He could tell that it would be a hot day since even at 7:00 a.m. it was already warm. He stepped into the bathroom and splashed water on his face, but he did not shave. He had learned long ago in Vietnam that a freshly shaved face will reflect light and give away a man's position. He would rather be hard to see than fashionable.

He stepped back into the sleeping room and began to slip on his equipment. He hesitated for a second as he looked at his Kevlar soft body armor vest. If he wore it, he knew it would be hot and uncomfortable. Still, he would rather be hot and sweaty than have a hole blown through his middle. He slipped on the vest, put on his shirt, and carefully checked and holstered his pistols.

McCarter poured condensed milk into a steel mug of tea and stirred in some sugar.

"Take this, Mack. It'll wake you up."

Bolan was saved by a knock on the door. He opened it, and Captain Vargas stepped in. He was tall for a Bolivian and made a dashing appearance in his leopard-spotted camouflaged uniform. He wore a large automatic pistol in a brown leather holster and binoculars slung over his left shoulder.

He showed his perfect white teeth in a flashing smile.

"Good morning, gentlemen. I trust you slept well. Are you ready? It is time to go see the red zone. I see you are having tea."

"Yeah," Bolan said smoothly. "Captain Green brews some remarkable tea. We've saved a cup for you." Before McCarter could say anything, Bolan took the mug and handed it to Vargas.

The Leopards' captain smiled politely as he raised the cup to his lips.

"Many thanks, Captain Green. I am fond of tea."

He took a sip and shuddered faintly.

"A remarkable flavor. What is in it?"

"It is rather good, isn't it? I start with the best tea I can get, brew it double strength, and add condensed milk and four lumps of sugar."

Vargas's pride would not let him stop now. The honor of the Leopards was at stake. He drained the steel mug in several big swallows.

"A truly remarkable taste. We Bolivians are fond of tea, but we do not make it this way."

"I would offer you another cup, but that's all there is. I can make some more when we get back."

"I will look forward to it," Vargas said with the determined air of a man who suffers for his country.

"Now we must go. Sergeant Chavez and his men are waiting at the briefing hut."

Bolan and McCarter picked up their M-4 carbines and followed Captain Vargas outside. It looked like a splendid morning. The sky was a bright blue, and the sun was shining brightly. Bolan hated to think how hot it would be in four or five hours.

"How large is the patrol?" he asked Vargas.

"One squad commanded by an experienced sergeant, a driver, and an officer in command."

"Ten or eleven men? Isn't that a very large police patrol?" McCarter asked.

Vargas smiled. "Perhaps if we were going to patrol downtown La Paz, but not here in the Red Zone. A strong patrol is necessary here. If we send out two or three men, they may not come back."

McCarter nodded solemnly.

"Like Northern Ireland during the troubles," he said softly. McCarter's tours in Northern Ireland with the SAS had not been happy ones. Bolan knew that McCarter did not like to talk about it, but his memories were bitter.

"Here we are, gentlemen," Vargas announced. "A quick prepatrol inspection, and we will be off. Colonel Suarez is a strong believer in prepatrol inspections."

Bolan and McCarter followed him into the briefing hut. A Leopards sergeant and eight men were waiting inside. All wore their unit's leopard-spotted combat fatigues and were armed with M-16 rifles. The sergeant and Captain Vargas exchanged salutes.

"This is Master Sergeant Chavez, gentlemen. His squad will be our patrol. Are we ready, Chavez?"

"Patrol ready for inspection, sir!" Chavez snapped.

Captain Vargas moved slowly along the line of waiting Leopards, checking each man's weapons and equipment. Bolan was pleased to see that he was not a spit-and-polish officer. He was not interested in starched uniforms or the shine on the men's boots. He checked each man's weapon and looked to see that each had a full canteen. He nodded his approval and spoke to the waiting men.

"We are honored today to have with us Captain Green, who is affiliated with the British army and Mr. Belasko from the American Department of Justice. They are here to provide us technical assistance and to observe our methods. They know that the Leopards are the best unit in Bolivia. I have told them this is the best squad in the Leopards. You must do your best today, men. I do not wish to look like a liar."

The men grinned. A chorus of, *"Sí, Capitán"* ran down the line.

"Before we go, I will ask Mr. Belasko to inspect our weapons. I am told he is a famous expert. I am told he killed half the *narce* gunmen in La Paz, and the rest tremble in their boots when they hear his name."

Bolan would have to speak to Mary Swenson about telling war stories, but it just might be helpful to have the reputation of a dangerous man. He checked each M-16 quickly but carefully. The rifles showed signs of hard use and were well worn, but they were clean and looked ready for action. He was less happy with the spare magazines and ammunition. The 30-round aluminum magazine has always been a weak point of the M-16 rifle, easily damaged and subject to wear. That was bad. No automatic rifle would work well if its magazines weren't in good condition.

Captain Vargas noticed Bolan's frown.

"Is there a problem?"

Bolan saw no reason to beat around the bush.

"There's no problem with the rifles, Captain, but most of your magazines are in poor shape. They could cause feeding problems, particularly in full automatic fire, and they ought to be replaced right now if that's possible. Also, your men have only two spare magazines apiece. I'm not trying to tell you your business, but if you're expecting any trouble, I'd be more comfortable if each man had at least four spare magazines."

Vargas frowned. "I would do as you say if I could, but unfortunately, I cannot. We got our M-16 rifles and their magazines in 1990. Since then, we have tried to get spare parts, but without success. We have no more magazines. I think the army is jealous that mere policemen have such modern weapons."

"Give me ten minutes, and I think I can fix it. After all, the best squad in the Leopards can't go second class."

He left the briefing hut and walked back to his quarters. He went to one corner of the room, stopped in front of a large black plastic case and punched his personal identification number into the cipher lock. The case held spare weapons, parts and ammunition. John Kissinger had packed it, personally, and Bolan knew that he would have put in everything but the kitchen sink. In one corner of the case were several packages of 30-round magazines for the Stony Man team's M-4 carbines. They were identical to those used with the M-16. Bolan picked up several packages, then paused and thought for a moment.

The patrol had a great deal of firepower. At close range, its gunners would be lethal, but if they had to reach out and touch someone at long range, they had no weapon suitable for the task. Bolan did not believe in taking unnecessary chances. He reached inside the case and pulled out a rifle.

It was not a pretty weapon. Its dull-black, nonreflective finish and matte-black plastic stock gave it an almost cheap look. It was a Remington 700-P sniper's rifle fitted with an advanced day or night telescopic sight. It had been an excellent rifle when it left the Remington custom gunshop. When John "Cowboy" Kissinger, the Stony Man Farm armorer, had finished fine-tuning it, it was superb. Bolan loaded it with .308 M-852 National Match ammunition manufactured at Lake City Arsenal, some of the most accurate military rifle ammunition in the world. When Mack Bolan did his part, the combination would put five shots in a three-quarter-inch-diameter group at a range of one hundred yards. If he had to trade shots with someone at long range, he could count on the ugly Remington. He slung it over his shoulder and started back for the briefing hut.

Everyone looked at him as he reentered the hut. He handed Vargas the packages of spare M-16 magazines, and the captain distributed the new magazines to his men. Bolan heard a low murmur of approval. At least this big American was not all talk. The Leopards happily began to transfer their ammunition to their new magazines.

"Tell them not to load more than twenty-eight rounds in the magazines, Captain," Bolan instructed.

"As you say," Vargas responded. He looked surprised, but he gave the order.

"I am sure you are right," he said, "but I do not understand. Are they not 30-round magazines?"

Bolan shook his head. "They'll hold thirty rounds and work when they're new and clean. If we went to the range and fired right now, they would all probably work perfectly. It's different when you're out in the bush all day and you have dust on your weapons and magazines. It gets worse if you have been firing steadily and you have powder fouling on your weapons. The first round or two out of the magazine are the hardest for the weapon to feed. Load twenty-eight rounds, and the chances of having malfunctions goes way down.''

Vargas nodded, and Bolan knew he was filing the information away for future reference.

"One other thing, Captain," Bolan added. "I notice you're armed only with a pistol. If you don't mind my saying so, it might be better if you also carried a rifle or a carbine."

Vargas frowned. "We do not have enough M-16s to go around. The colonel does not approve of his staff officers carrying M-16s when there are not enough to arm all the men, and I do not trust our old M-1 carbines. I have a very fine pistol, and I can shoot it well. I will be all right."

Bolan had thought something like that might be the case. He unslung the M-4 Ranger carbine from his left shoulder and handed it to Vargas.

"Here, carry this M-4 carbine. It's a shorter, lighter version of the M-16. That's a 40 mm grenade launcher under the rifle barrel. I'll show you how it works. It gives you a lot of extra firepower."

He handed Vargas the nylon web pouches that carried the M-4's spare ammunition.

Vargas stared at the ugly, dull black weapon in his hands as if it were the most beautiful thing in the world. He had been in several firefights during his four years with the Leopards. He knew that firepower could be the difference between life and death.

He sighed. "That is very kind of you, Mr. Belasko, but Colonel Suarez does not approve of his officers accepting gifts, even from our friends."

"Let's not think of it as a gift, Captain. Let's say it's

a research project. You use it for a few months and write me a report. Tell me if you think it would be a good weapon to rearm the Leopards. I will tell the colonel I asked you to do it as a personal favor. You can say you could not refuse.''

Vargas grinned and slung the M-4 over his shoulder.

"You are right," he said. "I am a gentleman. I cannot possibly refuse your request, but as you Americans say, I owe you. I will buy you the finest dinner to be had in Chimore. Perhaps I can introduce you to some charming young ladies?''

"Perhaps," Bolan said with a smile. Somehow, he did not think General Stuart had asked him to go to Chimore to enjoy the nightlife, but he could not insult his hosts.

Captain Vargas looked at his watch and frowned. "We are already two minutes late. If there is nothing more, let us go quickly. The colonel does not approve of officers who are late starting their patrols.''

They followed Vargas outside. A shiny red Dodge pickup truck was waiting, its driver behind the wheel. McCarter stared at the big Dodge. It did not resemble any military or police vehicle he had ever seen.

"It is a beauty, is it not?" Vargas inquired. "We got it from a *narcotrafficante* who had no further use for it. The motor pool has done an excellent job. You can hardly tell where the bullet holes were unless you look very closely.''

Vargas climbed into the back of the truck and motioned for Bolan and McCarter to sit next to him. He took a folded map out of his leopard-spotted camouflage jacket, unfolded it and attached it to his clipboard. He pointed to the center of the map.

"We are here, just north of the main road that runs from Chimore to Cochabamba on the eastern side of the

Chapare. We are going west, to the village of Paractito. It will take us an hour to get there, but in ten minutes we will pass through Sinahota. You will find it a very interesting place. We call it 'Little Chicago.' It is the real heart of the Chapare. Ninety percent of Bolivia's coca-leaf crop is grown within a hundred miles of Sinahota. It is a great place to get rich. The drug lords come here to do business. They buy coca leaves and coca paste. They fight over territory and settle old scores. They have some marvelous shootouts in the streets of Sinahota. They can be very entertaining, but be ready to duck when you hear automatic weapons firing.''

Bolan smiled. No one had to tell him to duck when the guns began to shoot.

''It sounds like a fun place, Captain,'' he remarked.

The truck reached the main road and turned west. Bolan relaxed and watched the passing scenery. The lush greenery of a well-watered tropical rain forest was spectacular. They passed a number of trucks heavily loaded with sacks of green leaves driving slowly toward Sinahota.

''What are those trucks carrying, Captain?'' McCarter asked.

''Coca leaves, Captain Green. To make cocaine, you must start with coca leaves. Each of those sacks holds one hundred pounds of coca leaves. A sack is called a *carga*. They are going to Sinahota to the coca market. A *carga* may sell for anywhere from fifty to two hundred dollars U.S. We will stop in Sinahota and check the price. That will tell us how well we are doing. If the drug dealers have avoided us, demand will be strong and the price will be high. If we have made some successful raids, some of the buyers will be scared away, and the price will fall.''

McCarter looked surprised.

"You mean they buy and sell coca leaves in public? Why don't the local authorities put a stop to it?"

"It would not be to their best interest to do so," Vargas said. "Sinahota lives on the coca trade. Everyone who goes to the market must pay a tax on each sack to the town government. Sinahota's local government runs on the money from their coca leaf tax. They are so prosperous that they put in an electric power plant last year. They even have an ice-cream parlor and cold beer."

McCarter shook his head. "It sounds like a bloody strange way to run things."

Vargas laughed.

"I am sure you do things differently in England, Captain, but this is Bolivia. It is not illegal to grow, sell or use coca leaves, only to make cocaine from them. That is what we try to stop. It does make things very interesting, but look. Here is Sinahota. You can see for yourselves."

Bolan saw a rusty sign by the side of the road that proclaimed in Spanish and English that "Possession or transportation of cocaine, cocaine products, or precursor chemicals is strictly forbidden." Someone had put half a dozen bullets through the sign.

The Executioner looked around as the truck slowed. At first glance, Sinahota looked like any other town he had seen in the Chapare, sprawling groups of small buildings and shacks on both sides of the road, women street vendors hopefully offering fried fish and chicken, soft drinks and beer. Then he saw sign after sign proclaiming that the finest beer, food, billiard halls and dance halls with charming young ladies were available at remarkably low prices.

Some cars parked along the streets were rusty old Chevrolets and Fords, but a startling number were shiny new Mercedes. Here and there, among the men in faded jeans and women in brightly colored skirts, he saw men in beautifully tailored tropical denim pants and jackets and expensive Panama hats. They all seemed to wear stylish wraparound French sunglasses and gold chains and rings. None of them were walking alone. Six or eight young men strolled along, each warily scanning the street and wearing loose-fitting jackets despite the morning heat.

"If you want to see some real drug lords, there they are. *Narcotrafficantes* and their bodyguards," Vargas said. "Some of them are very interesting people. Here is one now who is worth looking at."

He tapped on the back window of the pickup and signaled Sergeant Chavez to stop. Bolan found himself staring at a tall man in denim and gold. He had a woman in a black dress on his left arm and eight bodyguards in a semicircle around him. The bodyguards glared at the red truck. One or two hands started to ease toward their briefcases but stopped when they saw the muzzles of the Leopards' M-16s pointed casually at them. Vargas swung down from the back of the truck. Bolan followed him. McCarter moved silently around the vehicle, keeping it between him and the group on the street.

The tall man smiled and spoke in Spanish.

"Good day, Vargas. How does it go with you?"

"Splendidly, as always. What is the price of coca leaves today?"

"A hundred dollars a sack, Vargas. You must send out more patrols."

He glanced at Bolan. "Who is your large friend?"

It was Vargas's turn to smile.

"He is my new associate, the Bullfighter. You will be seeing more of him in the future."

Bolan did not understand why Vargas had called him a bullfighter, but he saw a wave of tension run through the men facing him. A tall, dark man with knife scars on his face started to slide his right hand under his jacket. Bolan reacted instantly, his .44 Magnum Desert Eagle seeming to appear in his right hand as if by magic. The man with the scarred face found himself staring down the huge muzzle. His hand froze.

The Executioner heard safeties click off behind him. The Leopards looking over the side of the truck had picked their targets and were ready to fire. Bolan caught a flicker of motion to his right. McCarter had stepped out from behind the front of the vehicle. His eyes were cold as he stared over the sights of his M-4 carbine.

"Freeze! If anyone moves, I'll kill him!"

McCarter's voice carried total conviction. He had flanked the drug lord and his men. They would have to turn ninety degrees to fire at him, and if they tried, they would be caught in a deadly cross fire from McCarter and the Leopards in the truck. They froze. They were not cowards, but they were not ready to die for nothing.

The drug lord smiled and moved his hands palms down, slowly, away from his sides.

"There is no need for all these guns. I am sure we are all friends here. We want no trouble. Lobo, put your hands at your sides. Vargas, perhaps you can persuade your large friend to put away his pistol."

Vargas nodded. Bolan waited until both of the bodyguard's hands were at their sides, then holstered his big .44. He had made his point.

The captain laughed softly.

"I am afraid I have forgotten my manners. This is El Cuchillo, the Knife. He is a famous drug trafficker. He is a true Bolivian, not a damned Colombian. This charming young lady is La Alta, and you have already met his chief bodyguard, El Lobo.

The bodyguard glared at Bolan, but he made no move to draw a weapon. He was not sure he understood the game Captain Vargas was playing. Everyone seemed to have no name and to go by some colorful nickname, and there seemed to be a casual, almost friendly relationship between Vargas and El Cuchillo. Bolan kept his eye on El Lobo. His nickname meant "the Wolf," and it suited him. Bolan knew the man would kill him in an instant if he thought he could get away with it.

He glanced at the tall woman in black. She was worth looking at. She was about thirty and beautifully built. She had a superb figure and was dressed to show it. Her dress could not have been tighter unless it were painted on. She had dark, glossy black hair, a burnished copper skin and exotic features that Bolan could not place. She was a striking sight, but the Executioner would not have called her a charming young lady. She was glaring furiously at Vargas and him. If looks could kill, they would both have died instantly.

"Say something nice, Alta," Vargas said tauntingly. "You know how fond I am of you."

Alta spit on the ground.

"You are a pig, Vargas. You were born a pig, and you will die a pig. And when you are dead, I will dance on your grave!" she said in a low, husky voice that vibrated with hatred.

She glared at Mack Bolan. "And you, gringo, we do not want your kind here. We will send you home in a coffin!"

Vargas slapped her hard across the face, still smiling while he did it.

"Watch your tongue, daughter of a whore. Show more respect for men in authority. Would you like me to take you back to our base for a little questioning? We have some splendid new equipment in the interrogation room. After I question you there for a few hours, you will be a good little girl, very respectful and eager to please.''

She glared at Captain Vargas, but she did not speak. She could see his left hand poised to slap her again.

"That is better," Vargas said, grinning wickedly, running a hand casually along the exposed bustline of the woman's low-cut dress. "I am sorry that I do not have time to strip search you today. I know how much you enjoy it. Perhaps next time."

He climbed back into the red truck. Bolan and McCarter followed him, careful not to turn their backs on the *narcotrafficantes*. Vargas tapped on the cab's rear window and motioned to the driver to start the engine. They drove slowly down the main street.

Bolan thought it over as they rode along. He was not sure he understood everything that had just gone on. He was surprised that Captain Vargas seemed to be on such casual terms with a known drug lord. It almost looked as if Vargas was on the take, but if that were true, Colonel Suarez would never have suggested that he and McCarter go on Vargas's patrol.

McCarter stared at Vargas.

"Captain Vargas," he said finally, "I'm not trying to tell you how to run your business and you *are* in command, but you shouldn't have slapped that woman or touched her as you did."

Vargas smiled with the air of a magician pulling a rabbit out of a hat. He held out his left hand. In its palm was a small, folded piece of yellow paper. He unfolded it carefully and passed it to McCarter.

"Perhaps you are right, Captain Green, but I find such interesting things there. See what she had hidden in her bra? Here is the location of the place we are going to raid and the positions of the guards. Alta is my mailbox, and a very attractive one, too.''

McCarter was astonished.

"You mean she is one of your informants? Bloody hell, the woman is a marvelous actress. I would have sworn that she hated your guts.''

"It is not all acting. She truly hates policemen. She would not weep if she saw me dead, but she is a *trafficante*. This way she and El Cuchillo can pass me information, and no one suspects.''

McCarter could see that, but he was still puzzled. "Why do they want to tell you anything?" he asked.

"This is a new factory, recently established. It is run by Colombians, and like most Bolivians, they do not like Colombians, particularly those who take business away from them. They will be very happy if we destroy it. Colonel Suarez will be happy, and the American government will be happy. Everyone will be happy.''

"Except the Colombians," McCarter said.

Vargas smiled coldly. "Perhaps they will not care. The note says they are heavily armed and will probably fight, not surrender. If they do, we will kill them all.''

CHAPTER TEN

The Red Zone, Central Bolivia

The Leopards in the back of the truck were laughing as they drove away. They clearly thought they had won that round. Their captain had put the whore in her place, and the big gringo had made El Lobo back down. They would have some good stories to tell when they got back to camp. Vargas looked quite pleased with himself. Even McCarter was smiling, now that he saw what had happened as a clever piece of undercover work.

Bolan was glad everyone was happy, but there were a few things that he did not understand about the incident.

"You say Bolivians don't like Colombians. I thought they were the ones who bought most of the Bolivian cocaine. If they bring in so much money, why are Colombians so unpopular?" he asked Vargas.

"We take their money, but that means only that we do business, not that we like them. Do not take this personally, but we are an isolated and clannish people. We do not like foreigners of any kind, and perhaps we have good reasons."

Bolan looked at Vargas.

"Mind telling me why?" he asked.

"Not at all. It will help you understand us much better. Do you know much about the history of South America?"

"Not much," Bolan said honestly.

Vargas nodded. He was used to that. Most Americans he met seemed to know very little about South America.

"Bolivia became an independent country in 1825 when we drove out the Spanish. The country was twice as big then as it is now. We had common borders then with Brazil, Chile, Argentina, Peru and Paraguay. We have fought wars with all of them and lost every one. They took away half of our country. Some Bolivians dream of taking back these lost lands, but it will never happen. Most of these countries are far richer and more powerful than Bolivia will ever be. You can understand why we do not love foreigners."

Bolan nodded. He had no trouble understanding. If the United States had lost half its territory to other countries, Americans probably would not like foreigners, either.

"There's one other thing I don't understand," Bolan said. "You know that El Cuchillo and his men are drug traffickers. Why don't you arrest them and put them in prison?"

"Indeed, I know they are *narcotrafficantes,* but I cannot prove it in a court of law. Unless I catch them in the act or I have very strong evidence, I have no right to arrest them."

They reached the outskirts of Sinahota. Just before the shacks ended and the coca fields and jungle began, an asphalt road turned off through the trees. They drove a few hundred yards, and Bolan was surprised to see a huge metal building that resembled a hangar at a major airfield. A dozen trucks were parked by the big front door. Groups of men were unloading the bulging sacks of green coca leaves, placing them on dollies, wheeling them inside.

Women were sitting at wooden tables selling food, beer and soft drinks. Several young men and women were moving through the crowd, trying to sell straw hats decorated with flamingo feathers, animal skins and Indian handicrafts. A few men were lounging around, eating and drinking, watching the crowd. If anyone was worried by the arrival of the Leopards, they did not show it. It might have been a scene from some rural county fair, but the crop that was being bought and sold was not going to end up in salads. Probably half the cocaine entering the United States started here.

Captain Vargas ordered his driver to stop the truck near the door. He took Sergeant Chavez and four of his men, motioned to Bolan and McCarter to follow him, and strode through the doorway. The huge building was bustling with activity. Men were feeling and smelling green coca leaves, bargaining furiously, and lifting the bulging sacks of green leaves onto weighing scales. A pungent odor filled the hot air.

"What is that odd smell? It almost smells like fresh spinach," McCarter asked.

Vargas smiled cheerfully. "That is the smell of fresh coca leaves, but the farmers who grow coca plants will tell you that it is the smell of money."

Bolan looked around. Most of the men were dressed in work clothes and straw hats, and looked like farmers. Here and there were men dressed in the denim suits and gold chains that seemed to be the uniform of the local drug lords. They moved from table to table examining the coca leaves and bargaining with the farmers. There was no paperwork involved. Deals were sealed with a handshake and immediately settled with cash. The presence of Vargas and his patrol certainly was noticed, but it seemed to have no effect on business.

"Who are the men buying the leaves? Do you know who they are?" Bolan asked.

Vargas shrugged. "Some of them. Others are new. Some of the drug lords prefer to buy in person. Others hire middlemen. In either case, no records are kept. The farmers know it is not wise to ask, and as long as their money is good, they do not care. Now, if I were to question those men, they would all say they are honest businessmen, wholesalers who buy the leaves and sell them to Indians and poor peasants who chew them as their ancestors have done for hundreds of years."

Bolan was puzzled. "Everyone chews coca leaves in Bolivia?"

"Not everyone. It is considered a lower class, Indian habit. Let us say most people do. I do not do it anymore. Colonel Suarez does not approve of officers who do, but when I was a wild young man I used to like to chew the leaves now and then. I suppose Americans do not do it because you have no coca leaves. Would you like to try it? I know several coca farmers here who grow the finest leaves in the Chapare."

"You can just walk up and buy them?" Mack Bolan asked. It was still hard for him to believe the casual way the Bolivians seemed to accept the coca trade.

Vargas laughed.

"The only problem would be to get them to take my money, but Colonel Suarez does not like his officers to accept gifts."

Bolan was not about to start chewing coca leaves, but he was curious.

"What does it do to people who chew it?" he asked.

"Not much. You put about thirty leaves in your mouth after you dust them with a powder made from potatoes and wood ash. That helps draw the juice out. It has a bitter taste, but you swallow it anyway. It makes your mouth and lips numb. The novocaine that dentists use is made from coca. Then you will feel peaceful and relaxed. It takes away your appetite and makes you feel strong. It also takes away pain and tiredness. I am not sure the juice from the leaves is really a narcotic, but people who have used it for a while do not want to be without it. No matter what the government does, it will not be able to stop people from growing coca and selling the leaves."

Bolan did not like the sound of that, but he was not a diplomat or a lawyer. Persuading the Bolivians to change their laws was not his job.

"All right, but there is one other thing I don't understand. Those people we talked to back there, you know they're drug dealers. They were in Sinahota to buy coca leaves. Why did you let them go?"

Vargas smiled.

"You must remember that my men and I are not soldiers. We are all members of the National Police. I am a graduate of the National Police Academy, not the Military Academy. The same is true of Colonel Suarez and the other officers in the Leopards. We would only come under the control of the military in time of war or grave national crisis."

Bolan nodded. "I understand what you're saying, Captain, but I'm not sure why it is important. Whether you're a soldier or a policeman, isn't it your mission to destroy the cocaine trade?"

"It makes much more difference than you think," Vargas replied. "If I were a soldier and we were truly at war with the drug cartels, I could attack and destroy them wherever they were found. I could call in air strikes on the drug factories, ambush their vehicles, plant land mines on the roads in the areas they control. I would take the drug lords prisoner and put them in prison camps without trials until the war was over. They would have no lawyers and no trials. But I am not a soldier, and legally, there is not a war. I must obey the constitution of 1967. I can kill people only if they attack my men or resist arrest, and I can arrest them only if I have hard evidence that they have committed a crime.''

Bolan shook his head, but he understood. Vargas was a Bolivian National Police officer. He could try hard to destroy the cocaine trade, but what he did must conform to Bolivian law. That made things far more complicated than they had seemed back in Washington.

''I understand,'' he said. Captain Vargas did not know the big American well, and thought that Bolan was politely agreeing with him. He might not have been happy if he had known what the Executioner was really thinking. He had come to Bolivia to disrupt the cocaine trade. Bolan had decided a long time ago that he would not let the laws of any country shield dangerous criminals and terrorists. If the Bolivian authorities would not agree to take decisive action against the drug cartels, *he* would act, and let the diplomats and lawyers pick up the pieces.

''Excuse me a few moments,'' Vargas said. ''I must talk to some people here before we leave. It would be best if you and Captain Green are not with me. People do not know you. They will speak much more freely if I do not have foreigners with me.''

Bolan understood. No one was going to mistake McCarter or him for Bolivians. He watched as Vargas started to circulate across the floor, stopping here and there to talk briefly with the men behind the tables. Bolan noted that the farmers treated Vargas with great respect, pulling off their hats and showing him their coca leaves. Once or twice, Vargas asked to see their papers and checked them briefly. Some of the men offered Vargas coca leaves or a soft drink but he refused with a smile.

The Executioner stopped at a farmer's table and stared at the sacks of coca leaves, trying to look like a real connoisseur. The farmer stared at Bolan in alarm. Whatever he was, he was not a Bolivian.

"Good day. How may I serve you?" he asked.

"You have fine merchandise," Bolan said politely. "If I were to buy fifty sacks, what would your price be?"

The farmer relaxed a little.

"You will excuse me. I do not want to seem impolite, but I do not know you. If you buy, how will you pay and how are you called?"

"I pay in American dollars. Men call me El Matador."

The Bolivian's face froze. Bolan could almost smell his fear.

"Please. I am a poor man. I have a wife and children. Whatever you say is fine with me."

Bolan was puzzled. Somehow, he had frightened the man to death by saying people called him the bullfighter. He was about to say something else when he heard voices growing steadily louder behind him. One of them was McCarter's. He turned.

The Briton had been trapped by a stocky Indian woman wearing the traditional native costume of a brightly embroidered blouse, long multiple layered skirts, and what looked for all the world like a brown derby hat decorated with pink flamingo feathers. She was determined to sell McCarter a finely woven brightly colored wool blanket. She draped the blanket over the tall Englishman's shoulders. McCarter was protesting politely in his limited Spanish, but she would not take no for an answer.

"Muy grande, senor," she said in her soft Bolivian accent.

She saw that Mack Bolan was watching and appealed to him. *"Muy grande y muy barato, senor!"*

"Very grand and very cheap," Bolan agreed. McCarter turned red and glared at Bolan. The Indian woman doubled her efforts, draping the brightly colored blanket fashionably around McCarter's broad shoulders.

Someone touched Bolan's left sleeve gently. He pivoted to the left instantly but did not draw his Desert Eagle when he saw a thin, gray-haired man holding an old model Polaroid camera.

"Photographs, *senor?* The finest souvenir of your visit to the market in Sinahota! Very good and very cheap!" the thin man said hopefully.

Bolan smiled and pointed at McCarter and the Indian woman. She threw an arm around McCarter and smiled broadly as the camera flashed. Bolan stepped forward.

"How much?" he asked.

"For you, only fifty pesos," she beamed.

Bolan handed her the money and pointed at McCarter. *"Timido,"* he said.

She smiled and put the money inside her blouse. She patted McCarter on the shoulder. *"Sí, timido,"* she agreed. Bolan paid the photographer. The photograph was excellent. It was hard to tell which was more colorful, the blanket or McCarter's face.

Bolan heard someone chuckling softly. Sergeant Chavez was standing there, fighting a losing battle to keep from laughing.

"Pardon, gentlemen. Captain Vargas says we leave in three minutes," he said.

Bolan nodded. "Tell him we'll be there as soon as Captain Green finishes shopping."

"Why did you tell that woman I was timid?" the Briton demanded.

"You need to work on your Spanish, David. *Timido* doesn't mean afraid. It means you're shy. In this case, shy with the ladies."

Somehow his explanation did not seem to make McCarter happy.

"What do you intend to do with that picture?"

Bolan looked thoughtful. Maybe I'll get it enlarged and hang it on the wall of the conference room at Stony Man."

"Bloody hell, Mack. I think you put that woman up to it. I'll get even with you one of these days, see if I don't!" McCarter said as he walked out.

Bolan grinned as he followed McCarter out. He had been the victim of the Briton's practical jokes more than once. It was about time he got even.

Outside, two young men dressed in the worldwide uniform of T-shirts and jeans swooped hopefully down on them. They had wool blankets and animal skins draped over their arms. They took one look at McCarter and let him pass. The look on his face told them instantly that he was not in a mood to buy. Their attention turned to Bolan, stepping into his path, standing side by side, about two feet apart.

The one on Bolan's right held up a beautiful golden yellow animal skin, spotted with black markings, draped across both arms. He smiled, flashing beautiful white teeth, as he held out the skin toward the Executioner.

"See, *senor,* the skin of a jaguar from the forests of the Gran Chaco. There is no finer souvenir in all of Bolivia. And you will not believe the price. Only three hundred American dollars! You cannot refuse such a bargain!"

It was a beautiful skin, but Bolan did not approve of killing rare animals to make souvenirs, and he did not collect exotic items on his travels.

"No, thank you," he said politely. "It's a beautiful skin, but I travel a great deal and I have no place to keep souvenirs."

The young man did not want to take no for an answer. He began to bargain rapidly, but Bolan's attention had shifted to the other man. He had said nothing, simply standing there staring at Bolan. Perhaps he did not speak English and let his partner make the pitch, but he looked nervous and tense, and there was something strange about the look on his face. His eyes were wide, and his cheeks were flushed. Was he using something? Coca leaves? No, Vargas said they made you feel happy and peaceful. Whatever it was, the man was not feeling that way. As Bolan looked at him, he shifted his stance into a slight crouch. The Executioner suddenly realized he could not see the man's right hand. It was concealed behind his thigh.

Bolan started to take a step back to open his distance from the pair when the first man shouted *"Ahora!"* and seized the big American's right wrist in a two-handed death grip. Bolan was trained in several hand-to-hand-combat systems. He knew how to break that hold, but not without using his left hand and he knew he did not have time for that. He saw the sunlight glint on a polished blade as the man on his left brought a large double-edged knife from behind his thigh and swung it in a wide, flashing horizontal arc.

"El Viejo sends you this!" the man yelled as he struck.

Bolan tried to block the blow, but he was off balance and he could not get enough strength into the block. The attacker's hand flashed through and Bolan felt the shock of the blow as the point of the knife slammed into his left side. The Executioner tried to jerk his right hand free, shaking the smaller man who gripped it like a terrier shook a rat. No good; the smaller man hung on.

The man with the knife struck again, smiling as he drove the point of the blade straight at Bolan's chest, aiming for his heart. The big American felt the shock of the blow as the knife struck home. This could not go on much longer. Bolan's left hand flashed down into his left-hand pants pocket, gripped the butt of his small Smith & Wesson Model 940 revolver and drew it in one smooth motion.

The man with the knife realized that something was wrong. Bolan should be lying on the ground pumping out his lifeblood. Somehow, he was still standing. The man snarled as he drew back his knife and started to aim a thrust at his adversary's throat. Bolan pulled the trigger of the hammerless Smith & Wesson the instant the deadly little revolver cleared the edge of his pocket. Its two-inch barrel was pointing low as he pulled the trigger, and the 940 drove a high-velocity 9 mm hollowpoint bullet through his attacker's right thigh. The man staggered but he did not fall. The knife was still in his hand. Bolan leveled the Smith & Wesson at the center of the man's chest and pulled its trigger twice in a fast double tap. The range was less than six inches. The two 9 mm hollowpoints tore through the man's chest, inflicting terrible damage, but still the man remained standing.

Bolan knew this attacker was mortally wounded, but he was not dead yet. It was impossible to kill a man instantly with a hand held weapon unless you hit the brain or cut the spinal cord. Any other wound gave your attacker what experts call ''the dead man's five seconds,'' the period when the dying man's body still functioned and he may take you with him. He was still trying to bring up his knife.

The Stony Man warrior did not hesitate. He thrust the Smith & Wesson under the man's jaw and pulled the trigger as fast as he could. Two 9 mm bullets tore upward through the man's skull and killed him instantly. The deadly little Smith & Wesson clicked as Bolan pulled the trigger again. It achieved its small size by holding only five shots, and they were gone.

Bolan dropped the weapon, made a fist with his right hand, reached through the wrist of the man who was still holding on tightly, grabbed his hand and pulled up and back as hard as he could. The man held on like grim death, but all the strength of Bolan's upper body was pulling against the man's two thumbs. Bolan broke the hold. His clasped hands shot up and back, almost touching his forehead, then shot downward as he drove both hands into the bridge of the man's nose with every ounce of his strength. The man staggered backward, blood spraying from his shattered nose. His hand started to go under his shirt.

The Executioner reached for his Desert Eagle, but before he could draw and fire, he heard the repeated, sharp blasts of a 9 mm pistol firing as fast as someone could pull the trigger. The man he had struck on the nose shuddered as half a dozen bullets smashed into his chest. He fell heavily and lay still. McCarter moved swiftly to Bolan's side and holstered his Browning. He opened his first-aid kit and pulled out a trauma dressing.

"Hold still, Mack," he ordered. "There's blood on your shirt."

Bolan looked down. McCarter was right, but thank God it was not his.

The Briton opened Bolan's shirt and stared at the glossy white woven fabric of soft body armor. He could see the places where the knife had struck, but the strands of Kevlar were stronger than steel. The armor had been stressed, but it had held.

Bolan heard feet pounding as Sergeant Chavez and four of his men approached. They formed a semicircle around Bolan and McCarter and menaced the crowd with their M-16s.

"If anyone moves toward us or draws a weapon, kill them!" Chavez ordered.

People shrank back, many of them raising their hands. None of them doubted that the Leopards would shoot at the slightest provocation.

"How is your friend?" Chavez asked McCarter.

"I don't think he is seriously injured, but I can tell better when I get him back to the truck."

Chavez nodded. "You are right. This is not a safe place. One moment, and we will go."

He moved quickly to the two dead men, searched their bodies, dropped a few items into his pocket and snapped an order. They moved as a group back to the red truck, the Leopards keeping the crowd covered with their M-16s. Vargas and the rest of the patrol were waiting, weapons ready. Vargas saw that Bolan and McCarter were on their feet and moving under their own power. He did not waste time asking questions. He gave an order, and the Leopards began to climb on the truck, pointing their weapons back at the crowd. Anyone who tried anything would be cut to pieces by the concentrated fire of half a dozen M-16s.

No one seemed to like the odds. Bolan and McCarter climbed on the truck. Vargas took one last look around and followed them. Chavez handed Vargas a number of items and climbed into the cab. The driver started the truck, and they moved away, back toward the main road.

McCarter insisted on taking off Bolan's shirt. The

Leopards looked at Bolan's soft armor vest and smiled. The big gringo knew many good tricks. He was a hard man to kill.

"I don't see anything serious. You'll have a couple of nice bruises, but you'll live," McCarter reported.

Bolan shrugged. He had been bruised before, and the worst bruise was better than a stab to the heart.

"I am glad you are not wounded," Vargas stated. "You would be amazed at how many reports I would have to fill out if you were killed on my patrol. Now, I must ask you one question. Do you feel like continuing on the raid, or shall we return to the base?"

"I'm all right," Bolan said flatly. "If you still think we've got the element of surprise, let's go." The attack had not put him in a good humor. He could think of no one in Bolivia who would try to have him killed like that except the drug cartels. He would enjoy a chance to pay them back.

Vargas's smile broadened. They had reached the main road. He gave an order, and the driver turned right, toward the west. He had laid out the items Chavez had given him across his knees. He picked up something and carefully handed it to Bolan. It was a superbly made knife, with an eight inch, double-edged, razor-sharp blade, with a brass cross guard. Bolan had seen it before, and he was not likely to forget it.

"Here. Sergeant Chavez says you must have this. Consider it a souvenir of Sinahota."

CHAPTER ELEVEN

The Red Zone, Central Bolivia

Mack Bolan felt the tension slowly fade as they drove down the road. He ejected the fired cartridge cases from his Smith & Wesson and reloaded before slipping it back into its pocket holster. It was not a big gun or a glamorous one, but it had just saved his life. It might do it again.

Captain Vargas was watching him intently.

"Tell me, Mr. Belasko. What happened back there? Were there threats? Some kind of confrontation?"

"As far as I know, nothing happened. Those two men just stopped me as I was going out the market door. They said they wanted to sell me a jaguar skin. Then all hell broke loose, and they were trying to kill me. I don't know why. I was lucky I was wearing my soft body armor."

Vargas did not think it was a matter of luck.

"So you think it was pure chance that they attacked you? They just wanted to kill a foreigner, and you were there?"

"Maybe, but there is one thing I remember. The man who stabbed me with the knife yelled something as he attacked. He said, 'El Viejo sends you this.' I don't know anyone called El Viejo. Do you?"

Vargas thought for a moment. "No. It means 'the old

one,' of course, and it is typical of the nicknames *narcotrafficantes* use, but I have never heard of anyone who used that name. I will call the Intelligence section in La Paz when we get back to the base. Perhaps they will have something in their files.''

Bolan shrugged. ''Maybe they wanted to rob me, or maybe it was political. Maybe they wanted to kill a foreigner.''

''It's not as simple as that,'' McCarter said. ''I was the first one through the door. If they were just after a foreigner, they would have attacked me. They didn't. Make no mistake, they were after Mike. They meant to kill him, not anybody else.''

''But why?'' Vargas said softly. ''That is the question.''

He was still looking at the items Sergeant Chavez had taken from the men Bolan and McCarter had killed. He opened a black leather wallet and took out an ID card.

''Jose Garcia. That is like saying John Smith. But here is something interesting. Perhaps it is the answer to our question.''

He handed a stiff piece of paper to Bolan. It was a glossy, black and white, three by five inch photograph. There were three people in the picture—Mack Bolan, Mary Swenson and Sergeant Johnson. It clearly had been taken outside the front entrance of the American embassy in La Paz. The picture was clear and sharp, obviously taken by an expert with a telephoto lens. Someone had added two small details. A red circle had been drawn around Mack Bolan's head and a green circle around Mary Swenson's. Bolan turned the picture over. Someone had written US $50,000 in the lower left-hand corner.

Bolan passed the picture to McCarter who stared at it intently, a look of suspicion in his green eyes.

"I do not think there can be any doubt about it. This is clearly an instruction to kill Mr. Belasko and Captain Swenson and an offer to pay for it," Captain Vargas said.

"Not necessarily. In fact, probably not," McCarter said. Captain Vargas lifted one eyebrow and stared at the Briton.

"I do not understand, Captain Green. What other interpretation is there?" Vargas asked.

"There are three people in the picture. Someone took the trouble to mark two of them. Undoubtedly because they were the two flying to the Chapare area. Now, I think that we can be sure that there must be more than one picture, many more."

"Why do you say that?"

"The red zone is a large area. One team of assassins could not possibly cover it all. More important, how could anyone have known Mike would be at the Sinahota coca leaf market? You only decided to go after you met your informants, so that no one could be sure where you got your information. No one can possibly have known that in advance. I believe there are many more copies of this picture circulating," McCarter said firmly.

Bolan frowned. McCarter was probably right. The thought that dozens of photographs were circulating with instructions to kill him on sight was not a happy one. It was hard to defend yourself if anyone you met may suddenly whip out a weapon and try to kill you.

"Now, look at the markings on the picture. They were done by hand with felt-tip colored pens, one red, one green. What do we conclude from that?" McCarter asked.

Vargas looked puzzled. "I think that is obvious. It means the two people who are marked are to be killed."

"I don't believe so. Stop and think. You are sitting at a desk marking copies of the picture, many copies. If a ring around the head means kill Striker and Captain Swenson, why use two colors? No one is going to use a pen and put it down and pick up another every time they mark a copy of the picture unless it means something. Now we know what the red ring means because they tried to kill Mike. If he hadn't thought fast and been wearing body armor, he would be dead. So the green ring around Captain Swenson's head means something different,'' McCarter said.

Bolan thought it over. It was hard to fault McCarter's logic. Vargas seemed to feel the same way.

"Very good, Captain Green. You should have been a detective. Let's see, perhaps it means that Mr. Belasko is to be killed first or that Captain Swenson is not to be killed for some reason, even if the two of them are found together.''

Bolan smiled grimly. "You could be right. She's on the U.S. embassy staff. If she was assassinated, it would cause a hell of an uproar, media attention, questions in Congress, that sort of thing. Nothing like that is going to happen if I'm killed. Not very many people would really care.''

"There is another interpretation,'' McCarter said coldly. "Perhaps it means don't kill her under any circumstances. Perhaps it means she is one of them.''

Vargas stared at him. "That is hard to believe.''

"Really? Think it over. She's been here in Bolivia several years. That's long enough for them to buy her if she could be bought. She's a U.S. army officer, on the staff of the military commander of Blast Furnace. She knows everything that's going on. What would she be worth to the cartels?''

Vargas frowned. His usually cheerful attitude vanished

as McCarter's words sank in. "Millions. Millions of dollars," he said softly.

"She killed a number of cartel gunmen in La Paz. It wasn't faked. I was there and I saw the bodies," Bolan objected.

"Gunmen are cheap, Mike. How many of them would the cartel be willing to sacrifice to have an agent at the heart of Blast Furnace? Think. Disregard the fact that she's a tall, sexy blonde. How well do you really know her?"

"Not well," Bolan admitted. "I met her in La Paz. All I really know is that General Stuart seems to trust her."

"I doubt that I have any authority to arrest her. She has diplomatic immunity. What will you do if you decide that she is guilty?" Vargas asked.

"We'll have to take her out of the game," Bolan stated.

"We must have real proof first. We will think of some test when we get back to the base. Feed her some false information, and see if the cartel reacts to it," Vargas suggested.

Bolan nodded. If Mary Swenson had sold them out, he'd have to be absolutely sure she was guilty.

"Very well. That leaves one question. Do we go on with the raid?"

McCarter nodded. "Let's get at it."

Paractito, The Red Zone

THE SUN WAS GETTING HOTTER and hotter as they drove along the main road. It was close to noon. Sergeant Chavez opened a picnic chest and handed out cold roast pork sandwiches and a local cola soft drink that tasted like liquid bubble gum. One sip was enough to convince Bolan that he did not want another. Even McCarter, who loved soft drinks, could not choke it down. The sandwich was greasy and the pork was tough, but Bolan ate it anyway, following the old soldier's philosophy that you never knew when you would have a chance to eat again. He took an antimalaria pill and washed it down with a few swallows of lukewarm water from his canteen.

"How long till we get there?" he asked Vargas.

The captain was studying his map and looking at landmarks.

"We are almost there now," he replied and signaled the driver to stop the truck. "Now the fun starts." He motioned to four of his men to follow him and dismounted.

"Come along if you like," he said to Bolan and McCarter. "I will show you how we fearless Leopards operate."

Bolan nodded. That was what they were there for. They climbed down from the truck and followed Vargas into the trees. The captain began to move, following the road to the west, but staying ten yards inside the cover of the trees. They walked for five minutes. Vargas motioned for everyone to halt and put his finger to his lips to signal for quiet.

He moved silently forward and lay prone just inside the edge of the trees. He beckoned for Bolan and McCarter to join him. Vargas pointed down the road. A dirt track led off the main road to the north. There was no traffic on the road. The Leopards' red Dodge truck had to have already passed by the intersection. Two hundred yards away, close to the intersection, a young man was sitting beside the road. He was wearing an embroidered Indian shirt and faded blue jeans, and he did not appear to have a care in the world. It might have been a scene from a tourist brochure, but Bolan could see a new handheld radio in one hand.

Vargas grinned wickedly.

"Let's go talk to that young man. I am sure he is an honest citizen who will be glad to aid his country's police," he said softly. "Let us do it quietly. We do not want to fire a shot unless we must. If the people we are after hear shooting, they will vanish into the jungle."

"If it comes to that, perhaps I can take care of it if you have no objections," McCarter offered.

He reached into a pocket in his camouflage fatigue jacket and drew out a small, sleek automatic pistol with a cylindrical sound suppressor attached to the barrel. The small pistol was a .22-caliber Walther PPK, a model widely used by British Intelligence and special operations troops. With its special subsonic ammunition, it was deadly accurate and as silent as a firearm could be.

"I will be glad of your assistance, Captain," Vargas said. "But take him alive if you can. I would like to interrogate him."

"If I can," McCarter said and slipped silently through the trees toward the lookout. Bolan and Vargas watched him disappear into the trees. Bolan stared through the telescopic sight of his Remington 700-P sniper's rifle. If anything did go wrong, he could back up McCarter with a perfectly aimed shot in less than a second. A few minutes crawled by, then the lookout set down his radio and stood up to stretch his legs. He lifted a small pair of binoculars, which were slung around his neck, and looked up and down the road.

He turned and suddenly froze in horror as McCarter seemed to appear from nowhere to stand twenty feet behind him. He stared as if hypnotized at the muzzle of the small Walther pointed steadily at the middle of his forehead. Bolan had heard many men speak contemptuously of .22-caliber pistols but never when one was pointed at them. All the fight had gone out of the young man instantly. McCarter's combat shooting stance and rock-solid, two-handed grip on his pistol was utterly convincing.

McCarter ordered the young man to kneel and clasp his hands behind his neck. He waved quickly with his left hand, signaling Bolan and Vargas that it was safe to come forward. The captain snapped an order, and the group moved forward. The young man seemed remarkably glad to see the Leopards' spotted uniforms.

"Help me, Captain. Please protect me. I am a Bolivian, and this foreigner is going to kill me," he gasped.

Vargas stared at him coldly. "No true Bolivian works for the Colombians. Still, I will give you one chance. Do exactly as I say, and I will not let the foreigner kill you. Now, how often do you check in on your radio, and where is the drug factory?"

"Please, Captain. If I tell you, they will kill me."

"Perhaps, if they catch you. However, if you do not tell me, he will kill you now."

McCarter played his part perfectly and smiled cruelly.

"I don't think he's going to talk. Let's not waste any more time, Captain. I'll take him fifty yards back into the bush and take care of him. No one will ever find his body."

Words spewed frantically out of the young man's mouth like champagne from an uncorked bottle.

"Please, Captain, don't let him kill me. My name is Jorge Claro. I do this because I need the money. They pay me good money. I call in on the radio every hour whether I see anything or not and report to them at once if I see anything suspicious. There is a pit for making paste on the farm of Julio Mezo. I have heard that the Colombians have set up a factory somewhere on his land, but I have never been there. That is God's truth, Captain."

"Very well, we will see if you are telling the truth. Now, you are going with us. If you try to warn anyone or to escape, I will kill you. That is God's truth, Jorge."

Vargas checked his watch and smiled as he saw the red truck coming back up the road. "Right on time. You can always depend on Chavez."

"Now, gentlemen, let us go pay a call on Julio Mezo."

VARGAS GAVE THE SIGNAL. The driver stepped on the gas, and the red Dodge shot around a curve in the road and screeched to a stop. Vargas yelled, "Go! Go!" and his men tumbled out of the truck, clutching their M-16s. Bolan saw three rusty corrugated iron huts, a battered old truck and a dilapidated enclosure with a few farm animals inside. The Leopards had obviously done this sort of thing before. They separated into pairs and ran toward the huts and the truck. A man and a woman stepped out of one of the structures. The man had a double-barreled shotgun in his hands. He dropped it as if it were red hot and threw up his hands when he saw the Leopards' distinctive spotted uniforms and the black M-16s in their hands.

Two grinning Leopards herded the man and woman over to Captain Vargas.

Both were dressed in worn work clothes. They appeared to be in their midfifties. The woman glared at Vargas with pure, undisguised hatred in her eyes. The man was trembling. The sight of a Leopard captain and two heavily armed foreigners did nothing to calm his fears.

"Please, Captain, do not harm me. Do not arrest us. There must be some misunderstanding. I am only a simple farmer."

Vargas stared at him coldly.

"You are Julio Mezo? This is your farm?"

"Yes, sir. I am only a small farmer. Please believe me. I have done nothing wrong!"

"Oh, and what do you grow here?"

"Coca leaves, but it is legal. I have a permit. I only grow them to sell at the Sinahota market, just to make a little money. I am a poor man, sir. I must feed my family."

Vargas sneered. "You are a poor liar, Mezo. I think you make paste, perhaps even snow. I think I will arrest you and send you to Santa Cruz for trial. We will see how you like the new prison in La Paz."

Mezo shuddered. His wife said something in Spanish using words that Bolan did not understand, but he was sure they were not complimentary. She spit on the ground, narrowly missing Vargas's boots. He slapped her hard.

"Perhaps ten years in prison will improve your manners, woman."

Bolan heard shrieks and screams. Sergeant Chavez and some of the men were returning. They were herding six young women ahead of them. They looked dazed and confused. All of them were wearing old blue jeans, cut off to make ragged shorts, which was surprising. Bolan had not seen a woman wearing shorts anywhere in Bolivia. A seventh woman was doing the shrieking. It was obvious that she did not want to accompany the policemen. Chavez had overcome her reluctance by grabbing a handful of her long black hair and pulling her along.

He held her in front of Captain Vargas. She was bent over, and hissing and snarling.

"Be careful of this one, Captain. She does not like policemen. She tried to run into the jungle, and when I caught her, she tried to bite," Chavez said with a smile.

Vargas was not amused. "Put the handcuffs on her. We will teach her to respect the National Police."

Bolan looked at the woman as Chavez handcuffed her hands behind her back. She was different, a tall, pretty girl, perhaps twenty-five or so, and dressed much better than the other women. She wore a low cut embroidered blouse and a long, full skirt that came nearly to her ankles. It was pretty enough, but it did not look like anything a sensible woman would wear to do farm work.

Chavez was smiling broadly.

"Look at this, Captain," he said and lifted the woman's long skirt above her waist with the muzzle of his M-16. She said something in sizzling Spanish so fast it was hard for Mack Bolan to follow. She seemed to be saying that Chavez lived by selling the services of his mother and sisters to anyone who had a dollar. Chavez slapped her casually, but did not lose his good humor.

Strapped to the inside of her left thigh by elastic bands was a small two-way radio identical to the one they had taken from the lookout. Vargas took the radio out of its straps and looked at it closely.

"Who are you, and where did you get this radio?"

The young woman glared at Vargas and refused to answer.

"Shall I beat it out of her, Captain?" Chavez inquired.

"We do not need to beat her. We have seen this kind of radio before. She is a *trafficante*. We will take her back to base. After a few hours in the interrogation room, she will sing like a bird and beg to tell us all she knows."

Mezo wrung his hands. "Please, Captain, she is my daughter, Maria. Do not take her away. She is only a stupid, silly girl. She takes the drug lord's money and carries the radio because it makes her feel important, and she thinks she loves him. She is not a criminal. You know how young girls are. Do not send her to prison.''

"You are all going to prison, you, your wife and your daughter," Vargas said coldly.

He walked over to the six young women being guarded by two Leopards. Bolan noticed again that the six girls seemed as if they did not really understand what was happening. Vargas stopped by the nearest of the six and took her firmly by the ankle. She moaned softly, but she offered no resistance.

Vargas bent the girl's knee, took her left foot in one hand, and lifted and examined it carefully. He nodded. "Look," he said to Bolan and McCarter. Bolan looked. At first, he did not see anything unusual. Then he noticed that the skin on the girl's feet and calves was pale, almost white, contrasting oddly with the darker tan color of the rest of her skin. It looked as if she was wearing stockings, but her feet were bare.

"Look closely at her feet. Look carefully," Vargas directed.

Bolan looked. At first glance, the girl appeared to be a healthy young woman, but a closer look showed that her feet were in bad condition. The pale skin color looked as if the skin had been burned with acid. The bottoms and sides of her feet showed thin red cracks and red spots that looked like healed sores or ulcers.

"See, the signs are unmistakable. She is a *pisacoca,* a stomper. They all are," Vargas said.

"Beg your pardon? Just what is a stomper?" McCarter inquired.

"You know that coca leaves are made into coca paste, and the paste is then refined in a drug factory to make cocaine?" Vargas asked.

Bolan nodded.

"I know that much, but I don't know the details," he said.

"You want to make the paste as soon as you can. It is much more concentrated, easier to hide, and easier to fly to the factories. It is really a simple process. One of your DEA agents once told me it is as easy as making apple pie."

Vargas paused.

"Now I have never made an apple pie. In fact, I have never seen one, but I do know how to make coca paste. Most Bolivians do. You dig a pit in the ground and line it with a plastic sheet. To make one kilogram of paste, you need ninety-six kilograms of coca leaves, eleven liters of kerosene, one liter of strong sulfuric acid and four kilograms of lime.

"You should be near a river or a stream," Vargas continued. "You will need plenty of water. You put the coca leaves in the pit and soak them in water and lime for a few hours. That draws out the alkaloids, which are the base material. Then you add the kerosene to break the leaves down. Now you use your stompers. They walk up and down the pit in pairs and stomp the leaves with their bare feet. It goes on for ten or twelve hours. The stompers are given coca leaves to chew and coca paste to smoke. That keeps them going, but coca paste is thirty to forty percent cocaine. It is very addictive. Once the stompers are hooked, they are slaves. They will do anything their masters want just to get more paste.

"The liquid in the pits is very corrosive. It damages the stompers' feet. By the look of her feet, she has been stomping for two or three years. If she keeps on doing it, in another year or two, her feet will be rotting. They will have to be amputated to save her life, but she does not care. She is an addict. She will do anything for coca paste.''

McCarter was revolted. "It never fails to amaze me how people can be so cruel to fellow man. People who would do that don't deserve to live.''

Vargas shrugged. "There is a lot of money to be made. Two hundred dollars' worth of leaves, a hundred dollars' worth of chemicals, and a few stompers and you have a kilogram of paste that you can sell for a thousand or two thousand dollars. It is cheaper to use addicts for stompers. All you have to give them is a little food and some coca paste.''

"After the leaves are stomped, what happens next?'' McCarter asked.

"You throw away the leaves, treat the liquid with the sulfuric acid and more lime, filter it through a sheet, and you have wet paste. Dry it, and it is ready to sell. Then it goes to a factory where it is refined into pure cocaine. Making paste is a very profitable business, five or six hundred percent profit, sometimes more. Bolivia produced over a thousand tons of paste last year. Of course, it is illegal under the 1988 Coca Control Law. Mezo and his wife will go to prison if I find an active paste pit on their land.''

"Why don't you close down the paste pits?'' McCarter asked.

"I wish to God we could, but there are more than ten thousand pits in the red zone, and all it takes to start a new one is a shovel and a few hundred dollars' worth of supplies. All we can do is make an example of those we catch.''

"Then why are we here?'' McCarter asked. "It would seem that we're wasting our time.''

"I do not think so,'' Vargas said. "I think that Mezo

has a drug factory on his land. He is refining paste and making cocaine. That is a very serious offense, isn't it, Mezo? You and your wife will die in prison, and your daughter will be an old woman when she gets out.''

Mezo began to moan. ''For the love of God, Captain, I did not want to do it. The Colombians made me do it. They had guns. They said they would kill me if I refused. I had no choice. Please, please, I am only a poor farmer. Have mercy on my family, I beg you!''

''I believe he is telling the truth, Captain,'' Sergeant Chavez said in a kindly voice. ''You know what these Colombians are like. Surely you can be lenient if he co-operates completely.''

Bolan realized that the good cop-bad cop routine was the same the whole world over, because it worked so often.

''We shall see,'' Vargas said. ''Talk is cheap, Mezo. Show me some cooperation.''

''I am telling the truth, Captain. Follow me and I will show you.''

Vargas nodded. Mezo led them past the three huts and about twenty yards into the trees. He pointed to a patch of sandy ground next to a large red rock.

''Here, Captain. Here is where they hide things.''

Sergeant Chavez knelt, drew a large folding knife and probed the sandy soil. Bolan heard a dull sound as the blade contacted wood. Chavez brushed the soil aside. He had uncovered an eight-foot-square wooden door with rope handles. He and another Leopard lifted it and set it aside. There was a pit about four feet deep under the door. Bolan caught a strong odor of chemicals and saw stacks of boxes and plastic sacks piled on the floor.

Chavez jumped into the pit and began to examine its contents. Some of the boxes seemed to contain canned food and beer. He slit open a black plastic sack and handed it up to Vargas with an air of triumph. The captain reached into the sack and took out a transparent plastic package filled with a snow white powder.

Vargas beamed and showed it to Bolan and McCarter.

"There you are, gentlemen. Cocaine hydrochloride, a kilogram of pure cocaine. You see, we are not wasting our time, Captain Green. What else do you see, Sergeant?"

"Food, supplies, some chemicals for refining, nothing unusual, except for this." He handed up a large, heavy brown cardboard box. Vargas opened it and stared at row after row of flat, brown rectangular boxes. Each was marked 20 Cartridges, 5.56 mm NATO, Lake City Arsenal 1994. It was new, fresh, American-made ammunition for M-16 rifles. Chavez handed up a second smaller, lighter cardboard box, and the captain opened it. The box held twenty long, black curved magazines. Vargas looked puzzled.

He handed one to Bolan and McCarter. The magazine was empty. The Executioner slipped one of the M-16 cartridges between the magazine's feeding lips. It fit perfectly. The magazine was made out of tough black plastic. It was obviously meant for use with some type of automatic rifle, but Bolan could not remember seeing one like it before. The only markings were a cryptic 101/102 on the magazine floor plate. He slipped it into a pocket. He would show it to John Kissinger when he got back to the Leopards' base. If anyone could identify it, he could.

Bolan was sure of one thing. The ammunition and the magazines indicated that the men running the drug factory were serious. Vargas checked the hand-drawn map he had gotten from Alta.

"This would not be here if the factory were not operating. I think it is time that we paid these *narcotrafficantes* a visit,'' he said.

McCarter nodded. That was what they were there for.

"I would suggest you distribute these cartridges among your men, Captain," he said. "We may get a warm reception when we get there."

CHAPTER TWELVE

The Red Zone, Central Bolivia

The Leopards moved quietly down the jungle trail with their M-16s ready. The heat was bad and the humidity was worse, but Vargas's men were alert. Bolan could sense their excitement. Raiding paste pits was all in a day's work, but a cocaine factory run by Colombians was new and different. They would have a great story to tell when they got back to base. They smiled at Bolan and McCarter. It seemed that the big gringos had brought them luck. Bolan hoped so, but he could feel the tension slowly building.

He looked up and down the trail. He had no real complaint about Vargas's arrangements. Sergeant Chavez and another Leopard had taken the point and were out of sight ahead. Vargas was leading the rest of the patrol with the M-4 Ranger carbine Bolan had given him in his hands. Bolan and McCarter were next in line, and the rest of the patrol followed in single file, a five-yard interval between each man.

The driver had been left behind with the truck and instructions to deliver Julio Mezo, his wife and the six stompers to the police post in Sinahota. Vargas had said it was not very secure. The Mezos could probably bribe their way out, but he did not care. They were no longer important to him. What he wanted was the factory and the people who operated it. Maria Mezo was going with the patrol. She was not exactly a volunteer, but she had little to say about it. She had been gagged and was still handcuffed, although her hands were in front of her now so that she could protect her face from branches along the trail. One of the Leopards led her by a rope around her neck.

The patrol seemed ready. Vargas and Chavez had checked each man's weapon carefully before they had moved out. They had made sure that each Leopard had a round in the chamber of his M-16 and its safety selector switch set on safe. A single accidental shot would warn the *narcotrafficantes* and spoil the raid. Vargas had stressed that no one was to fire unless fired upon, and Chavez had made it crystal clear that anyone who violated the captain's order would wish he had never been born.

This certainly made sense, but Mack Bolan knew that what was bothering him was no specific detail but a subconscious feeling that something was about to go wrong. He felt a certain foreboding. He knew part of it came from the scene around him. The tropical rain forest, the sunlight filtering through the tops of the trees, and the short dark men in camouflage fatigues with M-16 rifles in their hands all reminded him powerfully of hundreds of patrols he had led in Vietnam.

Perhaps that was it. Vargas was pushing hard, going straight down the well-used trail. Bolan understood why he was doing it. He wanted to get to the factory rapidly before he lost the element of surprise. The Leopards could move much faster along the trail than by slipping through the bush. Vargas thought of *trafficantes* as criminals trying to escape, not enemy soldiers who might try to ambush him at any moment.

Bolan's hard earned instincts honed by dozens of desperate firefights warned him that there might be an ambush around the next bend in the trail. Still, it was Vargas's patrol. The Executioner had volunteered to go along with it as an observer. He was not in command, and he knew that two men trying to give orders at the same time was a recipe for disaster. Unless he had some specific warning or suggestion, he would let Vargas run his show.

The captain suddenly signaled for the patrol to halt. The man who was on the point with Chavez had slipped back down the trail. His face was shining with excitement. He did not waste time on formalities.

"*Zepes,* Captain, many *zepes,* about two hundred meters ahead."

Bolan shook his head. He was going to have to work on improving his Spanish. He would have sworn that the Leopard had said that there were ants ahead. He could not imagine why an elite unit like the Leopards would be concerned about a swarm of ants. Vargas did not look concerned. He was obviously excited.

"Good work, Reyes. Lead the way," he ordered.

Reyes slipped silently back up the trail. Vargas motioned to Bolan and McCarter to follow him. They moved silently along the trail. It did not seem to be a good time for asking questions. Bolan slung his scope-sighted Remington Model 700-P over his shoulder and drew his 9 mm Beretta 93-R. The Remington was a superbly accurate and powerful rifle, but its bolt action had to be worked by hand for each shot, and it only held six cartridges. In a close range fight, the Beretta was a better weapon. He listened intently as they moved along the trail. At first, he heard only the whine of insects and the sigh of a faint breeze in the tops of the trees. Then he heard the sound of running water, growing steadily louder.

Reyes stopped and pointed ahead. There was a bend in the trail in front of them, and Bolan could see that there was an opening in the forest ahead. Vargas dropped into the prone position and wriggled forward. Bolan and McCarter followed silently. In front of them, the big American saw a shallow slope and the trail leading down to the bank of a wide, fast-running stream and to a rope and plank suspension bridge where a second trail joined it along the near bank of the stream.

A group of twenty or thirty people waited patiently by the bridge. Each one carried a large pack that held either boxes or cylindrical metal containers. Across the bridge, a man with a pack was talking to two suspicious men carrying black, short barreled automatic rifles. He showed them some papers and pointed back at the waiting group of men and women. Finally, the two men nodded and signaled the waiting group to cross the stream. They began slowly across the bridge in groups of three or four, each group waiting for the one ahead to cross before they followed.

Vargas beamed. "See those people with the packs? They are hired by the *trafficantes* to carry food, fuel, coca paste and chemicals for refining cocaine to a drug factory. We call them *zepes,* ants, because they go along trails in single file carrying heavy loads like ants. They are a very good sign. There would not be so many if it were not a large factory. And see those two guards? We are very close, and the factory is in operation."

"What next?" Bolan asked. Vargas thought for a moment. While he waited, Bolan put his Beretta 93-R back in its holster and unslung the Remington. He estimated the far end of the bridge was about two hundred yards away. At that range, the two guards were perfect targets for a sniper's rifle.

"We need to get across the stream and into the factory area quickly," Vargas said. "They cannot move their supplies and equipment now, even if there is a warning of some kind. We are too close. But the men can run into the jungle. I want to arrest them. The problem is how we can cross the bridge. If we are halfway across and they open fire with automatic weapons, they will kill us all."

Bolan nodded. He was glad Vargas saw that. If it were defended, the bridge was a death trap. He turned the magnification setting on his AN/PVS-10 sniper's sight and set it for its full 8.5 power magnification. That let him see details clearly even at long range, but it reduced his field of view.

"I can take out both guards in three seconds, but I can't do it quietly," he said. Bolan spoke with calm conviction. The light was good, and there was no cross wind. Under those conditions, he could place five shots inside a two-inch circle ten times out of ten at two hundred yards. If he fired, the two guards were dead men.

Vargas nodded and studied his hand-drawn map again.

"The factory should be just over that little rise beyond the bridge, perhaps three or four hundred yards from here. If they hear shots, the experts who 'cook' the paste to make it into cocaine will run. My information is that there are six to eight guards. All will have automatic weapons. They may run, or they may stay and fight. It is hard to say, but there are twelve of us, counting you two. If we can surprise them, we should win."

Bolan sensed that Vargas was nervous. It was the first major raid he commanded, and he was well aware that Bolan and McCarter were noting his every move. Vargas was simply having a hard time making up his mind. Bolan thought for a moment. He and McCarter could go a few hundred yards upstream and ford it, then slip back and take out the guards silently. It would take time, but it would be quiet. He was about to suggest the option to Vargas when something happened behind him.

He heard a man yell in pain, a woman shrieking loudly, and feet pounding on the trail behind him. Instinctively, he dropped his rifle and drew his .44 Magnum Desert Eagle but he was lying prone. Before he could be sure of what was happening and twist into a firing position, Maria Mezo shot past him, running toward the bridge. Vargas lunged for her ankles as she passed. He caught the bottom of her long skirt, but the thin fabric tore away. Maria tore the gag from her mouth and screamed as she ran.

"Alerta! Alerta! Leopardos!"

Reyes had been standing a few feet behind the command group. Maria had taken him by surprise, but he was on his feet and did not have to waste time getting up. Instantly, he lunged after the fleeing girl, drawn by the instinct of a good police officer not to let a suspect escape. Maria ran towards the bridge, her long legs flailing. Reyes pounded after her, but he was slowed by fifty pounds of weapons and equipment.

Bolan snapped his Remington 700-P to his shoulder and stared through its telescopic sight. No good. Reyes was running right behind Maria, directly in the line of fire. He heard McCarter swear bitterly. He did not have a clear shot, either. Besides, the Executioner knew the Briton would hesitate to shoot an unarmed woman who was running away. For that matter, so would he. He would have shot her instantly if she had been coming at him with a lethal weapon, but shooting her in the back as she ran away from him would be too much like cold-blooded murder.

Reyes lunged forward and caught her just as she set foot on the bridge. Bolan heard the sudden snarl of high-power weapons firing on full automatic. Half a dozen bullets struck Reyes, and he staggered and fell. Maria had been hit. She swayed on her feet, spots of blood starting to appear on her blouse. The guards did not know who she was, or perhaps they did not care. A second, long burst cut her down.

One of the guards had dropped into a prone position. The other was standing, admiring his work. Bolan placed the cross hairs of his sight on the man's chest. Through the telescope's 8.5 power magnification, he saw the look of satisfaction on the man's face as he squeezed the trigger. The Remington roared and sent a .308-caliber full-metal-jacketed bullet tearing through the man's chest. He died instantly. Instinctively, Bolan's right hand moved with blurring speed as he worked the Remington's bolt, ejected the smoking cartridge case, and drove a fresh round into the chamber.

Bolan heard bullets whine overhead as the second guard fired at them and the snarl of McCarter's M-4 carbine as he returned the fire. Vargas was on his feet, running toward where Reyes lay bleeding at the end of the bridge, firing his M-4 carbine from the hip as he ran. The Executioner heard men yelling as the rest of the patrol swept by him and followed their captain toward the bridge. It was brave, but it was not smart. Vargas's heroic action might get his entire patrol killed.

The big American swung his rifle smoothly to the left. He could see the head and shoulders of the man who was firing at McCarter. Bolan placed his cross hairs on the center of the man's forehead and squeezed the trigger. He hurried his shot a bit. The .308-caliber bullet struck two inches below the point of aim, but it made no difference.

The man died instantly. Bolan opened the bolt of his Remington and shoved two fresh .308 cartridges into the magazine. He closed the bolt and swept the far side of the stream with his telescopic sight. He held his fire; he could see nothing to shoot at.

The bridge was swaying and vibrating as Vargas led his Leopards across.

McCarter kept his sights on the little rise behind the far side of the bridge. He shook his head as he watched the Leopards charge across.

"It reminds me of the charge of the Light Brigade, Mack. It's magnificent, but it isn't war."

McCarter and Bolan waited tensely. There was no particular reason for the drug dealers to have placed a second guard post where the trail crossed over the rise. But if they were as close to the drug factory as they thought, the opposition had to have heard the crack of Bolan's rifle unless they were deaf or asleep. Vargas and his men had reached the far side of the bridge. Bolan was relieved to see that they were spreading out and forming a skirmish line, not charging straight up the trail. He had not liked McCarter's reference to the charge of the Light Brigade. Vargas was an excellent police officer, but he did not appear to completely grasp the power of modern infantry weapons. One well-sited machine gun could take out the entire Leopards' patrol if they were bunched up.

Vargas signaled to advance, and he and his men began to move up the slope toward the top of the shallow rise. That was not smart, and he was still wearing his shoulder straps. Bolan shook his head. Both things identified Vargas as an officer and the patrol commander. If there were snipers lying in wait, they would concentrate their fire on him.

"I hate to interrupt you when you are thinking, Mack,

but I believe it's time for us to move," McCarter said. "If we stay here much longer, we'll be completely out of it."

"All right," Bolan said. "I'll go first. You cover me."

"You're a much better shot with a sniper's rifle, faster and more accurate at long range. But I can run faster than you. I should go first."

"Go, then. I'll cover you."

"Right." McCarter got to his feet, crouching forward ready to run. There was no cover at all until he crossed the bridge. To crawl or wriggle forward prone would only leave him exposed to hostile fire for a longer time. He would run.

"You are an experienced sniper, Mack. If you were up there, where would you be?"

"In the trees close to the point where the trail crosses the rise. That would give me the best field of fire."

McCarter nodded. "Too right. Well, I won't give him a good target. I'll zigzag until I'm on the bridge and make him lead me."

"Just don't zig when you should zag."

McCarter grinned. "Thanks for the advice, mate."

Bolan placed his sights on the point where the trail crossed the rise. He saw nothing but dirt and trees, but that did not mean anything. Any good sniper would remain concealed until he opened fire.

"Go!"

McCarter shot forward in a spray of sand, burst out of the tree line and sprinted for the end of the bridge. He ran cleverly, not running all out, but varying his speed and abruptly zigzagging, changing his angle to give anyone aiming at him a hard shot. That was just as well. Bolan saw the sandy soil a foot behind McCarter suddenly spray upward as a bullet smashed into it. He heard the sound of the rifle's muzzle blast just behind the strike of the supersonic bullet. The rifle boomed again. Bolan had no time to see what had happened. Only fast and accurate shooting would save McCarter now.

Bolan stared through his scope, still seeing no one. The rifle boomed again. This time, he saw branches move two feet to the right of the trail. That was interesting. There was no wind. The hostile rifleman had made an error. He had not realized that his rifle's muzzle blast would disturb the branches and give away his position. Bolan snapped the cross hairs of his sight on the trembling branches and pulled the trigger. It was not a perfect shot, but he saw dirt fly behind the bush. Instantly, he worked the Remington's bolt and fired a second shot. He was not certain that he had scored a hit, but at least the concealed rifleman had other things to worry about besides shooting McCarter.

A bullet smashed into the ground six feet in front of Bolan and hurled a fountain of sand into the air. Several more bullets tore by to the left and right. Bark flew, and leaves and twigs rained to the ground. Bolan nodded grimly. The man firing at him had a semiautomatic rifle. That gave him the edge in speed of fire but not in accuracy. The firing suddenly stopped. The rifleman had to be changing magazines.

Despite the swarm of bullets passing by, Bolan had kept his cross hairs on the center of the spot where he had seen the bushes move. He triggered the Remington and sent a 173-grain .308 bullet to the exact center of his target. He saw leaves and twigs fly as the heavy bullet tore through. The light bullet from an M-16 might have been deflected by striking a branch, but not the .308 Match bullet. Three times heavier and with twice the striking energy, it smashed through to the center of the enemy sniper's position.

Instantly, Bolan worked the bolt action again and again and put one bullet one foot to the left and another to the right of his initial aim point. He saw the bush shudder, letting him glimpse the dimly seen form of a man with a big rifle. He had one shot left in the Remington, one shot to make it good. He did not hesitate. He squeezed the Remington's trigger, and the big rifle roared. He saw the man shudder and fall, dropping his rifle and rolling a few feet down the trail.

Bolan immediately pressed five fresh cartridges into the Remington's built-in magazine, closed the bolt and fired again. The sniper's body jerked as the heavy bullet tore through it. The Executioner was not being vindictive. The odds were overwhelming that the man he had hit was dead, but his life and McCarter's depended on his being absolutely sure. He peered through his scope. The Briton had crossed the bridge and had taken cover behind some rocks twenty feet beyond.

McCarter swept his arm forward, signaling Bolan to go. He aimed his M-4 Ranger carbine up the trail, ready to provide covering fire. The Executioner got to his feet and took three deep breaths to fill his lungs with air. He did not like this. He had the experienced infantryman's inherent distrust of leaving cover to move across open terrain. But he exploded forward, running hard down the slope. Instinctively, he imitated McCarter's tactics, never running in a straight line or at the same speed for more than a few seconds. No one fired at him, but the bridge was the real killing zone.

When he reached the bridge, he saw why Vargas had not paused to help Reyes. His body had been riddled with a precisely aimed burst. He had to have died instantly.

Maria Mezo was crumpled in a pathetic heap. She was another young life that the drug lords had to account for. Someone should make them pay, and Mack Bolan was prepared to be that someone, but first he had to get across the bridge.

The bridge shook and swayed as the Executioner ran across it. It seemed to take forever. He felt completely exposed, but no one fired. He shot across the bridge and threw himself down beside McCarter. The big Briton did not appear to be the worse for wear. Bolan saw the last of the Leopards vanish over the top of the rise, then heard shooting and screaming.

"Let's go, Mike," McCarter said.

"I'm with you." Bolan took a deep breath. He could hear more firing over the ridge. "There must be more of them over there."

"Too right, there are!" McCarter snapped a fresh 30-round magazine into his M-4 carbine and got to his feet. "Come on." He started up the trail. Bolan followed five yards behind, careful not to bunch up so that one burst could hit them both.

McCarter paused by the body of the sniper Bolan had shot, examining the man's rifle as the Executioner studied the man's body. He was not dressed in casual clothes like the guards. He was wearing camouflage combat fatigues, but Bolan could not place the pattern. The man had pale skin, as if he were European. He looked out of place in central Bolivia.

McCarter held out the rifle. "SVD."

It was a Russian army SVD Dragunov sniper's rifle complete with its four power scope. It was not nearly as accurate as Bolan's Model 700-P Remington, but it would consistently hit man-sized targets at roughly seven hundred yards, and its high-powered .30-caliber cartridge was lethal at those ranges. McCarter slung the SVD over his left shoulder and took the dead sniper's ammunition belt.

"The bloody thing may come in handy."

Bolan nodded. The SVD could outrange and outpenetrate an American M-16. It would be a good idea to show it to Captain Vargas and see if he had seen similar weapons in the red zone.

They paused at the top and confronted a scene of total confusion. The little ridge formed a shallow cup about two hundred yards in diameter, overgrown with scattered trees. It was not at all what Bolan had expected to see. He had raided drug factories in Colombia when he had operated against the Medellín cartel. There, the equipment was housed in commercial buildings that might have been ordinary industrial facilities.

Here, he saw some makeshift bamboo houses on short stilts and tents made out of green plastic sheeting, two diesel generators, and groups of silver colored metal tanks and cylinders that had to hold chemicals. There were a number of metal tanks connected by a tangle of pipes and hoses. A few bodies were scattered here and there. Men and women were running about, yelling and screaming. Most of them were the *zepes* Bolan had seen at the bridge. Four men were being held at gunpoint by a grinning Leopard. Captain Vargas's other men were trying to arrest some people as others ran off into the trees.

Vargas was standing in the middle of the confusion. One Leopard was standing behind him with the patrol's old-fashioned radio on his back.

"There you are, gentlemen," Vargas said as they approached. "What kept you?" Vargas said.

"A sniper near the trail," Bolan said brusquely.

McCarter nodded and held out the Dragunov.

Vargas frowned. "We did not see him."

Bolan and McCarter exchanged glances but said nothing. Vargas had made a mistake, and he knew it. At least, no one had been killed. The captain was a smart young man. Perhaps he would learn from his mistake. Bolan hoped so. If not, he would not live long enough to make major.

Vargas smiled. There was a look of triumph on his face.

"This is splendid. A large drug factory and most of the people running it. I only regret that I did not have enough men to surround the place and capture them all. But I am happy. I think we have killed or captured all the Colombians. Colonel Suarez should see this. He will be pleased."

"Is Colonel Suarez coming here?" Bolan asked.

"He will fly out if I can get this radio to work. He keeps a reaction force and a helicopter standing by when we have patrols out."

Bolan glanced at the radio. It was a long-obsolete U.S. Army model that looked old and tired. No wonder Vargas was having trouble. Bolan was not an electronics genius, but he knew a lot about tactical radios. He had been using them most of his life.

"Your signal may be blocked by the ridge lines. Get it up on the high ground, and you'll probably be able to get through."

Vargas beamed. He liked the man. The big American was a splendid soldier, and he seemed to know the answers to the Leopards' problems. Vargas thought Belasko had brought them luck. He hoped he was right about the radio. He was savoring the thought of reporting the raid to Colonel Suarez.

"Let's give it a try," he said. He started to walk back up the slope.

Bolan was turning to follow him when he heard a sound

that froze his blood, the unforgettable thumping sound of supersonic bullets tearing through a human body. The radioman shuddered. Shards of metal and plastic flew from the radio strapped to his back. He was dead before he started to fall.

The snarling chatter of a .30-caliber machine gun was clearly audible. Bolan threw himself down and into Captain Vargas's legs as he fell, and they hit the ground together. The machine gun fired again, and a 6-round burst shot through the space where they had just been standing. A second machine gun began to chatter, and Bolan heard the higher pitched snarl of automatic rifles opening fire. Green tracers were streaking from the opposite ridge line down into the cup in the ground that held the drug factory. The scene around him erupted into panic as the two machine guns began to search and traverse, spraying the area with burst after burst of lethal bullets.

McCarter ducked and rolled away, splitting the target. The machine gunner paid no attention. More green racers clawed at Bolan and Vargas. Bolan thought he was after Vargas, who was wearing his captain's insignia and had visibly been giving orders.

Sergeant Chavez was shouting, *"Refugio! Refugio!"*

It was excellent advice, but there was very little cover to take. Neither the thin tree trunks nor the walls of the bamboo houses would stop full-metal-jacketed .30-caliber bullets. There was nothing to do but shoot back. McCarter had rolled behind one of the diesel generators. Bolan heard the dull bloop of a 40 mm grenade launcher as McCarter engaged one of the machine guns with his M-203. The high-explosive grenade arched through the air and detonated on the opposite slope. Branches and leaves flew. McCarter started to push a new grenade into his grenade launcher.

He had obviously been close, but he had missed the machine gunners. Still, he had certainly attracted their attention. McCarter was under real threat with both weapons spitting sustained fire at his position. Bolan saw swarms of bullets strike the diesel generators and ricochet away. The generators emitted showers of blue sparks and dull black smoke. The Briton had reloaded, but the intense incoming fire forced him to keep his head down.

Bolan shouted to Vargas to toss him the M-4 carbine. Vargas complied, throwing him the nylon pouches that held the grenades, as well. The Executioner flipped up the grenade launcher sight, aimed and triggered the weapon. The grenade arched through the air and detonated. It had to have been close, but the machine gun kept firing. The sound of the hostile automatic rifle fire was growing louder. Covered by their machine guns, the riflemen were moving in.

Bolan thought fast. To stay where they were would be fatal. To move without neutralizing the machine guns would be suicidal. He opened another web pouch and took out two grenades. He checked the markings and nodded— smoke. He slipped one of the smoke grenades into the M-203 and yelled at McCarter.

"Smoke! Fire smoke!"

The Briton nodded. Bolan saw him slip a smoke grenade into his M-203. McCarter held up his left hand to indicate that he was ready. Bolan pointed to him, then to the left. McCarter nodded. He would fire at the left-hand machine gun. The Executioner aimed through the grenade launcher sight and squeezed the trigger. He felt the recoil of his weapon against his shoulder and knew his grenade was on the way. Instantly, he pumped the action of his M-203, snapped in his second grenade and fired again.

His first grenade had struck and was spewing thick,

gray-white smoke in front of the right-hand machine gun. Now it was joined by the second. McCarter's grenades arrived, and a cloud of smoke formed in front of the left-hand machine gun. Momentarily, the guns were masked. Their gunners could no longer see their targets. Bolan knew the 40 mm grenades could not produce a gas cloud large enough to screen the machine guns for long.

"Get your men out of here," he shouted at Vargas. "Get up to the top of the ridge. Stay there and set up a defensive position and fight. Don't make a break for the bridge. You'd never make it across."

The Leopard captain did not argue. Bolan heard him shouting orders.

Vargas did not ask for the M-4 carbine. He had picked up the radioman's M-16. He knew the American was far better with the M-203 grenade launcher clipped under the M-4's barrel. Bolan heard Sergeant Chavez shouting orders and saw the Leopards falling back toward the trail that led up the ridge.

Vargas fired a burst at the hostile riflemen. The smoke had taken them by surprise. They did not want to charge without their heavy fire support. The captain was firing to make them keep their heads down as his men fell back.

"Time to go, my friend. That smoke will not last much longer," he said.

Bolan smiled grimly. He did not get to his feet.

"You go ahead. I'm going to delay our friends."

Vargas did not like it, but he was not stupid enough to argue in the middle of a firefight. "God be with you," he said and was gone.

Bolan heard a whistle blowing. Whoever was in charge of the opposition was trying to get them moving forward again. Bolan heard the louder crack of the SVD as McCarter opened fire. Something long and thin came hissing down from the opposite slope trailing gray-white smoke. Bolan recognized it instantly as an RPG-7 rocket grenade. It struck one of the diesel generators and detonated in an orange flash. McCarter stopped firing. Bolan hoped the Briton had not been hit, but he had no time to go and see. The smoke from their M-203 grenades was starting to dissipate. He had to do something now.

He moved his hand from the grenade launcher to the M-4 carbine's pistol grip and peered through the carbine's peep sight. Long ago at Army sniper training school, one of his instructors had said "a rifle is just a long-range, remote-control, hole-punching device." Bolan had always remembered that. He used the carbine that way now. He aimed at a stack of the silver colored metal tanks and cylinders that held the chemicals used to make cocaine. He fired rapidly, his carbine set for semiautomatic fire, one precisely aimed shot for each pull of the trigger. He put two or three shots through each container. Colorless liquids began to run down out of the tanks and pool on the ground. Vapor clouds began to simmer upward from the pools.

Bolan had not been counting his shots. He kept squeezing his trigger until he saw a red dot fly from his carbine, signaling his last round. The red streak came from burning chemicals in the base of the bullet. The round struck. For half a second, nothing. Then there was a yellow flash, and the containers seemed to disappear in a blast of orange flame. Some of the containers exploded. Bolan kept his head down as metal fragments whined by and flaming fragments rained to the ground. Another group of cylinders caught fire and began to burn and explode. Thick black smoke began to billow up and spread across the devastated drug factory. Bolan could hear someone screaming hoarsely. It was bad enough where he was. It had to be a close approximation of hell in the center of the cup.

Bolan snapped a fresh magazine into his M-4 carbine. It was time to go. He kept low and dashed for the ruined diesel generators. A third group of chemical containers went up in flames. The flimsy bamboo buildings were burning briskly. McCarter was keeping low, peering through the SVD's telescopic sight. He ducked as an explosion rocked the ground.

"Let's get the hell out of here!" Bolan told him.

McCarter nodded and got to his feet.

They ran back up the slope as machine guns fired, but their gunners were firing blind. Reaching the top of the rise, they threw themselves down. Captain Vargas looked up.

"We are all here, Mr. Belasko, those of us who are still alive."

He was pressing a handkerchief against his left cheek. Blood had run down his uniform jacket, but he still managed to smile.

"You certainly do know how to eradicate a drug factory," he said. "I must remember your methods."

They both ducked as an RPG-7 rocket grenade hissed in and detonated ten feet below their position.

"They have not given up. We cannot stay here forever. What do you recommend? The smoke is thick. Shall we make a run for the bridge?" Vargas asked.

Bolan shook his head. "There's no cover while we run for the bridge. Once we're on the bridge, one good man with an automatic rifle could kill us all before we get across."

Vargas nodded. He did not like what Bolan said, but he knew it was true.

"What, then?"

Bolan thought that since they had a little cover here, they could hold out for a while.

"Time to call for help," he said.

He took out his tactical radio from its web belt pouch and pushed the emergency call button. A green light began to blink. The small radio was broadcasting a high-power, coded pulse. No one from the rest of the Stony team was listening continuously, but they would have a radio on, and it should be emitting a pulsing audio alarm. The steady high-power pulsing would drain his battery rapidly, but Bolan did not care about that. Unless they got help quickly, there would be no tomorrow.

Bolan ducked as another RPG-7 rocket grenade hissed in and detonated. A tree crashed down behind him, and steel fragments whined by. He was running out of hope when his radio crackled into life and he heard Gadgets Schwarz's voice.

"Striker, this is Gadgets. What's your situation?"

"We've run into an ambush. We are outnumbered and are taking heavy fire. We have casualties. We need help immediately. Over."

"Roger, Striker. Your message understood. What is your location?"

Bolan thought hard.

"Do not have exact map coordinates. Approximate location is a few miles past the town of Sinahota and north of the main road. You won't have any trouble finding it when you get close. There's one hell of a fire. Over."

"Roger, Striker. Your message understood. We're on the way. Over."

Another RPG-7 round hissed in, trailing gray white smoke. Its five-pound, high-explosive warhead exploded, and steel fragments filled the air. Something tore the radio out of Bolan's left hand and sent it tumbling away. He did not try to retrieve it, as he could see half of its electronic components strewed on the ground. It really did not matter. The team would get there as fast as was humanly possible. In the meantime, he would do his talking with his guns.

CHAPTER THIRTEEN

The Red Zone, Central Bolivia

Jack Grimaldi slipped into the helicopter's pilot seat and quickly began the engine-starting sequence. Gadgets Schwarz strapped himself into the copilot's seat and started to check the weapons and sensors. The fuselage of the special operations Black Hawk shook as the rest of the team loaded themselves and their equipment into the passenger compartment. Grimaldi looked out his side window. Colonel Suarez and a group of Leopards were racing toward their standby helicopters. Grimaldi saw Carl Lyons running toward the Black Hawk, carrying a small arsenal of weapons and equipment. The pilot grinned and kept his fingers poised over the engine starter switches. He knew he would never hear the last of it if he left Able Team's leader behind.

Grimaldi pushed the engine starter switches and felt the Black Hawk shudder as the twin T700-GE-701 turbine engines began to whine. The whine deepened to a howl as he went to full power and lifted the helicopter into the air. Almost instantly, the Leopards' airstrip vanished behind him, and he was skimming low and fast over the carpet of green trees. He checked his displays. Both engines were running smoothly. He was—

"Look out, Jack!" Gadgets Schwarz shouted.

Grimaldi looked through the canopy. Straight ahead, a red-and-white helicopter was going to land at the Leopards' airstrip. Instantly, he pulled the Black Hawk's nose up and hard left. There was no time for anything else. The red-and-white helicopter seemed to fill the Black Hawk's canopy, and then it was gone. Grimaldi felt the aircraft shudder as it passed through the other helicopter's rotorwash, but he felt no impact. It had been close. Too damned close, but they had survived. He brought the Black Hawk back on course and took her down again.

"Who the hell was that?" he snarled.

Schwarz shrugged.

"Damned if I know. It was some kind of commercial Bell Huey. I was too busy praying to see anything else."

Looking in his rearview mirror, Grimaldi was surprised to see the other helicopter turning as if to follow. Perhaps its pilot wanted to complain. Grimaldi smiled. Maybe his takeoff had bent a few commercial aviation rules, but he was not going to worry about that now.

Grimaldi concentrated on his flying. They were skimming over the tops of the trees at one hundred feet, headed for Sinahota. He kept his eyes on the multifunctional display. The MFD converted the data from the helicopter's infrared sensors and radar into a clear picture of the scene ahead. Even in broad daylight, the infrared sensors could see through dust and smoke far better than the human eye. He would use their capabilities to keep the Black Hawk near the treetops. If the opposition had any kind of anti-helicopter capability, he had better come in low and fast. He leveled off at seventy-five feet.

Gadgets Schwarz was finishing his checks and arming the weapons systems. A row of green lights on the weapons control console came on. The Black Hawk was carrying two 19-round 2.75-inch multiple rocket launchers under each stubby wing. They were ready to fire. Grimaldi checked the fixed .50-caliber machine gun he controlled. It was loaded and on safe, ready to fire with the flick of a switch. Gary Manning was checking and mounting the .30-caliber GE minigun door guns. They were as ready as they would ever be. Now it was time for tactics.

"I'm going straight for Sinahota. Mack says there's a large fire near his position. We should see the smoke when we get close to Sinahota. We should be there in about ten minutes. Have you heard anything more from him?"

Schwarz shook his head. "Negative. I can't raise him or McCarter. Just get us there as fast as you can."

Grimaldi glanced at his instruments. The turbine rpm of each engine was on the red line. They were making 185 miles per hour. There was no way he could go any faster. He could only hope Bolan and the Leopards could hold on until they got there. The radio silence was ominous. Grimaldi could think of no good explanation.

He was too busy flying to try communicating. Even with all the helicopter's electronic marvels, flying fast at low altitude demanded his continuous attention.

"See if you can contact Mack," he said to Schwarz.

Gadgets nodded and pushed his transmit button.

"Striker, this is Gadgets. Come in, Striker."

He repeated the call several times. Nothing.

Then the incoming message light flickered on.

"Gadgets, this is Dagger. Striker is otherwise occupied at the moment. Would you like to speak to me?"

Gadgets would have known that voice with its precise British accent anywhere.

"Dagger, this is Gadgets. We are airborne and inbound for your position. What's your situation?"

"Somewhat dicey, mate. I estimate we're outnumbered three or four to one, and the opposition has machine guns, automatic rifles and—"

Schwarz heard the sound of a nearby explosion.

"Bloody bastard! Not you, him, and, as I was saying, rocket launchers."

"Understood, Dagger. Sounds like you are having a hot time."

"You could say that. Anything else I can do for you? Make it quick. They're coming on again, and I'm going to be busy."

Grimaldi looked inquiringly at Schwarz. "Do they have colored smoke grenades?" he asked.

McCarter picked up Grimaldi's question. "Roger, Jack. We have four smoke grenades, two red and two yellow."

"Stand by to mark each end of your position with one red and one yellow. We'll be there in approximately three minutes."

Grimaldi and Schwarz heard the crackle of automatic rifle fire and the dull boom of grenades, then McCarter's voice above the uproar.

"Understood, mate. Dagger out."

Schwarz was staring out the cockpit windscreen.

"My God, look at that, Jack!" he said suddenly.

Grimaldi checked the terrain-following radar to be sure there were no obstacles immediately ahead. He looked up. A huge plume of dark black smoke was spreading into the sky.

The Stony Man pilot could see the target area ahead now. It looked like a shallow cup or bowl scooped out of the earth. A broad stream flowed to the south. Bolan's group should be on the south rim of the cup, but "should be" was not good enough when you were about to blow the hell out of an area. He spoke urgently into his headset.

"Striker, this is Jack. We will be arriving at your position in sixty seconds. I'm going to make a firing pass. Mark your position in thirty seconds."

"Roger, Jack, your message understood. Be careful. These people have machine guns and RPG-7s. They could have shoulder-launched SAMs."

"Roger, Striker. Keep your head down."

Grimaldi grimaced. He did not like the idea of shoulder-fired, surface-to-air missiles. They were impossible to detect before they fired and lethal if they hit a helicopter. But the Black Hawk had been designed to go in harm's way. Its engine exhaust ducts had been fitted with infrared suppression kits to reduce its infrared signature and make it harder for infrared homing missiles to lock on. The helicopter also carried an ALQ-144 infrared jammer and a flare dispenser. They would have to depend on them.

"I see the markers, Jack. Red and yellow smoke," Schwarz announced.

Grimaldi saw them, too. Time to do it!

"All right, we're going in. Gary, stand by to engage targets to the right. Gadgets, arm the rocket pods and give me infrared countermeasures now!"

Schwarz pushed a button, and the ALQ-144 began to pulse, emitting incredibly bright flashes of infrared light. The flashes were almost invisible to the human eye, but blinding to the seekers of infrared missiles trying to home in on the Black Hawk.

Manning, crouched behind the gun in the Black Hawk's right-hand door, saw some green tracers flashing from the trees below. He aimed the .308 GE M-134 minigun and fired. The squat cylindrical Gatling gun exploded into life. Streams of red tracers shot out from the Black Hawk's side and smashed into the ridge below. Having set the firing rate to a maximum of six thousand rounds per minute, Manning fired only a four-second burst as the Black Hawk swept by the target area, but in those four seconds the minigun poured four hundred rounds into the ground below. Trees shuddered and branches flew as the high-velocity bullets swept the ridge like a giant scythe.

The helicopter shuddered as it absorbed the minigun's recoil and bounced in the superheated air around the fire. Grimaldi fought his controls to maintain his course and speed. They were past the target area now. The pilot pulled the Black Hawk into a hard left turn that would have made its designers nervous.

"Ready to fire rockets!" He lined the aircraft's nose on the northern side of the cup. Someone down there was unhappy. Green tracers clawed at the Black Hawk and flashed past the cockpit canopy. Grimaldi squeezed his trigger and sent a burst of .50-caliber machine-gun bullets in reply. The cylindrical rocket launchers under the stub wings were suddenly wreathed with halos of orange fire as Schwarz launched the rockets.

Grimaldi saw the orange burning dots of the rocket motors as the rockets accelerated away, trailing lines of white smoke. Each of the four rocket launcher pods was firing a rocket every second. The hostile ridge line erupted in explosion after explosion as the swarm of rockets struck and detonated. Trees were falling, dust and dirt filled the air. Grimaldi pulled the Black Hawk's nose up and felt the dull black helicopter shudder as Manning fired another burst.

"Look out, Jack!" Schwarz yelled.

The pilot swore. The red-and-white helicopter was sailing over the cup at two hundred feet, flying straight and level as if it were making a sight-seeing run. What was that idiot trying to do? Grimaldi had no time to think about it. The other helicopter was just another threat to avoid. It did not appear to be attempting any hostile actions, but a midair collision at low altitude would ruin Grimaldi's day. He brought the Black Hawk around in another hard turn and went howling back for another rocket run.

Manning's voice crackled in Grimaldi's headset.

"Missile launch four o'clock!"

Schwarz did not hesitate. He pushed the button, and the Black Hawk's ALE-39 flare dispenser began to shoot infrared flares into its wake. Grimaldi saw the missile flashing upward, streaming gray smoke as its solid propellant rocket motor burned. He knew the missile's infrared guidance unit was searching for a heat source, trying to lock on and home in on the Black Hawk. He was too low to take evasive action, and he knew that the Black Hawk could never outfly the missile. All he could do was depend on the helicopter's countermeasures and pray.

The missile flashed upward. Its guidance unit searched the sky ahead, looking for its target. The Black Hawk was not a strong infrared source, and the bright pulses from its infrared jammer and the explosions of light from the flares dazzled and confused it. The guidance unit expanded its search pattern. There! Higher and to the right was a clear, unambiguous target. The missile locked on, flashed forward, struck the heat source and detonated.

MACK BOLAN SAW the slim, deadly missile strike the red-and-white Bell helicopter and explode. The missile had struck the engine exhaust duct. The aircraft staggered. Sparks and shattered pieces of metal flew from the damaged engine, followed by flames and greasy black smoke. The helicopter went down like a stricken bird, striking the ground heavily fifty feet down the slope from Bolan. Its rotors shattered, it skidded along, tipped over on its side and began to burn. As flames began to envelope the rear of its fuselage, Bolan heard a woman's voice screaming frantically.

Instantly, he was on his feet running down the slope toward the crashed helicopter. No one shot at him. The Black Hawk's low-level attacks seemed to have demoralized the opposition. He reached the red-and-white helicopter. There were several small holes in the fuselage, and smoke was beginning to drift out.

The woman was screaming hoarsely. "Help! For God's sake, help! Get me out!"

There was something familiar about her voice, but he could not place it. He heaved on the cockpit door, but it was jammed. The frantic woman, screaming steadily, was beating on the door window with both fists. One corner of Bolan's mind recognized her. She was Anne Bayne, the WWN television correspondent. He was too busy to wonder what she was doing here. The fire was spreading. If he did not get her out in the next 30 seconds, she would burn alive.

He drew his .44 Magnum Desert Eagle and blasted the door's hinges apart with a few quick shots. He grabbed the door and heaved. It tore open with a metallic screech. Bayne rolled out coughing and wheezing, and Bolan was faintly amused to see that she was clutching the nylon case that held her camcorder. He pulled her to her feet. Her face was red, and tears streamed down her cheeks. She was coughing and wheezing from the smoke, but other than that she seemed all right.

"Anyone else?" he shouted.

She shook her head. "They're both dead," she gasped.

"Come on, then. We have to get out of here. The fuel tanks may go."

Bolan pulled her from the burning wreck and led her

stumbling up the slope. He did not think he had to worry about another attack. There was nothing left of the drug factory that had been in the bottom of the cup but half a dozen raging fires. He got Bayne behind some cover and took out his canteen. He let her gulp a few swallows of tepid water and poured the rest over her face.

She was still pale and shaken, but he did not blame her. Burning to death trapped in a crashed aircraft was a horrible way to die. She took a few more swallows from the canteen. The water seemed to revive her.

"Thanks a lot. I owe you. I thought I'd had it until you showed up." She paused and shuddered. "I thought I was going to burn alive."

She stared at Bolan.

"I know you. You were with Captain Swenson at the Santa Cruz airport. You're Mike Belasko."

She glanced at the scene of destruction below.

"Mind telling me what's going on here, Belasko?"

"The Bolivian National Police staged a raid on a drug factory. I'm assisting them. The raid was a success. The drug factory has been eradicated," he said smoothly. The explanation was brief and to the point. Not only did it not give anything away, it was the truth.

Anne Bayne took out her camcorder and panned across the scene below. Fred Byrnes had been right when he called her a pushy bitch, but you had to admire her dedication. Two minutes after being dragged out of a burning helicopter, she was utterly determined to get her story.

Now she was photographing the burning red-and-white helicopter. She swung the camera and filmed Bolan for a few seconds. It was perfectly natural, but he did not like it. He would have to get the film, but this was not the right time or place.

"What happened to my helicopter? Some kind of engine failure?" she asked.

"Off the record?"

Bayne nodded and turned off her camcorder.

"You were hit by a shoulder-fired, surface-to-air guided missile."

The woman stared at him. Her face was blank with surprise.

"You're not kidding, are you?"

"No."

"Jesus Christ, Belasko! They shot me down with a guided missile? I thought this was the war on drugs, not World War Three!"

Bolan shrugged. He had learned a long time ago never to underestimate his enemies.

Bayne started to say something else, but her voice was lost in the whine of engines and the sound of rotors. Grimaldi had brought the Black Hawk to a perfect hover and was slowly coming in for a landing. Just before the helicopter's wheels touched down, four men clad in dull black raid suits leaped out of the passenger compartment. Each clutched a M-249 E-1, ready to fire. The small machine guns fired the same .223-caliber cartridge as the M-16 rifle, but they carried a 200-round belt in their plastic assault magazines.

Carl Lyons, the first out, dropped to a prone position and scanned the area. Two more olive drab helicopters were setting down. Colonel Suarez and two squads of Leopards poured out, clutching M-16 rifles. A medic began to treat the wounded.

Suarez walked up to Mack Bolan and Anne Bayne. He lifted one eyebrow when he saw the tall redhead. He took out his field glasses and surveyed the burning, exploding scene below. He looked at Bolan and smiled.

"You do have some interesting approaches to drug eradication, Mr. Belasko. A few more raids like this one, and I shall be able to retire."

CHAPTER FOURTEEN

The Leopards' Base, Chimore, Bolivia

The Leopards' Spartan conference room was crowded. Colonel Suarez had summoned all available officers for the debriefing. That was unusual, but the most astounding rumors were circulating about Captain Vargas's patrol. Most were very hard to believe, but the sight of three black automatic rifles, a blackened and burned machine gun, and an RPG-7 rocket grenade launcher displayed on a table near the door told them that it certainly had not been an ordinary patrol.

Vargas gave the debriefing. He looked a little pale, and there was a bandage on his cheek, but he seemed all right otherwise. Bolan thought Vargas did a good job. He outlined each action the patrol had taken and explained why he had decided to do what he did. He did not make excuses. He admitted the mistakes he had made, and gave credit to Sergeant Chavez and his men.

"Everything seemed to go well until we were down in the drug factory arresting suspects," Vargas concluded. "Two .30-caliber machine guns suddenly opened fire, and we were counterattacked by twenty or thirty men with automatic rifles and rocket launchers. It was a deliberate ambush. They were not trying to rescue their people. They were after the patrol. They intended to kill us all. I wish to give full credit to Mr. Belasko and Captain Green. They screened the machine guns with smoke grenades and set fire to the drug laboratory chemicals. Under cover of the smoke and flames, we retreated back up the ridge. We were trapped there, but they called in their helicopter, which drove off the *trafficantes* with rockets and machine guns. I regret to say that we lost three men killed and two wounded.''

Colonel Suarez nodded.

''Mr. Belasko, do you or Captain Green have anything to add?'' he asked.

Bolan did not want to make any long comments on other people's operations. Still, he did have a few things worth saying.

''Our team armorer identified the captured weapons. The machine guns were standard Russian PKM .30-caliber, belt-fed machine guns. The sniper's rifle was a standard SVD. The automatic rifles are something new. They're AK-102s, an improved version of the AK-74 rifle chambered for the American M-16 cartridge. They're so new they haven't been issued to the Russian army. They're manufactured at the Russian Izhmash plant for export sales.

''We also were fired on with RPG-7s and surface-to-air missiles,'' he continued. ''Whoever we were fighting, they were extremely well armed.''

Suarez nodded grimly. ''This is very serious. They are better armed than we are. Their rifles are as good as our M-16s, and we have no machine guns or rockets. Where did the *trafficantes* get such weapons?''

''The world is full of weapons. The drug cartels' profits last year were eight or nine billion dollars. They can buy anything they need.''

Suarez knew that what Bolan said was true, but he did not like to hear it. If the red zone was about to be flooded with modern high-tech weapons, his already difficult job might become impossible.

"What are your observations, Captain Green?"

"One or two minor points, Colonel. Most important, the enemy ambush was directed at your Leopards. Whoever planned it intended to kill as many of your men as possible."

Suarez looked skeptical.

"How do you know that it was not aimed at you and Mr. Belasko?"

"Logical analysis, Colonel," McCarter replied. "Think about it. Captain Vargas did not know the location of the drug factory until he talked to his informants in Sinahota. We were there in less than an hour. The force that ambushed us could not possibly have been moved into position in that short a time. They must have been in place for days, waiting for you to make a raid. No one could have known in advance that Mike and I would be with the patrol. No, they were there for your patrol."

Suarez thought it over.

"I cannot fault your logic, Captain. What is your other point?"

"That they will try again, Colonel. We were told in La Paz that your Leopards are the only really effective anti-narcotics force operating in the cocaine production area. From what I have seen, I believe it. If Operation Blast Furnace is going to succeed, you and your men are critical. I believe the drug lords have decided to take you out and our team, also."

McCarter paused for emphasis.

"They won't stop with one attempt. We must be prepared to be attacked at any moment. They'll strike at us any way they can with whatever they think will work. They will not stop until we are destroyed."

Suarez frowned. "Just what do you include in your 'whatever,' Captain?"

"I don't believe they would try nuclear weapons or long-range guided missiles," McCarter replied. "Other than that, anything their money can buy."

"Is your friend joking?" Suarez asked Bolan.

"I'm afraid not. He makes jokes now and then, but not about things like that."

As Suarez was about to respond, there was a disturbance at the door.

Bolan heard the guard protesting, then a loud voice.

"I do not care what he is doing. I must see him immediately. Get out of my way."

A tall, gray-haired man strode into the conference room. He was wearing a beautifully tailored, tropical weight tan military uniform. His shoulder straps showed the insignia of a colonel in the Bolivian army. He looked around the room. He did not seem to like what he saw.

Seeing him, Colonel Suarez smiled coldly.

"Gentlemen, this is Colonel Hector Zuazo, the chief of staff of the eighth division at Santa Cruz. I believe you know my officers. These gentlemen are Captain Green and Mr. Belasko. They are assisting us in our antinarcotics operations. Welcome to Chimore. How may we assist you?"

Colonel Zuazo looked disdainfully at Bolan and McCarter.

"What I have to say is a Bolivian matter, Suarez. It does not concern these Americans. I suggest you ask them to leave."

"These men are attached to our organization to assist

us in operations. They have already been of great value. We have no secrets from them.''

Colonel Zuazo froze for a moment, his eyes hard.

''Very well, Suarez, but it is your responsibility. What I am about to say must not go beyond this room. The military intelligence service has adviscd us that there is a strong possibility of a coup to overthrow the government. If it happens, it will probably occur in the next five to ten days. The general says we must be prepared to defend the government and the constitution.''

Colonel Suarez was not impressed. ''There are always rumors about coups. Why does the general believe this one?''

''You are isolated out here in the jungle, Suarez. Perhaps you do not know that there have been large-scale demonstrations against the government in La Paz, Cochabamba, Oruro and Potosi.''

''Who is it this time, Colonel?'' Suarez inquired skeptically. ''The tin miners, the coca farmers, or the Revolutionary Leftist Movement Party?''

''All of these, Suarez, and more. These demonstrations are remarkably well organized and financed. Their propaganda is remarkably similar. It calls on all Bolivians to unite and take up arms against the American invasion and overthrow the corrupt government that has been bought and paid for by the *yanquis*. It is not without effect. People are disturbed by this Operation Blast Furnace that your American friends have begun.''

Zuazo smiled nastily at Bolan and McCarter.

''I understand how they feel, Suarez. It seems to me there are far too many Americans in Bolivia.''

McCarter smiled back.

''With all due respect, Colonel, I'm not an American

and I have never been. I am a loyal subject of Her Majesty, the Queen. Would you like to see my passport?"

Zuazo flushed. He knew McCarter was making fun of him, and he did not like it.

"That will not be necessary, Captain," he said curtly.

Suarez smiled. It was obvious that he liked seeing Zuazo make a fool of himself.

"Very well, Colonel. Let us suppose that there is a serious coup. What is your general's plan and what do you want me to do? Remember that, under the law, the military can only give orders to the National Police in time of war or foreign invasion."

"I am well aware that you are a policeman, not a soldier, Suarez," Zuazo said with a sneer. He pronounced "policeman" as if it were a dirty word.

"Your role would be simple. If there is a coup, the eighth division will move from Santa Cruz to Cochabomba. The sixth division may be ordered to move from Trinidad. You have men near each place. If the army moves against the coup, we wish your Leopards to move in and maintain security in both places. I am sure this is a suitable role even for the National Police."

Colonel Suarez stared at Zuazo icily.

"Tell your general that if this happens, the National Police will maintain order. You may depend on it."

They exchanged salutes, and Colonel Zuazo stalked out of the room.

Colonel Suarez indicated that the meeting was over. His officers filed out of the conference room. The colonel motioned for Bolan and McCarter to remain.

"We have a serious problem, gentlemen. Zuazo would not have come here unless the army thought there was a serious possibility of a coup. If the army is united against it, they would rather deal with it without any help from the National Police,'' he said quietly.

McCarter spoke up. "You said 'if,' Colonel. Do you mean part or all of the army may be involved in the coup?''

Suarez shrugged his shoulders. "It is certainly possible. The sixth division at Trinidad supported the last coup attempt. The generals will do what seems best for them."

Bolan frowned. He did not like the sound of that. For that matter, he had no idea what the Bolivian army could do. If there was a major coup, was the army strong enough to stop it?

"Just how large is the Bolivian army, Colonel?'' he asked.

"It has ten regular divisions," Suarez said.

Bolan was impressed. Ten divisions was a formidable fighting force. The American army had only twelve. The Bolivians probably lacked modern equipment, but it sounded as if they should be able to handle any coup.

Colonel Suarez saw Bolan's expression.

"It is not as grand as it sounds. Our entire army consists of twenty thousand officers and men. Our divisions have only fifteen hundred to two thousand men, hardly enough to make up a brigade in your army. It is not very efficient, perhaps, but it provides many positions for generals and colonels."

"May I ask a question, Colonel?'' McCarter said.

"Of course," Colonel Suarez replied.

"Well, I realize it may be none of my business, but you and Colonel Zuazo seemed to be at swords' points from the instant he walked in. Do you dislike each other personally, or is there a problem between the army and the National Police?''

"I see that very little escapes you, Captain Green. The

answer is both. Colonel Zuazo does not like me. I despise him, and the army hates the National Police, particularly the Leopards.''

McCarter looked baffled. "I don't doubt you, Colonel, but I don't understand. I realize that you're two completely different organizations, but surely you must cooperate on important issues like national security and the war on drugs.''

Suarez shrugged. "Perhaps it should be so, but it is not. This is not England or the United States. We have sixteen thousand officers and men in the police. Most of our men are armed with rifles or submachine guns. The army has never liked an independent National Police Force, particularly one of this size. They believe the police should be part of the army. We disagree.''

Suarez paused, then added, "I am telling you this because it affects your mission. Consider it confidential. I would not like to be quoted in the La Paz newspapers. The war on drugs has made things much worse. The army does not want to get involved. They do not see how they would win. If all the *trafficantes* would assemble neatly in one place like an army and attempt to overthrow the government, the army would probably fight them and win. But the *trafficantes* are not stupid enough to do that. It is more like your war with the Vietcong in Vietnam. The *trafficantes* are spread over vast areas, most of which is covered with jungle. They are scattered in small groups in hundreds of places. They can only be fought by squads and platoons. Our generals do not want to break up their precious divisions for police work. The Leopards were created because the army did not want the mission.''

Suarez looked around the room and continued softly.

"That is not the only reason. Did you note Zuazo's pretty uniform? It cost more than a colonel's monthly pay, and he has two new Mercedes. I drive a 1984 Honda that continues to run only by the grace of God. I cannot prove it in a court of law, but I am sure all the senior military officers in Santa Cruz and Trinidad are paid handsomely by the *trafficantes* to keep out of the war on drugs. We can count on no help from them.''

"You think this coup is real?" Bolan asked.

Suarez shrugged.

"Probably, and you must understand that if this coup succeeds, your mission here is over. The new government will be totally opposed to your Operation Blast Furnace. All U.S. personnel will be ordered to leave the country immediately. I may have to join you. I think I will be removed from my command and placed under arrest within twenty-four hours. In fact, I will be lucky if—''

Suarez stopped. There was an odd whining, rumbling noise that grew steadily louder and louder until the building itself vibrated.

"What in the name of God is that?" Suarez asked.

Sergeant Chavez burst into the room without knocking. His face was flushed with excitement.

"Colonel," he gasped, "Captain Vargas asks that you come quickly. There is an airplane, a gigantic airplane."

CHAPTER FIFTEEN

The Leopards' Base, Chimore, Bolivia

Sergeant Chavez had not been exaggerating. The pale gray plane making a low pass over the Leopards' base was huge. Bolan recognized it instantly. It was a U.S. Air Force Lockheed C5B transport plane. He had seen them before, but a C5B making a low pass was a remarkable sight. It seemed to fill half the sky. He understood why C5 crews called their airplanes "aluminum clouds."

Bolan's tactical radio emitted a series of plaintive beeps. Someone wanted to talk to him. He pushed the respond button and heard a soft, Southern drawl.

"Striker, this is Gray Cloud. Come in, Striker."

"Gray Cloud, this is Striker."

"Striker, I have some packages for you. All I need is the password, and I'll drop them anywhere you say."

"Roger, Gray Cloud. Granite Home. I say again, Granite Home. Out."

Bolan turned to Suarez. The colonel was staring at the immense plane as it flew by. Bolivia was an isolated country, far away from the United States, but the C5 was a strong reminder that the U.S. could project its power anywhere in the world.

"Colonel, that plane is delivering some equipment I

requested. With your permission, I would like to have it airdropped on the base.''

"Certainly, at the end of the airstrip."

Bolan relayed the instructions and watched while the C5 turned slowly and came back over the base at five hundred feet. The tail loading door swung smoothly open, and parachute after parachute poured out and floated downward.

"There you are, Striker. It's been nice doing business with you. Before we go, there's someone who wants to speak with you."

Bolan heard a different voice.

"Striker, this is Eagle Six. I'll be in Santa Cruz in half an hour. I expect to be operational in twelve hours. Talk to you then. Eagle Six out."

"Understood, Eagle Six. Striker out."

The rumbling roar of the C5B's engines deepened as the huge plane turned east and headed for Santa Cruz. Colonel Suarez stared at the shower of parachutes touching down.

"You are getting a remarkable amount of equipment. And 'Striker' certainly is an appropriate name," he said.

"Christmas is coming early this year. Let's see what we got."

Half an hour later, the equipment canisters had been collected and brought to the conference room. Bolan, Colonel Suarez, and Captain Vargas were opening and inventorying their contents. The Leopards' officers' faces were shining with enthusiasm as they pulled out weapons and ammunition.

"Mother of God, Striker, you have enough weapons here to arm a division!" Suarez said.

"I tried to pay attention to what you told us you needed when we arrived, Colonel. There should be four hundred

M-16 rifles, forty M203 grenade launchers, twenty M-249 SAW light machine guns, ammunition, spare parts, and two hundred sets of night-vision equipment, plus a battalion set of tactical radios.''

"All for us?'' Suarez asked. He seemed to have trouble believing it. "What must we do to get all this equipment?''

Bolan grinned. He had never been much for paperwork.

"Write down the serial numbers, I suppose, and you can give me a receipt if you like.''

Suarez shook his head in amazement. "You would not believe the paperwork I have had to go through to get a few rifles and a little ammunition. And even if it is approved, it takes months to get it, and now it drops from the sky. You must have some very influential friends.''

Bolan did have one friend in Washington who did have an astounding amount of influence, but he was not about to talk about him.

"You have my undying gratitude. If you will accept a medal, I will try my best to get you one.''

Bolan shook his head. He appreciated the offer, but he did not know what he would do with a medal. It had been a long time since he wore a dress uniform, and a medal would look odd on his dull black raid suit.

"Thanks,'' he said politely, "but I'll settle for an all-out training program. If that's agreeable to you, Colonel, let's get started.''

BOLAN AND COLONEL SUAREZ worked late into the night to organize the training program, which was in full swing by morning. The Leopards' base sounded like a war zone. The sounds of rifle and machine gun fire and the dull boom of exploding grenades filled the air.

Gary Manning was giving rifle instruction, checking

each man's weapon to be sure it was in perfect shape, and teaching the tricks of assault firing. T.J. Hawkins was an artist with a light machine gun. He was running the machine gun course, while Rosario Blancanales was teaching basic M-203 grenade launcher. Carl Lyons and David McCarter had converted an old building into a "fun house" where graduates of the rifle and machine-gun course were confronted with targets that appeared by surprise and fast moving shoot-no-shoot decisions. Calvin James was instructing another group in hand-to-hand combat.

Colonel Suarez had divided his men into twenty-man groups, which were rotating between the courses. It made larger classes than Bolan would have liked, but at least each man got some individual instructions. The Leopards obviously liked their training. They were enjoying their new weapons and the chance to fire vast amounts of ammunition. The training was hard and fast, but it fit their image of themselves as an elite unit. Everyone had heard the story of Captain Vargas's patrol. If the *trafficantes* wanted to play rough, they would be ready. Bolan saw smiling faces everywhere as bullets tore through their targets.

They stopped by a quieter class where Hermann Schwarz was instructing a group of Leopards on handling their new radios. In a nearby building, Rafael Encizo had put blankets over the windows and was showing amazed Leopards the miracles of modern night-vision equipment. Colonel Suarez was pleased.

"You have a remarkable team, Striker, very skilled and professional."

Bolan certainly agreed with that. If there were any better men than those in Phoenix Force and Able Team, he had never seen them.

"Yes, we are making remarkable progress," Suarez continued happily. "Now, we must develop a plan to train the men at our base in Trinidad."

Bolan thought Suarez was a bit optimistic. They were certainly making a big improvement in the Leopards' combat power. Before, they had been lucky to fire five hundred practice rounds a year. They would fire two thousand rounds per man this day and the following one. Their instructors were outstanding. Morale was skyrocketing, but you did not make a man an outstanding combat shot in one or two days.

"Let's get a few pictures, gentlemen," someone said behind them. Bolan pivoted and drew his .44 Magnum Desert Eagle in one fast fluid motion.

Fred Byrnes was standing behind them, holding a 35 mm camera.

"Easy, Mike. It's just me, your friendly freelance journalist," Byrnes said.

"Make a little more noise the next time you come up behind me, Fred," Bolan suggested.

Byrnes stared at the .44's huge muzzle. It was a very impressive weapon when it was pointed straight at you.

"Damned right I will. Now put your cannon away. I want to take a few pictures."

Bolan slipped the big pistol back into its holster. You had to admire Byrnes's professional attitude. The CIA man maintained his cover most of the time.

Byrnes pointed the camera, and Bolan heard the shutter click several times. He wondered idly if Byrnes had any film in the camera.

"Thank you, gentlemen. If you'd like to see some of the pictures I took yesterday, Colonel, let's go to your office. Why don't you come along, Mike? I wouldn't want to publish any pictures of you or your team inadvertently.''

As they walked to Suarez's office, Bolan wondered what Byrnes was up to. The CIA agent seldom did anything without a good reason. Whatever he wanted, it was not just to show them pictures. A battered red and yellow jeep was parked outside the headquarters building. A young man in his early twenties, dressed in a bright red shirt and faded jeans, was languidly polishing the windshield.

"This is my assistant and driver, Pedro Sanchez. I hired him in Santa Cruz to help me with my equipment. Would you bring that aluminum case inside, Pedro?" Byrnes requested.

Sanchez flashed his white teeth in a big smile, pulled out the case and followed them inside. Colonel Suarez led them to his office. Fred Byrnes closed the door, he took a small black electronic device from his pocket and scanned the room.

"All clear," he said.

Byrnes's assistant suddenly underwent a remarkable transformation. He snapped to attention and saluted Colonel Suarez smartly.

"I am Ensign Julio Tejada, Colonel. I am on special assignment with the military Intelligence service. I believe I have information you will want to hear."

Suarez returned Tejada's salute.

"Very well, Ensign, proceed. I am always happy to receive information."

Tejada stared suspiciously at Mack Bolan. The big American did not blame him. He knew he did not look like a Bolivian officer.

"What I have to say is very confidential, Colonel. Will you certify this man's need to know?"

Suarez nodded.

"I have been assigned to investigate corruption in the navy. I regret to report that it is extremely widespread. The *trafficantes* have succeeded in bribing most of the senior naval officers in the area. I even have evidence that cocaine is being smuggled on board navy patrol boats."

"I suspect you are correct. Have you reported this?" Suarez asked.

"Repeatedly, Colonel. I am told I am doing good work, but nothing ever happens. I am afraid the *trafficantes* have eyes and ears at headquarters. Now I have learned something very important. The *trafficantes* have stepped up cocaine production in the Trinidad area. They have very large amounts of coca paste, but they are running short of the key chemicals needed to convert it to cocaine. They are moving large quantities of acetone and ether down the Mamore River. The chemicals are being transported on barges. They will be on the water tonight. I hear that they are heavily guarded. If they can be captured or destroyed, it will be a major blow to the cartels."

Suarez frowned. "This is valuable information, Ensign. I believe the navy has patrol boats on the Mamore. Have you informed the squadron commander?"

"No, Colonel. If I were to do that, I might as well call the trafficantes on the telephone direct and tell them to delay their shipment for a few days. That would save the squadron commander the price of a phone call."

"What you say is true, Ensign, but why are you here? What do you want me to do?" Suarez said.

"You are the only man I know who might do something about this," Tejada replied. "You have an excellent reputation. Men call you 'the poor colonel' because you cannot be bribed."

Suarez smiled. "God knows I am a poor man. Tell me, Tejada, how is it that you are here with Mr. Byrnes?"

"Mr. Byrnes and I have a common informant, who suggested that I talk to Mr. Byrnes. As you know, he is an agent of the American CIA. He recommended I talk to you. He said you would capture or destroy the chemical shipment if you could."

Suarez thought hard. "God knows I would like to, but Trinidad is more than two hundred miles from here. If I alert my base there, I cannot be sure the *trafficantes* will not be alerted. If I try to fly men from here, my helicopters will have to land at Trinidad and refuel. Once we are there, there is another problem. If we cannot use navy patrol boats, how will we intercept smugglers on the river?"

Mack Bolan had been listening. He was surprised to learn that landlocked Bolivia had a navy that operated in the middle of a jungle, but he would worry about that some other time.

"I may have the answer, Colonel. Our MH-60K Black Hawk has the range for the mission. We can fly direct from here. If you're willing to destroy the barges, it has the weapons to do it. It's your call. Give us the word, and we'll go."

Suarez looked skeptical. "There will be no moon tonight, Striker. Can you operate in the dark?"

"Perfectly, Colonel."

Colonel Suarez smiled wickedly.

"You are a bad influence, Striker. I shall probably be reprimanded for exceeding my authority, but I cannot resist the temptation. Get your helicopter ready. We go."

CHAPTER SIXTEEN

Trinidad, Central Bolivia

The Black Hawk droned on. Jack Grimaldi was flying the dull black helicopter without running lights, and it was almost invisible in the moonless night. He ran his eyes over the pilot's displays. Everything was in the green. The twin T700-GE-701 gas turbine engines were running smoothly. Mack Bolan, in the copilot's seat, had checked out the rocket launchers. Grimaldi had already checked out the fixed .50-caliber machine gun he controlled. Gary Manning had reported that both the .30-caliber miniguns were ready to fire.

They were all set. All Grimaldi had to do was get them there. He concentrated on his flying. They were skimming over the jungle, holding a steady six hundred feet and headed for Trinidad. Grimaldi kept his eyes on the multifunctional display. The MFD converted the data from the MH-60K's infrared sensors and radar into a clear picture of the scene ahead. Even on the darkest night, the infrared sensors could see as if it were bright daylight. He was not using the radar. He intended to keep it off until he really needed it. The radar emitted pulses of radio frequency energy when it was turned on. Those pulses could be detected on the ground. The infrared sensors did not radiate. They were completely passive, sensing heat radiated from objects outside the Black Hawk. No one could detect it.

Colonel Suarez stood behind the two cockpit seats, staring at the displays. He was used to helicopters, but not the MH-60K.

Jack Grimaldi checked the navigation display.

"Estimated time until arrival at Trinidad is ten minutes," he announced.

Colonel Suarez shook his head.

"This is a marvelous machine, but I do not understand. How can you know precisely where you are? It is as black as a witch's heart outside."

Grimaldi was tempted to say they used black magic, but Colonel Suarez might not be amused.

"We're using the Global Positioning System, Colonel. That's a large system of orbiting satellites. Our GPS receiver is receiving radio signals from three of them. It uses the combined data from the three satellites to continuously compute and display our position. It tells me where we are to fifty yards or less. If you could give me the exact coordinates, I could fly you to your base at Trinidad and land you within fifty yards of the flagpole."

Suarez looked amazed.

"Your American technology is marvelous. I would sell my soul to the devil for six helicopters like this one."

Grimaldi grinned wickedly. "I don't think the devil has any to sell. He can't get a high enough security clearance."

Bolan smiled. Jack Grimaldi would crack a joke if you told him the world was about to come to an end. He got up from the copilot's seat and motioned to Colonel Suarez.

"Why don't you sit here, Colonel? You'll have a better view. I want to check things in back," Bolan said.

Suarez smiled. He knew exactly how Mack Bolan felt. He had done it himself a hundred times. He was the commander and felt responsibility pushing on him. He had already checked everything twice, but as the precombat tension mounted, he felt he had to do it again.

Bolan stepped back into the passenger compartment. Ensign Tejada was sitting quietly in the back of the compartment. The young naval officer had changed into dark blue navy fatigues and was holding an M-16 rifle across his knees. He was staring quietly at the men from Phoenix Force and Able Team who filled the rest of the compartment. They were a formidable sight in their dull, nonreflective, black raid suits. With their blackened faces, and night-vision goggles pushed up on their foreheads, they looked like creatures from another world. Bolan was glad they were on his side.

He glanced around the dimly lit compartment. He had nothing more to say. His men were professionals. They did not need speeches or detailed instructions. They knew what to do as well as he did. Gary Manning and T. J. Hawkins gave the door guns their final checks. Gadgets Schwarz was monitoring the air waves for any unusual radio traffic in the area. Carl Lyons was running an oily rag over his assault shotgun. Rafael Encizo was putting an exquisitely sharp edge on his fighting knife. David McCarter and Fred Byrnes were talking quietly.

"Five minutes," he announced.

He stepped back into the cockpit. The scene in the MFD had changed. They were flying north along a broad river. Ahead in the darkness, he could see a glowing patch of lights gleaming through the night. That had to be Trinidad. Bolan heard a change in the sound of the engines as Grimaldi reduced power and started to take the Black Hawk down. He changed places with Suarez, slipping into the copilot's seat.

Grimaldi leveled off at two hundred feet. "We're on course and on time, Striker," he reported. "What do we do now?"

"We must search up the river. The *trafficantes* must be somewhere north of Trinidad," Colonel Suarez said.

"That may not be necessary," Bolan said as he slipped on his headset. He pushed two buttons on the communications control panel and waited until a green light came on. The MH-60K's SATCOM antenna was locked on a U.S. communications relay satellite floating high above the equator. He was ready to transmit.

"Hold her as steady as you can, Jack," he said.

Bolan pushed the button.

"Granite Home, this is Striker. Acknowledge, Granite Home."

"Striker, this is Granite Home. Over."

The satellite signal was not as clear as usual. It was hard to maintain a perfect antenna lock from a moving, vibrating helicopter, but he had no trouble recognizing Hal Brognola's voice. He reminded himself to be careful what he said as he pushed the transmit button. The narrow beam of the SATCOM was focused on the relay satellite. In theory, it could be intercepted only by another satellite in a similar orbit or a ground station immediately below the Black Hawk. That was fine, but Bolan did not like to trust his life to theories.

"We have reached the operations area, Granite Home. At planned location. Leopards' commander on board. Ready to start operation. Do you have target information for us?"

"Affirmative, Striker. There are seven targets twenty-six miles north of Trinidad on the Mamore River. They are proceeding south at six knots."

"Roger, Granite Home. I copy. Twenty-six miles north of Trinidad. By the way, we received the shipment. Tell Barbara it made everyone here very happy."

"Roger, Striker. Barbara reports there's nothing negative on Mary Swenson. And speaking of happy, a mutual friend of ours in Washington is very happy about that drug factory you destroyed. There were some great pictures on WWN. We need the publicity. He says keep up the good work. Granite Home out."

"Message understood, Granite Home. We'll do the best we can. Striker out."

Bolan frowned. It sounded as if there were high-level political trouble in Washington. Well, there was nothing he could do about that. Hal Brognola would have to handle that. Bolan had more immediate problems. He was glad to learn that Mary Swenson probably was not one of them. He switched off the SATCOM and spoke to Grimaldi.

"The barges are twenty-six miles up river, Jack. Let's go!"

Colonel Suarez was astounded. "How can you possibly know that?" he asked.

"We have friends in high places. I sent a message back to the States before we took off. A U.S. reconnaissance satellite has been tracking the barges for the past half hour. All we have to do is go get them."

Bolan turned to the weapons control console and checked the weapons systems. As he finished, a row of green lights on the control console came on. The four 19-round, 2.75-inch, multiple rocket launchers under the Black Hawk's stubby wings were armed and ready to fire. They were effective weapons. Their 70 mm, high-explosive warheads would be effective against any unarmored targets, but they were not particularly accurate. He would have to fire them in groups to be sure of getting hits. Once they were gone, they could not be replaced until the Black Hawk returned to the Leopards' base at Chimore.

He was less certain about the machine guns. If the barges had steel decks, the .30-caliber bullets from the Miniguns probably could not penetrate them. Grimaldi's .50-caliber machine gun almost certainly would, but it had a limited ammunition supply. He really did not have enough information to make a detailed plan. He would wait until he saw the barges before he made a final decision.

"What is your plan, Striker?" Colonel Suarez asked.

That was a nice way of putting it. Mack Bolan had no legal authority in Bolivia, and Suarez was a senior officer of the Bolivian National Police. Bolan was not sure what he would do if Suarez vetoed his plan. If there was going to be trouble between them, it was best to find out now.

"We should see them in two or three minutes. They'll hear our engines, but they won't see us unless they have night-vision equipment. As soon as we've identified the targets, I want to hit them hard and fast. Tejada's informant said they were heavily defended. I want to do as much damage as possible before they can react."

Suarez frowned. Bolan could see that something about his plan bothered him.

"I am an officer of the National Police. I do not know if I can attack those barges. We are not certain that they are *trafficantes,* and they have committed no hostile acts."

A stream of green tracers streaked upward through the dark, searching for the Black Hawk as it flashed over the line of barges. A second machine gun joined in, then a

third. The tracers were large and bright, probably from
Russian .51-caliber heavy machine guns. That was bad
news. The Black Hawk had not been designed as a gun-
ship. The bottom of the fuselage was lightly armored. It
should stop bullets from rifles and light machine guns, but
bullets from heavy machine guns would tear through it
like tissue paper.

"I think they're hostile, Striker," Grimaldi said wryly.

"I agree," Suarez stated. "They are very hostile."

Bolan was convinced. "Let's go. Rocket run!" he
snapped.

They were past the line of barges now. Grimaldi pulled
the Black Hawk around in a hard right turn and put the
dull black helicopter into a shallow dive.

"Ready to fire rockets!" He lined the MH-60K's nose
on the last barge. The image of the barge in the MFD
seemed to grow larger and larger as the Black Hawk shot
toward it at 180 miles per hour. Green tracers flashed past
the cockpit canopy. Grimaldi squeezed his trigger, and the
Black Hawk's .50-caliber machine gun roared to life. He
could see the big Browning's tracers as bright glowing
dots that flashed across the MFD screen and merged with
the image of the barge. Bolan pushed the button, and the
cylindrical rocket launchers under the Black Hawk's
stubby wings were surrounded by halos of orange fire as
he launched the 2.75-inch rockets.

Grimaldi saw lines of glowing fire from the rockets as
they accelerated toward the barges. Each of the four
rocket launcher pods was firing a rocket every second.
The surface of the river erupted in explosion after explosion as the swarm of rockets struck the water and detonated. Fountains of water shot up, and the Stony Man pilot
could see glowing balls of fire as four rockets struck the
barge and their high-explosive warheads detonated. Gri-

maldi pulled the Black Hawk's nose up, and they streaked over the line of barges.

"That was fun. Want to do it again?" Grimaldi asked.

Bolan shook his head. He did not think that it was smart to repeat the same tactic. Better to do something else that could not be anticipated.

"Go in low, and use the guns," he ordered.

"Roger. Firing pass. Door gunners stand by for targets to the left and right. Grimaldi put the Black Hawk's nose down and dived. Suarez gasped. It looked as if they were going straight into the water. If they struck it head-on at this speed, it would be like crashing into a stone wall. It was a white-knuckle maneuver. Grimaldi was the best pilot Bolan knew, but there were times when Grimaldi flew at the outer edge of his aircraft's performance envelope. This was one of those times.

The Stony Man pilot leveled off and sent the Black Hawk straight at the leading barge. The turbines' whine rose to a howl as he went to full emergency power. The helicopter's landing wheels were less than twenty feet above the surface of the water. Grimaldi pulled his trigger. The Black Hawk shuddered as the .50-caliber Browning began to fire. They were going almost straight at the leading barge. Grimaldi could see his tracers as glowing dots in the MFD and bright flashes of metal striking metal as the .50-caliber bullets tore into the target at supersonic velocities. He fired again and again in quick, short bursts.

Someone was firing back. Green tracers flashed overhead. The enemy gunner was firing high, but now he had the big Browning's muzzle-flash to aim at. Grimaldi put two more fast bursts into the barge. He was hitting, but nothing seemed to happen. That might be deceiving. The .50-caliber Browning was firing API, armor piercing incendiary ammunition. It would take a few seconds for the incendiary action to take effect.

Grimaldi broke left and flashed past the barge.

"Gunner, targets left!" he snapped into the intercom.

Hawkins was ready, standing behind the minigun in the Black Hawk's left-hand door. He saw bursts of green tracers flash at the helicopter from the line of barges. Dozens of lights were flashing on the vessels' decks as their crews fired automatic rifles at the MH-60K flashing by. Hawkins aimed the .308 GE M-134 minigun and fired. The deadly little Gatling gun exploded into life. Burst after burst of red tracers shot out from the Black Hawk's side and swept the decks of the barges below. Hawkins had set the firing rate to the minimum rate—three thousand rounds per minute—but the minigun was still firing fifty shots per second, three times faster than a normal machine gun. He could see the red tracers ricocheting off the decks of the barges as the Black Hawk swept by.

The Black Hawk streaked past the last barge in the line. It was burning fiercely, flames leaping and smoke rising into the air. Hawkins held his fire. The crew had jumped overboard.

The MH-60K suddenly shuddered. Hawkins heard a sound of tearing metal as bullets struck the stubby wing and lower left fuselage. Grimaldi fought his controls to maintain course and speed. "Any damage or casualties?" he asked.

Hawkins took a quick look around the passenger compartment.

"No casualties. Checking damage now."

He flipped down his night-vision goggles, turned them on and looked out the door.

"Hits on the wing. There are holes in the outboard rocket launcher. No sign of fire."

"Roger, T.J.," Grimaldi responded. "Take a look to the rear. I'm getting some funny indications from the left main fuel tank."

Hawkins did not like the sound of that. He braced himself against the doorframe and looked back toward the Black Hawk's tail. Through his night-vision goggles, he saw a large bullet hole and a thin line of fluid or vapor streaming back from the helicopter's side.

"We took a hit on the fuel tank, Jack. We're losing fuel. I can see it, but there's no sign of fire."

Grimaldi switched to the right-hand tank and turned to Bolan.

"We're losing fuel, Striker. We don't have much time. What do you want to do now?"

Bolan clenched his teeth as he thought furiously. His blood was up. They had destroyed one barge and damaged another, but he would feel they had lost if the others got through with their cargoes of chemicals.

"Go in again, Jack, one more time. Let's give them everything we've got."

Grimaldi nodded. "All right." He spoke into the intercom.

"We're going in again. Gary, stand by to engage targets to the right."

The Stony Man pilot brought the Black Hawk around in a smooth turn and headed back to attack. The burning barge was like a bright beacon in the MFD. As they got closer, he was surprised to see that the barges were not dispersing. They were still maintaining a straight line, each barge following the one ahead. Grimaldi did not like that. They could not know that the Black Hawk would not attack again. It did not make sense. They would be much harder targets if they broke up their formation and dispersed.

Grimaldi could think of only one reason. They had to think they had something that would defend the group. The initial attack had been a surprise, but now the men on the barges had had time to react. If they had shoulder-fired, surface-to-air missiles, they would be ready now, Grimaldi knew. They had almost reached the barges. If he was going to do anything, he had better do it now. Maybe he was getting paranoid, but better safe than sorry.

"Mack, give me infrared countermeasures, *now!*" he said.

Bolan pushed a button, and the ALQ-144 infrared jammer began to pulse, once again emitting incredibly bright flashes of infrared light.

The images of the barges were growing on the MFD as the Black Hawk closed in at 180 miles per hour. Grimaldi lined the MH-60K's nose on the line of vessels. Green tracers flashed past the cockpit canopy. Grimaldi squeezed his trigger and the Black Hawk's .50-caliber machine gun roared into life.

Bolan pushed the button, and the cylindrical rocket launchers under the Black Hawk's stubby wings emitted halos of orange fire as the 2.75-inch rockets were launched.

The rockets streaked toward the barges below. Each of the four rocket launcher pods fired a rocket every three seconds. The salvos of rockets struck and began to detonate. Geysers of water erupted, and Grimaldi could see glowing balls of fire as rockets struck the barges and their high-explosive warheads exploded.

"Rockets gone!" Mack Bolan shouted.

Grimaldi pulled the Black Hawk's nose up, and they streaked over the line of barges. Manning's voice suddenly crackled in Grimaldi's headset.

"Missile launch at six o'clock!"

Bolan reacted instantly. He pushed a button, and the Black Hawk's ALE-39 flare dispenser began to shoot infrared flares behind the helicopter. The missile was coming from directly behind them. Grimaldi could not see it, but he knew the missile's infrared guidance unit was searching for a heat source, trying to lock on and home in on the Black Hawk. He could not take evasive action so close to the water. Even if he could, he knew the Black Hawk could never outfly the missile. All he could do was depend on the MH-60K's countermeasures.

The leading barge suddenly exploded. The fires started by the .50-caliber Browning's incendiary bullets had done their work. A huge column of flame and smoke shot upward. The Black Hawk was headed straight toward the blazing column. The MFD's detectors saturated as they were struck by the blinding blast of light and showed only a glowing white screen. Grimaldi did not need night-vision technology. The flames and smoke seemed to fill his canopy. He turned as hard as he dared, and the Black Hawk skimmed by the flames.

The missile flashed toward them. Its guidance unit searched ahead, looking for its target. The Black Hawk was not a strong infrared source, and the bright pulses from its ALQ-144 jammer and the explosions of light from the flares dazzled and confused it. Still it came on, searching for its target. Suddenly, the missile's guidance was blinded by an immense tower of flames. The missile flashed into the fire and was destroyed.

Grimaldi took the Black Hawk out into the darkness. He turned back for one last look. The sky was lit by multiple fires and explosions. Grimaldi turned, seeing a red light glowing on one of the displays. The rockets were gone, and they were low on machine-gun ammunition.

"We're getting low on fuel, Striker. The left tank is almost empty. We've got to go."

"We can land at the Leopards' base near Trinidad. We have helicopter fuel there," Colonel Suarez said.

Bolan nodded.

"Let's do it, Jack."

Grimaldi turned the Black Hawk toward Trinidad.

CHAPTER SEVENTEEN

The Leopards' Base, near Trinidad, Central Bolivia

Mack Bolan sat in a corner of the headquarters conference room, sipping strong black coffee. Colonel Suarez was conducting the debriefing. The local Leopards officers listened intently. A visit by their commanding officer in the middle of the night was most unusual. The tapes from the Black Hawk's sensor displays were fascinating. The tapes indicated they had destroyed five barges and damaged the rest. The loss of the chemicals the barges had carried would have a major impact on local cocaine production. Bolan was pleased.

Jack Grimaldi and Gadgets Schwarz were inspecting the Black Hawk. If the battle damage was not too severe, they would refuel and fly back to Chimore the following day.

Bolan glanced at his watch. It was nearly midnight. Maybe he would walk out to the airstrip and see how they were doing before he turned in.

He stepped out the door into the hot and humid darkness, lit only by two weak light bulbs. He saw a flicker of movement in his peripheral vision and turned. A tall man in civilian clothes stood near a parked jeep.

"Are you Belasko?" the man asked.

There was something in his voice that told Bolan the man was not happy. He had a rifle over his shoulder, but he was not making any threatening gestures. Bolan kept his right hand poised near the holster of his .44 Magnum Desert Eagle.

"That's right. Who are you?"

The tall man stepped into the light. Well over six feet, he wore a T-shirt and faded blue jeans, and was slightly balding. He might have been a tourist except for the M-16 rifle slung over his shoulder and the Glock pistol in a hip holster.

"I'm Frank Latimer, DEA special agent in charge of the Chimore-Trinidad area. You and I need to talk in private, Belasko."

Latimer did not offer to shake hands, and he glared at Bolan. The Executioner did not care. He had been glared at by enough experts in his time.

"How about tomorrow morning? I've had a long day."

"How about right now? I'm responsible for U.S. antinarcotics operations in this area. I've never heard of you. Nobody told me you were coming. All of a sudden, you show up and start conducting operations everywhere. I need to know who the hell you are, who you're working for, and just what the hell you think you're doing here."

Bolan sighed. No matter what you tried to do, when the U.S. government was involved, interagency politics reared its ugly head. He did not like Latimer's attitude, but in a way he could understand it. He remembered what Hal Brognola had told him. All U.S. government agencies had been directed to work together to support Operation Blast Furnace. Perhaps the man had not gotten the word. All right, he would talk to him.

"I need to go to the airstrip. Give me a lift, and we'll talk."

Latimer got in the jeep and started the engine.

"All right, Belasko, let's go."

Bolan swung into the passenger's seat.

"Go ahead, it's your nickel," the DEA agent said.

Bolan thought for a second. He remembered Fred Byrnes saying the CIA thought the DEA had been penetrated by the drug cartels. He had better be careful.

"I'm working for the Justice Department's office of special operations as part of Operation Blast Furnace. I was asked to form a team of experts to provide advanced military training to Bolivia antinarcotics units. When I arrived in La Paz, General Stuart asked me to go immediately to Chimore and support Colonel Suarez's Leopards. That's it."

Latimer looked skeptical. The DEA was part of the Department of Justice.

"If you're from the Department of Justice, why wasn't I told you were coming here?" he asked.

Bolan shrugged. "Damned if I know. I assumed you had been notified through channels. I guess someone screwed up."

Latimer seemed to relax a bit. He had worked for the government long enough to believe almost any administrative foul-up was possible.

"Yeah, that's probably what happened. You may not have heard Washington has recalled Bill Mitchell as country DEA drug attaché. They're replacing him with some Washington desk jockey who's never spent a day in Bolivia."

Bolan had never heard of Bill Mitchell, but he knew the country drug attaché was the highest ranking DEA officer in a foreign country where the DEA maintained an office. If Mitchell had been relieved, a shake up of the DEA's Bolivian office was under way.

"I hadn't heard that. It doesn't sound good."

Latimer nodded.

"Maybe I came on a little too strong, Belasko, but I heard that you, personally, led an attack on a drug factory. Is that true?"

"I accompanied a Leopards' patrol in the red zone. I wasn't in command. They found a drug factory. The *traficantes* opened fire. When people shoot at me, I shoot back."

Latimer actually smiled. "I can't argue with that. Listen, we're on the same side. We ought to work together. I've got two dozen DEA special agents in the area. Most of them are concentrated here in Trinidad. They're hard charging, gung-ho types, and they know the area. I've got a pretty good network of informants, too. Let's agree to pool our Intelligence and notify each other about our planned operations. What do you say?"

Bolan thought hard. On the face of it, the man's proposal sounded reasonable, but he remembered Fred Byrnes's warning. If Latimer's or one of the other DEA agents had sold out to the drug cartels, cooperating with him could be fatal. Besides, there was no way he could share the data produced by Stony Man's advanced technology and data analysis with anyone. They were arriving at the airstrip. Was there anything he could concede that might make Latimer happy? No, if there was anything that had made Stony Man's operations successful, it was its insistence on total secrecy. Bolan had never violated that secrecy. He was not about to start now.

Latimer braked the jeep to a stop. "Well?"

"Sorry, I can't do that. Some of my information comes from sources outside the Department of Justice. I can't share it with anyone unless they have the proper special clearances and advanced authorization from the organizations involved. I don't make the rules, and I can't change them. That's the way it is."

The DEA agent glared at Bolan.

"That's what I thought you'd say, Belasko. I don't think you work for the Department of Justice at all. I think you're some sort of paramilitary spook for the CIA. Well, you haven't heard the last of this by a long shot. I'm sending an official protest to Washington and the embassy in La Paz in the morning. I want you and your damned team out of my area of operations, and I want you out now."

Bolan was getting a little tired of Frank Latimer.

"That's your privilege. They can make up their minds in Washington," he said as he climbed out of the jeep. That did not make Latimer happy. He put the jeep in gear and drove away in a cloud of dust.

Bolan walked over to the helicopter flight line. He was surprised to see Captain Vargas standing by the Black Hawk.

Vargas smiled. "There you are, Striker. I hear you had a great deal of fun tonight. I am sorry I was not there to see the action."

Bolan examined the bullet holes in the Black Hawk.

"I wouldn't call it fun, but it was exciting while it lasted. Why are you here? I thought you were still down in Chimore."

"I flew up with a load of M-16 rifles for the troops here at Trinidad. It was not very exciting, but I am popular with the men who have new rifles. I was about to go looking for you. I have a message for you. Your General Stuart wishes to talk to you. He asks that you call him on your satellite radio. His call sign is Blaster."

"Thanks, I'll call him now," Bolan said.

He stepped into the helicopter's cockpit and turned on

the SATCOM. He waited for a few seconds until the green light came on. The radio was locked on to the satellite and ready to transmit. Bolan pushed the button.

"Blaster, this is Striker. Acknowledge, Blaster."

Someone should be listening. If Stuart wanted him to call, the general would have someone monitoring his SATCOM. Bolan waited for a few seconds and heard a familiar voice.

"Striker, this is Blaster. What is your situation? Why are you in Trinidad? Over."

"Blaster, we attacked a group of seven barges carrying chemicals used in manufacturing cocaine to the Trinidad area. Five destroyed and two damaged. Will return Chimore tomorrow. Over."

"That's damned good work, Striker, or should I say 'heroic American commando'? Over."

Bolan frowned. What the hell did General Stuart mean by that?

"Blaster, your message not understood. Please say again. Over."

Stuart chuckled. "I guess you haven't been watching TV lately. You haven't seen Anne Bayne's report. 'Operation Blast Furnace a success. Heroic American commandos and elite Bolivian police destroy giant cocaine factory.' Those were lovely pictures Bayne took. People in Washington just love them. Over."

Bolan was speechless and filled with a cold anger. He had risked his life to pull Anne Bayne from her burning helicopter. Had she spread his face and the team's faces over worldwide television?

"Blaster, have team identities been compromised?"

"Negative, Striker. Bayne did the right thing. Your faces are obscured by little flashing rectangles on the broadcast."

"Roger, Blaster. Message understood."

"That's why I asked you to call me, Striker. You seem to have gotten Bayne on our side. That's important. They are having diplomatic and political problems in Washington and at the UN. Blast Furnace is being called American imperialism and another Vietnam. Bayne's story is the kind of publicity we need to get public opinion on our side. Over."

"Roger, Blaster, understood."

"There's a problem, Striker. Anne Bayne heard that there was a big story breaking in Trinidad. She chartered a helicopter in Santa Cruz and flew to Trinidad this afternoon. I told Captain Swenson to go along and keep an eye on her. Swenson was supposed to check in and report this evening. She hasn't, and that's not like her. I'm afraid something has happened to her and Bayne. I understand our friend Fred is with you. He has a lot of contacts in Trinidad. I want both of you to go to Trinidad and find Anne Bayne. If she's in trouble, get her out. I know it sounds like baby-sitting, but it's important. We'll get a black eye if anything happens to her, and we can use some more favorable publicity. Do the best you can. Over."

"Roger, Blaster, message understood. Will comply. Striker out."

Bolan went back outside.

"Was your message important?" Vargas asked.

Bolan nodded. "I've got a problem. Give me a lift back to base headquarters. I've got to talk to Fred Byrnes."

They drove quickly back to the headquarters building. Byrnes was still in the conference room, looking at the maps of the Trinidad area on the wall.

Bolan explained the situation quickly. Fred Byrnes shook his head.

"I don't know, Striker. It's not going to be easy. I've

been to Trinidad. It's not a country village. It's the capital of the Beni district. Forty thousand people live there. If Bayne and Swenson are there, damned if I see how we can find them.''

Bolan frowned. ''It does sound almost impossible,'' he said.

Captain Vargas smiled expansively.

''It is not as difficult as you think. You, Striker, are a soldier, and Mr. Byrnes is a spy, but I am a policeman. I know how to find people, and I know Trinidad. You will see, we shall find them.''

Byrnes looked skeptical.

''It's still a city of forty-thousand people. How do we search it all?''

''That is the point. You must know where to look and not waste time on places where they will not be. For example, there is only one good place to stay in Trinidad if you have money, the Hotel Ganadero. Anne Bayne is a television newscaster. She will have an expense account. She would stay there. That is where we look first.''

Bolan nodded. It sounded as if Vargas knew his business, and he had the local knowledge that made all the difference in the world.

''Sounds good, but suppose they're not there? What then?'' he asked.

''That is how we start. There are many other ways to locate them. You say Anne Bayne came there to get a big story. The only big stories she could find in Trinidad would concern the drug trade. There are only a few places the *trafficantes* frequent in Trinidad. We will look there. Also, there is a National Police post in Trinidad. I know most of the officers there. Two tall American women, a blonde and a redhead, would be most unusual in Trinidad. It is likely they have been noticed.''

"All right," Bolan said. "Let's go."

Vargas smiled again. "I know you are impatient to be off, but we must do one or two things to get ready. I am incredibly handsome in my Leopards' uniform, and you look splendid in your black raid suit. However, if we go to Trinidad dressed like this and covered with weapons, no one will talk to us except the police. I think no more than six of us should go. That way, we can split into two three-man teams if required. Pick your men, give me half an hour, and we will be ready to go."

Bolan did not like the idea of a delay, but Vargas was right. If they didn't change their appearance, they would stick out like a sore thumb. He would leave that to the captain. He knew Trinidad. Bolan though for a minute. He had to pick his team. He would go, of course. He would take Fred Byrnes. His informants in Trinidad might be crucial. Rafael Encizo should go, since he spoke perfect Spanish. McCarter was an obvious choice, since this might be a hostage rescue situation and the SAS-trained commando had specialized in that type of operation. McCarter had participated in some of their biggest successes. Who else? Gary Manning. His all-around skill with a rifle and knowledge of high explosives made him useful in almost any situation. Bolan looked at his watch. He had just enough time to find and brief them.

Half an hour later they were driving into town. Vargas had done well on a car. He had gotten a fiery red Mercedes from the evidence building. Bolan was not so sure about the clothes. Vargas was dressed in a beautiful white linen shirt, several gold chains and expensive wraparound sunglasses. He fit the image of a rich young *trafficante* perfectly. Encizo was in the normal size range for a Bolivian. Vargas had gotten him a cream-colored linen suit. For Bolan, McCarter, and Manning, who were all six feet or taller, far larger than most Bolivians, Vargas had found the loosely woven short-sleeve shirts that local Bolivians wore as leisure wear. The results were striking, to say the least.

McCarter sat in the back, seething quietly in a pastel pink-and-blue shirt. Manning was wearing a dark green shirt embroidered with yellow-and-gold jaguars. Bolan had a red-and-gold shirt that had to have been made for a giant. It hung on him like a tent, but at least it let him conceal his Beretta 93-R. They certainly did not look like a group of hard bitten professionals. If they met a large group of *trafficantes,* they might not have to fire a shot. The *trafficantes* would probably die laughing.

They were driving past Trinidad's surprisingly large and modern airport on the northeast edge of town. It was past midnight, but the center of town was ablaze with lights. Trinidad did not fit the picture of a sleepy town deep in Bolivia's central jungle.

"Is there a fiesta?" Encizo asked.

Vargas shook his head. "No, it is always like this. The people who live in Trinidad are a relaxed and fun-loving lot. They love to drink and dance and enjoy themselves. They say you can buy anything you want in Trinidad. There are many pretty women who hope to catch the eyes of a rich *trafficante.* There is even a country club down by the river. You can go swimming there if you do not mind the crocodiles."

They soon pulled up in front of a large, white, Florida style building on Trinidad's main street. A sign proclaimed that it was the Hotel Ganadero, the finest in Trinidad. Bolan noticed that there were a number of other expensive cars parked in front of the hotel.

"Is this where the *trafficantes* hang out?" he asked.

Vargas shrugged his shoulders. "You will certainly see

trafficantes there, but your DEA rents two whole floors. Perhaps I should say that it is neutral ground. It has the best restaurant, the best bar and some of the prettiest women in Trinidad. Everyone of any importance goes there. It is not considered polite to shoot anyone inside the hotel. Outside, you are fair game."

He handed Bolan the car keys. "I will be back in ten minutes. You can wait in the bar if you like."

That did not seem like a good idea. There were five M-4 Ranger carbines, a Heckler & Koch sniper's rifle, and Fred Byrnes's 12-gauge shotgun in the trunk. It would be difficult to explain that if the car was stolen.

Byrnes got out of the Mercedes.

"I need to go inside and make a contact. I'd appreciate it if you'd come along, Striker, jut in case somebody isn't playing by the no-shooting-inside rule."

Bolan nodded. It would be interesting to see the inside of the hotel. He was not worried about the car. Anyone who tried to take it away from the men of Phoenix Force was in for a nasty surprise. He followed Byrnes into the lobby. A man was dozing behind the hotel desk. Another man in a porter's uniform spotted the two Americans and swept towards them like a hungry shark.

"I am Ramon. How may I serve you, gentlemen?"

Byrnes took a fifty-dollar bill from his pocket. Ramon stared at it as if he were hypnotized.

"I am looking for two ladies, tall and pretty, one a blonde and one a redhead. Have you seen them?"

"*Sí, senor.* They are staying here. They are staying in room 217. They ate dinner in the hotel restaurant and then went to the bar. That was several hours ago. I have not seen them since."

Byrnes handed him the fifty-dollar bill and took out another.

"Is Maximo here?" he asked.

"*No, senor,* he has gone home."

"Find him and tell him that El Patron wishes to speak to him at once. I will be in the bar, and if others have something to tell me about the two ladies, I will be suitably grateful, to them and to you."

Bolan knew enough Spanish to know that El Patron means the boss. The porter was impressed. He grabbed the second bill and was off in a flash.

"You're throwing your money around, Fred," Bolan said.

Byrnes grinned. "You can be damned sure it's not my money, Striker. But you'd be surprised how well it works. A little bribery goes a long way. All you have to do is find the right people. Let's wait in the bar. I'm sure my expense account will stretch for a couple of tall, cool drinks."

Bolan followed Byrnes into the bar. The CIA agent flashed a twenty-dollar bill at the hostess, and they were immediately ushered to a corner table. That was fine with Bolan. He liked to sit with his back to the wall in a public place. A cocktail waitress came and took their orders. The Executioner looked around the room. People were sitting at half a dozen tables. He would have bet that several of the men were carrying guns, but that seemed to be common in the Chapare area. No one seemed to be paying any special attention to the two Americans.

"Who's Maximo?" Bolan asked.

"He's my main man in Trinidad. He's expensive, but he's worth it. He's a full blooded Aymara Indian, and he hates *trafficantes.* Maximo's smart, and he's not afraid of the devil himself. Washington wants samples of cocaine from all the drug factories in the Trinidad area. Maximo has been getting them for me. He's got a lot of contacts in Trinidad. He may be able to help us find out what happened to Bayne and Swenson."

Bolan noticed Fred Byrnes's choice of words.

"You think something happened to them?"

"I'd bet money on it. Bayne came here after a story. That wasn't a smart move. Trinidad can be a dangerous place. Asking questions about the wrong people here can get you killed. They probably have her somewhere right now and are beating the hell out of her. When they're through with her, they'll kill her. That way, there's no chance they can be identified."

Bolan nodded grimly. Everything he knew said that Fred Byrnes was right. It was hard to sit there doing nothing, looking idly at the people in the bar. The urge to charge off and do something was strong, but he knew that would be foolish. He had not lived this long by acting on impulse. He knew that knowledge of the enemy and careful planning were essential.

The cocktail waitress returned with their order, but it was not the same girl. She wore the same black skirt and low-cut blouse as the other girl, but she was taller. She smiled and started to set the drinks down in front of them. Her hand seemed to slip and she spilled Bolan's beer over the table.

"Forgive me. A thousand pardons. Please do not be angry with me, sir," she begged as she bent over the table and started to wipe up the spilled beer.

She was bending low over the tabletop, her face close to Fred Byrnes.

"*Senor,* I am Consuelo," she said softly. "Ramon, the porter, says you want information about the two American women who were here tonight. I know what happened to them and where they were taken, but if the *trafficantes* find out I told you they will kill me. You must pay me enough money to get out of Trinidad. If you will do that, I swear on my mother's grave, I will tell you everything I know."

Byrnes smiled genially and placed a ten-dollar bill on the table.

"Accidents will happen," he said loudly. He sounded like a happy drunk.

"Ten thousand U.S. dollars if you tell me the truth. If you lie—" he gestured casually toward Mack Bolan "—my friend here will kill you."

The girl trembled. "I will not lie, *senor*. Meet me outside in five minutes."

Byrnes nodded casually. "Five minutes."

He waited a minute or two after the girl left the table, then he stood up.

"This place is dead. Let's go where there's some action."

They walked out of the bar and into the lobby. No one seemed to pay any attention as they left the bar.

Ramon was standing in the lobby, smiling broadly.

Byrnes handed him another fifty-dollar bill.

"For good service," the CIA agent said.

"A thousand thanks," Ramon said. "I have found Maximo. I have a message for you. Maximo will be at the usual place in half an hour. He has some packages for you."

Byrnes handed him another bill, and they stepped outside with Ramon's thanks ringing in their ears.

"I wish I had your expense account, Fred," Bolan remarked.

Byrnes grinned. "It does come in handy, but you should see the paper I have to fill out after a mission."

They stood looking at the street as if trying to decide where to go drinking next.

Captain Vargas came walking down the street and joined them.

"I hope you have had better luck than I have. The police know nothing."

"I think we've found a live one," Byrnes said.

Consuelo came walking rapidly out of the hotel lobby. She looked startled to see Vargas but did not protest when Byrnes took her by the arm and towed her to the red Mercedes. Bolan handed Vargas the keys, and they all got in the car.

"Which way, Consuelo?" Byrnes asked.

"West along the main street, about three miles out of town," she said softly. She was obviously frightened.

"Stop here," Byrnes ordered. Vargas pulled the Mercedes over. "I've got to meet my contact. The rest of you go check out Consuelo's story. I need one man to back me up. It would help if he spoke excellent Spanish."

Encizo spoke up. "I believe I just volunteered."

"All right," Bolan said. "Where do we meet?"

"Across from the police station," Byrnes stated. "That ought to be safe."

He handed Bolan a piece of paper. "Here's where I'm meeting Maximo, just in case I don't make it back. Vargas will know how to get there."

He and Encizo got out of the car. Captain Vargas pulled the Mercedes away from the curb, driving smoothly, but not fast enough to attract attention.

"All right, Consuelo," Bolan said, "tell us what you know."

"The two American women were in the bar when I came on duty. The redhead was behaving most unwisely. She asked several people about some important *trafficantes*. After a while, two men came in. I know one of them. He is a *trafficante*. He bribed the bartender to put something in the women's drinks. I was afraid to say anything. The blond woman drank her drink, but the redhead was too busy talking. The blonde began to act as if she were sick or very drunk. The *traficantes* persuaded the women to go with them. That is the last time I saw them.''

"You said you knew where they were," Bolan said.

"I do. One of the *traficantes* made a quick phone call at the bar. He said they had the two women and were taking them to the Casa del Dolor and would make them sing like birds.''

Bolan was not sure he understood her. "The house of pain?'' he asked.

"Yes, *senor*. It is an awful place. That is where the *traficantes* take people they think are spies and informers to torture and kill them.''

"How do you know where it is?'' Bolan asked skeptically.

"A *traficante* was interested in me. He works there. He took me there to show me what an important and dangerous man he was. He wanted to sleep with me. He told me that if I made him angry, he would see that I was taken there. I was afraid to refuse him. I slept with him for a few weeks until he found another woman he liked better. That is God's truth, *senor*. I swear it!''

Bolan looked at her closely. She was obviously frightened. She was either telling the truth, or else she was leading them into a trap. He took out his Beretta 93-R and let Consuelo stare at the menacing weapon.

"It had better be, for your sake. If this is a trap, you'll be the first to die.''

"It is true. We are almost there. You will see that I speak the truth. It is about half a mile down a side road just beyond that big grove of trees.''

They were outside of Trinidad now. There were only a few scattered lights along the road.

"Pull over, and stop by those trees," Bolan ordered.

Vargas stopped the car.

"You stay with the car, Gary," Bolan said to Manning as they got out.

"Why me?" Manning asked, not liking the idea of being left behind.

"David knows more about hostage rescue than any of us. Vargas is an officer in the National Police. He can arrest people. You can only shoot them."

Manning grimaced. "You're always right. Don't you find it hard being right all the time?"

"I'll try and save some for you.

"Come on," he continued, "let's go reconnoiter. We'll leave our rifles in the car and look like we're out for a peaceful moonlight stroll."

He turned to Vargas. "Bring the girl."

Consuelo protested. Vargas smiled and showed her his badge.

"You will either come voluntarily, or I will arrest you and you will come in handcuffs," he said firmly. Consuelo sighed and followed him reluctantly.

They moved quietly along the side road toward the lights in the distance. As they got closer, he could see a small wooden house. He signaled the group to get off the road and move quietly through the trees. They worked their way to within a hundred yards of the building.

"Keep her here and keep her quiet," Bolan said to Vargas. "Green and I will go take a closer look."

Vargas nodded. Bolan and McCarter slipped silently forward until they were within thirty yards. The cover was not good beyond that point. Bolan looked at the small house. It had a shabby dilapidated look. There were lights on inside. The window shades were drawn despite the heat. He listened intently. Nothing. Except for the lights, the house might have been deserted. Suddenly, a woman screamed, a shrill wordless shriek of pain. There was a moment's silence, and then the woman screamed again. Bolan knew the voice. It was Anne Bayne.

He did not like the situation, but he knew he had to act now. They were hurting Bayne very badly to make her scream like that. They might be killing her. She had to be rescued now, but the problem was how. He and McCarter had their pistols. Their M-4 Ranger carbines were in the car, but they were not the answer. Their 40 mm grenade launchers could blow the house to pieces with a few rounds of high explosive. They would also kill everyone inside. They had a few 40 mm CS tear-gas grenades, but tear gas does not work instantly, and a man with a gun didn't need to see very well to kill a helpless woman. They would have to go in and depend on complete surprise and fast and accurate shooting. That was the only way that made sense.

He touched McCarter's arm, pointed to the house and nodded. They were going in. The Briton nodded. He understood, but he pointed at the porch. He had seen something. Bolan looked carefully. At first, he saw nothing, then he caught a flicker of motion.

Now, he could see a man sitting on a chair in the shadows on the small front porch. The man seemed to be holding something across his lap. The dim light was not bright enough for Bolan to be sure what it was. He did not intend to take any unnecessary chances. McCarter had the only silenced weapon. Bolan pointed to the Briton and then at the man on the porch. McCarter gave the understood signal. He drew his small .22 Walther PP pistol. With its special, heavy bullet, subsonic ammunition, it was as accurate and as silent as a firearm can be. McCarter began to work his way toward the porch.

Anne Bayne was screaming again and again, short, hoarse screams of pure agony. Bolan heard a man laugh. The men inside were enjoying their work. He heard a soft, hissing noise as McCarter fired. The man on the porch slumped over quietly as if he had gone to sleep. The Phoenix Force commando moved silently onto the porch and signaled Bolan forward.

The Executioner heard more screams and laughter. No one inside had heard McCarter's silenced Walther. Bolan drew his Beretta 93-R and set it for 3-round bursts. His .44 Desert Eagle had more sheer power, but the Beretta was the better weapon if he had to engage multiple targets at close range.

McCarter moved smoothly forward and tried the door, being careful not to stand in front of it. It was not locked, and it opened inward. Bolan moved to the center of the door. He held his Beretta 93-R at shoulder level in a rock-solid, two-handed grip. The pistol's safety was off. He was certain he had heard three men's voices. He had taken out three targets in less than two seconds a hundred times on the Stony Man range, but the targets did not carry guns and they did not shoot back. Nor did they have hostages. He took a deep breath, let half of it out, and nodded to McCarter.

The Briton turned the knob and threw the door open in one fluid motion. Bolan took one quick step forward across the threshold and stopped in a perfect combat-shooting stance. Anne Bayne had been stripped and tied to a chair. Three men were clustered around her. The one on the left drew a big pistol from a hip holster. He was remarkably fast, but Bolan's Beretta was already out and in his hands. He squeezed his trigger before the man could fire. The Beretta 93R snarled and put three rounds through the center of the man's chest in less than a quarter of a second. He was dead before he hit the floor.

The Executioner pivoted from the waist and swung the Beretta's front sight smoothly to the right, keeping his eyes, hands and sights in perfect alignment. The man in the center was holding an electric shock baton in his right hand. He seemed to be frozen by surprise. The baton was very effective for torturing women, but it was not a very effective weapon in a gunfight. Bolan pulled the trigger. The Beretta 93-R fired three shots so fast that the individual muzzle blasts merged into each other. Three 9 mm hollowpoints smashed into the man's chest. He dropped the shock baton and staggered backward. Bolan could see a black automatic pistol thrust through his belt. He fired again, and the man fell heavily.

The third man had an AK-47 slung over his shoulder, and he tried desperately to bring it into play. Bolan pivoted slightly to bring his sights on. Before he could fire, he heard soft, repeated hissing noises as McCarter fired his deadly little Walther. The man's head jerked back, and he fell limply, like a puppet with its strings cut.

Mack Bolan pulled the gag from Bayne's mouth.

"Where's Mary Swenson?" he snapped.

"In the next room," the woman gasped. "Watch out. I think there's a man in there."

The door to the next room was closed. Bolan was not about to charge through it heroically. People who did that sort of thing didn't live long. Either he or McCarter had to make the entry. He had the best weapon if there was more than one man to take out. Almost without thinking, he slipped a fresh magazine into his Beretta 93-R. Very gently, being careful not to twist the knob, he tried the door. It was locked. He moved to the left, out of line with the door, and pointed at the lock. McCarter nodded and moved silently forward. He positioned himself carefully, standing just to the right of the door jamb. He looked at Bolan and nodded. He was ready.

The Executioner aimed the Beretta 93-R at the center of the door. He would be ready to fire immediately as soon as he saw the situation inside the room.

He looked at McCarter and shouted, "Go!"

The Briton drew up his right leg until his knee almost touched his chest, then he drove his heel into the door just above the lock. McCarter put every ounce of his weight into his kick. The flimsy lock broke, and the door shot open. Bolan saw a bed, two chairs and a blur of motion as someone threw himself across the room and dived out the window. Bolan held his fire. He was not sure where Mary Swenson was.

Swenson was sprawled on the bed, not tied down, but lying limp and motionless. Was she unconscious? No. She stared vacantly at Bolan as he moved into the room. Her eyes were wide, and her pupils were dilated. She seemed to have no idea what was happening.

"Mike?" she asked. "What's going on? Where are we? I thought I heard shots."

Bolan stared at her. Her voice was slow and slurred. He felt a cold knot in his stomach. It looked like she was on drugs. He had been suspicious of Mary Swenson in La Paz. If she was a drug addict, the drug lords owned her, body and soul.

Captain Vargas stepped into the room, pistol in hand. He had moved to the house quickly when he heard shots. Bolan pointed to Swenson.

"What's the matter with her? Is she on drugs?"

Vargas examined her closely.

"Yes, but it is not cocaine or heroin. I have seen it

before. It is *burundanga,* a drug they make in Colombia,"
Vargas explained. "The main effects are a total loss of
willpower, and sleepiness. She does not really know
where she is or what is happening to her. She will remember very little. It works almost like a truth serum.
She will tell anyone anything she knows and do anything
she is told to do. There is no antidote, but the effects will
probably wear off in a few hours or a day or two. Still,
we should get her to a doctor. An overdose can be fatal."

"Bloody hell," McCarter said. "Why would anyone
take a drug like that?"

"No one would. It is not a drug people take. It is a
drug they are given. It has almost no taste or smell. It is
easily slipped into many kinds of food or drinks. Criminals in Colombia use it to rob or kidnap people. We never
used to see it in Bolivia. It is another gift the damned
Colombians have given us."

McCarter wrapped a sheet around Swenson. He and
Captain Vargas followed Bolan into the front room.

Bolan cut Anne Bayne loose and handed her her
clothes. She glared at the bodies on the floor.

"Lousy bastards! They enjoyed hurting me. They were
having a ball. I'm glad you killed them. I hope they burn
in hell!"

"Glad to give you a hand," Bolan said. "Now, I need
your help, Anne. It's important. I need to know everything
that happened."

"All right. We got to town and checked in at the hotel.
I'd heard rumors something big was going to happen in
Trinidad. I had a few local contacts and the names of two
men who were supposed to be willing to talk if the price
was right. I spread a little money around and put out the
word I was in town. We had dinner and went to the bar.
We had a couple of drinks. All of a sudden, Mary started

acting funny, like she was falling down drunk and didn't know where she was. Two men were sitting at the next table. One of them said he was a doctor. He looked at Mary and said she was coming down with some kind of jungle fever. He said we had to get her to a hospital right away or she might die."

She paused for a minute and looked unhappy.

"I guess I was stupid, but I was scared she was going to die. We went outside, and they called a cab. Once we got inside, they pointed a gun at me. They brought us here. They took off my clothes and tied me to that damned chair. They told me I was going to sing like a bird before they were through with me, but they worked on Mary first. She didn't try to fight back or resist. She was slow and dazed, but she answered every question they asked her. There wasn't any reason for them to hit her. They just did it for fun. Then they started working on me with that damned electric baton."

She shuddered for a second.

"That was bad. They seemed to think I work for the CIA. I would have told them everything I knew, but I didn't know anything. I was afraid they were going to kill me. You were a mighty pretty sight when you stepped through the door."

Bolan nodded. He was sorry she had had a bad time, but at least she was alive. She had told her story well, like a good reporter, but there was one thing he needed to know.

"Are the two men who brought you from the hotel still here?"

"One of them is, that bastard with the baton. The other one left ten minutes ago after they finished questioning Mary Swenson."

"That is bad, very bad," Captain Vargas said. "She

will have answered any questions they asked her. You must assume the *trafficantes* know anything she knew. Did she know anything that threatens your team or your mission?''

Bolan thought hard. What did Mary Swenson really know? She knew him only as Mike Belasko. She knew the code names of some members of the Phoenix Force team, but she knew nothing about who they really were or where they came from. She knew their mission with the Leopards, but that was hardly a secret anymore. He was about to say she could not have told the *trafficantes* anything really important when it hit him. Fred Byrnes! She knew Fred Byrnes was a CIA agent. She knew he was running the CIA's antidrug operations in Bolivia. If she had told the *trafficantes* that, Byrnes was in a hell of a lot of trouble, and Rafael Encizo was with him.

CHAPTER EIGHTEEN

Trinidad, Central Bolivia

Captain Vargas drove the big red Mercedes smoothly back toward Trinidad. It was nearly two hours past midnight. There was little traffic on the streets. Although they drove fast, the seconds seemed to be crawling by. Bolan was afraid that Byrnes and Encizo were walking into a trap, and there was no way to warn them. Vargas had proposed they contact the National Police and get some back up. Bolan had rejected that idea. The Bolivian police radios did not operate on the same frequencies as the advanced models used by Phoenix Force. If they went to the police station, the delay could be fatal.

"Where is this place?" he asked.

"It is a park near the center of town, close to the central plaza. We will be there in three minutes, but we must be careful when we get there. The *trafficantes* will not have sent just one man to kill Mr. Byrnes. Do you want to go to the police station first? I can identify myself and get a backup squad," Vargas suggested.

Bolan shook his head. That would take five or ten minutes. Every second could be critical. If Byrnes and Encizo needed help, they would need it now. The streets seemed almost deserted. Vargas was driving as fast as he could. The Mercedes's tires were squealing as he took corners as rapidly as he dared. Bolan was thinking hard. He had not ignored Vargas's warning. The *trafficantes* had not hesitated to send a death squad after him in La Paz. They might very well have done the same for Byrnes now. The head of CIA antidrug operations in Bolivia was a tempting target. They had better be prepared for the worst.

He turned to McCarter and Manning.

"We may be outnumbered. As soon as the car stops, get your rifles out of the trunk. I'll cover you. We'll decide on a plan when we see how the park's laid out."

The two men nodded. The three of them had worked together a long time. Each knew what the others could do. There was no need for long discussions. Bolan unleathered his Beretta 93-R, unfolded the forward hand grip in front of the trigger guard, and attached the metal folding stock and locked it in place. The Beretta was not a perfect weapon, but it concentrated the firepower of a ten pound submachine gun in a two-and-a-half-pound package. He lived in a hard and dangerous world. It was nice to always have the firepower of a submachine gun with him.

"What do you want me to do?" Vargas asked.

"As soon as we get out, drive a block away and park. Wait five minutes. If we aren't back by then, drive the women to the police station and come back with a platoon."

"I understand. See those trees ahead? That is the park. Ready?"

Bolan nodded. Vargas slammed on the brakes as they reached the park and brought the Mercedes to a screeching halt. Bolan threw the passenger door open and rolled out, staying low, keeping the body of the car between him and the park. The engine block is the only part of a car that will stop bullets. He moved forward, crouched behind the engine and aimed over the hood. He saw nothing but trees and thick green hedges.

As McCarter and Gary Manning bailed out and dashed for the trunk, Bolan saw a sudden flicker of motion in the bushes that formed the hedge. He swung the pale green, glowing night sights of the Beretta on the motion and flicked off the safety. A man stood up with his hands raised high above his head.

"Do not shoot, *senor*. It is Maximo. Senor Byrnes needs help. He is in great danger."

Bolan glanced to his left. McCarter had out his M-4 Ranger carbine and was aiming it at the hedge.

"Cover me," Bolan shouted and raced forward toward Maximo, staying low, keeping his Beretta in the assault fire position, ready to shoot instantly.

"Put your hands down, but keep them where I can see them. Now, where is Senor Byrnes?" he snapped. He kept the muzzle of the Beretta pointed at Maximo's chest. Byrnes seemed to have trusted the man, but Bolan was not sure he could.

Maximo saw the cold, deadly look in Bolan's eyes and stared down the muzzle of the Beretta 93-R. He knew that if the American decided he had sold out to the *trafficantes*, he was a dead man.

"Senor Byrnes is in the center of the park with another man I do not know. He speaks like a Cuban, but Senor Byrnes vouched for him. I met him there to deliver the packages."

Bolan relaxed a little. Like most Cubans, Encizo did speak Spanish with a distinct accent. He still kept his Beretta pointed at Maximo's chest. There were still a few questions he wanted answered.

"What are these packages, Maximo?"

"Senor Byrnes wanted a sample of cocaine from every drug factory in the Trinidad area. Why, I do not know. He tells me what he wants me to do, not why I do it. I got the last samples today and delivered them to him just now. He was very pleased."

"Why are you here if Byrnes is still in the park?" Bolan demanded.

"Senor Byrnes has rules. We are never to enter or leave a meeting site together. Tonight, I left first. He would wait ten minutes. Then he would leave."

It sounded like the truth. It was a typical CIA procedure, one Byrnes was likely to use when meeting with one of his informants.

"All right, what is this great danger?"

"As I was leaving, a group of men came into the park. I stepped into the trees, and they did not see me, but I heard them say they would kill the gringo spy. I decided to try to find help. When I got to the edge of the park, a man was waiting in the trees just by the path. He had a large pistol. I think he was waiting for Senor Byrnes if he escaped from the others."

Bolan felt the adrenaline begin to flow. He did not like the idea of a killer with a big pistol lurking in the dark.

"Where is this man?" he asked.

Maximo pointed into the bushes to his right. "There, *senor.*"

Bolan pivoted from the waist and centered the sights of his Beretta on the bushes.

"Do not be concerned, *senor.* He was doubtless a very fierce *trafficante,* but he was not very good in the dark. I killed him. Here, I will show you."

Maximo moved three steps to the right and pointed down. A young man in dark clothes lay on his back. A large black automatic pistol lay on the ground beside him. His throat was neatly cut from ear to ear. Bolan picked up the pistol. It was a 9 mm Glock 18 machine pistol, the same type his attackers had carried in La Paz. The dead man's body was very convincing. He no longer doubted Maximo.

Bolan signaled for McCarter and Manning to come forward.

The Briton came first, moving fast and staying low. Manning followed him, but stopped five yards away and took cover. Only fools bunched up when they know they may be fired on.

"Who is this person?" McCarter asked suspiciously. "Where is Byrnes?"

"This is Maximo. He's one of Fred's agents. Fred is—"

Bolan heard a loud, booming crack that he identified as the muzzle blast of a short-barreled .357 Magnum pistol. It was Fred Byrnes's gun. The night was suddenly shattered by the repeated sounds of gunfire. Byrnes was firing repeatedly and was being answered by the ripping, snarling sound of 9 mm automatic weapons. Encizo and Byrnes were outnumbered and outgunned. The tactical situation called for a cool and cautious approach. The problem was they did not know precisely where the fight was taking place or the position of the enemy. If they played it by the book, they were almost certainly going to be too late.

They stared at each other in the dim light, then McCarter smiled.

"You are a better shot than I am, Striker. Cover me."

The Briton dashed down the path. He held his M-4 carbine low in the assault fire position. He moved forward about fifty feet and took cover, dropping prone in a clump of bushes beside the path. Now Bolan sprinted forward. Ten lunging steps, and he suddenly was out of the trees and into an open central area of the park. He could see a small fountain surrounded by a low stone wall. He saw the brilliant muzzle-flash of Fred Byrnes's pistol and the smaller, dimmer flash of Encizo's .45 automatic.

Someone spotted him. Bright yellow flashes flickered from the trees across the open area as a long burst from a 9 mm machine pistol came straight at him. Bolan threw himself down and rolled. Dirt flew from the ground as high-velocity 9 mm bullets tore into the path. The burst was too long. The Glock 18 was a deadly weapon, but it lacked the muzzle compensator and the 3-round-burst limiter that made his own Beretta 93-R so effective. The repeated recoil of a 15-round burst made the Glock uncontrollable. Each round of the burst went higher than the one before. The middle rounds tore into the trees above Bolan's head. The final shots were ten feet high.

Bolan heard the snarling crackle of McCarter's M-4 carbine as he fired one short, well aimed burst after another at the enemy's muzzle-flash. A second Glock opened fire, sending 9 mm full-metal-jacketed bullets streaking at Bolan. The Executioner rolled to the right, looking desperately for cover. He saw a small stone bench and hurled himself behind it. Stone splinters flew as 9 mm bullets struck the bench and screamed away into the night.

The bench was a solid block of stone. Even full-metal-jacketed, high-velocity bullets would not penetrate it. Bolan was safe as long as he stayed behind it and the men firing at him did not move, but he would be totally vulnerable if he was flanked. He rolled to the right edge of the bench and snapped a 3-round burst at a hostile muzzle-flash. He probably had not hit the man behind the Glock, but he had come close. That would give the man firing at him something to think about and spoil his aim.

McCarter and the other man were trading shots. The Briton suddenly swore bitterly, and the sounds of his M-4 carbine firing abruptly stopped. He did not sound as if he had been hit. He sounded furious.

"That bloody little man hit my carbine's stock," McCarter snarled.

Bolan took a quick look. A bullet had struck and shattered the stock of McCarter's M-4 carbine. Like all variations of the M-16 rifle, it carried its operating spring inside its plastic stock. The spring was dangling from a large tear. Without the operating spring in place, McCarter's weapon would not fire. With the proper spare parts and a few tools it could be fixed in five minutes, but there was absolutely nothing they could do to fix it now.

Bolan thought quickly. The hostile fire had slowed. Only one or two weapons were firing semiautomatically. The answer was obvious. Someone on the other side was using his head. Some of the enemy were moving to flank them. They could not stay here. The stone bench would provide no cover at all against lateral fire. They had to move. There was only one question—forward or back? Going back to the shelter of the trees was tempting, but Bolan rejected that. He knew it is much easier to fire accurately moving forward.

It would be risky, but they had to take the chance. McCarter had drawn his 9 mm Browning Hi-Power and was glaring at the trees.

"Let's go for the fountain. Ready?"

"Ready!" McCarter snapped.

Bolan rolled out to the right of the bench and aimed his Beretta at the trees in front of them.

"Go!" he shouted.

McCarter was on his feet instantly, running for the fountain. Bolan sent two, fast, 3-round bursts into the trees. The Phoenix Force commando ran skillfully, avoiding moving in a straight line and varying his speed to make himself a difficult target. Encizo saw him coming. Bolan heard the dull boom of the Cuban's .45 Colt automatic as he added to the covering fire. The Executioner saw flickering muzzle-flashes in the trees as the enemy fired at McCarter. Bolan saw dirt fly, but the bullets missed the Briton, striking the ground three feet behind him. The big American was not surprised. Even fairly good shots had trouble hitting a moving target, and the bad light made it worse. He sent two more 3-round bursts at the enemy's muzzle-flashes.

McCarter reached the low stone wall around the fountain and threw himself down behind it. Now it was Bolan's turn. He took two seconds to slip a fresh, 20-round magazine into the Beretta 93-R. He was not looking forward to the run. McCarter had taken the enemy by surprise, but now they would be expecting Bolan to move. They were probably aiming at the bench. But he knew that waiting would not make it any easier. He rolled out to the left, staying down until he had gone ten feet. He fired a quick 3-round burst and lunged forward.

For a second, nothing happened. Then he heard the snarling sound of rapid, full automatic fire as 9 mm bullets flashed at him. He fired again and heard the boom of Encizo's .45 and the higher pitched bark of McCarter's Browning as they gave him covering fire. Bolan ran forward, resisting the tendency to run all-out in a straight line. Dirt flew to his left as a swarm of bullets tore into the ground. The man who was firing had good eyes and fast reflexes. He changed his aim and emptied his magazine at Bolan in one long burst. The executioner felt a burning sensation as something plucked at his left sleeve. No time to worry. He was almost there. One last effort and he cleared the low stone wall and dropped down behind it.

Encizo grinned. "Welcome to the party, Striker."

Bolan looked around as he gasped for breath. McCarter was still trading shots with the enemy, while Encizo had stopped firing. Fred Byrnes lay on his side with his back to the low stone wall. Bolan could see a slowly growing spot of blood on his left side. The man was still conscious. He had his .357 Magnum Colt Python in his right hand, but he was pale and shaken.

"Hello, Striker. I'm damned glad to see you," he said hoarsely.

The situation was not good. They were pinned down. The low stone wall provided excellent cover against bullets but only if they stayed prone behind it. Encizo and Byrnes had to be low on ammunition. Worst of all, the enemy could shift their positions in the trees without being seen. There was no way to predict their next firing position. They certainly had the advantage, but Bolan had one card left to play.

He pushed the transmit button on his tactical radio and spoke urgently.

"Gary, this is Striker. All friendlies are at the fountain. All other targets are hostile. Move up, and take them out."

Bolan listened for a second, then heard Gary Manning's reassuring voice.

"Roger, Striker. On the way."

The best practical rifle shot in Phoenix Force was on the way. Manning was an excellent shot on a rifle range. In the woods, against moving targets, he was superb.

The big Canadian moved forward to the line of trees and brought his big black-and-gray rifle smoothly to his shoulder. It was a .308-caliber Heckler & Koch PSG-1 sniper's rifle. It had been a remarkably accurate rifle when it left the factory. When Cowboy Kissinger finished tuning it, it was a masterpiece. As the butt of the rifle touched Manning's shoulder, a tiny pressure sensor activated the AN/PAS-13 thermal sight. To the human eye, the two *trafficantes* who were firing at Bolan and McCarter were almost impossible to see, concealed by the darkness, trees and bushes. But Manning's sight saw them in the infrared. The hotter the target, the brighter it appeared in the sight. He could see their heat-generated images glowing through the colder foliage.

Manning placed his cross hairs on one of the images and squeezed the trigger. He saw the man stagger as the heavy .30-caliber bullet struck home. Instantly, the Phoenix Force commando realigned his sight and fired again. This time, the man he had hit fell heavily and lay still. With one quick fluid motion, Manning swung his cross hairs onto the second man. He could see bright, glowing flashes in his infrared sight as the man fired back. The man was firing continuously, spraying the trees that concealed Manning. The big Canadian felt the cool contempt of a true professional for an amateur. He was a marksman and totally despised the "pray and spray" style of shooting. He squeezed the trigger of the big Heckler & Koch, and the firing stopped abruptly.

The enemy had had enough. In his sight, Manning saw them break and run toward the far side of the park. There were three of them. They were staying within the trees, but Manning's infrared sight let him see them clearly. You had to lead a running man, even with a high-velocity rifle. The big Canadian pivoted smoothly, keeping his vertical cross hair a foot in front of the man's body and squeezed the trigger. The man spun and fell. The drug gunner behind him almost tripped and fell over his body. For a few seconds, he was almost stationary. That was a mistake. Manning put his cross hairs on his chest and squeezed off a fast shot. The man collapsed to the ground in a heap.

The third man panicked and broke cover. Manning sighted in and started to squeeze his trigger. Before he could fire, he heard Bolan's Beretta snarl and saw the man stagger and go down.

There was a sudden, startling silence. Manning maintained his position and scanned the area through his infrared sight, but there was nothing left to shoot.

"You're clear, Striker," he shouted.

He waited, ready to provide covering fire, as his friends around the fountain moved quickly back toward his position. Bolan was the rear guard. Manning grinned as he passed.

"Thanks, Striker. This time, you did save a few for me."

"I always try to keep a promise. Wait a minute, and be sure no one follows us."

He moved quickly down the path to the street. McCarter had opened the first-aid kit on his web ammunition belt and was treating Fred Byrnes's wound. Bolan looked quickly. Byrnes had been wearing a soft armored vest under his shirt. It had not been strong enough to stop a hard-jacketed 9 mm bullet, but it had absorbed some of the bullet's force before it had plowed along his ribs.

"What do you think?" he asked McCarter. The Briton was not a doctor, but he had seen and treated a lot of bullet wounds.

"It doesn't look too serious. I'll put on a trauma dressing, then we should get him back to the base. He may need some blood plasma."

Captain Vargas had brought the car back.

"You must have been having an exciting time, but I am probably not the only one who heard all that shooting. I suggest we leave immediately."

Bolan nodded and waited for Manning while the rest of the team piled into the Mercedes. Manning came quietly, slipping through the dark like a ghost.

"All clear, Striker," he reported.

"Let's go," Bolan said.

Vargas started the engine as the two men climbed in the car.

"Where to?" he asked Bolan.

"Byrnes is hit. It's obviously a gunshot wound. It might be a little hard to explain. Let's go to your base."

Vargas pulled the vehicle away from the curb smoothly and began to drive down the deserted streets of Trinidad as fast as he dared.

"Something strange is going on," he said. "There should be more traffic, even at this time of night."

Bolan saw flickering red lights ahead as they turned the corner. Two jeeps with National Police markings were partially blocking the road. The policemen manning the roadblock were alert, and they had their carbines ready in their hands.

Something loomed up in the dark behind them. It was an impressive, six wheeled armored car with Bolivian army markings. Its turret was traversed so that its cannon was pointing straight down the street at the Mercedes. The cannon looked like an 85 or 90 mm. Its gaping muzzle made an extremely effective argument for law and order. Bolan was glad they had Captain Vargas with them. Whatever this was, it was not a routine traffic stop.

Vargas stopped the car immediately. A National Police officer wearing the insignia of a lieutenant walked over to the car.

"Captain Vargas?" he inquired.

Vargas handed the lieutenant his ID.

The lieutenant looked at it and saluted.

"I have a message for you, Captain. Colonel Suarez requests that you return to your base as soon as possible."

"Thank you, Lieutenant. We are on our way now." Vargas paused and gestured quietly at the army armored car. "What has happened? Why is the army out in the streets?"

The lieutenant leaned in through the driver's window and spoke softly.

"There is a nation-wide joint alert for the army and the National Police. There has been more rioting in La Paz and Cochabamba. People have been killed. A number of illegal radio stations have suddenly started broadcasting. They call themselves the National Front and tell the people to rise up and overthrow the government. Tonight they began to call on the army to join with the people. There are reports that the commander of the seventh division at Cochabamba has joined the revolution."

Vargas looked grave. "What about the soldiers here? What does the commander of the sixth division say?"

The lieutenant shrugged his shoulders. "So far, he has ordered his soldiers to support the police in maintaining order. But there are rumors that he will join the revolution if it appears that it will succeed. His officers and men await his decision."

"Thank you, Lieutenant. Now I must go."

The lieutenant waved them through the roadblock. Vargas accelerated rapidly as soon as they were through. The tires squealed as the Mercedes shot through the night.

"What does it mean?" Bolan asked.

"It could be very bad. We have had many coups in Bolivia. If the generals are united, the coups are usually bloodless because no one can resist the army. If the army and the National Police are divided, it may mean civil war. The last time this happened, it was a bloody affair and thousands of people were killed.''

Bolan did not like the sound of that. The Leopards were part of the National Police. If they were drawn into a civil war, he and Phoenix Force would be right in the middle of it. He needed to talk to General Stuart and find out what the United States was going to do. For that matter, he needed to know what the Leopards would do.

''What will Colonel Suarez do?'' he asked.

''The colonel is a man of very strong principles. He feels that his duty is to the Bolivian constitution. As long as the government has done nothing that violates the constitution, he will defend it.''

Bolan thought hard as they drove on through the night. The situation seemed to be spinning out of control. He was too isolated out here in Trinidad. He had no idea what the United States would do if a civil war broke out in Bolivia. He needed to contact Hal Brognola or General Stuart and find out just what was going on.

They reached the Leopards' base. The main gate was heavily guarded by Leopards in full combat gear. They drove to the base clinic and left Mary Swenson and Fred Byrnes there. Anne Bayne announced that she would stay with them. Bolan asked Vargas to drive him to the air strip. There were lights burning around the Black Hawk. Gadgets Schwarz and T. J. Hawkins were on guard.

Gadgets motioned to Bolan as soon as he got out of the car.

''General Stuart wants to talk to you immediately. He says he will be monitoring the SATCOM.''

Bolan stepped into the helicopter's cockpit and turned on the SATCOM. He waited for a few seconds until the green light came on. The radio was ready to transmit. Bolan pushed the button.

"Blaster, this is Striker. Acknowledge, Blaster."

After a few seconds, Bolan heard General Stuart's voice.

"Striker, this is Blaster. Were you able to accomplish your mission? Over."

"Blaster, mission accomplished. Bayne and Swenson recovered. Over."

"Good work, Striker. What is their condition? Over."

"Blaster, both were tortured, but neither is seriously injured. However, there is a problem. Captain Swenson was drugged with a kind of truth serum. You must assume that she told anything she knows to the *trafficantes*. Over."

"Understood, Striker. Has your team been compromised?"

"Probably not, Blaster, but the *trafficantes* have identified Fred Byrnes, and his operations may have been compromised. His organization should be informed. They may need to get him out of the country."

"Roger, Striker. Message understood. Are you aware of the situation developing in Bolivia?"

"Roger, Blaster. I have been briefed by Colonel Suarez."

"What does Colonel Suarez say he will do, Striker?"

"Support the current government, Blaster. However, the Leopards' antidrug efforts will probably stop until this crisis is over."

"Understood, Striker. I want you and your entire team ready to move on short notice. It may be necessary to evacuate you to La Paz or to the *Hornet*. If I order you out, bring Swenson and Bayne with you. Byrnes, too, if he wants. I'll contact you early tomorrow morning. Over.''

"Roger, Blaster. Your message understood. Will comply. Striker out.''

CHAPTER NINETEEN

La Paz, Bolivia

Mack Bolan was sleeping soundly when they reached La Paz. He had had very little sleep in the past twenty-four hours, and even the C-130's vibrations and uncomfortable seats could not keep him awake. Gadgets Schwarz shook his shoulder lightly and held out a strong cup of Air Force coffee.

"Time to wake up, Mack. We're almost to La Paz."

Bolan sipped the coffee gratefully and looked out the window. The C-130 was passing over La Paz as it climbed up to land at the international airport. At first glance, the city looked the same as it had four days earlier, but a closer look showed columns of black smoke drifting upward from several points. Apparently, the rioting in the city had been severe.

He glanced around the passenger compartment as the C-130 began to turn into its final landing approach. McCarter and Manning were talking quietly, Byrnes was dozing in his seat, Lyons was staring out a window and Kissinger was studying a Heckler & Koch armorer's manual. Bolan had been unwilling to fly to La Paz alone. In theory, he was just going to meet with General Stuart and his staff, but experience had taught him that things were never predictable. The rest of the team was still at the Leopards' base at Chimore. He did not like to split the team, but he was not willing to shut down the operation with the Leopards.

A few seats away, Captain Vargas sat with Anne Bayne and Mary Swenson. Colonel Suarez, unwilling to leave his battalion and fly to La Paz, had sent Vargas to represent him. The captain was smiling and joking, trying to cheer up Mary Swenson, without much luck. The woman was better, but she was still pale and shaken. She looked worried. Maybe what had happened to her in Trinidad was not her fault, but she had revealed classified information. She did not know how the Army would look at that, and she was not looking forward to reporting to General Stuart. In the back, he saw Frank Latimer, the DEA special agent in charge of the chimore-Trinidad area. The man still seemed unhappy. He was pointedly ignoring Bolan. Bolan did not mind. He had nothing more to say to Latimer and no time to spend arguing.

The C-130 touched down smoothly and taxied down the runway. The international airport had changed in four days. U.S. military transport planes, C-130s, and big four engined C-141 Star Lifters were spotted near the runways. A huge U.S. Marine Corps CH-53E heavy transport helicopter was touching down near a group of U.S. Army Black Hawks.

Bolivian National Police troopers were still in evidence, but groups of heavily armed U.S. Marines were everywhere, guarding the aircraft and helicopters and patrolling the airport. Whatever the lawyers and diplomats might say, Bolan knew that the United States armed forces controlled the international airport. The C-130 braked to a stop, and the passengers started to disembark.

Someone waved at Bolan as he walked down the ramp.

It was Sergeant Johnson from the U.S. embassy. He was wearing body armor and a Kevlar helmet and had an M-16 A-2 rifle slung over his shoulder. It looked as if things had been rough in La Paz.

Johnson walked rapidly over to meet Bolan.

"Mr. Belasko," he said quickly, "please assemble your party and follow me. General Stuart wants to see you in a hurry."

Bolan made sure he had everyone off the plane, then followed Sergeant Johnson toward one of the Black Hawks. He would have liked to ask Johnson a few questions, but the sergeant had no time for conversation. He was concentrating on getting the Black Hawk rapidly loaded and off the ground. They climbed into the helicopter's passenger compartment. The pilot started the twin engines as soon as Johnson closed the door.

The sergeant sat in one of the Spartan seats next to Bolan.

"Things have been rough in La Paz?" Bolan inquired.

"Damned right! We've had anti-American demonstrations, riots and attacks on American civilians. That's funny, in a way. Bolivians don't like any foreigners very much, but they never seemed to be mad at Americans. Not enough to try and kill them, anyway."

"I've been out in the bush. What's our government doing?"

"The State Department is taking this talk of a revolution seriously. They have advised all civilians except U.S. government personnel to leave the country. General Stuart is taking action to get them out. You saw the airport. We've taken it over. He has established a safe area for American civilians in La Paz, and he's using those big Marine helicopters from the *Hornet* to take them up to the airport and Air Force transports to fly them out. The local State Department types say he's exceeding his authority. They're complaining to Washington. The general told them very politely to go to hell.''

Johnson paused and smiled. It was obvious that Stuart was the kind of general he approved of.

"What's the Bolivian government doing?"

"I don't go to meetings at that level, Mr. Belasko. All I know is what I see. The National Police seem to be loyal to the government. They're trying to keep the riots under control. I don't know about the Bolivian army. People say a lot of their generals are sitting on the fence, waiting to jump in bed with the winning side. That's all I know. You'll probably find out more at the general's meeting.''

Bolan nodded and looked out the window. The Black Hawk was slanting steadily toward the center of La Paz. It was a spectacular view. The city was spread out below him, filling from rim to rim the bowl of the huge three-mile-wide canyon. It was a beautiful sight, but the Executioner remembered that a million people lived in La Paz. If the coup had widespread public support, he did not see how the National Police could possibly keep things under control.

They were almost to the center of the city now, but there was still a group of twenty modern high-rise buildings still farther to the east. Bolan was surprised when the Black Hawk's pilot hovered and started straight down. He knew they had not yet gotten as far as the embassy.

"Where are we landing?" he asked Johnson.

"The La Paz professional soccer stadium. It's the only place in La Paz big and flat enough to handle a lot of helicopters. It's a damned good thing it isn't the soccer season, or we'd be at war with Bolivia tomorrow."

The U.S. embassy, La Paz

THE TRIP TO THE EMBASSY had been educational. Bolan and his party rode in an embassy station wagon, convoyed by two Marine Hummers mounting .50-caliber machine guns. The entrance to the embassy was protected by a sandbag wall topped with razor wire. The only opening was just wide enough to let one person enter at a time. The Marines who manned it were not the regular guards but heavily armed, combat-ready troops from the *Hornet.* Looking up, Bolan could see sharpshooters with scope-sighted rifles on the roof. General Stuart was not taking any chances.

Johnson led Bolan's group inside. Despite the fact that the Marines knew Johnson, they insisted on calling inside and verifying that the general would authorize each person to enter the building. Bolan understood. With their weapons and black raid suits, the men from Phoenix Force and Able Team were not a reassuring sight to a facilities guard.

The sergeant escorted them to a lounge. He took a piece of paper from his pocket and checked it.

"Access to the general's meeting is controlled for security reasons. Mr. Belasko, Captain Green, Mr. Byrnes, if you'll follow me, I'll take you to the meeting. If the rest of you ladies and gentlemen will wait here, I'll have the kitchen send up some coffee."

"Sergeant, I would like for my associate, Mr. Schwarz, to attend the meeting," Bolan stated. "I believe he may have some information that will interest the general. I will vouch for his security clearance."

Johnson thought it over. Strictly speaking, it was against his instructions, but Belasko seemed to have a lot of clout with the general.

"Very well, gentlemen, please follow me."

He led them down a corridor, spoke to a Marine guard,

opened the door and ushered them into the room. General Stuart sat at the head of a large conference table. Half a dozen officers in American Army, Navy and Marine Corps uniforms sat around the table. The general made the introductions. The officers stared curiously at the newcomers. None of them had had time to change clothes. In their dusty, dull black raid suits, they looked out of place in a conference room. Fred Byrnes attracted a few stares, since there were still a few bloodstains on his coat.

"Be seated, gentlemen, and let's get the meeting under way."

"Thank you, General," Bolan said smoothly. "But first, my associate, Mr. Schwarz, would like to brief you on the psychodynamics of the current situation. He's an expert in conflict resolution and may be able to tell us how to resolve this crisis without violence."

Stuart looked at Bolan as if he thought he had gone crazy. Then he smiled. He did not know what Bolan was up to, but he knew whatever it was, it was not a joke.

"Certainly. I'm sure we need that information. Proceed, Mr. Schwarz."

Gadgets Schwarz opened a flat plastic box, the size and shape of a laptop. He pushed two buttons and stared at it intently as he spoke.

"Gentlemen, the psychodynamics of the current situation in Bolivia are quite complex, but I believe you will all agree that the key factor may be expressed by the ratio of omega to delta multiplied by beta. Therefore—"

Schwarz pushed a button.

"Got it!" he said triumphantly.

"Got what?" the general inquired.

"A voice-activated microphone. It's under the table about two feet to your left. I'm jamming it. It will sound like sensor failure on the other end of the line."

Gadgets stood up and moved casually to the head of the table. He drew his knife and cut something away from the bottom of the table. He looked at it for a second and then handed the tiny object to the General.

"It's a Japanese design, battery operated, turns on whenever anyone speaks in the room and turns off when they quit. It's a very advanced design, as good as anything we've got. It has a short transmission range, though. Whoever was listening is probably within a thousand yards of here."

Stuart glared at the tiny object in his hand.

"Goddamn it! The embassy security officer swept this room this morning and swore it was clear," he said furiously. He turned to one of the Army officers sitting at the table. "Go find him, and tell him to get in here immediately."

The general looked at Schwarz and smiled.

"I see you know more than psychodynamics, Mr. Schwarz. Just what is that black box you have there?"

"It's a multifunctional electronic device. It contains a microprocessor and a number of multifrequency sensors and transmitters."

Gadgets looked around the room. It was obvious he had lost half the group. He shook his head slightly. It was hard for him to understand how intelligent people could fail to understand a simple technological device. Well, he would try again. They were military men. He would put it in their terminology.

"It's a miniaturized electronic warfare system. It detects electronic devices, classifies them and neutralizes them. Of course, there are limitations due to its small size and relatively low power. I could detect a radar thirty miles away, for example, but I couldn't jam."

The officers nodded and looked wise. They understood what Gadgets's black box did, if not how it did it.

A worried-looking civilian was ushered into the room.

Stuart glared at him coldly and held out the eavesdropping device.

"You searched this room this morning, Miller, and you certified that it was clean. Look at this! Mr. Schwarz found it in two minutes!"

Miller looked as if he wished he had never been born. He could think of nothing to say.

Schwarz spoke soothingly.

"I'm sure that Mr. Miller did his best, General. I just have better equipment. "

"Damned right you do!" Stuart turned to Bolan. "I'd like Mr. Schwarz to make an immediate security sweep of all critical areas of the embassy. Miller can watch and see how it's done."

Bolan nodded. Schwarz picked up his black box. He and Miller left the room, then the meeting started. Bolan could see that the group still looked worried. To find out that you had almost broadcast your plans and situation to your enemy was extremely sobering. Each of the officers gave a simple, no-nonsense briefing. They covered the deployment of Marines in La Paz, the availability of helicopters and airplanes, and events in the past twenty-four hours. It was interesting, but Bolan wondered why General Stuart had asked him to attend. Maintaining order and evacuating civilians made sense, but it was not his kind of mission.

Fred Byrnes had been using a security phone in one corner of the room. General Stuart looked at him as he hung up.

"Does the CIA have anything for us, Mr. Byrnes?" he asked.

"Our La Paz staff has been working night and day. This antigovernment, antiAmerican movement is very well organized and extremely well financed. There are half a dozen illegal radio stations broadcasting propaganda around the clock. The streets of all the major cities are flooded with leaflets and posters. A lot of the anti-American demonstrations appear to be genuine, but there are well armed and trained hit squads operating under cover of the demonstrations. They are the ones attacking Americans. There also is evidence that groups are working to provoke violent clashes between the demonstrators and the National Police. They want martyrs."

"What's the situation with the military and the security forces?"

"So far, two army divisions have gone over to the rebels. Two others say they're loyal to the government but have refused orders to move against the rebels. They say all Americans should leave Bolivia to insure peace. There are signs that the Bolivian air force may join the revolution within a few hours."

The general frowned. It was not good news. The situation in Bolivia was deteriorating rapidly, and Washington was breathing down the back of his neck. There were times when he found it hard to remember why he had ever wanted to be a general.

"What are your conclusions, Mr. Byrnes?"

"Well, I think it's obvious. This so-called revolution is being run by a well-organized group of people who don't care who they kill and who have money to burn. There's only one group like that in Bolivia—the *trafficantes*. I think it's obvious that they're masterminding the whole show."

He paused for a second.

"There's something else. I just got a message from CIA

headquarters in Virginia. It's off the record, and I'll deny I ever said it if it comes to that, but I think you have to know. The opposition party is preparing to launch a major campaign against the President over Blast Furnace. They'll accuse him of violating the *War Powers Act* and getting the United States involved in a civil war in Bolivia. They think they can win the next election on the issue. Several key members of the President's party agree. They're putting tremendous pressure on him to cut his losses and cancel Blast Furnace now.''

Bolan heard a murmur of remarks run around the conference table. The senior officers sitting there knew how to express themselves forcefully. "Goddamned politicians,'' was the mildest expression he heard.

"Damn it, General,'' an Army Lieutenant Colonel with the dagger badge of the Special Operations Command on his left sleeve said. "Let's not just sit here and let those bastards beat us. We've got the Rangers and Marine Force Recon. The CIA knows where the drug factories are, and we have the helicopters to get there. We can wipe them off the face of the earth in twenty-four hours if you give the word. Let's go!''

General Stuart took a deep breath. If Bolan had ever seen a U.S. Army general suffering from severe temptation, it was now.

Stuart looked at the Ranger colonel and smiled.

"God only knows I'd like to give that order, but I can't. When I graduated from West Point and got my commission, I swore an oath to defend the Constitution of the United States. So did all of you. The Constitution says the President is the commander-in-chief of the armed forces. As long as he does not give us illegal orders, it's our sworn duty to obey his orders. I've never violated that oath, and I never will. We stand by until we get a decision from the President.''

The conference-room door suddenly opened, and Gadgets Schwarz walked in.

''Excuse me for interrupting your meeting, General, but we've got a problem. A serious problem.''

Stony Man Farm, Virginia

THE WEATHER WAS BEAUTIFUL in the Shenandoah Valley. The sky was a hazy blue, and the leaves of the trees were turning color. Barbara Price had no time for the beauties of nature. She was sitting in the Stony Man operations center, staring at her computer. She was looking at a string of U.S. Intelligence reports on events in Bolivia. She was good at sifting masses of reports and extracting the critical data. She had been doing this for hours, and she was not happy. Things seemed to be going to hell in Bolivia, and her team was in the middle of it.

Aaron Kurtzman came up behind her and handed her a cup of black coffee. Price had drunk too much coffee already, but she drained the cup quickly. At least, the caffeine would help keep her awake.

The cybernetics expert looked at her closely.

''You have been here nearly sixteen hours, Barbara. No one can go on forever. Go get some sleep. I'll relieve you.''

Price shook her head and brushed her blond hair back from her forehead.

''Hal should be here in a few minutes. He's about to leave for a meeting at the White House. I talked to Striker on SATCOM about ten minutes ago. I need to brief Hal on what he said. Then I'll take a break. You can—''

Price stopped abruptly. A window on her computer

screen was flashing rapidly. All the computers were hooked together so that they could exchange information over a local area network. Someone was sending her a priority interrupt message. She touched a key on her computer and read.

Barbara. Reuters reports that a U.S. Marine Corps CH-53 helicopter crashed near La Paz, Bolivia. Seven U.S. Marines and fifty civilian passengers were killed.

Carmen.

"Good God! That's all we needed. Blast Furnace seems to be blowing up in our faces," Kurtzman said.

Hal Brognola entered the operations center and walked quickly over to Barbara Price's work station.

"What's going on?" he inquired.

Price pointed to her computer screen.

Brognola read the message and shook his head.

"That's bad. It's going to increase the pressure on the President to cancel Blast Furnace and pull all our people out of Bolivia."

He glanced at his watch.

"I've got to go. This is one meeting I'd better not be late for."

Price handed him a computer printout.

"Here's the latest Intelligence summary."

"Thanks, I'll read it on the way. Have we heard anything from Striker?"

"Yes, I talked to him ten minutes ago. He's in the U.S. embassy in La Paz. He says this coup attempt has halted antidrug operations in Bolivia and that he knows the locations of most of the cocaine factories in Bolivia. He wants to know if he's authorized to take independent action to destroy them.''

Brognola frowned.

"I don't know. The situation in Washington is changing too fast. Call Striker back and tell him I'll see the President and do my damnedest to get him an answer.''

CHAPTER TWENTY

The U.S. embassy, La Paz, Bolivia

General Stuart turned to Gadgets Schwarz.

"I'm not sure I need any more problems, Mr. Schwarz, but fill me in."

Schwarz had never been particularly impressed by people in authority, but he liked General Stuart's straightforward, no-nonsense attitude.

"All right. I conducted a security sweep of the critical areas of the embassy as requested. I found four clandestine listening devices. I neutralized them and turned them over to Mr. Miller."

"Good work, Mr. Schwarz. What's the problem?"

"During the sweep, I detected a radio-frequency message that I'm sure was beamed at the embassy."

"Were you able to read it, or was it in code?" Stuart asked quickly.

Schwarz frowned.

"There wasn't anything to read. I should have explained that I'm using the word 'message' in the broad technical sense, the transmission of information by any means. The message I picked up was digital. It consisted of a string of ones and zeros. Now, it's certainly possible to convert a message in any language to a digital format, but this is almost certainly a computer-to-computer message. I've seen this type of message before, and there's no doubt in my mind. It's an external source communicating with a fusing system.''

''A fusing system?''

''Yes, sir. That's the part of a large bomb that triggers the explosion. I've seen this message pattern before, when I was in Lebanon a few years ago. It was designed and manufactured in East Germany and widely distributed to terrorist groups in the Middle East.''

''Let me be sure I've got this straight, Mr. Schwarz. You're telling me there's a bomb in the embassy?''

Schwarz shook his head.

''Probably not in the embassy, but close by. It's probably a very large bomb. Based on the message format, I conclude that the bomb's live and that it's armed.''

''Exactly what do you mean when you say 'armed,' Mr. Schwarz?'' Stuart asked. ''Do you mean that it's ready to go off?'' Bolan admired Stuart's coolness. He might be staring death in the face, but if it frightened him, you could not tell.

Schwarz shook his head. ''No, sir. You have to be very careful with a large bomb. You don't want it to explode until you have delivered it to your target. People who know what they're doing use what ordnance experts call 'an arming, fusing and firing system.' When the bomb is not armed, it is basically inert and safe to handle and transport. In theory, it's impossible for the bomb to detonate when it's not armed unless it's in a large fire or something external explodes in contact with it. Fusing is the next step. When certain preset conditions are met, all safety features are disabled, and the bomb is ready to be fired. The firing command is the final step. It's sent by the fuse when something initiates fuse action, and then the bomb detonates.

"That can be done in many different ways—contact, time, pressure or command. That's determined by the bomb's fuse designer. This bomb is definitely armed. It may be fused. Based on the message I intercepted, this bomb will be detonated by a remote command. Somebody will decide it's time for it to go off and will push a button. There could also be a backup timer counting down to a preset detonation time. I would have to look inside the bomb to determine that."

"Can you give me any idea how big the bomb is or where it's located?"

Gadgets nodded. "It's almost certainly a car bomb, containing several thousand pounds of high explosives. There's a large truck parked in front of the embassy delivering food to the kitchen. I think I detected a response to the message coming from it."

The Marine Corps colonel sitting next to Stuart spoke suddenly.

"We'd better evacuate the building immediately, General. I've seen what these things can do. I was in Beirut in 1983. One truck bomb blew the Marine barracks to pieces. We lost 241 Marines. Let's not wait. Let's get our people out now!"

"That wouldn't be a good idea," Bolan said. "I'm sure all entrances and exits to the embassy are under surveillance. If they see large numbers of people starting to leave, they'll just push the button."

"Well, what the hell can we do? We can't just sit here and wait for them to blow us up," Stuart said angrily.

"I think I've located their observation point. The message originated from the third floor of that commercial building across the street. If we can take that out, maybe we can move the truck,'' Schwarz said.

Stuart grimaced. Everything he knew told him to hit back, not just wait passively.

"All right, how do we do it? If they see a group of soldiers or Marines head their way, they're likely to get suspicious.''

McCarter had been sitting quietly, listening to the discussion.

"I believe a few of my associates and I can take care of it, General,'' he said. "We don't look very military if we conceal our weapons. We'll go out the back in twos and threes, circle around and pay those chaps a visit.''

Stuart and his officers stared at McCarter. They did not like the idea of letting someone they did not know handle such a critical mission. But they saw McCarter's sand colored beret with its winged dagger badge. Every special operations officer in the world would have recognized it as the symbol of his former regiment, the SAS. They were no exception.

General Stuart did not waste time debating.

"All right, Captain, do it!''

McCARTER LED THE RAIDING PARTY quietly up the stairwell toward the building's third floor. The building had elevators, but the Briton did not like elevators when he was leading a raid. The indicator panels told when elevators were moving, the elevators made noises when they stopped on a floor, and last but not least, they were a death trap if someone was standing outside with an automatic weapon when the doors opened. Walking took longer, but they were far more likely to reach their objective alive.

When they reached the top of the stairs. McCarter slowly opened the door a crack and peered down the hall.

A man was sitting in a chair sixty feet away, looking at the elevator doors. He might have been the janitor except for the black AK-49 assault rifle he held across his knees. McCarter considered using his silenced .22 Walther pistol but rejected it. He could not be sure of a fatal shot at that range. If the people on the third floor had the device that triggered the bomb, it was absolutely necessary that the guard be taken out quickly and silently. Whatever weapon they used had to kill him instantly.

McCarter motioned to Kissinger. He was carrying a silenced Heckler & Koch MP-5 SD-6 9 mm submachine gun. It was as accurate as a rifle out to a hundred yards, and Kissinger was a superb shot. McCarter opened the door a few inches more and pointed down the hall. The Stony Man armorer nodded, pushed the MP-5's selector switch to semiautomatic and took careful aim. The guard stood no chance whatsoever. He would never know what hit him, but the Briton felt no compassion. He had been fighting terrorists half his life, and he hated them with a burning passion. If a man wanted to blow up a building full of people, he deserved what he got.

Kissinger squeezed the MP-5's trigger in a fast double tap. McCarter heard a faint hiss as two 147-grain subsonic bullets struck the guard in the side of the head. The man slumped and slid to the floor as if he had fallen asleep. The only sound was made by his rifle as it dropped to the floor.

McCarter waited for a few seconds, but there was no reaction. He pushed the door open quietly and motioned to his teammates to move down the hall. There were office doors on either side. He signaled Schwarz to check the offices on the street side. Gadgets held his black box in both hands, placed a small, flat microphone against the walls and listened intently. Carl Lyons moved a few feet behind him. His 12-gauge Atchisson assault shotgun was ready for action. If anyone suddenly stepped out of an office and saw Schwarz, it would be the last thing he would ever see.

Gadgets checked three offices, then a fourth. He nodded and pointed. Bingo! McCarter moved silently forward and listened. He could hear men talking inside. He heard the words *la bomba* more than once. He looked at Schwarz and raised one eyebrow inquiringly.

Gadgets listened intently, then held up four fingers. McCarter nodded. Schwarz could hear four people talking behind the door. That did not mean that there could not be more. Someone might be asleep or simply sitting quietly, not talking. The Briton thought hard. He could not be absolutely sure the office contained the transmitter that would send the command to detonate the bomb, but it seemed likely. His attack plan had to consider that there were at least four armed men to be taken out. They had to be killed or completely neutralized before any of them could push the button.

He considered his options. Flash-stun grenades? No, a man could be dazed and dazzled and still push a button. CS tear gas? No, it might take twenty or thirty seconds to become effective. There was really no alternative but to go in and shoot to kill. Very well, who would be the first man through the door? The Briton had been trained in the SAS tradition that an officer always led, no matter how great the danger might be. It was tempting to go in first himself, but what counted was not how he felt, but accomplishing the mission.

He looked at the three members of his team, Lyons, Kissinger and Schwarz. The answer was obvious. In his career as an LAPD detective sergeant, the Ironman had led more room raids than the rest of the team combined.

There was one other factor. Across a room, his 12-gauge Atchisson assault shotgun was the deadliest weapon they had. McCarter pointed to Lyons the Able Team leader, then pumped his fist at the door. Lyons nodded his understanding. They were going in, and he would make the initial entry.

McCarter moved to the left of the door, one pace behind Lyons and one pace to his left. Kissinger took up a similar position to the Ironman's right. As soon as Lyons stepped through the door, they would be clear to fire into the far corners of the room. Schwarz moved quietly forward, staying flat against the wall. He reached carefully over and tried the doorknob. McCarter could see it turn. The door was unlocked.

He looked at Lyons, who nodded. He was ready. McCarter brought up his left hand and then snapped it down. Execute! Schwarz twisted the knob and threw the door open. Lyons found himself looking into the face of a man less than five feet away. He had been walking toward the door when it suddenly opened. He had an AK-47 automatic rifle in his hands, the muzzle resting across his chest. For a fraction of a second, he and Lyons stared at each other, both surprised by the sudden unexpected confrontation. The man tried desperately to bring his AK-47 to bear, but Lyons's shotgun was already pointed straight at his chest, and he pulled the trigger.

The big, black shotgun roared and bucked. Lyons had loaded it with Winchester 12-gauge Magnum buckshot shells. Twelve .33-inch, hardened, round lead shots smashed into the man's chest. He died where he stood and fell heavily. The report of Lyons's shotgun was terrible in the confined office space. The room exploded into a blur of action as the blast waves echoed from the walls.

Lyons took one long step through the door, and his ice

blue eyes swept the room. A man sat at the window, staring through a large, tripod camera. Behind him a second man was sitting at a table with a telephone and two or three electronic devices. Another man was rolling off a couch to Lyons's left, drawing a pistol as he moved. The two men near the window were the threat. One of the black boxes on the table could be the detonating device.

The Able Team leader pivoted from the waist, keeping his eyes, hands and shotgun muzzle in perfect alignment. The man sitting at the table lunged for something on the tabletop. The man at the camera whirled, his hand flashing toward an automatic pistol in a holster on his belt. Lyons pulled the Atchisson's trigger three times as fast as he could and sent a hailstorm of buckshot at the two men. The man at the table went down. The other man was hit. He staggered backward but he was still on his feet, and now his pistol was in his hand.

Lyons fought the recoil of his big shotgun and tried to bring the muzzle to bear. Too late. He and the man fired simultaneously. The Able Team commando felt a blow on his chest like a fast jab from a boxer as a high-velocity 9 mm bullet smashed into his body armor. He had fired a little high, but it did not matter. Twelve buckshot struck the man in the face, and he died instantly.

Lyons caught a blur of motion to his right. Someone was swinging a Remington 12-gauge pump shotgun toward him. He knew he would not be able to pivot and fire his Atchisson in time, but his step into the room had partially cleared McCarter's line of fire. He heard the crackling snarl of the Briton's M-4 Ranger carbine as the man fired a long fast burst. Half a dozen full-metal-jacketed .223-caliber bullets struck the shotgunner in the head and chest. The Remington suddenly became too heavy for him to hold. It dropped from his nerveless hands as he slumped toward the floor.

Lyons heard Kissinger shout a warning. He started to pivot back to the left. He felt a hard, smashing blow on his side as he swung and staggered as he completed his turn, but he was off balance and out of his firing stance. The man who had shot him was aiming again. He knew he had hit Lyons, but he had failed to kill him. He knew that his adversary had been wearing body armor. He was a dangerous man. Using his sights, he took half a second to aim at Lyons's head.

The Able Team leader had no time to recover his combat stance and aim precisely. He simply shoved the barrel of his shotgun at the man who was less than fifteen feet away and fired. The 12-gauge assault shotgun roared and bucked as Lyons pulled the trigger again and again as fast as he could. The room seemed to shake and vibrate as the muzzle blasts of the individual shots blended into one sustained roar and each blast sent twelve more deadly buckshot hissing at his opponent.

It was not pretty shooting, but it was effective. Lyons saw the man stagger as buckshot tore into his left arm and shoulder. The shock of the impact twisted him to the left. He pulled the trigger of his big automatic, but the bullet went wide. Lyons fired again and kept firing until his Atchisson clicked on empty. The man with the pistol lay sprawled on the floor, bleeding from several wounds. Although seriously wounded, he still held the big automatic in his right hand, still trying to aim at Lyons. The Atchisson was slow and awkward to reload. He dropped it and quickly drew his .357 Magnum Colt Python, firing two fast double-action shots as soon as the big revolver cleared the holster. He saw the man's body jerk as two .357 Magnum hollowpoints struck home. The automatic slipped from the man's right hand, and he lay still. Lyons swept the room with the muzzle of the big revolver. Nothing moved. The fight was over. He bent and picked up his beloved shotgun. He felt a sudden shudder of reaction. It had been close, too damned close!

McCarter and Kissinger were in the room now, and the Stony Man armorer Kissinger began to search the bodies. McCarter motioned to Schwarz to come forward and examine the electronic hardware on the small table.

He picked up one black box the size of a cellular telephone.

"This is it!" he said excitedly. "This is the remote detonator."

"Splendid. Fine piece of work, mates," McCarter said. "Secure and search the area. Gadgets, check that electronic equipment and see if you can figure it out and see what it does. Cowboy, as soon as you're through checking our friends, watch the door."

He walked over to the window to get a good line of sight to the embassy and pressed the transmit button on his tactical radio.

"Striker, this is Dagger. The target is secure. You're free to move out."

"Roger, Dagger, on the way. Striker out."

McCarter considered his options. Bolan and Manning were going to investigate the truck. He could either stay where he was or go back to the embassy. They were vulnerable in their present location. They could be attacked by a superior force at any time. He would pull back to the embassy as soon as they finished searching the bodies. They would be relatively safe there as long as the bomb did not go off.

McCarter heard the sound of a sudden blow and a man groaning hoarsely.

"Try that again and I'll kill you!" Kissinger snarled.

The Briton whirled, ready to fire, but Kissinger had the situation under control. The man who had sat at the table and reached for the detonator was alive. He was lying on the floor, grimacing in pain as the armorer stood on his right wrist and ground down with all his weight pressing downward. The man was bleeding heavily from a wound in his left thigh. A Glock automatic lay a few inches from his right hand, but he had stopped trying to reach it. He was staring at the gaping black muzzle of Kissinger's .45 Colt Gold Cup National Match automatic. All the fight had gone out of him.

"Please, I am wounded. Who is in command here? I will die if I do not get to a doctor," the man gasped in heavily accented English. Kissinger kicked the Glock away and handed McCarter two small booklets.

One was a relatively new German passport issued to Manfred Werner. The second was more interesting. It was an older passport in the same name, but issued by the old Communist East German Republic. McCarter looked at the entry and exit stamps and smiled grimly—Syria, Lebanon, Iran, Iraq, Libya. Mr. Werner was a well-traveled man.

"Please, someone help me. I am dying. For God's sake, help me."

McCarter stared down at Werner. The look in his green eyes was as cold as death.

"I'm in command here, Herr Werner. I don't care whether you live or die. Can you give me one reason why I should help you?"

"I am a German citizen. I am merely a technical expert. I have nothing to do with these Bolivian madmen. Call the German embassy. They will confirm what I say."

McCarter smiled down at Werner without a trace of

humor. He hated terrorists with a burning passion. As far as he was concerned, Werner was a terrorist of the worst sort, the kind who killed for money, not convictions.

"Don't talk like a bloody fool. You helped plant a truck bomb in front of the American embassy. You were trying to detonate the bomb when you were shot. You were perfectly willing to kill dozens of innocent people. You did it for money. If I were a bloody Hun like you, I'd torture you to death. Since I'm not, I'll simply leave you here to bleed to death."

Werner's face contorted in agony as a spasm of pain shot through his bleeding thigh.

"I have information, valuable information, about the bombings these Bolivians are planning, where the bombs are made and stored. If I die, you will never learn this. Help me, and I will tell you everything!"

McCarter thought it over. As much as he hated terrorists, the information might save thousands of innocent lives. "Very well, Werner. I'll see that you get medical attention and get safely out of Bolivia. In return, you'll tell me everything you know. If you lie to me, you'll not have to worry about bleeding to death. I'll kill you personally."

The Briton turned to Kissinger to follow him to the office door.

"Put a tourniquet on his leg and keep him alive until I get back. I'm going over to the embassy to get Fred Byrnes. He needs to talk to Herr Werner. The CIA is used to dealing with scum like him."

"Got it. I've got to hand it to you, David. That was a beautiful bluff you ran. You almost had me believing you were going to leave him there and let him bleed to death."

McCarter lifted one eyebrow and stared at Kissinger for a second.

"What an odd thing to say, John. You've known me long enough to know that I never bluff."

BOLAN AND MANNING walked out the front door of the embassy and moved casually toward the back of the parked truck. They had the keys. The truck driver and his partner had been terrified when the grim-faced Marine Corps guards had arrested them. They swore they knew nothing about the bomb. That might or might not be true. It did not matter. Bolan had one overwhelming problem. How could he deal with an immense bomb? Manning unlocked the doors, and they stepped into the back of the truck. Besides a few scattered boxes of canned goods, the back of the truck was almost empty. Manning pointed to the sides of the cargo compartment. Metal doors were arranged in one long solid row on either side. Manning reached out and touched a door on either side.

"Refrigerator doors, but they don't feel cold," he said.

Manning checked one of the doors carefully.

"No booby traps that I can detect. Here we go!"

He swung the heavy door open smoothly, and Bolan looked inside. The dimly lighted refrigerator compartment was filled with large plastic drums. The air inside had a strong oily smell. Manning shone a mini-flashlight on the drums. The amazingly bright beam showed a large triangular label that proclaimed that the drums contained ammonium nitrate fertilizer. Manning swung his flashlight beam along the compartment. Between and around the drums were pressurized gas cylinders. Their labels read *propane* in Spanish and English.

Manning opened a second door, then a third. Each compartment was the same—row upon row of the big drums and silvery cylinders. Bolan waited patiently for the big Canadian to finish his inspection. If he had to stand inside an armed bomb, there was no one he would rather be with than Gary Manning, who radiated cool competence. He was an expert who was qualified in all common military and industrial explosives, particularly those used by terrorists. The commanding officer of Germany's elite GSG-9 counterterrorist force had once described Manning as absolutely brilliant at defusing bombs.

They reached the front of the compartment. Manning shone his flashlight on a small black plastic box attached to the wall. A wire led up to the roof.

"There's the fuse," he said with a nod as he drew a small flat tool kit from his belt. Carefully, delicately, Manning checked the box.

"No antitamper device," he said quietly as he opened the lid of the black box, then disconnected two wires.

"Pretty simple design, Mack. Defusing it is as easy as taking candy from a baby."

Bolan discovered that he had been holding his breath. He released it. It was a big truck, and there were an awful lot of those drums and cylinders.

"Just how bad is it, Gary?"

Manning thought for a few seconds.

"It's an ammonium fertilizer bomb, of course. That's very hard to detonate in the pure condition. The diesel oil sensitizes the fertilizer and makes it easy to detonate. The propane creates a fuel-air explosive effect that makes the blast much stronger. It's hard to predict the exact explosive power, but I'd say it should be somewhere between twelve thousand to twenty thousand pounds of TNT. There wouldn't have been much left of the embassy building if this baby had gone off."

He shone his flashlight slowly and carefully around the truck's cargo compartment.

"I'd better check to be sure there's not a backup fuse. I'd really be embarrassed if there was and somebody pushed the button."

"Great idea, Gary," Bolan agreed.

Someone tapped lightly on the back doors. Bolan drew his .44 Magnum and pivoted smoothly.

"Are you there, Mack?" McCarter asked cautiously.

"Yeah. Gary's just finishing defusing the bomb. Come on in," Bolan replied.

The doors swung open. McCarter and Fred Byrnes stepped into the truck as Manning finished his inspection. The CIA agent looked around the interior of the truck.

"This is all one big bomb?" he asked.

Manning nodded. "It's the latest and greatest in home-made bombs. You can buy everything they used at your local hardware store except the fuse. It was made in East Germany before the wall came down."

"Yes, I know. Byrnes and I have just concluded an interesting chat with a Manfred Werner. In exchange for a new passport, fifty thousand dollars and transportation out of Bolivia, Herr Werner has told us everything he knows. We now know where the bombs are put together and the names of most of the key people involved. Werner was the expert on the fusing systems."

"That leaves us with one hell of a big problem," Byrnes stated. "We're sitting on top of a screaming disaster waiting to happen. What are we going to do with this goddamned bomb?"

Bolan smiled grimly.

"What do you do when you get a package in the mail that you didn't order and you don't want? You mark it 'Return to Sender.'"

CHAPTER TWENTY-ONE

La Paz, Bolivia

Captain Vargas drove the bomb truck slowly and carefully through the streets of La Paz. Next to him, Gadgets Schwarz gave his remote detonating device one last check. He had replaced the original detonating device with two of his own. All that was necessary to detonate the bomb was to press two buttons, and he was careful not to touch them. The thought that he and Vargas were sitting on top of twenty-thousand pounds of high explosives was very sobering.

Mack Bolan, Gary Manning and John Kissinger were following a hundred yards back in an embassy station wagon. It was nice to have a little backup in case things went wrong.

"There it is, just ahead. See that big building surrounded by a wall? It's just as Werner described it. All we have to do is get past the gate guards, and we'll deliver our little surprise," Vargas said.

Schwarz nodded and slipped his remote detonator into his jacket pocket. He tried to look relaxed and unconcerned as Vargas turned in and drove towards the gate.

A man with an AK-47 in his hands stepped out of the gate house.

"*Alto!*" he said and held up his left hand. Gadgets noticed there were two more men standing by the gate, casually pointing AK-47s at the truck. If this was merely the local security guards, they were mightily impressive. Gadgets had his Beretta 93-R ready in its shoulder holster. Its weight was reassuring. He could draw and fire it in less than a second, but he did not like the idea of a fire-fight while he was sitting on a bomb.

The guard walked to the driver's door and stared at Vargas suspiciously.

"Who are you? What are you doing here?"

Vargas smiled with the air of a man who is compelled to deal with idiots.

"I am Vargas, of course. I have brought the truck back from the American embassy because Werner said I should. Something has gone wrong with it. Martinez says it must be fixed."

The guard relaxed and nodded. Vargas had mentioned the right names. He had no particular reason to be suspicious. He waved his hand, and the other two guards opened the gate. Vargas put the truck in gear and drove smoothly toward the building. It was a large, single-story building with several large doors, big enough for large trucks to drive through. Four trucks identical to the one they had captured were lined up near the front wall. Two jeeps were parked nearby.

"Put it next to the other trucks," Schwarz said. Vargas nodded and parked the vehicle. No one seemed to be watching them as they stepped out of the truck. They strolled casually back toward the gate as if they did not have a care in the world. The guards might have been a little suspicious if they had seen them coming back so soon, but their attention had been diverted. Kissinger had pulled the station wagon up to the gate. As the guard stepped forward, Bolan and Manning suddenly opened fire with silenced 9 mm Heckler & Koch submachine guns. The guards collapsed to the ground as bursts of heavy, subsonic bullets struck them.

Schwarz and Vargas hurried through the gate and climbed into the station wagon. Kissinger had left the engine running. He turned the car and drove rapidly down the street.

"Stop here," Schwarz said after they had traveled about a thousand yards.

He took out his remote detonator, pulled out the telescoping antenna and pushed a button. A green light came on.

"I've put a five-minute delay in the firing circuit. That gives us a little more time to get clear," he explained.

He turned to Captain Vargas. "Would you like to do the honors, Captain?"

Vargas nodded and took the remote detonating device.

He pushed the firing button, and a red light came on.

"Firing command accepted. Fuse action underway. Let's get the hell out of here!" Schwarz said urgently.

The captain looked back at the building in the distance and smiled coldly. He did not like people who built bombs to kill civilians.

"*Adios,* go with God," he said.

EL VIEJO WAS SITTING at his desk, smiling as he studied the large map of La Paz on his office wall. The map was studded with colored pins and marked here and there with colored tape. It would have meant nothing to anyone who did not know his code, but to El Viejo it told everything, where the next riots would occur, where the bombs would explode, where various army and National Police units were stationed, and the immediate location of key players like the president of Bolivia and the American ambassador.

He was enjoying himself immensely. He could not remember when he had had so much fun. When he was young, he had been impressed by the generals in their brilliant uniforms. He would have loved to go to the army military academy and become an officer, but his father had been a poor farmer without money or influence. That morning, he had bought a general and two colonels. Now, he was coordinating his attacks. Before the sun set, he would destroy the U.S. embassy and probably overthrow the government of Bolivia. That was better than being a general.

He heard a soft knock on the door. It was probably his assistant, Roberto, with some fresh report, but he took no chances. He picked up his 9 mm mini-Uzi and aimed at the door.

Roberto walked into the room with a stack of papers in his hands.

"Good day, Roberto," El Viejo said politely. He set his Uzi on safe and put it back on his desk. "How are things going? You have the latest reports?"

He had been busy bribing generals and colonels. He needed to know if the situation had changed while he was occupied.

Roberto nodded. "Yes, most things are going well."

El Viejo had caught the word "most." Well, he had never thought that Operation Thunderbolt would go perfectly.

"What is the problem?"

"Something has apparently gone wrong with the attack on the American embassy. The American general was there with his key officers and the CIA chief. The truck bomb was in place. Our men were waiting to explode the bomb until the American ambassador returned from his meeting at the presidential palace. Then something went wrong with the bomb. It did not respond to some signal. Our group across the street from the embassy was investigating. They stopped communicating suddenly, and all attempts to contact them again have failed. I am not sure what it means. Perhaps something has just gone wrong with our communications equipment.''

El Viejo frowned. It did not seem likely that several pieces of electronic equipment had simply failed simultaneously. He did not believe in coincidences. This smelled like enemy action.

"Have the Americans seized the truck?" El Viejo asked.

Roberto hesitated.

"I do not believe so, but the truck drove away from the American embassy fifteen minutes ago. Where it went I do not know."

El Viejo reached for the telephone on his desk and dialed a number.

"Get me Martinez. Get him now!"

He waited tensely for a few seconds. His instincts told him that something was wrong. He was not sure what, but he had lived through thirty years of the cocaine wars by never ignoring a subconscious warning.

"Martinez, what is happening?" he snapped.

"Four more trucks are ready now. Four more are in preparation. They will be ready in two or three hours."

"What about the first truck? I hear that there is a problem."

"Werner reported that there was some problem with the fuse. The delivery team returned it about five minutes ago. I will have it checked and—''

Martinez suddenly stopped talking. He had not hung up. The line had gone dead.

El Viejo started to dial again, then he heard an appalling noise like an immense clap of thunder. The building shook as the tremendous roar was repeated again and again. He glanced out the window. A huge ball of fire was rising up into the sky. El Viejo knew what had happened. The bomb factory had been less than a mile away. Now he knew that it was gone.

Roberto stared out the window at a colossal column of black smoke spreading rapidly upward. "May God have mercy on their souls," he said piously.

El Viejo snarled. He did not think God had anything to do with it. It was the Americans! They might think they had defeated him, but they were wrong. He still had one trump card to play. He dialed another number.

"Get me General Morales immediately!"

CHAPTER TWENTY-TWO

The U.S. embassy, La Paz, Bolivia

The mood in the U.S. embassy was mildly hilarious. There was nothing like escaping a close brush with death to make fighting men happy. General Stuart was treating everyone to two beers in the embassy lounge and giving full credit for saving the embassy to the team from Stony Man. The hardened combat veterans on Stuart's staff loved blowing up the opposition with their own bomb. They no longer considered Bolan's team to be some kind of weird CIA paramilitary spooks. They were experts in special operations, and they were willing to accept Bolan and company as members of their exclusive fraternity.

McCarter was proclaiming that the enemy had been "hoist by his own petard," when Sergeant Johnson dashed into the room and headed straight for General Stuart.

"Sir, Captain Swenson is on the phone. She says there's something on TV you've got to see."

Stuart frowned. Messages like that usually meant trouble. There was a TV set in a corner of the lounge. The general turned it on and began to run rapidly through the channels. He stopped suddenly, and Bolan heard a familiar voice.

"This is Anne Bayne, World Wide News, in La Paz, Bolivia, with a breaking news story. In a startling move that escalates the rapidly developing crisis in Bolivia, dissident units of the Bolivian army have seized the presidential palace in Bolivia and are holding the president and several of his key cabinet officers hostage. A spokesman for the group that seized the palace say that they have acted out of the highest patriotic motives and to save the people of Bolivia from ruthless foreign domination. They haven't made any formal demands so far but say they plan to hold a news conference in the next few hours.

"There are unconfirmed rumors that the U.S. ambassador and several members of his staff were in the palace at the time of the coup and may also be hostages. In a related development, the minister of national defense has assumed control of the government. He urges the people to be calm and stay in their homes. He says that the armed forces will insure the safety of the republic. This is Anne Bayne in La Paz. Stay tuned to WWN for further developments."

The mood in the room changed instantly.

General Stuart snapped orders.

"Put everyone on maximum alert. If the ambassador's being held prisoner, we need a plan to rescue him. Let's look at alternate approaches. I want a plan for a Marine ground attack using all the resources we've got on the *Hornet*, including air cover by Hawker Harriers. Also, take a look at an air assault by the Rangers with helicopter landings directly on the palace grounds. See if it makes any sense to combine the two attacks. Let's get moving, gentlemen."

The bustle of activity swirled around Bolan. He did not intend to get involved, at least not yet. It was possible that a few good men could slip into the presidential palace and get the ambassador and the Bolivian president out. He needed to know more about the layout of the palace and how it was defended. He looked around the room. His team was sitting quietly. They saw no reason to panic. If the time came to take action, they would be ready.

Captain Vargas was standing at the bar.

"What do you think is going to happen?" Bolan asked.

Vargas frowned. "A bloody coup or a civil war unless we are lucky. We may seem like a comic opera country to you. We have had many bloodless coups, but when we fight, we fight seriously. When the army is divided or there are radical revolutionary groups, tens of thousands of people can be killed. I hope to God it can be prevented."

"Maybe we can prevent it," Bolan said. "Let's you and I do a little quiet planning. We have some superior night-vision equipment. If we can figure a way to make a clandestine entry after dark, there's a good chance we can get your president and our ambassador out. Can you get us a set of blueprints of the presidential palace?"

Vargas nodded. Anything was better than sitting around doing nothing while his country went to hell. A few men raiding the palace in the dark sounded crazy, but he had seen Striker and his team do some remarkable things. He would not bet a month's pay that they could not do it.

"At once, Striker. Is there anything else you need?"

"See if you can find out how many men seized the palace, how they're armed and how they're deployed."

"I can help you with that," Mary Swenson said. Bolan had not noticed her entering the room in the midst of the uproar. She was rather oddly dressed for an Army officer on duty. She was wearing a T-shirt and blue jeans, and a plastic identification badge that said she worked for World Wide News.

"I just got back from the presidential palace," she said. "I've got some videotapes I think you'll want to see. Come on, I have to brief the general."

Bolan followed her to a table where Stuart and several of his officers were pouring over a map of La Paz.

"Excuse me, General, I've got something I think you need to see," Swenson said.

Stuart raised one eyebrow when he saw how she was dressed, but he halted his meeting immediately.

"Gentlemen, this is Captain Swenson. She has some information for us."

Swenson slipped a videotape into the VCR and turned on the television set.

"General Stuart ordered me to keep an eye on Anne Bayne and keep her out of trouble. She got a tip that a major story was breaking at the presidential palace. Her cameraman was killed in a helicopter crash two days ago. I know how to operate a camcorder, so I changed into civilian clothes and went to the palace pretending to be her cameraman. I shot the tape that was broadcast a few minutes ago."

"That's fine, Captain, but we already saw your tape, and we're busy," the Marine Corps colonel said.

Swenson smiled. "No, you didn't, Colonel. You saw the edited version that WWN broadcast. I've got a lot more footage that shows where the rebels are digging in, where they have emplaced their antiaircraft guns, things like that. I thought that information might be useful in your planning."

The Marine Corps colonel's expression changed immediately.

"Damned right, Captain. We need to see it at once!"

She turned on the VCR. They saw the familiar scene of the front of the presidential palace, and Anne Bayne was talking to three men in uniform. The scene shifted as Swenson panned the camera.

"They didn't care about me. They saw the camera, and they wanted publicity. That's why they called Anne Bayne. I just tried to look like a stupid blond gringa who was shooting background footage. Some of it's not too exciting, but there—those are twin Oerlikon 20 mm automatic antiaircraft guns and some shoulder-fired, surface-to-air missiles, probably SA-7s. I think they're expecting a helicopter assault. There and there they are digging machine-gun emplacements and mortar pits. They'll provide interlocking fields of fire to defend the palace grounds. I saw no signs that they are emplacing land mines.

"There are some of the soldiers. Their uniforms and equipment indicate that they're regular Bolivian army infantrymen. Their shoulder patches indicate that they are part of the first division. Their morale seems good, and they're confident they can hold the palace."

The officers around the table were visibly impressed. Swenson had taped the scene with the eye of a trained soldier. This was just the kind of information they needed to plan an attack.

"How many of them do you think there are, Captain?" Stuart asked.

"I would estimate two to three hundred, General. From a few remarks I overheard, they expect to be reinforced sometime tomorrow."

The tape came to the end. The staff officers immediately rewound it and ran it again, studying every detail.

"That's damned good work, Captain. Where did you leave Anne Bayne?"

Swenson smiled. It was obvious that she was back in General Stuart's good graces.

"She's waiting across the plaza from the palace, sir.

The rebels told her they might hold a news conference fairly soon. She's waiting for it. Wild horses couldn't drag her away from a place when she thinks she can get a story.''

Stuart got to his feet.

"I'm going to try to get in touch with the minister of national defense and see if I can find out what the Bolivian government is going to do. Then I'll call Washington and see what they're willing to let us do. In the meantime, finish those attack plans and be prepared to give me your recommendations.''

Stuart left for the communications room. Captain Vargas returned with the plans of the presidential palace. He, Bolan and McCarter began to study them intently, looking for an approach that might make a covert entry possible. Swenson stayed with them and answered their questions when she could. Bolan could see one major gap in their information. They did not know where the hostages were located in the palace, whether they were being held in one place or scattered in small groups. The palace was a large building. It would be extremely difficult to search it without being detected by the rebel defenders. Vargas had been inside the palace several times. He could think of several possible places where the hostages might be held, but there was no way he could be sure.

General Stuart came back into the room. He did not look happy. The buzz of conversation stopped as everyone looked at him expectantly.

"I've talked to the minister of national defense. He doesn't want to say much on the phone. He's afraid the lines have been tapped. He's coming over to the embassy to meet with us here. I also talked to Washington on SAT-COM. They authorize us to use all necessary force to protect U.S. citizens and the embassy. At least for now, they won't authorize us to take any offensive actions or provide combat support to Bolivian forces. There are supposed to be some negotiations underway to free the president and our ambassador. If those fail, Washington may authorize us to assault the palace, so let's get those assault plans finished.''

He sat down at the table with his staff officers to look at their maps. Bolan, McCarter and Vargas continued to look at the palace plans. A helicopter landing looked like the best approach, but helicopters weren't quiet. The moment they got close to the roof, everyone in the building would know they were there. There had to be some other way that would preserve the element of surprise.

Sergeant Johnson walked over to their table.

"Excuse me, Captain Vargas, but there is a woman at the front entrance. She says she works for the Bolivian government and that you can vouch for her. She says her name is Lida Almagro."

"Mother of God! Lida Almagro," Vargas gasped. He was on his feet and out of the room in a flash.

"Who's Lida Almagro, his girlfriend?" Bolan asked.

"I don't think so. She's a little too old for Captain Vargas," Johnson said.

Swenson laughed so hard McCarter had to slap her on the back.

"She's not Vargas's girlfriend," she gasped. "She's his boss!"

Captain Vargas was back in a minute. He ushered a tall, gray-haired woman into the conference room. She peered at General Stuart through her steel-rimmed glasses.

"General Stuart? I am Lida Almagro, the minister of justice."

Stuart smiled politely. "I'm pleased to meet you, *senora*. Are you with the minister of national defense?"

"Unfortunately, no. He is not coming. He was killed half an hour ago. They put a bomb in his car. I am here in his place. Let us not waste time. I believe I am the highest ranking member of the Bolivian government in La Paz who is not dead or a prisoner. I have come to request your assistance to resolve this crisis."

"I'll do anything in my power to honor your request as long as it does not violate the orders of my government," Stuart said formally.

"That is understood, General. What I request is the use of some of your airplanes and helicopters to move units of the National Police to La Paz. I ask you to provide them with a fighter escort to protect them in case they are attacked. I can no longer be sure of the loyalty of our air force. I am not asking for any U.S. troops to take part in combat. I ask only that you provide the logistical support to move my men here."

Stuart nodded. "Nothing you request violates my orders, Madam Minister. We have C-130 transports and Black Hawk helicopters available. Marine Hawker Harriers will provide the escort. If you'll give me the details, I'll get my people started on it immediately."

Lida Almagro smiled coldly. "I have one other favor to ask, General, before you go to any great trouble. I must find out if I have any loyal men to move. I understand that you have satellite communications with the UMOPAR base at Chimore?"

"We should have. Striker, are your people with the Leopards monitoring their SATCOM?"

Bolan nodded. "They'll have the audible alarm on."

"Then I wish to speak to Colonel Suarez as soon as possible," Lida Almagro said.

They moved to the communications room, and Bolan

keyed the SATCOM. He waited thirty seconds and heard Rosario Balancanales's familiar voice.

"Pol, this is Striker. We have an urgent message for Colonel Suarez. Please ask him to get on the SATCOM as soon as possible."

"Roger, Striker. Wait one, I'm on the way."

Two minutes went by, then they heard Colonel Suarez's voice.

Lida Almagro took the microphone.

"Colonel, this is the minister of justice. Are you aware of the situation in La Paz?"

"Yes, Minister. I have seen the television reports. I assume they are true."

"Colonel, I am the acting head of the government. I remind you that, as an officer of the National Police, you report to me. I remind you that you have sworn an oath to defend the constitution of the republic and obey all lawful orders from your superiors."

"Minister, you do not have to remind me of these things. I am a man of honor. I have given my word. I will keep it. What are your orders?"

"The army will not move against the rebels. You must. Assemble your battalion. Bring it to La Paz. The Americans will provide planes to transport you. Retake the presidential palace. Kill or capture the traitors who have seized it. Do you understand?"

"Yes, Minister. I will carry out your orders to the letter. I will report to you as soon as I reach La Paz."

"God willing, I will see you here, Colonel, but I may not be alive when you get to La Paz. In that case, no one has the authority to countermand the orders I have just given you. You are to retake the palace. No matter what it costs, you must retake it."

CHAPTER TWENTY-THREE

La Paz, Bolivia

Captain Vargas was leading the attack as the Leopards moved slowly down the street toward the presidential palace. They were careful to leave no pockets of resistance behind them. Their progress was punctuated by the chatter of automatic rifles and the dull boom of hand grenades. Bolan would have liked for them to move faster, but he knew they were doing the best they could. Most of them had been in action against the *trafficantes'* gunmen in the Chapare, but they were not used to fighting in built-up city areas.

Mary Swenson was moving with the small command group, keeping General Stuart informed about the action as the Leopards' attack moved forward. Gary Manning and Gadgets Schwarz were moving with Bolan, their weapons ready. The Executioner suddenly heard shouts from the leading squad.

"*¡Carros blindado! ¡Carros blindado!*"

They were shouting, something about some kind of cars. For a second, Bolan did not understand. Then it hit him. Armored cars!

He looked quickly through his binoculars and found himself staring at a six wheeled armored car. He had seen one like that in Trinidad. He remembered what Vargas had called it. "It's an EE-9 armored car," he said. Gadgets Schwarz was pleased. "That's right, Striker," he said. "Made in Brazil, fifteen tons, one 90 mm cannon, two .30-caliber machine guns, one and a quarter inches of armor plate, and a crew of three."

Vargas was impressed. The American seemed to know everything.

Bolan scanned the area. There were at least four EE-9s moving toward them, as well as at least three other vehicles, all the same model. They were like the EE-9s but had larger, boxy hulls and no cannon. He pointed them out to Captain Vargas. "What are those?"

"EE-11 Urutus. They are the armored personnel carrier version of the EE-9. They mount no cannon, as you can see, but they have machine guns and can carry twelve infantrymen protected by armor." Bolan made a quick calculation, and he did not like the odds.

"Who do you think they are?"

"I do not think. I know! I recognize the markings. They are an army mechanized battalion from the first division at Viacha. But see that red diagonal stripe painted on their sides? That means they have gone over to the rebels. They are well-trained troops who are responsible for internal security in this area. They will almost certainly attack as soon as their force is assembled. The Leopards have no antiarmor weapons. Rifles and machine guns will not stop them. Unless you have some kind of antiarmor weapons, they will drive us back."

Bolan frowned. It was worse than Vargas thought. He had seen armor versus infantry before. Even the bravest men could succumb to what the Germans call "Panzer fever," the unreasoning fear of men attacked by armored cars who know that they have no weapons that can destroy them. Unless he could do something, it was likely that the Leopards would break and run. He pushed the button on his tactical radio and spoke quickly.

"Cowboy, this is Striker. Our leading elements have encountered armored fighting vehicles. Get the AT-4s up here immediately. Bring all of them. Striker over."

Kissinger had been monitoring the tactical frequency to follow the progress of the attack, and he replied instantly. "Roger, Striker. AT-4s on the way. Cowboy out."

It did not sound good. By modern standards, the EE-9s and EE-11s were obsolete, 1970s technology. A company of modern American main battle tanks would have destroyed them in ten minutes, but they had no tanks. They would have to depend on the AT-4s. They were the only real antiarmor weapons the team had.

Kissinger had moved fast and was passing out the AT-4s. Bolan laid four carefully against the side of the building. Captain Vargas stared at them, unimpressed. Their fiberglass-reinforced plastic launchers looked like three-foot-long sections of ugly, olive-drab pipe. Bolan had never seen one used in combat. He'd been told by the Rangers that they were wonderful, and he hoped to hell they were right.

He was about to find out the hard way. The late-morning quiet was suddenly broken by the rumble of engines. Vargas had been right. The rebels were coming. The rumble of the engines deepened as the attacking force moved out, the EE-9s leading, the EE-11s following about twenty yards behind. Bolan saw a bright yellow flash from the turret of the leading EE-9 as its gunner sent a 12-pound 90 mm high-explosive shell shrieking into the Leopards' position. The round struck the side of a building. Chunks of concrete flew and broken glass rained to the ground.

Bolan waited tensely, but there was no barrage. The rebel commander had only forty-four cannon rounds per vehicle. He was conserving his ammunition. The EE-9s were firing occasionally as they moved forward to cover their advance, but the serious shooting would come when they got in close.

The Executioner picked up an AT-4 and swung the weapon to his shoulder. It did not seem like much to stop a thirteen-ton armored fighting vehicle, but it was all he had. He pulled back the cocking lever on the top of the AT-4. He was ready to fire. The EE-9s were advancing in a loose line, about fifty yards apart. One of them was coming straight toward Bolan. It caused him concern, but it would give him a good shot. The AT-4 was not a guided weapon and had to be aimed like a rifle. It was up to Bolan to get a hit. Things would get very bad very rapidly if he missed.

Bolan placed his sights on the front of the EE-9, which was camouflaged in a mottled green and brown pattern. It looked ugly to him, but not half as ugly as the 90 mm cannon and machine gun protruding menacingly from the front of its turret. The machine gun suddenly emitted a series of rapid, yellow flashes. Bolan ducked as a burst of .30-caliber bullets struck the concrete a few feet in front of him. He did not think the EE-9's gunner had seen him. He was just firing on general principles to discourage anyone with antiarmor weapons.

He aimed again. The armored vehicles were coming on steadily. The EE-9's machine gun fired again. This time, the bullets were off to his left. Bolan kept his sights on the target. Few things were more difficult than restraining yourself from shooting back when fired upon. The temptation to fire was almost overwhelming. Every nerve in Bolan's body shrieked for him to pull the trigger, but the

EE-9s were at least two hundred yards away. In theory, the AT-4s could score at that range, but a hit was much more likely if he held his fire until the target was closer.

Two hundred yards, one hundred, the EE-9 was coming straight at him now. He did not have to lead the target. Steady, steady, now! Bolan squeezed the trigger and felt the launcher quiver as the AT-4 fired. There was no recoil. The 6.6 pound 84 mm High Explosive Anti Tank projectile shot toward the EE-9 at 985 feet per second. Bolan saw a bright yellow flash as it struck the armored vehicle just under its turret and detonated. Had it been an ordinary high-explosive projectile, it would have failed completely. However, the AT-4's HEAT round was designed to penetrate armor. The exploding warhead vaporized its metal liner and drove the jet of superheated metal forward. The blast penetrated the hardened steel armor and sprayed the interior of the EE-9 with white hot gas and molten metal. The ready rounds for the EE-9's 90 mm gun detonated in a shattering series of explosions. The armored car shuddered to a halt, spewing orange flames and dark black smoke.

Mary Swenson sprinted down the street followed by Sergeant Chavez, each of them carrying two more AT-4s. The captain's face was flushed with the excitement of being in her first battle.

"Kissinger says these are the last ones we've got. Better make them good."

Bolan heard the sound of diesel engines growing louder. He needed all the help he could get.

"Do you know how to use an AT-4, Sergeant?" he asked Chavez.

"I am sorry, Striker. I do not. We have no such weapons in the Leopards."

"I do. I've fired them at Fort Benning. Let me take a shot," Swenson said eagerly.

Bolan nodded. The more qualified AT-4 gunners, the better.

"Go ahead. Aim just below the turret," he said.

Swenson dashed to the other side of the street to get a better firing angle, followed by Chavez with the other AT-4s.

The Executioner grabbed another AT-4 and looked for a new target. Two EE-9s were advancing toward him, one staying a few yards back to cover the other. Bolan aimed carefully and squeezed the trigger. The 84 mm projectile struck and detonated near the driver's vision slit. For a few seconds, nothing seemed to happen. Then, the EE-9's hatches flew open, and the crew bailed out frantically. Smoke and flames began to pour from the open hatches.

The second EE-9 came straight for him. The gunner seemed to have spotted Bolan's position. He could see bright yellow flashes as a .30-caliber machine gun fired burst after burst. Chips of concrete flew as the bullets struck the corner of the building and ricocheted away. He was pinned down, but Swenson had a shot. She aimed carefully and fired. Her projectile struck the EE-9 just below the turret. Bolan heard her shout in triumph as the EE-9 was shattered by a series of internal explosions.

Swenson grabbed another AT-4 and took three steps into the street to engage another target. An EE-11 gunner saw her move and fired a burst from his .50-caliber machine gun. Three of the huge bullets struck her. She was wearing body armor, but it could not stop .50-caliber armor-piercing bullets. She fell and lay still in a pool of spreading blood. Sergeant Chavez raced toward her and tried to drag her back to cover. The EE-11 gunner cut him down with a long burst. He was dead before he hit the street.

Bolan snatched up another AT-4, aimed at the EE-11 and pulled the trigger. He saw a yellow flash as the projectile detonated and the armored vehicle started to burn. The crew bailed out, but a light machine gunner cut them down. Chavez had been a popular man.

The Stony Man warrior picked up an AT-4 and looked around. Another EE-9 was burning brightly to his left. Gary Manning had gotten a hit. Bolan stared down the street. It was no good. They had slowed down the armored cars, but they had not stopped them. There were just too many of them.

Bolan pushed the transmit button on his tactical radio.

"Eagle, this is Striker," he said urgently.

General Stuart was monitoring the frequency, trying to follow the progress of the attack. Bolan could hear his voice clearly over the sounds of battle.

"Striker, this is Eagle. I hear cannon fire. What is your situation?"

"Eagle, the rebels have launched a counterattack with armored cars. We're using AT-4s, but we aren't going to stop them. It's all over unless we get air support immediately. I say again, immediately!"

Stuart did not reply for a few seconds, and Bolan could almost hear him thinking. A 90 mm cannon shell slammed into a nearby building and exploded. The general had better not take too long making up his mind.

"Striker, I am not authorized to provide combat support to Bolivian forces. Confirm your position. You are about six blocks from the American embassy, and the armored cars are headed towards the embassy. I am authorized to use any force necessary to protect our embassy from attack. Does it appear to you that these armored cars intend to attack it?''

Bolan smiled grimly. Stuart was the kind of general he liked.

"Eagle, this is Striker. It's clear to me that they intend to attack and destroy the American embassy unless you stop them.''

"Roger, Striker. We can't have that. Stand by for fast movers inbound your area. Bayonet Leader, this is Eagle. Your target is armored vehicles moving on the American embassy. You are authorized to attack with all weapons. Take them out, Bayonet!''

"Roger, Eagle. Your message understood. Attacking now.''

Bolan waited tensely for a minute or two. He hoped Bayonet Leader, whoever he was, would not waste time getting there. The armored cars were getting closer, and most of their AT-4s had been fired. Then he heard the rumbling whine of jet engines growing closer.

"Striker, this is Bayonet Leader. I'm approaching your position. Confirm that all armored vehicles in the area are hostile.''

"Bayonet Leader, confirmed all armored vehicles in the area are hostile.''

"Roger, Striker. Keep your heads down. Bayonet Flight attacking now!''

The sound of jet engines rose to a roar. Bolan looked up at the astounding sight of a camouflaged Marine Corps Hawker Harrier flying a hundred feet above the street, barely clearing the roofs of the buildings as it came. Something streaked from under one of the Harrier's wings and shot toward the leading EE-9. The missile struck and detonated. The turret of the armored car blew off, and the hull exploded in a ball of orange flame. Bolan could see flickering yellow flashes around the muzzle of the Harrier's 30 mm cannon as it put a burst into another EE-9.

The Harrier flashed by and pulled up. The Leopards stared up in awe and cheered as a second jet flew down the street, cannon blazing and antiarmor rockets flashing out from under its wings. Another EE-9 began to burn and explode. An EE-11 was stopped fifty yards away. Bursts of bullets from one of the Leopards' .223 light machine guns were beating on its armor, but they glanced off harmlessly. Bolan placed the sights of the AT-4 on its side and pulled back the cocking lever. Before he could fire, a number of objects arced from the EE-11 and struck the ground around it. Gray-white smoke began to billow up. The armored vehicle was firing its smoke grenade launchers, laying down a smoke screen to cover its withdrawal. The rebels were pulling out. Bolan no longer had a target, but he did not care. He had seen enough EE-9s and EE-11s to last him a lifetime.

He watched as two more Harriers attacked and turned the armored cars' retreat into a rout. He pushed the button on his tactical radio.

"Eagle, this is Striker. Bayonet Flight's attack completely successful. We're resuming our attack on the palace. Striker out."

The attack moved steadily forward past the burned-out armored cars. The fight had gone out of the survivors of the rebel mechanized battalion. They were throwing down their weapons and surrendering to the advancing Leopards. The command group turned a corner, and Bolan could see the plaza and the presidential palace looming ahead. He was surprised to hear the firing slack off and almost stop. He could hear the Leopards' squad leaders shouting, "Cease-fire! Cease-fire!" What the hell was going on? This was no time to slow down the attack. They should finish the enemy off before they could reorganize.

A Leopard corporal dashed up to Vargas and saluted.

"Captain," he gasped, "they have stopped firing. An officer has come out of the palace carrying a white flag. He asks to speak to our commander. It looks as if they are surrendering. Sergeant Ortiz asks for your orders."

It looked to Vargas as if he had just won his first battle. It would not hurt his chances for promotion if he had just led the men who rescued the president of Bolivia.

"Tell Sergeant Ortiz I want this officer brought to me. Tell him to remain alert in case this is some kind of trick."

The corporal was back in a minute escorting a man in the uniform of a Bolivian army lieutenant. He was wearing a red armband and carrying an improvised white flag in one hand. He looked at Vargas coldly. He did not salute him.

"You are the commander of the attack force?"

"I am Captain Vargas of the National Police. Do you wish terms for your surrender? I can promise only that you will not be killed and that you will receive a fair trial for treason."

The lieutenant sneered.

"It is we who will give you terms, Captain Vargas. If you do not cease fire and stop your advance on the palace, we will execute our hostages. We will begin with the American ambassador. If you continue your advance or make another attack, we will kill the president and all the other hostages. Take these words to your American masters, Leopard."

The American embassy, La Paz, Bolivia

THE GLOOM IN THE EMBASSY conference was thick enough to cut with a knife. The rebels in the presidential palace were outnumbered and surrounded, but they held the trump cards. Lida Almagro finally broke the silence.

"What is your opinion, Colonel Suarez? If I order you to resume the attack, can you take the palace?"

"Yes, Minister. I will suffer heavy casualties, but I will take it in thirty minutes. However, if the rebels are serious, there is no way I can prevent them from killing the president and the other hostages."

Almagro sighed. "Then there is no other choice. The government must negotiate."

Stuart frowned. "With all due respect, madam, I would advise you not to do that. Negotiating deals with terrorists is always bad policy."

"I am aware of that, General, but what other choice is there? If there was a reasonable chance of success, I would order Colonel Suarez to attack again. But he says there is not. If the president is murdered, we will have civil war. Hundreds of thousands of people will die. We cannot allow that. We must negotiate."

Mack Bolan and David McCarter had been listening quietly to the discussion.

"I think there is an alternative. The SAS has one of the best hostage-rescue records in the world. Do you remember how they retook the Iranian embassy in London a few years back? Captain Green was a member of that SAS raiding party. He's an expert in this kind of operation. He has a plan I think you should hear," Bolan said.

Almagro was impressed. Like most people involved in antiterrorist activities, she was familiar with the SAS. Their raid on the Iranian embassy was universally regarded as a textbook example of hostage rescue.

"We would be pleased to hear your plan, Captain," she said.

"Thank you, Madam Minister," McCarter said formally. "In many ways, this situation is like that of the Iranian embassy rescue. The presidential palace is held by terrorists who threaten to execute their hostages if any moves are made against them. To prevent this, we must introduce a small but effective team into the palace without alerting the rebels. This team will kill the terrorists guarding the hostages and safeguard them until Colonel Suarez and his Leopards have recaptured it. I must emphasize that the rescue team must act ruthlessly wherever that is necessary. We will not issue warnings. We will not attempt to arrest the terrorists. We shall simply kill them if they offer the slightest resistance. If this plan is acceptable, I recommend that we go in shortly before dawn and that Colonel Suarez attacks as soon as we have rescued the hostages."

General Stuart had not missed the word "we" in McCarter's plan.

"I gather you are suggesting that you lead the assault team?"

"I rather thought Striker and I should do that, General. We do have a certain amount of experience in these affairs."

"That's a brilliant plan, Green," Stuart said. "I see only one small problem. How do you get your team inside the palace without being detected?"

"I've thought of that, General. Here are the construction plans for the palace. Note that the roof is large and basically flat. We have aircraft and HALO equipment available. We will use them."

General Stuart laughed. "By God, Green, I like your

style. You go in without knocking, as we say in the Rangers. All right, it's a go if the minister agrees.''

Everyone looked at Almagro. She was thinking hard. She was not sure she understood exactly what HALO meant, but she knew General Stuart was an expert in these matters. If he approved the Briton's plan, it had to be good.

''Very well, gentlemen, I approve your plan. I authorize any actions you must take. Go with God.''

CHAPTER TWENTY-FOUR

La Paz, Bolivia

The big Air Force Lockheed C-130H transport climbed steadily upward through the dark. Mack Bolan sat in one of the cramped nylon web seats in the troop compartment and worried. There was really nothing else for him to do until they got to the target. He was strapped snugly but uncomfortably into his web equipment and his parachute harness. He had put on his equipment half an hour before. His legs were numb, and his back was aching and throbbing from the constriction of his harness and his seat. Bolan liked C-130s. They were strong, reliable aircraft that always got you there. For all their strong points, though, they had obviously not been designed for passenger comfort.

The C-130 was one of the new H models, specially designed and equipped to support American special operations missions. The plane and its crew were from the Air Force's 8th Special Operations wing. Bolan had worked with them before. He knew they were some of the best aircrews in the business, but this jump was going to be difficult at best. Jumping into the heart of a large city at night was not a standard-operating procedure.

He did not have time to worry about it. They had taken

off from the international airport and would be over the target as soon as they reached thirty thousand feet. Sergeant Garcia, the U.S. Air Force jump master, suddenly appeared, moving quietly through the dimly lighted compartment. He looked at Bolan for a second to be sure he had the right man. In the dark, Bolan looked like all the other members of the team in their dull black, nonreflective uniforms, Kevlar helmets and combat gear. None of them were wearing anything shiny or reflective. They were not going to make things easier for enemy snipers.

"Mr. Belasko?" Garcia inquired. Bolan nodded. "Captain Lee says to tell you we are on final approach for the drop zone. Course and location are confirmed by the inertial navigation system and satellite global position system."

Bolan nodded. He told himself to settle down and relax, but that was not easy to do. A high-altitude, low-opening parachute jump was not the safest thing in the world. They had all done it before, but they had never jumped into the center of a city, which worried Bolan. He knew that there are no unimportant details in a HALO jump. Small mistakes could kill you.

The steady whine of the C-130H's four turboprop engines changed as the pilot throttled back and leveled off. Sergeant Garcia came slowly down the aisle, breathing from the oxygen bottle on his chest.

"Jump party get ready!" Garcia's voice rang through the troop compartment, loud and clear over the whine of the C-130H's engines. The assault team stared at Garcia intently. He gestured upward with both hands.

"Jump party! Stand...up!"

The six members of the assault team heaved themselves to their feet, each man fighting the drag of 120 pounds of parachutes, weapons and combat equipment. Bolan could feel the shoulder straps of his parachute harness cutting deeper into his shoulders.

"Check equipment. Prepare for troop compartment depressurization!" Garcia shouted.

Quickly, Bolan checked Gary Manning's equipment, and Manning checked his. Now for the critical step. Everyone in the troop compartment had to go on oxygen. The big C-130H had been climbing steadily since it left the La Paz international airport. It was currently at thirty thousand feet. The C-130H's aft compartment had to be depressurized now. The HALO jump required opening the tail door. If the pressure inside the troop compartment did not match that of the thin outside air, a hurricane of air would blast through the compartment the instant the door was opened. That meant Bolan and the rest of the jumpers had to start to breathe oxygen from the two individual bailout bottles strapped to their harnesses before the door was opened. Each bottle could supply thirty minutes of oxygen. The bailout bottles and their oxygen masks would keep them alive until they were below ten thousand feet.

The four-minute warning light was on. They were all breathing from their bailout bottles now. Garcia gave each man a final equipment check. He looked closely to see that everyone's heads and faces were covered by their jump helmets and oxygen masks. Their boots, gloves and insulated jumpsuits protected the rest of their bodies. It was sixty degrees below zero outside, and the air would be howling past the C-130H's fuselage at 130 knots when they jumped. It was going to be like stepping into an ice-cold hurricane. Any unprotected skin meant instant frostbite. Bolan and Manning checked each other's equipment one last time and gave each other the thumbs-up ready signal. Garcia nodded and pointed toward the tail door.

Slowly, careful not to tangle their equipment, the assault team moved toward the C-130H's tail door in a double line. Bolan and Manning first, then Carl Lyons and T. J. Hawkins. Gadgets Schwarz and David McCarter brought up the rear. Bolan would jump first. He would be the jump leader, the low man. The team would jump at five-second intervals. McCarter would jump last, the high man.

Two-minute warning. Bolan and Manning stood at the end of the cargo compartment facing the C-130's tail door. When the door opened, there would be nothing below them for thirty thousand feet but dark night air. The C-130's pilot was waiting until the last minute to open the door. Garcia signaled for the final oxygen check. Red warning lights came on, and Bolan heard the high-pitched whine of hydraulic motors as the C-130H's tail door was lowered and locked open in the horizontal position. Instantly, icy outside air rushed into the troop compartment. Bolan stared out at the amazing scene below. The lights of La Paz stretched like a vast field of jewels below him.

One-minute warning! Bolan looked back and made a thumbs-up gesture to the team, which was returned. None of them was having breathing problems or trouble with their other equipment. They were all ready to go. The thirty-second warning light came on, and there was a sudden change in the roar of the four engines as the pilot throttled them back. He was holding the C-130H as close to its stalling speed as he could in order to reduce the strength of the airflow around the big plane's fuselage. The aircraft began to shake and vibrate as its speed dropped to within a few knots of stalling. Satisfied, the pilot pushed the button. The ten-second warning light came on.

"Stand by!" Garcia shouted. That order was the last warning before the jump. Bolan felt a quick surge of adrenaline. There was nothing left for him to do now but go through the door.

Suddenly, the "go" light went on.

Bolan heard Garcia shout, "Go!..Go!..Go!" Bolan took two long strides along the ramp and dived out the open door into the darkness. Instantly, he was in free-fall. The slipstream buffeted and spun his body, turning him over and over. Looking back, he could see the moonlight reflected from the big wings and fuselage of the C-130H. The whine of its engines faded as it flew away and vanished into the dark. Bolan used his arms and legs to stop his spinning and turn his body to a facedown position.

He was falling faster and faster toward the great glowing bowl of lights below. The only sounds were the sighing of the air as it rushed past him and the rasping noise of his own breathing inside his oxygen mask. He looked down. All he could see was the sea of lights below. The scene did not seem to change. Bolan knew he was falling several hundred feet each second toward the center of the city, but he seemed to be hanging motionless in space. Now it was time to think like an assault team commander. McCarter should have jumped and cleared the aircraft by now. He should be above and behind the rest of the team.

"High man, give me a count," Bolan said. The sound of his voice activated the microphone on his throat, and the low-probability-of-intercept radio transmitted his message.

"I see five, Leader," McCarter reported. The Briton could see the entire team clearly, so they had to be close together. They were all falling through space toward the target now. Bolan looked down again. He no longer seemed to be suspended motionless in space. He was getting closer and closer to the lights below. La Paz was spread out below him.

He could identify the individual streets and see the illuminated plaza that marked the location of the presidential palace. He checked his altimeter—eight thousand feet. Now, it was time to concentrate on his landing. He was a bit to the left of the palace, but the special rectangular, MT1-XX ram-air canopy parachutes could be flown like hang gliders, allowing them to come down at angles as great as forty-five degrees. With any luck, the entire team should be able to come down on the palace roof.

He checked his altimeter again—three thousand feet. He kept his eye on his altimeter dial and grasped the rip cord's D-ring. He was counting to himself without thinking as he looked quickly to the left and right. All clear. Three! Two! One! Bolan pulled his rip cord. His pilot chute deployed, pulling his special high-performance, ram-air canopy parachute out of its pack and into the air. The canopy blossomed, and he felt a bone-jarring jolt as it filled with air and suddenly slowed his fall. He slipped his hands into his steering loops, ready to maneuver if he had to. A collision with another member of the team could ruin his landing. If it collapsed Bolan's canopy, it might ruin him.

"High man, give me a check," the Executioner said.

"Roger, Leader. All chutes are open. I have you in sight," McCarter responded quickly. Bolan felt a surge of relief. Now, it was time to concentrate on his landing.

He pulled on his parachute's steering loops and began to move left, toward the center of the palace roof. He had to make a good parachute landing fall now. Long ago, in jump school, his instructors had drilled it into him that no operational jump was worth a damn without a good PLF. The roof of the palace was getting closer and closer.

Now he was almost on top of the roof. He pulled on

the steering loops and went to full brake. His forward motion stopped immediately, and he went straight down.

He saw a sudden flash of movement below him. Someone was standing on the palace roof. Bolan pulled hard on his steering loops and slanted straight for the man, aiming his booted feet straight for the middle of the guy's back.

Bolan felt a jolt through every bone in his body as both feet struck with all his weight and the velocity of his fall behind him. The man went down as if he had been struck by a sledgehammer. The Executioner rolled and reached for the black nylon weapons case under his left arm, unsnapped it and pulled out his silenced 9 mm Heckler & Koch MP-5, submachine gun. There was a round in the chamber, and a full 30-round magazine was inserted in the receiver. Bolan flicked the MP-5's selector switch to automatic. Now he was ready to fight if necessary. He stayed prone just in case someone had heard his landing.

Someone had. He saw a figure silhouetted against the glow of the city's lights and the outline of the automatic weapon in his hands. Bolan did not hesitate. One warning shout and the plan was ruined. He centered his sights on the middle of the dark figure and pulled the trigger. Six heavy subsonic 9 mm bullets struck the gunner, punching him to the rooftop.

Bolan waited a second, then slipped out of his parachute harness.

He heard a soft sighing noise, and Manning came floating down from the sky, followed by Hawkins. Lyons landed hard and rolled, but he was on his feet instantly. Schwarz touched down, then McCarter. Bolan heard the soft sigh of parachute canopies collapsing. He looked at his watch. It would be dawn soon. Time to get going.

He could see a door to his left that had to lead down

into the main building. He beckoned to Schwarz and pointed to the door. The electronics expert moved forward and checked the door carefully, then gave Bolan a thumbs-up. The door was unlocked, and it was not alarmed. The Executioner motioned Manning to cover him and carefully opened the door. A ladder led down into what looked like an attic. There were boxes and crates here and there but no sign of a guard.

Bolan went quietly down the ladder. There was a dim light over a closed door that looked promising. He motioned to Manning to bring the team down as he moved to the door. It was unlocked, but Bolan knew it might be wired with an alarm. He waited until Schwarz checked it out, then slowly slipped it open a little and peered through the crack. He was looking down a long dimly lighted hallway. His eye caught a flicker of motion down the hall and froze.

Halfway down the hall, two men were standing in front of closed double doors. They were not wearing uniforms, but they were wearing red armbands and carried AK-47s. Bolan mentally checked the photographs that Vargas had shown him. This was it. The hallway was too long, and there was no cover. A close approach was impractical.

He signaled to Manning to come forward, and the big Canadian nodded. Bolan pointed to the left. Manning would take the guard on the left, and he would take the one on the right. They would fire together on the count of three. The Executioner eased the door open and slipped silently into the hall. Manning followed. Both were armed with silenced 9 mm Heckler & Koch MP-5 submachine guns.

Bolan placed his sights on the chest of the guard to the right and slipped his weapon's selector switch to full automatic. Manning nodded. He was ready. Bolan softly counted, "One, two, three!" and squeezed his trigger. The MP-5 vibrated gently and hissed softly as the submachine gun's sound suppressor absorbed and dissipated the sounds of the shots. Six heavy subsonic 9 mm bullets drilled into the guard's chest, and he went down. Manning's target was hit and slumped to the floor.

They waited tensely, but there was no reaction. No one behind the double doors had heard the quick, deadly attack. The two men moved silently down the hall. Gadgets Schwarz and McCarter joined them, while Lyons guarded the hall behind them. Hawkins moved up carrying a .223 SAW light machine gun. Bolan motioned to him to cover the doors at the far end of the hall. The SAW was not a silenced weapon, but Hawkins had loaded it with a 200-round belt in its plastic carrier. He was an expert with the weapon. If anyone attempted to move down the hall, he would make life extremely unpleasant for him.

Gadgets Schwarz placed a small, electronically amplified microphone against the door and listened intently. He frowned, shifted his microphone and listened again. Bolan waited tensely. If something was wrong, if the hostages had been moved, the assault team was in a lot of trouble. Schwarz looked at Bolan and opened and closed the fingers of his left hand rapidly seven or eight times. Gadgets thought there were thirty-five to forty people behind the doors. Then he held up five fingers and shrugged his shoulders. Bolan understood. Schwarz thought there might be four or five guards inside.

Bolan was satisfied that the hostages had to still be inside. All right, as General Stuart had said, it was time to go in without knocking. Bolan pointed to the lights. Schwarz took an odd-looking cylindrical device out of his pack and connected it to a wall socket. He looked at Manning and McCarter and touched one of the flash-stun hand grenades on his web harness. The two men nodded and pulled the grenades from their web belts. Bolan slipped a fresh 30-round magazine into his Heckler & Koch MP-5. He felt the adrenaline start to flow in the normal reaction most men felt when they were about to go in to kill or be killed.

Bolan activated his night-vision goggles, as did the rest of the team. Everyone was ready. Bolan brought his left hand up and then sharply down. Gripping his MP-5, he aimed at the center of the doors. Schwarz counted silently to five and pushed the button. The round, black cylinder made a sudden crackling noise. An immensely powerful electromagnetic pulse shot into the building's electrical system. Huge high-voltage surges flowed through the wiring. Fuses blew and wires burned out. The electrical system failed, and the palace was plunged into darkness.

Manning threw the doors open. He and McCarter lobbed their grenades inside and ducked back as the big Canadian slammed the door. Bolan saw a series of blinding flashes around the edges of the threshold and heard an incredibly loud series of explosions. The grenades were designed to be nonlethal, but the effects of the deafening blasts and eye-searing flashes inside the big room had to be terrible. Bolan heard shrieks and screams of panic. He looked at Manning and shouted, "Now!"

The Phoenix Force commando threw the doors open again. Bolan took two long, lunging steps into the room, keeping the metal buttstock pressed firmly against his shoulder, ready to fire. The room had no windows. Bolan's night-vision goggles showed him a scene of mass confusion as the people inside surged back and forth, slamming into one another and trampling those who had been knocked down as they tried desperately to escape.

Someone fired at the door from Bolan's left. His night-vision goggles showed the automatic weapon's muzzle-flash as a bright oval of light. The Executioner pivoted smoothly from the waist. He saw the shape of a man with a submachine gun and fired a fast burst the instant his sights were on him. A burst struck the gunner, and he went down hard.

"Behind you, Striker," McCarter shouted. Bolan threw himself down and rolled. A long, ripping burst of sub-machine-gun fire tore through the space where he had previously been. He twisted to try to bring his sights on target. Before he could fire, he saw the man who had been behind him stagger and fall as McCarter drilled him with subsonic 9 mm bullets. Bolan started to rise, but a screaming woman slammed into the warrior and fell on top of him, her arms and legs flailing madly. He threw her off with all his strength. He had no time to be gentle.

The room suddenly seemed to glow with light. Bolan heard the easily identifiable boom of a 12-gauge shotgun as someone fired three fast rounds at the door. He heard McCarter swear, and turned toward the shotgun's muzzle-flash. He caught a blur of movement as the shotgunner dived for the floor. The Executioner aimed just in front of the man and pulled the MP-5's trigger, letting the man fall into the burst. He hit the floor, and the shotgun slipped from his hands as he lay still.

There was a sudden silence, broken only by the moans and curses of the hostages as they tried to escape the hellish darkness that entrapped them.

Bolan filled his lungs and shouted with the command voice that dated back to his Army days.

"Be quiet! This is a United States hostage rescue team. Be quiet and stay in one placc. Wait for instructions before you move. Follow our orders, and you'll be all right."

Dim emergency lights suddenly flickered on. Bolan found himself looking at thirty dazed and panicked men and women, who stared at him in horror. With his night-vision goggles covering his face and his black raid suit, he was not a reassuring sight. A tall, distinguished-looking man in a blood-spattered, three-piece suit moved toward Bolan. The Executioner recognized him from photographs he had seen. He was the U.S. ambassador.

"Please, what's happening? We were told there would be no violence if we cooperated. They said no one would be hurt," he said in a trembling voice.

Bolan figured the ambassador had been too close to a grenade.

"Are you wounded?" Bolan asked.

The ambassador looked at his bloody hands.

"No, this is Betty Chandler's blood. She was my assistant press secretary. The lights went out and somebody shot her. She died in my arms."

He stared blankly at Bolan, his eyes running over his raid suit and the submachine gun in his hands.

"Who are you? Why was there so much shooting? Why did you kill the guards? They seemed like reasonable men. All they wanted to do was negotiate."

Bolan stared coldly at the ambassador. He refrained from pointing out that the guard's version of negotiations had been a burst of 9 mm bullets through Betty Chandler's head.

"This is an American hostage rescue team. We shot the guards to keep them from killing you. Take it easy and we'll get you out of here soon."

"Time to get going, Striker," McCarter said. "The sun is starting to come up."

"On the way." He and McCarter moved back toward the door.

"What's the matter with the ambassador? He seems to be on their side?" Bolan asked.

"It's the Helsinki syndrome, Striker. We've encountered it before in the SAS. When hostages are totally dependent on their captors and do not know whether they'll live or die, they begin to identify with the terrorists. They start to think that they're their friends, and their rescuers are their enemies. Fortunately, it wears off rather quickly. He will probably thank you tomorrow."

Bolan shook his head. He had no more time to ponder it. He heard the sudden snarling crack of a .223-caliber weapon as Hawkins fired a burst from his SAW. He looked cautiously down the hall. Two bodies were sprawled near the far doors.

"Somebody came to investigate the noise," Schwarz explained quickly. "T.J. took care of them, but there'll be more."

Gadgets was right. Time to get the Leopards' attack under way.

"Gary and I will take the roof. You hold the fort, David."

McCarter nodded. The hallway was not much of a fort, but he would hold it.

Bolan and Manning returned rapidly to the roof. Dawn was breaking. La Paz was a beautiful sight as the first rays of sunlight illuminated the taller buildings and the mountains surrounding the city. Manning slipped his Heckler & Koch PSG-1 sniper's rifle out of its container, checked the telescopic sight and moved to the edge of the roof. Mack Bolan removed his .308 Remington 700-P from its protective case and pulled a flare gun from a pouch on his belt. He laid out three flares, then loaded and fired them in rapid succession. The flares arched upward and burst brightly in the dawn sky—red, yellow, red, the attack signal.

Hundreds of small bright lights began to flicker and flash around the edges of the plaza as the Leopards opened fire. For a few seconds, the defenders were stunned. Then they manned their guns and fired bursts of rifle and machine-gun fire toward Colonel Suarez's advancing men.

Bolan joined Manning at the edge of the roof. They were above it all with a superb view of the battle. The Executioner dropped into his firing position as the noise of the battle swelled up from below. He smiled grimly as he swung the cross hairs of his scope on a rebel machine-gun emplacement. It was ironic to think that La Paz meant the city of peace. He did not have time to worry about that. His sights were on target, and he was concentrating solely on his shooting.

He squeezed the trigger, and the Remington bucked and roared. The machine gunner fell over his weapon. Bolan worked his bolt and fired again. A second man went down, sprawled over the sandbags of the emplacement. The rest of the crew broke and ran for the palace. The Stony Man commando let them go and aimed at a second machine-gun crew. He killed the gunner with his first shot, and the gun fell silent as the crew abandoned the weapon. He could hear Manning firing steadily, and he scored with every shot.

The rebels had positioned their weapons carefully. The emplacement provided excellent cover against fire from the front and the sides, but the men who planned the sites had never imagined that they would be attacked from above and behind. It was a fatal error. Bolan and Manning were superb riflemen, firing with the cool, professional detachment of master snipers. Man after man went down as their rifles roared repeatedly. Panic spread through the rebel force as death struck from behind, and their automatic weapons fell silent. Bolan could see men throwing down their weapons and raising their hands as the Leopards overran the defenders' positions.

A wave of Leopards reached the palace's huge front door. Some of the rebels still fought back. Bolan heard the snarling chaos of dozens of automatic rifles exchanging fire at point-blank range and the dull boom of 40 mm grenades as the Leopards blasted the defenders with their M-203 grenade launchers. Bolan heard a hoarse, wordless cheer as the Leopards poured into the palace.

Time to check on things below. He raced toward the room that held the hostages. As he opened the door to the hallway he heard the crackling snarl of Hawkins's SAW and the steady boom of Lyons's shotgun as they fired down the hall. McCarter was quieter but no less effective. He had set his silenced MP-5 for semiautomatic fire and was sending shot after precisely aimed shot down the hallway. A dozen bodies were sprawled on the hallway floor.

The firing suddenly stopped. There was no one left to shoot. He heard shouts from behind the far doors, then a man in a leopard-spotted uniform slipped through the doors, followed by others.

"Hold your fire, Striker," Colonel Suarez shouted.

More and more Leopards moved forward. Colonel Suarez came rapidly down the hall and entered the big room where the hostages had been held. Bolan followed. Suarez stopped in front of a stocky man with iron gray hair, snapped to attention and saluted perfectly.

"Mr. President, I am Colonel Suarez of the National Police. I have the honor to report that we have retaken the palace. You are free, and constitutional government is restored. I await your orders. God save the republic!"

The president embraced Colonel Suarez as all the Bolivians cheered proudly.

CHAPTER TWENTY-FIVE

The American embassy, La Paz

The late-afternoon sun was slanting down across La Paz, bathing the white buildings in pale gold light. General Stuart looked up and smiled as Mack Bolan entered his office.

"That was damned good work at the palace this morning, Striker. Damned good! The president is going to give you a high-level Bolivian medal. He says he never saw a prettier sight than you and your team."

"It did go well. Suarez and his Leopards did very well, too. I'm sorry about Mary Swenson, though."

Stuart's smile faded.

"I am, too. I knew her all her life. She came from an Army family. Her father was my sergeant major when I commanded the 2nd Ranger battalion. All she ever wanted was to be a soldier. I'm putting her in for the Silver Star. Maybe that will make her family feel better."

Stuart paused for a second and stared out the window.

"I asked to see you to talk about what we do next. The CIA is promising us the latest satellite data sometime today. I want to use it to plan some raids on the drug factories. If Washington will let me use the Rangers and the Marines, fine. If not, I'm going to meet with the president and the ambassador in a few minutes. I'll recommend that Colonel Suarez and the Leopards go back to Trinidad and conduct the raids. I'd like for you and your team to go with them if that's all right with you.''

Bolan nodded. Stuart's plan seemed to make good sense.

The colonel's phone rang.

"All right, I'm off to the meeting. It should take only a few minutes. Why don't you wait for me?''

Bolan agreed. He sat and studied the map on the wall. A helicopter assault seemed like the best plan. If he could use a company of Black Hawks, they could lift about 220 Leopards. They should be able to overwhelm any guard force at the drug factories. He was busy calculating flight times and distances when Stuart came back.

Bolan was startled. Stuart's appearance had changed. He looked stunned, as if he could not believe what was happening.

"Something wrong?'' Bolan asked.

"You aren't going to believe this, but we've had it. It's all over, Striker. The whole goddamned operation's down the drain.''

"What's wrong?''

"The president says he can't risk civil war destroying Bolivia. He's asked Washington to cancel Blast Furnace and get all U.S. military personnel out of Bolivia within forty-eight hours. All operations have been canceled. The president is going on TV to pledge a UN supervised election in six months. The rebels have agreed to a cease-fire. A UN peacekeeping force is coming in to keep things quiet. It's a screaming disaster. The *trafficantes* will run rings around a UN force. They might as well make co-caine-production legal.''

"What does Washington say?''

"It's not official yet, but the ambassador says he hears that our government will go along with it. You might as well pack your bags. It's all over. We're going home."

La Paz, Bolivia

EL VIEJO SAT IN HIS OFFICE and seethed. He should have been happy, but he was not. A dozen important men in the cartel had called to congratulate him on the success of his brilliant plan. It was true that he had succeeded. The threat of civil war had been enough to force the government to ask the American military to leave, but El Viejo felt he had suffered a personal defeat. His bomb assembly team had been destroyed. The seizure of the presidential palace had gone well, but the Americans had stormed the palace and rescued his hostages. He thought he knew who was responsible, and his personal honor demanded revenge.

The phone rang. Roberto answered it and handed it to him.

"It is El Verde for you."

El Viejo smiled as he took the phone. El Verde had cost him three million dollars over the past five years, but he was worth it. His information was always accurate.

"I have the information you wanted. The man who's leading the special American team is Mike Belasko. The other one is Fred Byrnes. My contacts confirm that he's the head of CIA operations in Bolivia. They're both in the American embassy at the moment."

El Viejo smiled. Your information is excellent, as always. Is there anything else you wish to say?"

"Just goodbye. I'm leaving the country tonight. The CIA investigations of American personnel in Bolivia are getting a little too close for comfort. So long, it's been a pleasure doing business with you.''

"One moment. I want those two men killed immediately."

"Good luck. There are Marines all around the embassy, and security is tight. Really tight. It's going to be hard for your people to get in."

"But you are already inside the embassy, my friend. How would you like to kill these two men for me?"

There was a long pause. El Verde was thinking hard.

"I'd like to oblige, but the risk would be very high. I'm afraid I'll have to say no."

"Would two million dollars deposited to your Cayman Islands bank account change your mind?"

El Verde laughed softly. "You do know how to make offers I can't refuse. Consider it done."

The American embassy, La Paz

MACK BOLAN WAS SITTING in the small room he had been assigned, cleaning and checking his weapons. His Beretta 93-R was not made of stainless steel. It required careful cleaning and oiling to prevent rust in the hot humid Bolivian climate. Someone knocked on the door, and Bolan's hand automatically went to the grip of his .44 Magnum Desert Eagle.

"Who's there?" he called.

"Fred Byrnes. I've just been over to our La Paz office. I've got some information I want to talk to you about."

"Come in, Fred, but I don't know what good talking is going to do. You've heard the word. The politicians have pulled the plug. All American military personnel have been ordered out of Bolivia."

"Yeah, I heard. Ain't it a bitch? But you aren't American military personnel. Neither am I. Just suppose we—"

Another knock sounded at Bolan's door.

"Who's there?" he asked.

"Frank Latimer, the DEA special agent in charge in Trinidad. You remember me? I need to talk to you and Fred Byrnes if he's there. The CIA office said he was on his way over here to see you."

"Come in," Bolan said. He did remember Latimer, but not with pleasure. As the man entered, Bolan motioned to him to sit down.

"I have an idea," Latimer said. "The President's canceled Blast Furnace and ordered the U.S. military out of Bolivia. That doesn't apply to the DEA. We stay. I've got thirty agents in the Trinidad-Chimore area. Byrnes has got the latest satellite data, so we know where the active drug factories are. Let's work together and go get them."

Byrnes nodded. "I've got the latest satellite reconnaissance data on the location of the drug factories. I was just here to talk to Belasko about that."

He unfolded a map and spread it on the table.

Latimer suddenly stabbed a finger of his left hand at the map.

"What the hell's wrong? That can't be right."

For a second, both Byrnes and Bolan stared at the spot on the map. There was nothing there. When they looked up, Latimer was holding a big .45-caliber Glock 21. The round cylinder of the sound suppressor was pointing straight at them.

"What the hell's the matter with you, Latimer?" Byrnes demanded.

Bolan did not ask. He knew.

"Don't move. This baby's as quiet as the grave."

"You lousy bastard! You've sold your country out!" Byrnes snarled.

"Don't make tiresome speeches, Byrnes. Just say your prayers."

Byrnes was not the kind of man who would sit there and wait to die. Despite the odds, his hand flashed toward his .357 Magnum pistol. He was not fast enough. Latimer shot him twice, the heavy .45-caliber bullets driving him backward as he desperately tried to bring his revolver up to fire.

Latimer's attention was distracted. Bolan drew his Desert Eagle and fired the moment its muzzle cleared leather. The DEA agent staggered, but he still had his Glock in his hand. The Executioner fired two times as fast as he could pull the trigger. Latimer was dead before he hit the floor.

Bolan turned to Byrnes, who was bent over, gasping for breath.

"You've gotten me into good habits, friend. I wear my soft body armor all the time now."

He looked down at Latimer's body.

"Well, I guess we know who the leak was. I'd like to have seen the bastard stand trial, but you shoot too goddamned straight."

Half an hour later, they were sitting in the embassy lounge. Bolan's room had been taken over by the team investigating the shooting.

"You said you wanted to talk to me before our friend dropped by," Bolan said.

"That's right. I don't like this pullout. Neither do you. I told you that I've got the latest satellite-reconnaissance data. I know where all the drug factories are located. Now, if I were a real hero, I'd go blow them all to hell. Well, it's no one-man job. It needs a first-rate strike team. Suppose I give you the data and we just go do it. If Washington doesn't like it, they can yell at us, but the drug factories will be gone. What do you say?"

Bolan smiled grimly. "It sounds like something a crazy CIA man would dream up. Give me half an hour. I have to talk to a few people."

Ten minutes later Bolan sat in the communications room and keyed the SATCOM.

"Granite Home, this is Striker. I need to speak to Hal immediately. Flash priority."

Barbara Price did not waste time asking questions. There was no higher priority. Two minutes later, Brognola was on the line.

"What's your situation, Striker?"

"Damned poor. You've heard what happened. They're canceling Blast Furnace."

"That's right. The President had no choice when the Bolivians asked us to leave. We're not at war with Bolivia. We can't occupy the country. We have to pull out."

"Do we? I have the latest target location data. I've talked to the team. We're all agreed. We're going in and destroy the drug factories."

"I'm sorry, Striker. I don't think I can get authorization for you to do that."

"You don't understand, Hal. I'm not asking for permission. I'm telling you what I'm going to do. I'm sorry if it causes you trouble, but we're going to destroy those cocaine factories. You can tell them it was entirely my idea. I'll accept complete responsibility."

"You know I don't play the game that way, Striker. I'll handle things here. You go in and wipe them out."

Bolan had thought he could count on Brognola. He had not been wrong.

"Roger, Granite Home. Breaking contact. Will continue mission. Striker out."

CHAPTER TWENTY-SIX

The Trinidad Area, Central Bolivia

Mack Bolan checked his watch. Two minutes to go. Gadgets Schwarz gave his remote-detonating device one final check and gave Bolan the thumbs-up sign. The Executioner took a quick drink of warm water from his canteen. He was hot, tired, sweating and dirty. He was not alone. The team showed the effects of twenty-four straight hours of operating in hostile country. They had left five burning and exploding drug factories in the jungle behind them. Now it was time for number six. Grimaldi should be in position near the recovery zone. Bolan did not want to break radio silence to check. It seemed probable that the enemy had intercepted some of their radio messages. He checked his watch again. Five seconds. He nodded to Gadgets Schwarz.

Gadgets pushed the button.

"This one's for Mary Swenson," he said. Gadgets had been fond of the captain.

Six hundred yards away the carefully placed charges fired, and the jungle exploded in a series of shattering detonations. A huge ball of orange fire rose over the treetops. Bolan was satisfied. As General Stuart had told him, *trafficantes* used a great many dangerous chemicals.

Time to go. Some very unhappy people were looking for them. He gave the signal and the team began to slip through the jungle like dull black phantoms.

The White House, Washington, D.C.

THE PRESIDENT'S SECRETARY ushered Hal Brognola into the Oval Office. The President was sitting alone, staring at a television set. On the screen Anne Bayne was standing in front of a Lockheed C-5B. Men in uniform were loading equipment into the giant transport.

"And so Operation Blast Furnace, which was begun with such high hopes, comes to an abrupt end as the last U.S. military personnel are withdrawn from Bolivia. This is Anne Bayne for WWN in La Paz, Bolivia."

The President clicked off the TV and stared at the dark screen. He did not look happy. He frowned as he looked up at Brognola.

"Do you have the latest satellite data?" he asked.

"Yes, Mr. President. I've just come from the National Reconnaissance Office. They're maintaining continuous multiple satellite surveillance of Bolivia. In the past twelve hours, they have observed major fires and explosions at six cocaine factories. I don't think there can be any doubt. Striker and the Stony Man team are attacking and destroying every known drug factory they can reach."

The President's frown deepened.

"Did you authorize these attacks, Hal?"

Brognola hesitated. He had never lied to the President, and he wouldn't start now."

"No, sir. Striker told me what he intended to do. He did not ask my permission, but I completely approve of what he's doing. If that is unacceptable, I am prepared to offer my resignation."

The President shook his head.

"Don't be silly, Hal. I can't spare you, and just between the two of us, it'll make me extremely happy if Striker blows every damned cocaine factory in Bolivia to hell! Let's just hope he doesn't get caught. Well, is there anything else? I have a big meeting in half an hour."

"Yes, sir, I'm afraid there is. The Bolivian army and the National Police are paralyzed by the crisis. The *traficantes* can operate freely. They know there's a small American team operating against them. They're mobilizing large numbers of men and helicopters to hunt them down and kill them. I'm afraid that they're going to succeed. I've talked to some of the special operations people at the Pentagon. They estimate that there's less than a five percent chance that Striker and his team will get out alive unless they get help.

"We sent them there, Mr. President. They're carrying out the task we assigned them. No matter what the political considerations are, I don't believe we can leave them to die trying. You're the only person who can help them. I'm asking you to authorize that help."

The President thought long and hard.

Brognola watched the seconds crawl by on the clock on the wall.

Finally, the President nodded. "You're right, Brognola. You usually are. All right, I'll send in a little plausibly deniable help."

He picked up the receiver of a gold colored phone on his desk.

"Get me the commanding officer of the Air Combat Command. Hello, General. This is the President. Flash priority. Execute Operation Vampire immediately."

The wheels of the Air Combat Command began to turn smoothly. Aircrews manned their planes and performed their final checks, and jet engines whined into life. One after another, dull-gray, bat-winged shapes lifted off their runways and headed south.

The Trinidad Area, Central Bolivia

BOLAN HEARD THE AUDIBLE ALARM on his tactical radio beep. Someone wanted to talk to him urgently. He strained to hear over the rattle and crackle of automatic weapons firing continuously.

"Striker, this is Vampire Leader. Come in, Striker."

"Vampire Leader. This is Striker."

"Striker, I'm inbound your position at thirty-two thousand feet with eight aircraft. What is your situation? Vampire Leader over."

"Vampire Leader, we're heavily outnumbered and under attack. Request all possible support immediately. Striker over."

"Roger, Striker. Where do you want it?"

Bolan transmitted his GPS coordinates and thought hard. The satellite positioning system was supposed to be accurate to fifty yards, but nothing was perfect. He had better add a little margin.

"Vampire Leader, put them one hundred yards in front of my position. Striker over."

There was a pause for a few seconds. Then Vampire Leader spoke again.

"Striker, you realize that is on top of your position. I can't guarantee that some of them won't land a lot closer to you than that. Do you want to move the strike farther away from your position?"

Bolan listened to the sounds of automatic weapons. They were getting closer. This was no time to be cautious.

"Vampire Leader, this is Striker. Negative, no change. Do it!"

"Roger, Striker. Will comply. Vampire Force, did you copy that?"

Vampire Leader waited a few seconds for replies Bolan could not hear.

"Very well. All Vampire aircraft, execute!"

Aboard Vampire Force's bat-winged B-2 stealth bombers, the weapons system operators checked their computers. The B-2s' bomb bay doors slid smoothly open. Streamlined olive-drab shapes began to drop from the bomb bays and arch toward the jungle below.

BOLAN FIRED TWO BURSTS at the trees behind him. The opposition was closing in for the kill. He loaded his last full magazine into his Ranger carbine. They had destroyed three more drug factories, but he was not sure they would make the pickup point where Grimaldi was waiting. Too many people were pursuing them. Whatever Vampire Leader was going to do, he had better do it soon.

He stopped, hearing a strange whistling-sighing sound that was growing louder. He had heard that sound before in Vietnam and a hundred other places. He flattened himself against the bottom of the ditch and yelled at the top of his lungs.

"Bombs. Bombs! Take cover. Take cover! Bombs!"

The rest of the Stony Man team instantly complied, but Captain Vargas did not understand what was happening, so McCarter pulled him to the ground.

The whistling-sighing sound grew louder. Bolan hoped to God Vampire Flight knew its business. It was going to be close. Then the world in front of his position suddenly exploded. The Executioner watched, awestruck, as dozens of thousand-pound bombs began to detonate. He had seen the B-52 bomber strikes in Vietnam and the astounding destruction they produced. He knew he was going to see it again now.

It seemed as if an invisible giant was stamping through the forest, closer and closer to the ditch. The ground shook, and the air vibrated as huge fountains of dust and dirt rose. The noise was incredible. Bolan clapped his hands to his ears and opened his mouth to relieve the pressure on his ears as the explosions walked through the trees toward the ditch. A giant hand seemed to strike his entire body again and again. Dust and smoke obscured everything. The acrid smell of burning high explosives filled the air.

The concussions abruptly stopped. There was a sudden deafening silence, broken only by rocks and branches raining back to earth. Bolan was dazed and shaken by the repeated blasts. He tried to think. There was no way to tell how many casualties the bombing had caused, but the opposition had to be disorganized. Now, he had to get his team organized and out of there before the enemy could recover and react.

He struggled to his feet and looked around. "Come on, Let's go! The smoke'll hide us. They can't see us now! Go! Go! Go!"

The men were dazed, but a voice they knew was telling them what to do. Clutching their weapons, they got to their feet and fell back through the smoke. They moved rapidly for several hundred yards and burst into the clearing where Grimaldi waited. He started the MH-60K's engines as they piled on board. Bolan slipped into the co-pilot's seat and checked his map. How far was it to the next cocaine factory? Grimaldi saw what he was doing and smiled.

"Don't worry about it, Sarge. They're not there any-more. Somebody named Vampire took care of them."

La Paz International Airport

MACK BOLAN WATCHED as the Air Force C-17 crew fin-ished loading. The Stony Man team and Fred Byrnes were already on board. Colonel Suarez had insisted on escort-ing them to the airport. He smiled at Bolan as an air force sergeant signaled that it was time for him to board.

"Goodbye, Striker. We have done some great things together. Do not forget us. Go with God."

They shook hands, and Bolan went up the ramp and into the C-17's huge interior. He took a seat with Byrnes and the team as the pilot started the engines and began to taxi out. In a minute, they were airborne. The Executioner looked back out the window as La Paz vanished in the distance.

Fred Byrnes was jovial. "Well, we made it. Got the job done and got out alive."

He reached into his attaché case and pulled out a bottle of liquor. He poured the whiskey into small paper cups and passed it around.

"Here's to you and your team, Striker. It's a pleasure to work with you. If we had enough men like you, we could save the whole damned world."

Bolan did not really want a drink, but the toast was important to Fred. He drank it and sat thinking.

"What's the matter, Striker?" Byrnes asked. "You don't look happy."

"I'm not. Blast Furnace was a great idea. We came down here with a good general and good men. We were all working together for a change. We were getting results, hitting the *trafficantes* hard. Then the politicians caved in, and it's all over. The drug cartel has billions of dollars. Those drug factories we destroyed will be rebuilt and operating again in six months. Damned right, I'm not happy."

"Well, maybe this will make you feel better. I was talking to headquarters before we left for the airport. They tell me that cocaine prices on the East Coast have more than doubled. That's enough to save thousands of lives."

McCarter was sipping his drink tentatively. When he drank, he preferred his regular cola soft drink, but he didn't want to hurt the man's feelings.

"Fred's right, Striker. We don't make policy or plan the wars. We just fight the battles. We accomplished every task we were handed. We did our duty. That's what counts in the end."

Bolan nodded. McCarter was right. They had gone in and done their job, and everyone on the team had made it out alive. That made it a good mission. Now he could relax until the next one.

Don't miss out on the action in these titles!

A violent struggle for survival
in a post-holocaust world

JAMES AXLER

DEATH
LANDS®

Watersleep

In the altered reality of the Deathlands, America's coastal waters
haven't escaped the ravages of the nukecaust, but the awesome
power of the oceans still rules there. It's a power that will let
Ryan Cawdor, first among post-holocaust survivors, ride the crest
of victory—or consign his woman to the raging depths.

A deadly kind of immortality...

THE Destroyer™

#110 Never Say Die

Created by
WARREN MURPHY
and RICHARD SAPIR

Forensic evidence in a number of assassinations reveals a curious link between the killers: identical fingerprints and genetic code. The bizarre problem is turned over to Remo and Chiun, who follow the trail back to a literal dead end— the grave of an executed killer.

Look for it in January wherever Gold Eagle books are sold.

James Axler

OUTLANDERS™

SAVAGE SUN

A reference to ancient mysterious powers
sends Kane, Brigid Baptiste and Grant to
the wild hinterlands of Ireland, whose stone
ruins may function as a gateway for the alien
Archons.

But the Emerald Isle's blend of ancient magic
and advanced technology, as wielded by a
powerful woman, brings them to the very brink
of oblivion.

Available December 1997,
wherever Gold Eagle books are sold.

Don't miss out on the action in these titles featuring
THE EXECUTIONER®, STONY MAN™ and SUPERBOLAN®!

The Red Dragon Trilogy

#64210	FIRE LASH	$3.75 U.S.	☐
		$4.25 CAN.	☐
#64211	STEEL CLAWS	$3.75 U.S.	☐
		$4.25 CAN.	☐
#64212	RIDE THE BEAST	$3.75 U.S.	☐
		$4.25 CAN.	☐

Stony Man™

#61910	FLASHBACK	$5.50 U.S.	☐
		$6.50 CAN.	☐
#61911	ASIAN STORM	$5.50 U.S.	☐
		$6.50 CAN.	☐
#61912	BLOOD STAR	$5.50 U.S.	☐
		$6.50 CAN.	☐

SuperBolan®

#61452	DAY OF THE VULTURE	$5.50 U.S.	☐
		$6.50 CAN.	☐
#61453	FLAMES OF WRATH	$5.50 U.S.	☐
		$6.50 CAN.	☐
#61454	HIGH AGGRESSION	$5.50 U.S.	☐
		$6.50 CAN.	☐

(limited quantities available on certain titles)

TOTAL AMOUNT	$
POSTAGE & HANDLING	$
($1.00 for one book, 50¢ for each additional)	
APPLICABLE TAXES*	$ _____
TOTAL PAYABLE	$ _____
(check ~~money order~~—please do not send cash)	

To order, comp~~lete~~ this form and send it, along with a check or money order for the total above, ~~paya~~ble to Gold Eagle Books, to: **In the U.S.:** 3010 Walden Avenue, P.O. Box 9077, Bu~~ffalo,~~ NY 14269-9077; **In Canada:** P.O. Box 636, Fort Erie, Ontario, L2A 5X3.

Name:_____

Address:_____ City:_____

State/Prov.:_____ Zip/Postal Code: _____

*New York residents remit applicable sales taxes.
 Canadian residents remit applicable GST and provincial taxes.

GOLD
EAGLE®

GEBACK18